*EVERYMAN, I will go with thee,*

*and be thy guide,*

*In thy most need to go by thy side*

# RUDYARD KIPLING

# Stories and Poems

EDITED WITH A BIOGRAPHICAL NOTE
AND AN INTRODUCTION BY
ROGER LANCELYN GREEN

DENT: LONDON
EVERYMAN'S LIBRARY

*This selection is published by permission of
Mrs George Bambridge and Macmillan & Company Limited
and Methuen & Company Limited*

© *Biographical Note and Introduction
J. M. Dent & Sons Ltd, 1970*

*All rights reserved
Made in Great Britain
at the
Aldine Press · Letchworth · Herts
for
J. M. DENT & SONS LTD
Aldine House · Bedford Street · London*

*This selection first included
in Everyman's Library 1970*

ISBN: 0 460 00690 8

# Contents

ROGER LANCELYN GREEN

RUDYARD KIPLING: A BIOGRAPHICAL NOTE AND
SHORT BIBLIOGRAPHY

INTRODUCTION

## STORIES

## POEMS

# Rudyard Kipling

## A Biographical Note

JOSEPH RUDYARD KIPLING was born on 30th December 1865 in Bombay, where his father John Lockwood Kipling had just been appointed to the newly founded Jamsetjee Jeejeebhoy School of Art, of which he was the first Principal and Professor of Architectural Sculpture. Kipling's mother, Alice, was one of the daughters of the Rev. George Macdonald, a Methodist minister; one of her sisters married Edward Burne-Jones, another Edward Poynter, and the third became the mother of Stanley Baldwin.

Kipling had vivid recollections of his Indian childhood, though he was taken back to England with his sister when he was six, and left in the care of Captain and Mrs P. A. Holloway at Southsea for nearly six years. During this period Kipling was intensely unhappy (a rather highly coloured version appears in his story 'Baa, Baa, Black Sheep') but, except for permanently impaired eyesight, six months of freedom at Goldings Hill on the border of Epping Forest with his mother and sister effected a perfect cure. He had begun his education at Hope House, Southsea, and in 1878 entered the United Services College, Westward Ho!, North Devon, of which Cormell Price, a family friend, was the first and greatest headmaster.

Kipling's years at Westward Ho! form the background to *Stalky & Co.* in which he appears as Beetle: the adventures were pure fiction, but the setting and much of the characterization had a factual basis.

At the age of seventeen, his literary bent already well developed, he returned to India as sub-editor of *The Civil and Military Gazette* at Lahore (where his father had become curator of the museum), and was promoted to *The Pioneer* of Allahabad in 1887. During his 'seven years' hard' in India, Kipling published his first collection of verse, *Departmental Ditties* (1886) and his volume of short stories, *Plain Tales from the Hills* (1888). These were followed by a series of stories of much greater excellence, most of which appeared in the Allahabad papers and were collected throughout 1888 in six paper-bound 'Railway Library' booklets, later made into two volumes as *Soldiers Three* and *Wee Willie Winkie*.

Sending these ahead of him, Kipling set out for England early in 1889, going by way of Japan and America, and reached London in October. He arrived known only to a few of the more discerning critics:

within three months he was the most famous writer in England, and his reputation soon spread to America.

Stories, mainly of India, were collected in *Life's Handicap* (1891) and *Many Inventions* (1893), and verses in *Barrack-Room Ballads* (1892) and, with a less successful novel, *The Light That Failed* (1890), these volumes, with reprints of his earlier works, set him among the great writers of the period.

In 1892 Kipling married Caroline Starr Balestier of Brattleboro, Vermont, U.S.A., where he lived until 1896, though spending two summers with his parents in England, at Tisbury, Wilts. During this period he wrote his most popular volumes, the two *Jungle Books*, and his longer story with an American setting, *Captains Courageous* (1897).

On his return to England he collected his adult stories of the period in *The Day's Work* (1898), wrote *Stalky & Co.* (1899), *Just So Stories* (1902) and his masterpiece, the picaresque novel of Indian life, *Kim* (1901).

He was also writing much verse at this period, some of it of a political nature which led to a general disparagement of his literary status from which he has scarcely yet recovered.

However, he was awarded the Nobel Peace Prize in 1907 and the gold medal of the Royal Society of Literature in 1927. He refused to accept all honours that might tie him to any political party, including the Poet Laureateship (twice), the Order of Merit and various titles. But he received honorary degrees from Oxford, Cambridge, Durham, Edinburgh, Paris, Strasbourg and Athens, and was Rector of St Andrews and Honorary Fellow of Magdalene College, Cambridge.

In 1902 the Kiplings settled at Bateman's, Burwash, Sussex, which he left to the National Trust, and which is kept as a memorial to him.

His Sussex home gave Kipling the setting for his historical tales in *Puck of Pook's Hill* (1906) and *Rewards and Fairies* (1910), besides some of the great stories of his middle period: 'They', 'Below the Mill Dam', 'An Habitation Enforced', 'My Son's Wife' and 'Friendly Brook'.

Tales of sailors predominate in *Traffics and Discoveries* (1904), and *Actions and Reactions* (1909) vary from science fiction ('With the Night Mail') to political allegory and stories of country life. *A Diversity of Creatures* (1917) explored some of these fields still further and ended in the psychological tragedy of the First World War.

His post-war collections, *Debits and Credits* (1926) and *Limits and Renewals* (1932), showed his genius at its most mature and contain stories which an increasing number of critics place among the most interesting and important that he ever wrote.

During his last years Kipling suffered increasingly from abdominal trouble, and wrote very little. He was just able to see the final collected and definitive edition of his works launched, and to write his fragment of autobiography, *Something of Myself*, to form an epilogue to this

Sussex Edition, and died in Middlesex Hospital on 18th January 1936 after an operation.

His ashes were buried in Poets' Corner, Westminster Abbey. The official biography by Charles Carrington did not appear until 1955, but a Kipling Society with headquarters and library at 18 Northumberland Avenue, London, was founded in 1927 to discuss and elucidate his works and issue the quarterly *Kipling Journal*. The following list is a short bibliography.

FICTION. *Plain Tales from the Hills*, 1888; *Soldiers Three*, 1888; *The Story of the Gadsbys*, 1888; *In Black and White*, 1888; *Under the Deodars*, 1888; *The Phantom Rickshaw*, 1888; *Wee Willie Winkie*, 1888; *The Light that Failed*, 1890; *Life's Handicap*, 1891; *The Naulahka* (in collaboration with Wolcott Balestier), 1892; *Many Inventions*, 1893; *The Jungle Book*, 1894; *The Second Jungle Book*, 1895; *Captains Courageous*, 1897; *The Day's Work*, 1898; *Stalky & Co.*, 1899; *Kim*, 1901; *Just So Stories*, 1902; *Traffics and Discoveries*, 1904; *Puck of Pook's Hill*, 1906; *Actions and Reactions*, 1909; *Abaft the Funnel*, 1909; *Rewards and Fairies*, 1910; *A Diversity of Creatures*, 1917; *Land and Sea Tales*, 1923; *Debits and Credits*, 1926; *Thy Servant a Dog*, 1930; *Limits and Renewals*, 1932.

OTHER PROSE. *The City of Dreadful Night*, 1890; *Letters of Marque*, 1891; *A Fleet in Being*, 1898; *From Sea to Sea*, 1899; *A History of England* (in collaboration with C. R. L. Fletcher), 1911; *The Harbour Watch* (play: acted but unpublished), 1913; *The New Army in Training*, 1915; *France at War*, 1915; *Fringes of the Fleet*, 1915; *Tales of the Trade*, 1916; *Sea Warfare*, 1916; *The Eyes of Asia*, 1918; *Letters of Travel*, 1920; *The Irish Guards in the Great War*, 1923; *A Book of Words*, 1928; *Souvenirs of France*, 1933; *Something of Myself*, 1937; *Brazilian Sketches*, 1940.

VERSE. *Schoolboy Lyrics*, 1881; *Departmental Ditties*, 1886, with additions 1886, 1888, 1890; *Barrack-Room Ballads*, 1892; *The Seven Seas*, 1896; *The Five Nations*, 1903; *Songs from Books*, 1912; *The Years Between*, 1919; *Verse: Inclusive Edition*, 1919, with additions 1921, 1927, 1933; *Verse: Definitive Edition*, 1940.

BIOGRAPHY AND CRITICISM. T. S. Eliot, *A Choice of Kipling's Verse*, 1942; C. E. Carrington, *Rudyard Kipling: His Life and Work*, 1955 (the authorized biography); J. M. S. Tompkins, *The Art of Rudyard Kipling*, 1959; J. McG. Stewart, *Rudyard Kipling: A Bibliographical Catalogue*, 1959; J. I. M. Stewart, *Eight Modern Writers*, 1963; Roger Lancelyn Green, *Kipling and the Children*, 1965; Louis L. Cornell, *Kipling in India*, 1966; J. I. M. Stewart, *Rudyard Kipling*, 1966; Bonamy Dobrée, *Rudyard Kipling: Realist and Fabulist*, 1967; W. Arthur Young and John H. McGivering, *A Kipling Dictionary*, 1967. *The Kipling Journal*, 1927–   ; in progress: published four times a year by the Kipling Society.

The publishers thank Mrs George Bambridge and Macmillan & Company Limited and Methuen & Company Limited for their permission to print the present selection.

All the stories and poems in this volume were printed in the thirty-five volume *Sussex Edition* (1937–9) of Kipling's works, collected and authorized by him during the last year of his life and published by Macmillan. The stories (except 'The Pit That They Digged' and 'Proofs Of Holy Writ') also appear in Macmillan's Uniform and Pocket Editions.

The separate verse volumes, except *Songs from Books* (Macmillan), are published by Methuen. The collected verse appears in the one-volume *Definitive Edition of Rudyard Kipling's Verse* (Hodder & Stoughton).

# Introduction

RUDYARD KIPLING is probably the most controversial figure in English literature. Before he was twenty-five such critics as W. E. Henley and Andrew Lang were hailing him as a likely successor to Dickens, while Henry James was writing: 'Kipling strikes me personally as the most complete man of genius that I have ever known.' Not ten years later Robert Buchanan declared that 'the vulgarity, the brutality, the savagery, reeks on every page of *Stalky & Co.*'—but Neil Munro was writing in the same year that 'surveying the work of Mr Kipling as a whole, the most fastidious must be impressed by the greatness of his genius, the scope and variety it displays, the essentially wholesome influence it creates'.

During the decade following his death we find James Agate describing him as 'the world's greatest master of the short story', and Somerset Maugham echoing this with the statement that Kipling was 'the best short-story writer that our country can boast of'—while H. E. Bates was declaring that 'the notion that Kipling was a great writer is a myth . . . no single syllable of Kipling has ever given a moment's pleasure', but T. S. Eliot was calling him 'the greatest Englishman of letters of his generation'.

Most of the more extreme anti-Kipling criticism, which sometimes reached the dimensions of pathological hatred, was inspired by political and not by literary judgment. As early as 1923 Edward Shanks wrote of Kipling's 'leap into a position in English political thought and feeling which, it is safe to say, no other English imaginative writer (even Milton not excepted) has ever occupied. Hence too comes the difficulty, which still exists, of looking at him dispassionately as an imaginative writer'. That is a difficulty which has not been altogether overcome even now.

At the beginning of 1890, when he was just twenty-five, Kipling leapt suddenly into fame, becoming at once both the most popular with the general readers and the most highly acclaimed by the literary critics of all the authors of the day. His popularity with the general reader he never lost: his collected verse and nearly all his prose continue to be reprinted frequently.

Kipling captured the British and American public with his stories and poems of India: stories and ballads of army life, tales of British officers and civilians with their wives on and off duty at Simla, sketches of native life, and a sprinkling of tales of oriental magic and mystery and of children in India, both black and white.

The very short, rather 'smart' and 'would-be clever' stories in *Plain Tales from the Hills* and *Soldiers Three* were already giving place to longer and infinitely superior works even before he left India early in 1889—and indeed by then he had written two, usually ranked among his greatest—'The Man Who Would Be King' and 'The Drums of the Fore and Aft'.

His reception in literary London seems to have stimulated his powers into a period of accomplishment almost as high as he ever achieved, and by which he is still apt to be judged with little reference to the later development of his genius. The majority of the stories were still set in India, including several of the greatest of the tales of the Soldiers Three, such as 'The Courting of Dinah Shadd', 'The Incarnation of Krishna Mulvaney', 'On Greenhow Hill', and 'My Lord the Elephant'. Other stories of India included two of his most famous—'The Man Who Was', and 'Without Benefit of Clergy',

Kipling collected these stories into *Life's Handicap* (1891) and *Many Inventions* (1893), including in the first several written before leaving India that might well have been left to oblivion. He also tried his hand at the novel (*The Light that Failed*, 1891) and the adventure story (*The Naulakha*, 1892), but in neither was able to reach the undoubted greatness of the best of the shorter stories.

He was living in America by the time *Many Inventions* appeared, and was beginning to write the jungle tales which have proved his most popular works. Mowgli, the Indian boy brought up by wolves, made his first appearance as a man in the adult story 'In the Rukh' in this collection—but entered another dimension when his earlier adventures were described in the first three stories of *The Jungle Book* (1894) and took his place securely among the great characters of fiction with his five further adventures in *The Second Jungle Book* (1895).

That volume also contained 'The Miracle of Purun Bhagat', a story that appeals to few young readers but is generally considered by adults to be one of Kipling's greatest, a sympathetic study of the Indian 'holy man' which ranks with that of the Lama in *Kim*.

From animals Kipling turned to machines, with somewhat less success in prose, but achieving one of his most remarkable narrative poems in 'McAndrew's Hymn'. The volume in which the tales of ships and railway engines were collected, *The Day's Work* (1898), also contained some of his last stories of India, such as 'William the Conqueror', 'The Bridge Builders' and 'The Tomb of his Ancestors', which show no falling away from the high level achieved in *Many Inventions*. It also contained 'The Brushwood Boy', a romantic love-story with a strangely evocative background of the dream life of two healthy and apparently unromantic young people, which has divided Kipling's admirers ever since.

These volumes also included a number of humorous or farcical stories. Indeed Kipling began to try his hand at this kind as early as *Plain Tales from the Hills*, achieving considerable success with the dry humour of 'Pig' and 'A Germ Destroyer' and 'The Pit that they Digged', but not always keeping his delight in immoderate laughter and the practical joke sufficiently in check in longer stories. He showed a much surer control of this difficult form in 'Brugglesmith' (*Many Inventions*) and 'My Sunday at Home' (*The Day's Work*), and achieved his masterpiece of humour with the connected tales of school life in *Stalky & Co.* (1899).

This book, however, failed to amuse a certain percentage of readers and critics who took it too seriously and were either shocked beyond words by this profane attack on the 'public school spirit' and the 'breathless hush in the close tonight', or interpreted it as a symptom of something much worse—as Robert Buchanan showed in the criticism already quoted, and as H. G. Wells was to do many years later in his *Outline of History*, where he twists one of the stories to serve his purpose of showing up 'the psychology of the British Empire at the close of the nineteenth century'.

The publication of *Stalky & Co.* coincided with the involvement in politics which alienated so many critics (but not the reading public) from Kipling the writer. 'What should they know of England who only

England know?' he had asked—and forthwith proceeded to tell the islanders about their possessions overseas and something of the lives lived there. In 'A Song of the English' he did little more than explore the Empire; when the Diamond Jubilee brought the great access of imperial pride to the Mother Country, Kipling's contribution was 'Recessional'—a plea for humility and a reminder of the transitoriness of all empires and civilizations. Kipling has too often been dismissed summarily as a 'Jingo': but 'Recessional' should be compared with Henley's 'England, my England'—and 'The Flag of Their Country' in *Stalky & Co.* should be read for one of the most devastating attacks on jingoism ever written.

Kipling did, however, believe passionately that British rule in the Empire was bringing benefits to those ruled far outweighing any temporary disadvantages—and at the beginning of this century the great wave of nationalism which has since swept over the world was no more than an uneasy shuffling in the background.

But the Boer War proved bitterly disillusioning, and even before it ended Kipling was warning his countrymen of their unreadiness, should a major European conflict break out, in poems such as 'The Islanders' —which damaged his reputation even more by its unequivocal demand for conscription and its slighting references to England's excessive preoccupation with sport.

No prophet of evil is welcome, though the First World War proved Kipling right (yet his last public speech in 1935, foretelling the Second World War, won just the sort of reaction he had experienced at the beginning of the century); but there was a change for the better in the critical reception of *Debits and Credits* (1926) and *Limits and Renewals* (1932), books which began to win Kipling a new public, in spite of the fact that the American critic Edmund Wilson dismissed them in 1941 as 'The Kipling that Nobody Read'. That same year T. S. Eliot issued *A Choice of Kipling's Verse* with a long and appreciative introductory study which caused some consternation to the critical pundits of the day. They were further shaken in 1952 when Somerset Maugham edited *A Choice of Kipling's Prose* (mainly early stories) with a similarly eulogistic introduction.

Genuine Kipling criticism, taking him simply as a great writer and making no more of his political opinions than if he had been Milton or

Swift or William Morris, began with an outstanding lecture by C. S. Lewis in 1948 and was developed in the full scale study by J. M. S. Timpkins, *The Art of Rudyard Kipling*, in 1958. Since then Kipling has been accepted academically as a 'great writer' by inclusion among the sacred eight in J. I. M. Stewart's volume of the *Oxford History of English Literature* (1963), and treated in scholarly and perceptive volumes by Louis Cornell in America and Bonamy Dobrée here, besides studies and essays by lesser writers.

But the politico-critical bias takes a long time to wear off. The younger generation, though it may have read the *Jungle Books, Just So Stories* and *Puck* in its childhood, is discouraged from proceeding to the adult Kipling by the ignorant and second-hand labels affixed to him, such as 'imperialist', 'jingo', 'sadist', 'pro-Fascist', 'racialist' and the like by their seniors and instructors, few of whom have read much Kipling, and fewer still his later stories and poems.

The present volume strives to present a fairly balanced selection from Kipling's works, so that the general reader may form his own opinion of his literary accomplishment as a whole, and then go on to read further —or abstain from doing so. 'Kipling is intensely loved and hated. Hardly any reader likes him a little,' said C. S. Lewis, but went on, while admitting that he was one of the few who did not belong fully to either party, to maintain that 'I have never at any time been able to understand how a man of taste could doubt that Kipling is a very great artist'.

Simple reasons of length have prevented the inclusion here of some of Kipling's most famous stories—many of which have been voted among his best. Had this book consisted of 'The Man Who Would Be King', 'The Drums of the Fore and Aft', 'The Courting of Dinah Shadd', 'The Brushwood Boy', 'An Habitation Enforced', 'The Village that Voted the Earth was Flat', 'The Wish House' and 'Dayspring Mishandled', it might have come nearer to a majority choice—but would have more than filled the volume.

To select has been difficult since, apart from a few general favourites, no gathering of Kipling's readers will ever agree even on his twelve best stories. I have tried to include as many favourites as possible, but also— since it is hoped that this may be an introductory volume to Kipling for many readers—a representative selection introducing some of his most famous characters.

Thus the short *Plain Tale* which opens it represents the typical Simla intrigues of Mrs Hauksbee and her friends, while 'The Pit that They Digged' is a good example of his humorous satires on Indian bureaucracy.

'The Man Who Was', one of Kipling's most famous stories, presents the British Army in India—in lieu of a Mulvaney story: the short, early tales of the Soldiers Three are too slight for inclusion, the later ones too long and the difficult dialects rather daunting at a first introduction.

'The Miracle of Purun Bhagat' shows Kipling's tender and sympathetic understanding of the religious and mystical side of the native Indian character, while 'The King's Ankus' presents Mowgli in one of his best adventures—and one which can be appreciated apart from the other stories in the series.

To choose an item from *Stalky & Co.* is more difficult, as most of the stories are sequent to each other. But 'Slaves of the Lamp' was the first written, and was intended to stand alone (apart from a sequel describing how Stalky put his peculiar school training to practical use years later as an army officer in India): it is also one of the two or three generally voted by boy readers as the best of the series.

*Just So Stories for Little Children*—the originality and imagination of which is only surpassed in its kind by *Alice* and approached by *Pooh*— had to be represented, and that chosen has probably the widest appeal to readers of all ages. Kipling's stories of the supernatural are represented by 'They', the most famous of them, which was suggested by the tragic death at the age of seven of his daughter Josephine, who also inspired the poignant poem 'Merrow Down'.

With 'An Habitation Enforced' we enter on Kipling's middle period, in which he developed as uncanny a knowledge of the basic England as he had earlier acquired of India. In it he captured perfectly the old life on an English estate which perished almost completely with the First World War. With it go such poems as 'Sussex', 'The Way Through the Woods', 'The Roman Centurion's Song' and 'The Land'. 'Marklake Witches', the most adult—and most moving—of the Puck stories, belongs to the same group.

The last four represent Kipling's final period when the war had brought disillusionment and suffering (see the poem 'My Boy Jack': his only son, John, killed in 1915), and with them a far deeper understanding of the human mind and much thought about physical and psychological suffering. 'The Gardener' is actually the only story included that has the war for its setting; but 'The Eye of Allah' and 'The Church that was at Antioch' show Kipling's earlier gifts deepened and widened—and should help to prove the conviction of many serious critics of recent years that his last three major collections, *A Diversity of Creatures* (1917), *Debits and Credits* (1926) and *Limits and Renewals* (1932), though many of the stories are difficult and even obscure, contain his best and most mature work. His last important story, the little known, uncollected 'Proofs of Holy Writ' (which John Buchan held to be his best), ends the selection appropriately with its relaxed atmosphere of peace in the shady garden of old age.

The poems keep pace with the stories, veering between verse and poetry, and again try to give a representative cross-section of his output in this field. Whether or not he ranks as poet rather than versifier is still being argued; but the fact remains that, after Shakespeare, he is the most quoted writer in the English language.

ROGER LANCELYN GREEN

1970

The date printed at the end of each story and poem is the
year of its first publication, which may precede its appearance
in the book named in the contents. The date of first publica-
tion of books is given in the contents and bibliography.

# STORIES

# Three—And An Extra

When halter and heel-ropes are slipped, do not
give chase with sticks but with *gram.*
*Punjabi Proverb.*

AFTER marriage arrives a reaction, sometimes a big, sometimes a
little one; but it comes sooner or later, and must be tided over by
both parties if they desire the rest of their lives to go with the
current.

In the case of the Cusack-Bremmils this reaction did not set in
till the third year after the wedding. Bremmil was hard to hold at
the best of times; but he was a beautiful husband until the baby
died and Mrs Bremmil wore black, and grew thin, and mourned
as though the bottom of the Universe had fallen out. Perhaps
Bremmil ought to have comforted her. He tried to do so, but the
more he comforted the more Mrs Bremmil grieved, and, conse-
quently, the more uncomfortable grew Bremmil. The fact was
that they both needed a tonic. And they got it. Mrs Bremmil can
afford to laugh now, but it was no laughing matter to her at the
time.

Mrs Hauksbee appeared on the horizon; and where she existed
was fair chance of trouble. At Simla her by-name was the
'Stormy Petrel'. She had won that title five times to my own
certain knowledge. She was a little, brown, thin, almost skinny,
woman, with big, rolling, violet-blue eyes, and the sweetest
manners in the world. You had only to mention her name at
afternoon teas for every woman in the room to rise up and call
her not blessed. She was clever, witty, brilliant, and sparkling
beyond most of her kind; but possessed of many devils of malice
and mischievousness. She could be nice, though, even to her own
sex. But that is another story.

Bremmil went off at score after the baby's death and the
general discomfort that followed, and Mrs Hauksbee annexed
him. She took no pleasure in hiding her captives. She annexed
him publicly, and saw that the public saw it. He rode with her,
and walked with her, and talked with her, and picnicked with her,
and tiffined at Peliti's with her, till people put up their eyebrows
and said, 'Shocking!' Mrs Bremmil stayed at home, turning over
the dead baby's frocks and crying into the empty cradle. She did

not care to do anything else. But some eight dear, affectionate lady-friends explained the situation at length to her in case she should miss the cream of it. Mrs Bremmil listened quietly, and thanked them for their good offices. She was not as clever as Mrs Hauksbee, but she was no fool. She kept her own counsel, and did not speak to Bremmil of what she had heard. This is worth remembering. Speaking to or crying over a husband never did any good yet.

When Bremmil was at home, which was not often, he was more affectionate than usual; and that showed his hand. The affection was forced, partly to soothe his own conscience and partly to soothe Mrs Bremmil. It failed in both regards.

Then 'the A.-D.-C. in Waiting was commanded by Their Excellencies, Lord and Lady Lytton, to invite Mr and Mrs Cusack-Bremmil to Peterhof on July 26 at 9-30 P.M.'—'Dancing' in the bottom left-hand corner.

'I can't go,' said Mrs Bremmil, 'it is too soon after poor little Florrie . . . but it need not stop you, Tom.'

She meant what she said then, and Bremmil said that he would go just to put in an appearance. Here he spoke the thing which was not; and Mrs Bremmil knew it. She guessed—a woman's guess is much more accurate than a man's certainty—that he had meant to go from the first, and with Mrs Hauksbee. She sat down to think and the outcome of her thoughts was that the memory of a dead child was worth considerably less than the affections of a living husband. She made her plan and staked her all upon it. In that hour she discovered that she knew Tom Bremmil thoroughly, and this knowledge she acted on.

'Tom,' said she,' I shall be dining out at the Longmores' on the evening of the 26th. You'd better dine at the Club.'

This saved Bremmil from making an excuse to get away and dine with Mrs Hauksbee, so he was grateful, and felt small and mean at the same time—which was wholesome. Bremmil left the house at five for a ride. About half-past five in the evening a large leather-covered basket came in from Phelps's for Mrs Bremmil. She was a woman who knew how to dress; and she had not spent a week of designing that dress and having it gored, and hemmed, and herring-boned, and tucked and rucked (or whatever the terms are), for nothing. It was a gorgeous dress—slight mourning. I can't describe it, but it was what *The Queen* calls 'a creation'—a thing that hit you straight between the eyes and made you gasp. She had not much heart for what she was going to do; but as she glanced at the long mirror she had the satisfaction of knowing that she had never looked so well in her life. She was a large blonde and, when she chose, carried herself superbly.

After the dinner at the Longmores' she went on to the dance—
a little late—and encountered Bremmil with Mrs Hauksbee on his
arm. That made her flush, and as the men crowded round her for
dances she looked magnificent. She filled up all her dances except
three, and those she left blank. Mrs Hauksbee caught her eye
once; and she knew it was war—real war—between them. She
started handicapped in the struggle, for she had ordered Bremmil
about just the least little bit in the world too much, and he was
beginning to resent it. Moreover, he had never seen his wife look
so lovely. He stared at her from doorways, and glared at her from
passages as she went about with her partners; and the more he
stared, the more taken was he. He could scarcely believe that this
was the woman with the red eyes and the black stuff gown who
used to weep over the eggs at breakfast.

Mrs Hauksbee did her best to hold him in play, but, after two
dances, he crossed over to his wife and asked for a dance.

'I'm afraid you've come too late, Mister Bremmil,' she said,
with her eyes twinkling.

Then he begged her to give him a dance, and, as a great favour,
she allowed him the fifth waltz. Luckily Five stood vacant on his
programme. They danced it together, and there was a little flutter
round the room. Bremmil had a sort of a notion that his wife
could dance, but he never knew she danced so divinely. At the
end of that waltz he asked for another—as a favour, not as a
right; and Mrs Bremmil said, 'Show me your programme, dear!'
He showed it as a naughty little schoolboy hands up contraband
sweets to a master. There was a fair sprinkling of 'H' on it,
besides 'H' at supper. Mrs Bremmil said nothing, but she smiled
contemptuously, ran her pencil through Seven and Nine—two
'H's'—and returned the card with her own name written above—
a pet name that only she and her husband used. Then she shook
her finger at him, and said laughing, 'Oh, you silly, *silly* boy!'

Mrs Hauksbee heard that, and—she owned as much—felt she
had the worst of it. Bremmil accepted Seven and Nine gratefully.
They danced Seven, and sat out Nine in one of the little tents.
What Bremmil said and what Mrs Bremmil did is no concern of
anyone.

When the band struck up 'The Roast Beef of Old England', the
two went out into the verandah, and Bremmil began looking for
his wife's dandy (this was before rickshaw days) while she went
into the cloakroom. Mrs Hauksbee came up and said, 'You take
me in to supper, I think, Mr Bremmil?' Bremmil turned red and
looked foolish. 'Ah—h'm! I'm going home with my wife, Mrs
Hauksbee. I think there has been a little mistake.' Being a man,
he spoke as though Mrs Hauksbee were entirely responsible.

Mrs Bremmil came out of the cloakroom in a swan's-down cloak with a white 'cloud' round her head. She looked radiant; and she had a right to.

The couple went off into the darkness together, Bremmil riding very close to the dandy.

Then said Mrs Hauksbee to me—she looked a trifle faded and jaded in the lamplight—'Take my word for it, the silliest woman can manage a clever man; but it needs a very clever woman to manage a fool.'

Then we went in to supper.

1886

# Beyond The Pale

Love heeds not caste nor sleep a broken bed.
I went in search of love and lost myself.
*Hindu Proverb.*

A MAN should, whatever happens, keep to his own caste, race, and breed. Let the White go to the White and the Black to the Black. Then, whatever trouble falls is in the ordinary course of things—neither sudden, alien, nor unexpected.

This is the story of a man who wilfully stepped beyond the safe limits of decent everyday society, and paid for it heavily.

He knew too much in the first instance; and he saw too much in the second. He took too deep an interest in native life; but he will never do so again.

Deep away in the heart of the City, behind Jitha Megji's *bustee*, lies Amir Nath's Gully, which ends in a dead-wall pierced by one grated window. At the head of the Gully is a big cowbyre, and the walls on either side of the Gully are without windows. Neither Suchet Singh nor Gaur Chand approve of their women-folk looking into the world. If Darga Charan had been of their opinion he would have been a happier man today, and little Bisesa would have been able to knead her own bread. Her room looked out through the grated window into the narrow dark Gully where the sun never came and where the buffaloes wallowed in the blue slime. She was a widow, about fifteen years old, and she prayed the Gods, day and night, to send her a lover; for she did not approve of living alone.

One day, the man—Trejago his name was—came into Amir Nath's Gully on an aimless wandering; and, after he had passed the buffaloes, stumbled over a big heap of cattle-food.

Then he saw that the Gully ended in a trap, and heard a little laugh from behind the grated window. It was a pretty little laugh, and Trejago, knowing that, for all practical purposes, the old *Arabian Nights* are good guides, went forward to the window, and whispered that verse of 'The Love Song of Har Dyal' which begins:—

Can a man stand upright in the face of the naked Sun; or a lover in the Presence of his Beloved?

If my feet fail me, O Heart of my Heart, am I to blame, being blinded by the glimpse of your beauty?

There came the faint *tchink* of a woman's bracelets from

behind the grating, and a little voice went on with the song at the
fifth verse:—

Alas! alas! Can the Moon tell the Lotus of her love when the Gate of
Heaven is shut and the clouds gather for the rains?
They have taken my Beloved, and driven her with the pack-horses to
the North.
There are iron chains on the feet that were set on my heart.
Call to the bowmen to make ready——

The voice stopped suddenly, and Trejago walked out of Amir
Nath's Gully, wondering who in the world could have capped
'The Love Song of Har Dyal' so neatly.

Next morning, as he was driving to office, an old woman
threw a packet into his dogcart. In the packet was the half of a
broken glass-bangle, one flower of the blood-red *dhak*, a pinch of
*bhusa* or cattle-food, and eleven cardamoms. That packet was
a letter—not a clumsy compromising letter, but an innocent
unintelligible lover's epistle.

Trejago knew far too much about these things, as I have said.
No Englishman should be able to translate object-letters. But
Trejago spread all the trifles on the lid of his office-box and began
to puzzle them out.

A broken glass-bangle stands for a Hundu widow all India
over; because, when her husband dies, a woman's bracelets are
broken on her wrists. Trejago saw the meaning of the little bit of
glass. The flower of the *dhak* means diversely 'desire', 'come',
'write', or 'danger', according to the other things with it. One
cardamom means 'jealousy'; but when any article is duplicated
in an object-letter, it loses its symbolic meaning and stands
merely for one of a number indicating time, or, if incense, curds,
or saffron be sent also, place. The message ran then—'A widow—
*dhak* flower and *bhusa*,—at eleven o'clock.' The pinch of *bhusa*
enlightened Trejago. He saw—this kind of letter leaves much to
instinctive knowledge—that the *bhusa* referred to the big heap of
cattle-food over which he had fallen in Amir Nath's Gully, and
that the message must come from the person behind the grating;
she being a widow. So the message ran then—'A widow, in the
Gully in which is the heap of *bhusa*, desires you to come at eleven
o'clock.'

Trejago threw all the rubbish into the fireplace and laughed.
He knew that men in the East do not make love under windows
at eleven in the forenoon, nor do women fix appointments a week
in advance. So he went, that very night at eleven, into Amir
Nath's Gully, clad in a *boorka*, which cloaks a man as well as a

woman. Directly the gongs of the City made the hour, the little voice behind the grating took up 'The Love Song of Har Dyal' at the verse where the Pathan girl calls upon Har Dyal to return. The song is really pretty in the vernacular. In English you miss the wail of it. It runs something like this—

> Alone upon the housetops, to the North
>     I turn and watch the lightning in the sky,—
> The glamour of thy footsteps in the North.
>     *Come back to me, Beloved, or I die!*
>
> Below my feet the still bazar is laid—
>     Far, far, below the weary camels lie,—
> The camels and the captives of thy raid.
>     *Come back to me, Beloved, or I die!*
>
> My father's wife is old and harsh with years,
>     And drudge of all my father's house am I.—
> My bread is sorrow and my drink is tears,
>     *Come back to me, Beloved, or I die!*

As the song stopped, Trejago stepped up under the grating and whispered—'I am here.'

Bisesa was good to look upon.

That night was the beginning of many strange things, and of a double life so wild that Trejago today sometimes wonders if it were not all a dream. Bisesa, or her old handmaiden who had thrown the object-letter, had detached the heavy grating from the brick-work of the wall; so that the window slid inside, leaving only a square of raw masonry into which an active man might climb.

In the day-time, Trejago drove through his routine of office-work, or put on his calling-clothes and called on the ladies of the Station, wondering how long they would know him if they knew of poor little Bisesa. At night, when all the City was still, came the walk under the evil-smelling *boorka*, the patrol through Jitha Megji's *bustee*, the quick turn into Amir Nath's Gully between the sleeping cattle and the dead walls, and then, last of all, Bisesa, and the deep, even breathing of the old woman who slept outside the door of the bare little room that Durga Charan allotted to his sister's daughter. Who or what Durga Charan was, Trejago never inquired; and why in the world he was not discovered and knifed never occurred to him till his madness was over, and Bisesa. . . . But this comes later.

Bisesa was an endless delight to Trejago. She was as ignorant as a bird; and her distorted versions of the rumours from the outside world, that had reached her in her room, amused Trejago almost as much as her lisping attempts to pronounce his name—'Christopher'. The first syllable was always more than she could manage, and she made funny little gestures with her roseleaf hands, as one throwing the name away, and then, kneeling before Trejago, asked him, exactly as an Englishwoman would do, if he were sure he loved her. Trejago swore that he loved her more than anyone else in the world. Which was true.

After a month of this folly, the exigencies of his other life compelled Trejago to be especially attentive to a lady of his acquaintance. You may take it for a fact that anything of this kind is not only noticed and discussed by a man's own race, but by some hundred and fifty natives as well. Trejago had to walk with this lady and talk to her at the Band-stand, and once or twice to drive with her; never for an instant dreaming that this would affect his dearer, out-of-the-way life. But the news flew, in the usual mysterious fashion, from mouth to mouth, till Bisesa's duenna heard of it and told Bisesa. The child was so troubled that she did the household work evilly, and was beaten by Durga Charan's wife in consequence.

A week later Bisesa taxed Trejago with the flirtation. She understood no gradations and spoke openly. Trejago laughed, and Bisesa stamped her little feet—little feet, light as marigold flowers, that could lie in the palm of a man's one hand.

Much that is written about Oriental passion and impulsiveness is exaggerated and compiled at second-hand, but a little of it is true; and when an Englishman finds that little, it is quite as startling as any passion in his own proper life. Bisesa raged and stormed, and finally threatened to kill herself if Trejago did not at once drop the alien *Memsahib* who had come between them. Trejago tried to explain, and to show her that she did not understand these things from a Western standpoint. Bisesa drew herself up, and said simply—

'I do not. I know only this—it is not good that I should have made you dearer than my own heart to me, *Sahib*. You are an Englishman. I am only a black girl'—she was fairer than bar-gold in the Mint,—'and the widow of a black man.'

Then she sobbed and said—'But on my soul and my Mother's soul, I love you. There shall no harm come to you, whatever happens to me.'

Trejago argued with the child, and tried to soothe her, but she seemed quite unreasonably disturbed. Nothing would satisfy her save that all relations between them should end. He was to go away at once. And he went. As he dropped out of the window she kissed his forehead twice, and he walked home wondering.

A week, and then three weeks, passed without a sign from Bisesa. Trejago, thinking that the rupture had lasted quite long enough, went down to Amir Nath's Gully for the fifth time in the three weeks, hoping that his rap at the sill of the shifting grating would be answered. He was not disappointed.

There was a young moon, and one stream of light fell down into Amir Nath's Gully, and struck the grating which was drawn away as he knocked. From the black dark Bisesa held out her arms into the moonlight. Both hands had been cut off at the wrists, and the stumps were nearly healed.

Then, as Bisesa bowed her head between her arms and sobbed, someone in the room grunted like a wild beast, and something sharp—knife, sword, or spear,—thrust at Trejago in his *boorka*. The stroke missed his body, but cut into one of the muscles of the groin, and he limped slightly from the wound for the rest of his days.

The grating went into its place. There was no sign whatever from inside the house,—nothing but the moonlight strip on the high wall, and the blackness of Amir Nath's Gully behind.

The next thing Trejago remembers, after raging and shouting like a madman between those pitiless walls, is that he found himself near the river as the dawn was breaking, threw away his *boorka* and went home bareheaded.

What was the tragedy—whether Bisesa had, in a fit of causeless despair, told everything, or the intrigue had been discovered and she tortured to tell; whether Durga Charan knew his name and what became of Bisesa—Trejago does not know to this day. Something horrible had happened, and the thought of what it must have been comes upon Trejago in the night now and again, and keeps him company till the morning. One special feature of the case is that he does not know where lies the front of Durga Charan's house. It may open on to a courtyard common to two or more houses, or it may lie behind any one of the gates of Jitha Megji's *bustee*. Trejago cannot tell. He cannot get Bisesa—poor little Bisesa—back again. He has lost her in the City where each man's house is as guarded and as unknowable as the grave; and the grating that opens into Amir Nath's Gully has been walled up.

But Trejago pays his calls regularly, and is reckoned a very decent sort of man.

There is nothing peculiar about him, except a slight stiffness, caused by a riding-strain, in the right leg.

1888

# The Pit That They Digged

MR HAWKINS MUMRATH, of Her Majesty's Bengal Civil Service, lay down to die of enteric fever; and, being a thorough-minded man, so nearly accomplished his purpose that all his friends, two doctors, and the Government he served gave him up for lost. Indeed, upon a false rumour the night before he rallied, several journals published very pleasant obituary notices, which, three weeks later, Mr Mumrath sat up in bed and studied with interest. It is strange to read about yourself in the past tense, and soothing to dicover that for all your faults, your world 'might have spared a better man'. When a Bengal civilian is tepid and harmless, newspapers always conclude their notices with this reflection. It entirely failed to amuse Mr Mumrath.

The loving-kindness of the Government provides for the use of its servants in the East luxuries undreamed of by other civilizations. A State-paid doctor closed Mumrath's eyes,—till Mumrath insisted upon opening them again; a subventionized undertaker bought Government timber for a Government coffin, and the great cemetery of St Golgotha-in-Partibus prepared, according to regulation, a brick-lined grave, headed and edged, with masonry rests for the coffin. The cost of that grave was 175 rupees 14 annas, including the lease of the land in perpetuity. Very minute are the instructions of the Government for the disposal, wharfage, and demurrage of its dead; but the actual arrangements are not published in any appendix to pay and pension rules, for the same reason that led a Prussian officer not to leave his dead and wounded too long in the sight of a battery under fire.

Mr Mumrath recovered and went about his work, to the disgust of his juniors who had hoped promotion from his decease. The undertaker sold the coffin, at a profit, to a fat Armenian merchant in Calcutta, and the State-paid doctor profited in practice by Mumrath's resurrection from the dead. The Cemetery of St Golgotha-in-Partibus sat down by the head of the new-made grave with the beautiful brick lining, and waited for the corpse then signing despatches in an office three miles away. The yearly accounts were made up; and there remained over, unpaid for, one grave, cost 175 rupees 14 annas. The vouchers for all the other graves carried the name of a deceased servant of the Government. Only one space was blank in the column.

Then Ahutosh Lal Deb, Sub-deputy Assistant in the Accounts Department, being full of zeal for the State and but newly appointed to his important post, wrote officially to the Cemetery, desiring to know the inwardness of that grave, and 'having the honour to be', etc. The Cemetery wrote officially that there was no inwardness at all, but a complete emptiness; said grave having been ordered for Mr Hawkins Mumrath, and 'had the honour to remain'. Ahutosh Lal Deb had the honour to point out that, the grave being unused, the Government could by no means pay for it. The Cemetery wished to know if the account could be carried over to the next year, 'pending anticipated taking-up of grave'.

Ahutosh Lal Deb said that he was not going to have the accounts confused. Discrepancy was the soul of badinage and defalcations. The Cemetery would be good enough to adjust on the financial basis of that year.

The Cemetery wished they might be buried if they saw their way to doing it, and there really had been more than two thousand burned bricks put into the lining of the grave. Meantime, they complained, the Government Brickfield Audit was waiting until all material should have been paid for.

Ahutosh Lal Deb wrote: 'Refer to Mr Mumrath.' The Cemetery referred semi-officially. It struck them as being rather a delicate matter, but orders are orders.

Hawkins Mumrath wrote back, saying that he had the honour to be quite well, and not in the least in need of a grave, brick-lined or otherwise. He recommended the head of the Cemetery to get into that grave and stay there. The Cemetery forwarded the letter to Ahutosh Lal Deb, for reference and order.

Ahutosh Lal Deb forwarded it to the Provincial Government, who filed it behind a mass of other files and forgot all about it.

A fat she-cobra crawled into the neglected grave, and laid her eggs among the bricks. The Rains fell, and a little sprinkling of grass jewelled the brick floor.

The Cemetery wrote to Ahutosh Lal Deb, advising him that Mr Mumrath had not paid for the grave, and requesting that the sum might be stopped from his monthly pay. Ahutosh Lal Deb sent the letter to Hawkins Mumrath as a reminder.

Hawkins Mumrath swore; but when he had sworn, he began to feel frightened. The enteric fever had destroyed his nerve. He wrote to the Accounts Department, protesting against the injustice of paying for a grave beforehand. Deductions for pension or widow's annuity were quite right, but this sort of deduction was an imposition besides being sarcastic.

Ahutosh Lal Deb wrote that Mr Mumrath's style was not one usually employed in official correspondence, and requested him to modulate it and pay for the grave. Hawkins Mumrath tossed the letter into the fire, and wrote to the Provincial Government.

The Provincial Government had the honour to point out that the matter rested entirely between Mr Hawkins Mumrath and the

Accounts Department. They saw no reason to interfere till the money was actually deducted from the pay. In that eventuality, if Mr Hawkins Mumrath appealed through the proper channels, he might, if the matter were properly reported upon, get a refund, less the cost of his last letter, which was under-stamped. The Cemetery wrote to Ahutosh Lal Deb, enclosing triplicate of grave-bill and demanding some sort of settlement.

Ahutosh Lal Deb deducted 175 rupees 14 annas from Mumrath's monthly pay. Mumrath appealed through the proper channels. The Provincial Government wrote that the expenses of all Government graves solely concerned the Supreme Government, to whom his letter had been forwarded.

Mumrath wrote to the Supreme Government. The Supreme Government had the honour to explain that the management of St Golgotha-in-Partibus was under direct control of the Provincial Government, to whom they had had the honour of forwarding his communication. Mumrath telegraphed to the Cemetery to this effect.

The Cemetery telegraphed: 'Fiscal and finance, Supreme; management of internal affairs, Provincial Government. Refer Revenue and Agricultural Department for grave details.'

Mumrath referred to the Revenue and Agricultural Department. That Department had the honour to make clear that it was only concerned in the plantation of trees round the Cemetery. The Forest Department controlled the reboisement of the edges of the paths.

Mumrath forwarded all the letters to Ahutosh Lal Deb, with a request for an immediate refund under 'Rule 431 A, Supplementary Addenda, Bengal'. He invented rule and reference *pro re nata*, having some knowledge of the workings of the Babu mind.

The crest of the Revenue and Agricultural Department frightened Ahutosh Lal Deb more than the reference. He bewilderedly granted the refund, and recouped the Government from the Cemetery Establishment allowance.

The Cemetery Establishment Executive Head wanted to know what Ahutosh Lal Deb meant.

The Accountant-General wanted to know what Ahutosh Lal Deb meant.

The Provincial Government wanted to know what Ahutosh Lal Deb meant.

The Revenue and Agriculture, the Forest Department, and the Government Harness Depot, which supplies the leather slings for the biers, all wanted to know what the deuce Ahutosh Lal Deb meant.

Ahutosh Lal Deb referred them severally to Mr Hawkins

Mumrath, who had driven out to chuckle over his victory all alone at the head of the brick-lined grave with the masonry foot rests.

The she-cobra was sunning herself by the edge of the grave with her little ones about her, for the eggs had hatched out beautifully. Hawkins Mumrath stepped absently on the old lady's tail, and she bit him in the ankle.

Hawkins Mumrath drove home very quickly, and died in five hours and three-quarters.

Then Ahutosh Lal Deb passed the entry to 'regular account', and there was peace in India.

1889

# The Man Who Was

The Earth gave up her dead that tide,
  Into our camp he came,
And said his say, and went his way,
  And left our hearts aflame.

Keep tally—on the gun-butt score
  The vengeance we must take,
When God shall bring full reckoning,
  For our dead comrade's sake.

*Ballad.*

LET it be clearly understood that the Russian is a delightful person till he tucks in his shirt. As an Oriental he is charming. It is only when he insists upon being treated as the most easterly of western peoples instead of the most westerly of easterns that he becomes a racial anomaly extremely difficult to handle. The host never knows which side of his nature is going to turn up next.

Dirkovitch was a Russian—a Russian of the Russians—who appeared to get his bread by serving the Czar as an officer in a Cossack regiment, and corresponding for a Russian newspaper with a name that was never twice alike. He was a handsome young Oriental, fond of wandering through unexplored portions of the earth, and he arrived in India from nowhere in particular. At least no living man could ascertain whether it was by way of Balkh, Badakshan, Chitral, Baluchistan, or Nepal, or anywhere else. The Indian Government, being in an unusually affable mood, gave orders that he was to be civilly treated and shown everything that was to be seen. So he drifted, talking bad English and worse French, from one city to another, till he foregathered with Her Majesty's White Hussars in the city of Peshawur, which stands at the mouth of that narrow swordcut in the hills that men call the Khyber Pass. He was undoubtedly an officer, and he was decorated after the manner of the Russians with little enamelled crosses, and he could talk, and (though this has nothing to do with his merits) he had been given up as a hopeless task, or cask, by the Black Tyrone, who individually and collectively, with hot whisky and honey, mulled brandy, and mixed spirits of every kind, had striven in all hospitality to make him drunk. And when the Black Tyrone, who are exclusively Irish, fail to disturb the peace of head of a foreigner—that foreigner is certain to be a superior man.

The White Hussars were as conscientious in choosing their wine as in charging the enemy. All that they possessed, including

14

some wondrous brandy, was placed at the absolute disposition of Dirkovitch, and he enjoyed himself hugely—even more than among the Black Tyrones.

But he remained distressingly European through it all. The White Hussars were 'My dear true friends', 'Fellow-soldiers glorious', and 'Brothers inseparable'. He would unburden himself by the hour on the glorious future that awaited the combined arms of England and Russia when their hearts and their territories should run side by side, and the great mission of civilizing Asia should begin. That was unsatisfactory, because Asia is not going to be civilized after the methods of the West. There is too much Asia and she is too old. You cannot reform a lady of many lovers, and Asia has been insatiable in her flirtations aforetime. She will never attend Sunday school or learn to vote save with swords for tickets.

Dirkovitch knew this as well as anyone else, but it suited him to talk special-correspondently and to make himself as genial as he could. Now and then he volunteered a little, a very little, information about his own sotnia of Cossacks, left apparently to look after themselves somewhere at the back of beyond. He had done rough work in Central Asia, and had seen rather more help-yourself fighting than most men of his years. But he was careful never to betray his superiority, and more than careful to praise on all occasions the appearance, drill, uniform, and organization of Her Majesty's White Hussars. And indeed they were a regiment to be admired. When Lady Durgan, widow of the late Sir John Durgan, arrived in their station, and after a short time had been proposed to by every single man at mess, she put the public sentiment very neatly when she explained that they were all so nice that unless she could marry them all, including the colonel and some majors already married, she was not going to content herself with one hussar. Wherefore she wedded a little man in a rifle regiment, being by nature contradictious; and the White Hussars were going to wear crape on their arms, but compromised by attending the wedding in full force, and lining the aisle with unutterable reproach. She had jilted them all—from Basset-Holmer the senior captain to little Mildred the junior subaltern, who could have given her four thousand a year and a title.

The only persons who did not share the general regard for the White Hussars were a few thousand gentlemen of Jewish extraction who lived across the border, and answered to the name of Pathan. They had once met the regiment officially and for something less than twenty minutes, but the interview, which was complicated with many casualties, had filled them with prejudice.

They even called the White Hussars children of the devil and sons of persons whom it would be perfectly impossible to meet in decent society. Yet they were not above making their aversion fill their money-belts. The regiment possessed carbines—beautiful Martini-Henry carbines that would lob a bullet into an enemy's camp at one thousand yards, and were even handier than the long rifle. Therefore they were coveted all along the border, and since demand inevitably breeds supply, they were supplied at the risk of life and limb for exactly their weight in coined silver—seven and one half pounds' weight of rupees, or sixteen pounds sterling reckoning the rupee at par. They were stolen at night by snaky-haired thieves who crawled on their stomachs under the nose of the sentries; they disappeared mysteriously from locked arm-racks, and in the hot weather, when all the barrack doors and windows were open, they vanished like puffs of their own smoke. The border people desired them for family vendettas and contingencies. But in the long cold nights of the northern Indian winter they were stolen most extensively. The traffic of murder was liveliest among the hills at that season, and prices ruled high. The regimental guards were first doubled and then trebled. A trooper does not much care if he loses a weapon—Government must make it good—but he deeply resents the loss of his sleep. The regiment grew very angry, and one rifle-thief bears the visible marks of their anger upon him to this hour. That incident stopped the burglaries for a time, and the guards were reduced accordingly, and the regiment devoted itself to polo with unexpected results; for it beat by two goals to one that very terrible polo corps the Lushkar Light Horse, though the latter had four ponies apiece for a short hour's fight, as well as a native officer who played like a lambent flame across the ground.

They gave a dinner to celebrate the event. The Lushkar team came, and Dirkovitch came, in the fullest full uniform of a Cossack officer, which is as full as a dressing-gown, and was introduced to the Lushkars, and opened his eyes as he regarded. They were lighter men than the Hussars, and they carried themselves with the swing that is the peculiar right of the Punjab Frontier Force and all Irregular Horse. Like everything else in the Service it has to be learnt, but, unlike many things, it is never forgotten, and remains on the body till death.

The great beam-roofed mess-room of the White Hussars was a sight to be remembered. All the mess plate was out on the long table—the same table that had served up the bodies of five officers after a forgotten fight long and long ago—the dingy, battered standards faced the door of entrance, clumps of winter-roses lay between the silver candlesticks, and the portraits of eminent officers deceased looked down on their successors from between the heads of sambhur, nilghai, markhor, and, pride of all the mess, two grinning snow-leopards that had cost Basset-Holmer four months' leave that he might have spent in England, instead of on the road to Thibet and the daily risk of his life by ledge, snow-slide, and grassy slope.

The servants in spotless white muslin with the crest of their regiments on the brow of their turbans waited behind their masters, who were clad in the scarlet and gold of the White Hussars, and the cream and silver of the Lushkar Light Horse. Dirkovitch's dull green uniform was the only dark spot at the board, but his big onyx eyes made up for it. He was fraternizing effusively with the captain of the Lushkar team, who was wondering how many of Dirkovitch's Cossacks his own dark wiry down-countrymen could account for in a fair charge. But one does not speak of these things openly.

The talk rose higher and higher, and the regimental band played between the courses, as is the immemorial custom, till all tongues ceased for a moment with the removal of the dinner-slips and the first toast of obligation, when an officer rising said, 'Mr Vice, the Queen', and little Mildred from the bottom of the table answered, 'The Queen, God bless her', and the big spurs clanked as the big men heaved themselves up and drank the Queen upon whose pay they were falsely supposed to settle their mess-bills. That Sacrament of the Mess never grows old, and never ceases to bring a lump into the throat of the listener wherever he be by sea or by land. Dirkovitch rose with his 'brothers glorious', but he could not understand. No one but an officer can tell what the toast means; and the bulk have more sentiment than comprehension. Immediately after the little silence that follows on the ceremony there entered the native officer who had played for the Lushkar team. He could not, of course, eat with the mess, but he came in at dessert, all six feet of him, with the blue and silver turban atop, and the big black boots below. The mess rose joyously as he thrust forward the hilt of his sabre in token of fealty for the colonel of the White Hussars to touch, and dropped into a vacant chair amid shouts of: '*Rung ho*, Hira Singh!' (which being translated means 'Go in and win'). 'Did I whack you over the knee, old man?' 'Rissaldar Sahib, what the devil made you play that kicking pig of a pony in the last ten minutes?' '*Shabash*, Rissaldar Sahib!' Then the voice of the colonel,'The health of Rissaldar Hira Singh!'

After the shouting had died away Hira Singh rose to reply, for he was the cadet of a royal house, the son of a king's son, and knew what was due on these occasions. Thus he spoke in the vernacular: 'Colonel Sahib and officers of this regiment. Much honour have you done me. This will I remember. We came down from afar to play you. But we were beaten.' ('No fault of yours, Rissaldar Sahib. Played on our own ground y'know. Your ponies were cramped from the railway. Don't apologize!') 'Therefore perhaps we will come again if it be so ordained.' ('Hear! Hear! Hear, indeed! Bravo! Hsh!') 'Then we will play you afresh' ('Happy to meet you.') 'till there are left no feet upon our ponies. Thus far for sport.' He dropped one hand on his sword-hilt and his eye wandered to Dirkovitch lolling back in his chair. 'But if by the will of God there arises any other game which is not the polo game, then be assured, Colonel Sahib and officers, that we will play it out side by side, though *they*,' again his eye sought Dirkovitch, 'though *they*, I say, have fifty ponies to our one horse.' And with a deep-mouthed *Rung ho!* that sounded like a musket-butt on flagstones, he sat down amid leaping glasses.

Dirkovitch, who had devoted himself steadily to the brandy—the terrible brandy aforementioned—did not understand, nor did the expurgated translations offered to him at all convey the point. Decidedly Hira Singh's was the speech of the evening, and the clamour might have continued to the dawn had it not been broken by the noise of a shot without that sent every man feeling at his defenceless left side. Then there was a scuffle and a yell of pain.

'Carbine-stealing again!' said the adjutant, calmly sinking back in his chair. 'This comes of reducing the guards. I hope the sentries have killed him.'

The feet of armed men pounded on the verandah flags, and it was as though something was being dragged.

'Why don't they put him in the cells till the morning?' said the colonel testily. 'See if they've damaged him, sergeant.'

The mess sergeant fled out into the darkness and returned with two troopers and a corporal, all very much perplexed.

'Caught a man stealin' carbines, sir,' said the corporal. 'Leastways 'e was crawlin' towards the barricks, sir, past the main road sentries, an' the sentry 'e sez, sir——'

The limp heap of rags upheld by the three men groaned. Never was seen so destitute and demoralized an Afghan. He was turbanless, shoeless, caked with dirt, and all but dead with rough handling. Hira Singh started slightly at the sound of the man's pain. Dirkovitch took another glass of brandy.

'*What* does the sentry say?' said the colonel.

'Sez 'e speaks English, sir,' said the corporal.

'So you brought him into mess instead of handing him over to the sergeant! If he spoke all the Tongues of the Pentecost you've no business——'

Again the bundle groaned and muttered. Little Mildred had risen from his place to inspect. He jumped back as though he had been shot.

'Perhaps it would be better, sir, to send the men away,' said he to the colonel, for he was a much privileged subaltern. He put his arms round the rag-bound horror as he spoke, and dropped him into a chair It may not have been explained that the littleness of Mildred lay in his being six feet four and big in proportion. The corporal seeing that an officer was disposed to look after the capture, and that the colonel's eye was beginning to blaze, promptly removed himself and his men. The mess was left alone with the carbine-thief, who laid his head on the table and wept bitterly, hopelessly, and inconsolably, as little children weep.

Hira Singh leapt to his feet. 'Colonel Sahib,' said he, 'that man is no Afghan, for they weep *Ai! Ai!* Nor is he of Hindustan, for they weep *Oh! Ho!* He weeps after the fashion of the white men, who say *Ow! Ow!*'

'Now where the dickens did you get that knowledge, Hira Singh?' said the captain of the Lushkar team.

'Hear him!' said Hira Singh simply, pointing at the crumpled figure that wept as though it would never cease.

'He said, "My God!"' said little Mildred. 'I heard him say it.'

The colonel and the mess-room looked at the man in silence. It is a horrible thing to hear a man cry. A woman can sob from the top of her palate, or her lips, or anywhere else, but a man must cry from his diaphragm, and it rends him to pieces.

'Poor devil!' said the colonel, coughing tremendously. 'We ought to send him to hospital. He's been manhandled.'

Now the adjutant loved his carbines. They were to him as his grandchildren, the men standing in the first place. He grunted rebelliously: 'I can understand an Afghan stealing, because he's built that way. But I can't understand his crying. That makes it worse.'

The brandy must have affected Dirkovitch, for he lay back in his chair and stared at the ceiling. There was nothing special in the ceiling beyond a shadow as of a huge black coffin. Owing to some peculiarity in the construction of the mess-room this shadow was always thrown when the candles were lighted. It never disturbed the digestion of the White Hussars. They were in fact rather proud of it.

'Is he going to cry all night?' said the colonel, 'or are we supposed to sit up with little Mildred's guest until he feels better?'

The man in the chair threw up his head and stared at the mess. 'Oh, my God!' he said, and every soul in the mess rose to his feet.

Then the Lushkar captain did a deed for which he ought to have
been given the Victoria Cross—distinguished gallantry in a fight
against overwhelming curiosity. He picked up his team with his
eyes as the hostess picks up the ladies at the opportune moment,
and pausing only by the colonel's chair to say, 'This isn't *our*
affair, you know, sir,' led them into the verandah and the gardens.
Hira Singh was the last to go, and he looked at Dirkovitch. But
Dirkovitch had departed into a brandy-paradise of his own. His
lips moved without sound, and he was studying the coffin on the
ceiling.

'White—white all over,' said Basset-Holmer, the adjutant.
'What a pernicious renegade he must be! I wonder where he came
from?'

The colonel shook the man gently by the arm, and 'Who are
you?' said he.

There was no answer. The man stared round the mess-room
and smiled in the colonel's face. Little Mildred, who was always
more of a woman than a man till 'Boot and saddle' was sounded,
repeated the question in a voice that would have drawn confi-
dences from a geyser. The man only smiled. Dirkovitch at the far
end of the table slid gently from his chair to the floor. No son of
Adam in this present imperfect world can mix the Hussars'
champagne with the Hussars' brandy by five and eight glasses of
each without remembering the pit whence he was digged and
descending thither. The band began to play the tune with which
the White Hussars from the date of their formation have con-
cluded all their functions. They would sooner be disbanded than
abandon that tune; it is a part of their system. The man straight-
ened himself in his chair and drummed on the table with his
fingers.

'I don't see why we should entertain lunatics,' said the colonel.
'Call a guard and send him off to the cells. We'll look into the
business in the morning. Give him a glass of wine first though.'

Little Mildred filled a sherry-glass with the brandy and thrust it
over to the man. He drank, and the tune rose louder, and he
straightened himself yet more. Then he put out his long-taloned
hands to a piece of plate opposite and fingered it lovingly. There
was a mystery connected with that piece of plate, in the shape of
a spring which converted what was a seven-branched candlestick,
three springs on each side and one in the middle, into a sort of
wheel-spoke candelabrum. He found the spring, pressed it, and
laughed weakly. He rose from his chair and inspected a picture on
the wall, then moved on to another picture, the mess watching
him without a word. When he came to the mantelpiece he shook
his head and seemed distressed. A piece of plate representing a

mounted hussar in full uniform caught his eye. He pointed to it, and then to the mantelpiece with inquiry in his eyes.

'What is it—Oh, what is it?' said little Mildred. Then as a mother might speak to a child, 'That is a horse. Yes, a horse.'

Very slowly came the answer in a thick, passionless guttural—'Yes, I—have seen. But—where is *the* horse?'

You could have heard the hearts of the mess beating as the men drew back to give the stranger full room in his wanderings. There was no question of calling the guard.

Again he spoke—very slowly, 'Where is *our* horse?'

There is but one horse in the White Hussars, and his portrait hangs outside the door of the mess-room. He is the piebald drum-horse, the king of the regimental band, that served the regiment for seven-and-thirty years, and in the end was shot for old age. Half the mess tore the thing down from its place and thrust it into the man's hands. He placed it above the mantelpiece, it clattered on the ledge as his poor hands dropped it, and he staggered towards the bottom of the table, falling into Mildred's chair. Then all the men spoke to one another something after this fashion. 'The drum-horse hasn't hung over the mantelpiece since '67.' 'How does he know?' 'Mildred, go and speak to him again.' 'Colonel, what are you going to do?' 'Oh, dry up, and give the poor devil a chance to pull himself together.' 'It isn't possible anyhow. The man's a lunatic.'

Little Mildred stood at the colonel's side talking in his ear. 'Will you be good enough to take your seats please, gentlemen!' he said, and the mess dropped into the chairs. Only Dirkovitch's seat, next to little Mildred's, was blank, and little Mildred himself had found Hira Singh's place. The wide-eyed mess-sergeant filled the glasses in dead silence. Once more the colonel rose, but his hand shook, and the port spilled on the table as he looked straight at the man in little Mildred's chair and said hoarsely, 'Mr Vice, the Queen.' There was a little pause, but the man sprung to his feet and answered without hesitation, 'The Queen, God bless her!' and as he emptied the thin glass he snapped the shank between his fingers.

Long and long ago, when the Empress of India was a young woman and there were no unclean ideals in the land, it was the custom of a few messes to drink the Queen's toast in broken glass, to the vast delight of the mess-contractors. The custom is now dead, because there is nothing to break anything for, except now and again the word of a Government, and that has been broken already.

'That settles it,' said the colonel, with a gasp. 'He's not a sergeant. What in the world is he?'

The entire mess echoed the word, and the volley of questions would have scared any man. It was no wonder that the ragged, filthy invader could only smile and shake his head.

From under the table, calm and smiling, rose Dirkovitch, who had been roused from healthful slumber by feet upon his body. By the side of the man he rose, and the man shrieked and grovelled. It was a horrible sight coming so swiftly upon the pride and glory of the toast that had brought the strayed wits together.

Dirkovitch made no offer to raise him, but little Mildred heaved him up in an instant. It is not good that a gentleman who can answer to the Queen's toast should lie at the feet of a subaltern of Cossacks.

The hasty action tore the wretch's upper clothing nearly to the waist, and his body was seamed with dry black scars. There is only one weapon in the world that cuts in parallel lines, and it is neither the cane nor the cat. Dirkovitch saw the marks, and the pupils of his eyes dilated. Also his face changed. He said something that sounded like *Shto ve takete*, and the man fawning answered, *Chetyre*.

'What's that?' said everybody together.

'His number. That is number four, you know.' Dirkovitch spoke very thickly.

'What has a Queen's officer to do with a qualified number?' said the colonel, and an unpleasant growl ran round the table.

'How can I tell?' said the affable Oriental with a sweet smile. 'He is a—how you have it?—escape—run-a-way, from over there.' He nodded towards the darkness of the night.

'Speak to him if he'll answer you, and speak to him gently,' said little Mildred, settling the man in a chair. It seemed most improper to all present that Dirkovitch should sip brandy as he talked in purring, spitting Russian to the creature who answered so feebly and with such evident dread. But since Dirkovitch appeared to understand no one said a word. All breathed heavily, leaning forward, in the long gaps of the conversation. The next time that they have no engagements on hand the White Hussars intend to go to St Petersburg in a body to learn Russian.

'He does not know how many years ago,' said Dirkovitch facing the mess, 'but he says it was very long ago in a war. I think that there was an accident. He says he was of this glorious and distinguished regiment in the war.'

'The rolls! The rolls! Holmer, get the rolls!' said little Mildred, and the adjutant dashed off bareheaded to the orderly-room, where the muster-rolls of the regiment were kept. He returned just in time to hear Dirkovitch conclude, 'Therefore, my dear friends, I am most sorry to say there was an accident which would have been reparable if he had apologized to that our colonel, which he had insulted.'

The followed another growl which the colonel tried to beat down. The mess was in no mood just then to weigh insults to Russian colonels.

'He does not remember, but I think that there was an accident, and so he was not exchanged among the prisoners, but he was sent to another place—how do you say?—the country. *So*, he says, he came here. He does not know how he came. Eh? He was at Chepany'—the man caught the word, nodded, and shivered—'at Zhigansk and Irkutsk. I cannot understand how he escaped. He says, too, that he was in the forests for many years, but how many years he has forgotten—that with many things. It was an accident; done because he did not apologize to that our colonel. Ah!'

Instead of echoing Dirkovitch's sigh of regret, it is sad to record that the White Hussars livelily exhibited un-Christian delight and other emotions, hardly restrained by their sense of hospitality. Holmer flung the frayed and yellow regimental rolls on the table, and the men flung themselves at these.

'Steady! Fifty-six—fifty-five—fifty-four,' said Holmer. 'Here we are. "Lieutenant Austin Limmason. *Missing*.' That was before Sebastopol. What an infernal shame! Insulted one of their colonels, and was quietly shipped off. Thirty years of his life wiped out.'

'But he never apologized. Said he'd see him damned first,' chorused the mess.

'Poor chap! I suppose he never had the chance afterwards. How did he come here?' said the colonel.

The dingy heap in the chair could give no answer.

'Do you know who you are?'

It laughed weakly.

'Do you know that you are Limmason—Lieutenant Limmason of the White Hussars?'

Swiftly as a shot came the answer, in a slightly surprised tone, 'Yes, I'm Limmason, of course.' The light died out in his eyes, and the man collapsed, watching every motion of Dirkovitch with terror. A flight from Siberia may fix a few elementary facts in the mind, but it does not seem to lead to continuity of thought. The man could not explain how, like a homing pigeon, he had found his way to his own old mess again. Of what he had suffered or seen he knew nothing. He cringed before Dirkovitch as instinctively as he had pressed the spring of the candlestick, sought the picture of the drum-horse, and answered to the toast of the Queen. The rest was a blank that the dreaded Russian tongue could only in part remove. His head bowed on his breast, and he giggled and cowered alternately.

The devil that lived in the brandy prompted Dirkovitch at this extremely inopportune moment to make a speech. He rose, swaying slightly, gripped the table-edge, while his eyes glowed like opals, and began:

'Fellow-soldiers glorious—true friends and hospitables. It was an accident, and deplorable—most deplorable.' Here he smiled sweetly all round the mess. 'But you will think of this little, little thing. So little, is it not? The Czar! Posh! I slap my fingers—I snap my fingers at him. Do I believe in him? No! But in us Slav who has done nothing, *him* I believe. Seventy—how much—millions peoples that have done nothing—not one thing. Posh! Napoleon was an episode.' He banged a hand on the table. 'Hear you, old peoples, we have done nothing in the world—out here. All our work is to do; and it shall be done, old peoples. Get a-way!' He waved his hand imperiously, and pointed to the man. 'You see him. He is not good to see. He was just one little—oh, so little—accident, that no one remembered. Now he is *That*! So will you be, brother soldiers so brave—so will you be. But you will never come back. You will all go where he is gone, or'—he pointed to the great coffin-shadow on the ceiling, and muttering, 'Seventy millions—get a-way, you old peoples', fell asleep.

'Sweet, and to the point,' said little Mildred. 'What's the use of getting wroth? Let's make this poor devil comfortable.'

But that was a matter suddenly and swiftly taken from the loving hands of the White Hussars. The lieutenant had returned only to go away again three days later, when the wail of the Dead March, and the tramp of the squadrons, told the wondering Station, who saw no gap in the mess-table, that an officer of the regiment had resigned his new-found commission.

And Dirkovitch, bland, supple, and always genial, went away too by a night train. Little Mildred and another man saw him off, for he was the guest of the mess, and even had he smitten the colonel with the open hand, the law of that mess allowed no relaxation of hospitality.

'Goodbye, Dirkovitch, and a pleasant journey,' said little Mildred.

'*Au revoir*,' said the Russian.

'Indeed! But we thought you were going home?'

'Yes, but I will come again. My dear friends, is that road shut?' He pointed to where the North Star burned over the Khyber Pass.

'By Jove! I forgot. Of course. Happy to meet you, old man,

any time you like. Got everything you want? Cheroots, ice, bedding? That's all right. Well, *au revoir*, Dirkovitch.'

'Um,' said the other man, as the tail-lights of the train grew small. 'Of—all—the—unmitigated——!'

Little Mildred answered nothing, but watched the North Star and hummed a selection from a recent Simla burlesque that had much delighted the White Hussars. It ran—

> I'm sorry for Mister Bluebeard,
> I'm sorry to cause him pain;
> But a terrible spree there's sure to be
> When he comes back again.

1890

# The Miracle Of Purun Bhagat

The night we felt the earth would move
    We stole and plucked him by the hand,
Because we loved him with the love
    That knows but cannot understand.

And when the roaring hillside broke,
    And all our world fell down in rain,
We saved him, we the Little Folk;
    But lo! he does not come again!

Mourn now, we saved him for the sake
    Of such poor love as wild ones may.
Mourn ye! Our brother will not awake,
    And his own kind drive us away!
                              *Dirge of the Langurs.*

THERE was once a man in India who was Prime Minister of one of the semi-independent native States in the north-west part of the country. He was a Brahmin, so high-caste that caste ceased to have any particular meaning for him; and his father had been an important official in the gay-coloured tag-rag and bobtail of an old-fashioned Hindu Court. But as Purun Dass grew up he felt that the old order of things was changing, and that if anyone wished to get on in the world he must stand well with the English, and imitate all that the English believed to be good. At the same time a native official must keep his own master's favour. This was a difficult game, but the quiet, close-mouthed young Brahmin, helped by a good English education at a Bombay University, played it coolly, and rose, step by step, to be Prime Minister of the kingdom. That is to say, he held more real power than his master the Maharajah.

When the old king—who was suspicious of the English, their railways and telegraphs—died, Purun Dass stood high with his young successor, who had been tutored by an Englishman; and between them, though he always took care that his master should have the credit, they established schools for little girls, made roads, and started State dispensaries and shows of agricultural implements, and published a yearly blue-book on the 'Moral and Material Progress of the State', and the Foreign Office and the Government of India were delighted. Very few native States take up English progress altogether, for they will not believe, as Purun Dass showed he did, that what was good for the Englishman must be twice as good for the Asiatic. The Prime Minister became the honoured friend of Viceroys, and Governors, and Lieutenant-Governors, and medical missionaries, and common missionaries, and hard-riding English officers who came to shoot in the State preserves, as well as of whole hosts of tourists who travelled up and down India in the cold weather, showing how things ought to be managed. In his spare time he would endow scholarships for the study of medicine and manufactures on strictly English lines, and write letters to the *Pioneer*, the greatest Indian daily paper, explaining his master's aims and objects.

At last he went to England on a visit, and had to pay enormous sums to the priests when he came back; for even so high-caste a Brahmin as Purun Dass lost caste by crossing the black sea. In London he met and talked with everyone worth knowing—men whose names go all over the world—and saw a great deal more than he said. He was given honorary degrees by learned universities, and he made speeches and talked of Hindu social reform to English ladies in evening dress, till all London cried, 'This is the most fascinating man we have ever met at dinner since cloths were first laid.'

When he returned to India there was a blaze of glory, for the Viceroy himself made a special visit to confer upon the Maharajah the Grand Cross of the Star of India—all diamonds and ribbons and enamel; and at the same ceremony, while the cannon boomed, Purun Dass was made a Knight Commander of the Order of the Indian Empire; so that his name stood Sir Purun Dass, K.C.I.E.

That evening, at dinner in the big Viceregal tent, he stood up with the badge and the collar of the Order on his breast, and replying to the toast of his master's health, made a speech few Englishmen could have bettered.

Next month, when the city had returned to its sun-baked quiet, he did a thing no Englishman would have dreamed of doing; for, so far as the world's affairs went, he died. The jewelled order of his knighthood went back to the Indian Government, and a new Prime Minister was appointed to the charge of affairs, and a great game of General Post began in all the subordinate appointments. The priests knew what had happened, and the people guessed; but India is the one place in the world where a man can do as he pleases and nobody asks why; and the fact that Dewan Sir Purun Dass, K.C.I.E., had resigned position, palace, and power, and taken up the begging-bowl and ochre-coloured dress of a Sunnyasi, or holy man, was considered nothing extraordinary. He had been, as the Old Law recommends, twenty years a youth, twenty years a fighter—though he had never carried a weapon in his life—and twenty years head of a household. He had used his wealth and his power for what he knew both to be worth; he had taken honour when it came his way; he had seen men and cities far and near, and men and cities had stood up and honoured him. Now he would let those things go, as a man drops the cloak he no longer needs.

Behind him, as he walked through the city gates, an antelope skin and brass-handled crutch under his arm, and a begging-bowl of polished brown *coco-de-mer* in his hand, barefoot, alone, with eyes cast on the ground—behind him they were firing salutes from the bastions in honour of his happy successor. Purun Dass nodded. All that life was ended; and he bore it no more ill-will or good-will than a man bears to a colourless dream of the night. He was a Sunnyasi—a houseless, wandering mendicant, depending on his neighbours for his daily bread; and so long as there is a morsel to divide in India, neither priest nor beggar starves. He had never in his life tasted meat, and very seldom eaten even fish. A five-pound note would have covered his personal expenses for food through any one of the many years in which he had been absolute master of millions of money. Even when he was being lionized in London he had held before him his dream of peace and quiet—the long, white, dusty Indian road, printed all over with bare feet, the incessant, slow-moving traffic, and the sharp-smelling wood smoke curling up under the fig-trees in the twilight, where the wayfarers sit at their evening meal.

When the time came to make that dream true the Prime Minister took the proper steps, and in three days you might more easily have found a bubble in the trough of the long Atlantic seas than Purun Dass among the roving, gathering, separating millions of India.

At night his antelope skin was spread where the darkness overtook him—sometimes in a Sunnyasi monastery by the roadside; sometimes by a mud-pillar shrine of Kala Pir, where the Jogis, who are another misty division of holy men, would receive him as they do those who know what castes and divisions are worth; sometimes on the outskirts of a little Hindu village, where the children would steal up with the food their parents had prepared; and sometimes on the pitch of the bare grazing-grounds, where the flame of his stick fire waked the drowsy camels. It was all one to Purun Dass—or Purun Bhagat, as he called himself now. Earth, people, and food were all one. But unconsciously his feet drew him away northward and eastward; from the south to Rohtak; from Rohtak to Kurnool; from Kurnool to ruined Samanah, and then up-stream along the dried bed of the Gugger river that fills only when the rain falls in the hills, till one day he saw the far line of the great Himalayas.

Then Purun Bhagat smiled, for he remembered that his mother was of Rajput Brahmin birth, from Kulu way—a Hill-woman, always home-sick for the snows—and that the least touch of Hill blood draws a man in the end back to where he belongs.

'Yonder,' said Purun Bhagat, breasting the lower slopes of the Sewaliks, where the cacti stand up like seven-branched candle-sticks—'yonder I shall sit down and get knowledge'; and the cool wind of the Himalayas whistled about his ears as he trod the road that led to Simla.

The last time he had come that way it had been in state, with a clattering cavalry escort, to visit the gentlest and most affable of Viceroys; and the two had talked for an hour together about mutual friends in London, and what the Indian common folk really thought of things. This time Purun Bhagat paid no calls, but leaned on the rail of the Mall, watching that glorious view of the Plains spread out forty miles below, till a native Moham-medan policeman told him he was obstructing traffic; and Purun Bhagat salaamed reverently to the Law, because he knew the value of it, and was seeking for a Law of his own. Then he moved on, and slept that night in an empty hut at Chota Simla, which looks like the very last end of the earth, but it was only the beginning of his journey.

He followed the Himalaya–Tibet road, the little ten-foot track that is blasted out of solid rock, or strutted out on timbers over gulfs a thousand feet deep; that dips into warm, wet, shut-in valleys, and climbs out across bare, grassy hill-shoulders where the sun strikes like a burning-glass; or turns through dripping, dark forests where the tree-ferns dress the trunks from head to heel, and the pheasant calls to his mate. And he met Tibetan herdsmen with their dogs and flocks of sheep, each sheep with a little bag of borax on his back, and wandering wood-cutters, and cloaked and blanketed Lamas from Tibet, coming into India on pilgrimage, and envoys of little solitary Hill-states, posting furiously on ring-streaked and piebald ponies, or the cavalcade of a Rajah paying a visit; or else for a long, clear day he would see nothing more than a black bear grunting and rooting below in the valley. When he first started, the roar of the world he had left still rang in his ears, as the roar of a tunnel rings long after the train has passed through; but when he had put the Muteeanee Pass behind him that was all done, and Purun Bhagat was alone with himself walking, wondering, and thinking, his eyes on the ground, and his thoughts with the clouds.

One evening he crossed the highest pass he had met till then— it had been a two-days' climb—and came out on a line of snow-peaks that banded all the horizon—mountains from fifteen to

twenty thousand feet high, looking almost near enough to hit
with a stone, though they were fifty or sixty miles away. The pass
was crowned with dense, dark forest—deodar, walnut, wild
cherry, wild olive, and wild pear, but mostly deodar, which is the
Himalayan cedar; and under the shadow of the deodars stood a
deserted shrine to Kali—who is Durga, who is Sitala, who is
sometimes worshipped against the smallpox.

Purun Bhagat swept the stone floor clean, smiled at the grin-
ning statue, made himself a little mud fireplace at the back of the
shrine, spread his antelope skin on a bed of fresh pine-needles,
tucked his *bairagi*—his brass-handled crutch—under his armpit,
and sat down to rest.

Immediately below him the hillside fell away, clean and cleared
for fifteen hundred feet, where a little village of stone-walled
houses, with roofs of beaten earth, clung to the steep tilt. All
round it the tiny terraced fields lay out like aprons of patchwork
on the knees of the mountain, and cows no bigger than beetles
grazed between the smooth stone circles of the threshing-floors.
Looking across the valley, the eye was deceived by the size of
things, and could not at first realize that what seemed to be low
scrub, on the opposite mountain-flank, was in truth a forest of
hundred-foot pines. Purun Bhagat saw an eagle swoop across the
gigantic hollow, but the great bird dwindled to a dot ere it was
half-way over. A few bands of scattered clouds strung up and
down the valley, catching on a shoulder of the hills, or rising up
and dying out when they were level with the head of the pass.
And 'Here shall I find peace,' said Purun Bhagat.

Now, a Hill-man makes nothing of a few hundred feet up or
down, and as soon as the villagers saw the smoke in the deserted
shrine, the village priest climbed up the terraced hillside to
welcome the stranger.

When he met Purun Bhagat's eyes—the eyes of a man used to
control thousands—he bowed to the earth, took the begging-
bowl without a word, and returned to the village, saying, 'We
have at last a holy man. Never have I seen such a man. He is of
the Plains—but pale-coloured—a Brahmin of the Brahmins.'
Then all the housewives of the village said, 'Think you he will
stay with us?' and each did her best to cook the most savoury
meal for the Bhagat. Hill-food is very simple, but with buck-
wheat and Indian corn, and rice and red pepper, and little fish out
of the stream in the valley, and honey from the flue-like hives
built in the stone walls, and dried apricots, and turmeric, and
wild ginger, and bannocks of flour, a devout woman can make
good things, and it was a full bowl that the priest carried to the
Bhagat. Was he going to stay? asked the priest. Would he need a

*chela*—a disciple—to beg for him? Had he a blanket against the cold weather? Was the food good?

Purun Bhagat ate, and thanked the giver. It was in his mind to stay. That was sufficient, said the priest. Let the begging-bowl be placed outside the shrine, in the hollow made by those two twisted roots, and daily should the Bhagat be fed; for the village felt honoured that such a man—he looked timidly into the Bhagat's face—should tarry among them.

That day saw the end of Purun Bhagat's wanderings. He had come to the place appointed for him—the silence and the space. After this, time stopped, and he, sitting at the mouth of the shrine, could not tell whether he were alive or dead; a man with control of his limbs, or a part of the hills, and the clouds, and the shifting rain and sunlight. He would repeat a Name softly to himself a hundred hundred times, till, at each repetition, he seemed to move more and more out of his body, sweeping up to the doors of some tremendous discovery; but, just as the door was opening, his body would drag him back, and, with grief, he felt he was locked up again in the flesh and bones of Purun Bhagat.

Every morning the filled begging-bowl was laid silently in the crutch of the roots outside the shrine. Sometimes the priest brought it; sometimes a Ladakhi trader, lodging in the village, and anxious to get merit, trudged up the path; but, more often, it was the woman who had cooked the meal overnight; and she would murmur, hardly above her breath: 'Speak for me before the gods, Bhagat. Speak for such a one, the wife of so-and-so!' Now and then some bold child would be allowed the honour, and Purun Bhagat would hear him drop the bowl and run as fast as his little legs could carry him, but the Bhagat never came down to the village. It was laid out like a map at his feet. He could see the evening gatherings, held on the circle of the threshing-floors, because that was the only level ground; could see the wonderful unnamed green of the young rice, the indigo blues of the Indian corn, the dock-like patches of buckwheat, and, in its season, the red bloom of the amaranth, whose tiny seeds, being neither grain nor pulse, make a food that can be lawfully eaten by Hindus in time of fasts.

When the year turned, the roofs of the huts were all little squares of purest gold, for it was on the roofs that they laid out their cobs of the corn to dry. Hiving and harvest, rice-sowing and husking, passed before his eyes, all embroidered down there on the many-sided plots of fields, and he thought of them all, and wondered what they all led to at the long last.

Even in populated India a man cannot a day sit still before the wild things run over him as though he were a rock; and in that wilderness very soon the wild things, who knew Kali's Shrine well, came back to look at the intruder. The *langurs*, the big grey-whiskered monkeys of the Himalayas, were, naturally, the first, for they are alive with curiosity; and when they had upset the begging-bowl, and rolled it round the floor, and tried their teeth on the brass-handled crutch, and made faces at the antelope skin, they decided that the human being who sat so still was harmless. At evening, they would leap down from the pines, and beg with their hands for things to eat, and then swing off in graceful curves. They liked the warmth of the fire, too, and huddled round it till Purun Bhagat had to push them aside to throw on more fuel; and in the morning, as often as not, he would find a furry ape sharing his blanket. All day long, one or other of the tribe would sit by his side, staring out at the snows, crooning and looking unspeakably wise and sorrowful.

After the monkeys came the *barasingh*, that big deer which is like our red deer, but stronger. He wished to rub off the velvet of his horns against the cold stones of Kali's statue, and stamped his feet when he saw the man at the shrine. But Purun Bhagat never moved, and, little by little, the royal stag edged up and nuzzled his shoulder. Purun Bhagat slid one cool hand along the hot antlers, and the touch soothed the fretted beast, who bowed his head, and Purun Bhagat very softly rubbed and ravelled off the velvet. Afterward, the *barasingh* brought his doe and fawn—gentle things that mumbled on the holy man's blanket—or would come alone at night, his eyes green in the fire-flicker, to take his share of fresh walnuts. At last, the musk-deer, the shyest and almost the smallest of the deerlets, came too, her big rabbity ears erect; even brindled, silent *mushicknabha* must needs find out what the light in the shrine meant, and drop out her moose-like nose into Purun Bhagat's lap, coming and going with the shadows of the fire. Purun Bhagat called them all 'my brothers', and his low call of '*Bhai! Bhai!*' would draw them from the forest at noon if they were within earshot. The Himalayan black bear, moody and suspicious—Sona, who has the V-shaped white mark under his chin—passed that way more than once; and since the Bhagat showed no fear, Sona showed no anger, but watched him, and came closer, and begged a share of the caresses, and a dole of bread or wild berries. Often, in the still dawns, when the Bhagat would climb to the very crest of the pass to watch the red day walking along the peaks of the snows, he would find Sona shuffling and grunting at his heels, thrusting a curious fore-paw under fallen trunks, and bringing it away with a *whoof* of impatience; or his early steps would wake Sona where he lay curled up, and the great brute, rising erect, would think to fight, till he heard the Bhagat's voice and knew his best friend.

Nearly all hermits and holy men who live apart from the big cities have the reputation of being able to work miracles with the wild things, but all the miracle lies in keeping still, in never making a hasty movement, and, for a long time, at least, in never looking directly at a visitor. The villagers saw the outline of the *barasingh* stalking like a shadow through the dark forest behind the shrine; saw the *minaul*, the Himalayan pheasant, blazing in her best colours before Kali's statue; and the *langurs* on their haunches, inside, playing with the walnut shells. Some of the children, too, had heard Sona singing to himself, bear-fashion, behind the fallen rocks, and the Bhagat's reputation as miracle-worker stood firm.

Yet nothing was farther from his mind than miracles. He believed that all things were one big Miracle, and when a man knows that much he knows something to go upon. He knew for a certainty that there was nothing great and nothing little in this world: and day and night he strove to think out his way into the heart of things, back to the place whence his soul had come.

So thinking, his untrimmed hair fell down about his shoulders, the stone slab at the side of the antelope skin was dented into a little hole by the foot of his brass-handled crutch, and the place between the tree-trunks, where the begging-bowl rested day after day, sunk and wore into a hollow almost as smooth as the brown shell itself; and each beast knew his exact place at the fire. The fields changed their colours with the seasons; the threshing-floors filled and emptied, and filled again and again; and again and again, when winter came, the *langurs* frisked among the branches feathered with light snow, till the mother-monkeys brought their sad-eyed little babies up from the warmer valleys with the spring. There were few changes in the village. The priest was older, and many of the little children who used to come with the begging-dish sent their own children now; and when you asked of the villagers how long their holy man had lived in Kali's Shrine at the head of the pass, they answered, 'Always'.

Then came such summer rains as had not been known in the Hills for many seasons. Through three good months the valley was wrapped in cloud and soaking mist—steady, unrelenting downfall, breaking off into thunder-shower after thunder-shower. Kali's Shrine stood above the clouds, for the most part, and there was a whole month in which the Bhagat never caught a glimpse of his village. It was packed away under a white floor of cloud that swayed and shifted and rolled on itself and bulged upward, but never broke from its piers—the streaming flanks of the valley.

All that time he heard nothing but the sound of a million little waters, overhead from the trees, and underfoot along the ground, soaking through the pine-needles, dripping from the tongues of draggled fern, and spouting in newly-torn muddy channels down the slopes. Then the sun came out, and drew forth the good incense of the deodars and the rhododendrons, and that far-off, clean smell which the Hill people call 'the smell of the snows'. The hot sunshine lasted for a week, and then the rains gathered together for their last downpour, and the water fell in sheets that flayed off the skin of the ground and leaped back in mud. Purun Bhagat heaped his fire high that night, for he was sure his brothers would need warmth; but never a beast came to the shrine, though he called and called till he dropped asleep, wondering what had happened in the woods.

It was in the black heart of the night, the rain drumming like a thousand drums, that he was roused by a plucking at his blanket, and, stretching out, felt the little hand of a *langur*. 'It is better here than in the trees,' he said sleepily, loosening a fold of blanket; 'take it and be warm.' The monkey caught his hand and pulled hard. 'Is it food, then?' said Purun Bhagat. 'Wait awhile, and I will prepare some.' As he kneeled to throw fuel on the fire the *langur* ran to the door of the shrine, crooned and ran back again, plucking at the man's knee.

'What is it? What is thy trouble, Brother?' said Purun Bhagat, for the *langur*'s eyes were full of things that he could not tell. 'Unless one of thy caste be in a trap—and none set traps here—I I will not go into that weather. Look, Brother, even the *barasingh* comes for shelter!'

The deer's antlers clashed as he strode into the shrine, clashed against the grinning statue of Kali. He lowered them in Purun Bhagat's direction and stamped uneasily, hissing through his half-shut nostrils.

'Hai! Hai! Hai!' said Bhagat, snapping his fingers. 'Is *this* payment for a night's lodging?' But the deer pushed him toward the door, and as he did so Purun Bhagat heard the sound of something opening with a sigh, and saw two slabs of the floor draw away from each other, while the sticky earth below smacked its lips.

'Now I see,' said Purun Bhagat. 'No blame to my brothers that they did not sit by the fire tonight. The mountain is falling. And yet—why should I go?' His eye fell on the empty begging-bowl, and his face changed. 'They have given me good food daily since—since I came, and, if I am not swift, tomorrow there will not be one mouth in the valley. Indeed, I must go and warn them below. Back there, Brother! Let me get to the fire.'

The *barasingh* backed unwillingly as Purun Bhagat drove a pine torch deep into the flame, twirling it till it was well lit. 'Ah! ye came to warn me,' he said, rising. 'Better than that we shall do; better than that. Out, now, and lend me thy neck, Brother, for I have but two feet.'

He clutched the bristling withers of the *barasingh* with his right hand, held the torch away with his left, and stepped out of the shrine into the desperate night. There was no breath of wind, but the rain nearly drowned the flare as the great deer hurried down the slope, sliding on his haunches. As soon as they were clear of the forest more of the Bhagat's brothers joined them. He heard, though he could not see, the *langurs* pressing about him, and behind them the *uhh! uhh!* of Sona. The rain matted his long white hair into ropes; the water splashed beneath his bare feet, and his yellow robe clung to his frail old body, but he stepped down steadily, leaning against the *barasingh*. He was no longer a holy man, but Sir Purun Dass, K.C.I.E., Prime Minister of no small State, a man accustomed to command, going out to save life. Down the steep, plashy path they poured all together, the Bhagat and his brothers, down and down till the deer's feet clicked and stumbled on the wall of a threshing-floor, and he snorted because he smelt Man. Now they were at the head of the one crooked village street, and the Bhagat beat with his crutch on the barred windows of the blacksmith's house, as his torch blazed up in the shelter of the eaves. 'Up and out!' cried Purun Bhagat; and he did not know his own voice, for it was years since he had spoken aloud to a man. 'The hill falls! The hill is falling! Up and out, oh, you within!'

'It is our Bhagat,' said the blacksmith's wife. 'He stands among his beasts. Gather the little ones and give the call.'

It ran from house to house, while the beasts, cramped in the narrow way, surged and huddled round the Bhagat, and Sona puffed impatiently.

The people hurried into the street—they were no more than seventy souls all told—and in the glare of the torches they saw their Bhagat holding back the terrified *barasingh*, while the monkeys plucked piteously at his skirts, and Sona sat on his haunches and roared.

'Across the valley and up the next hill!' shouted Purun Bhagat. 'Leave none behind! We follow!'

Then the people ran as only Hill folk can run, for they knew that in a landslip you must climb for the highest ground across the valley. They fled, splashing through the little river at the bottom, and panted up the terraced fields on the far side, while the Bhagat and his brethren followed. Up and up the opposite mountain they climbed, calling to each other by name—the roll-call of the village—and at their heels toiled the big *barasingh*, weighted by the failing strength of Purun Bhagat. At last the deer stopped in the shadow of a deep pine-wood, five hundred feet up the hillside. His instinct, that had warned him of the coming slide, told him he would be safe here.

Purun Bhagat dropped fainting by his side, for the chill of the rain and that fierce climb were killing him; but first he called to the scattered torches ahead, 'Stay and count your numbers'; then, whispering to the deer as he saw the lights gather in a cluster: 'Stay with me, Brother. Stay—till—I—go!'

There was a sigh in the air that grew to a mutter, and a mutter that grew to a roar, and a roar that passed all sense of hearing, and the hillside on which the villagers stood was hit in the darkness, and rocked to the blow. Then a note as steady, deep, and true as the deep C of the organ drowned everything for perhaps five minutes, while the very roots of the pines quivered to it. It died away, and the sound of the rain falling on miles of hard ground and grass changed to the muffled drum of water on soft earth. That told its own tale.

Never a villager—not even the priest—was bold enough to speak to the Bhagat who had saved their lives. They crouched under the pines and waited till the day. When it came they looked across the valley and saw that what had been forest, and terraced field, and track-threaded grazing-ground was one raw, red, fan-shaped smear, with a few trees flung head-down on the scarp. That red ran high up the hill of their refuge, damming back the little river, which had begun to spread into a brick-coloured lake. Of the village, of the road to the shrine, of the shrine itself, and the forest behind, there was no trace. For one mile in width and two thousand feet in sheer depth the mountain-side had come away bodily, planed clean from head to heel.

And the villagers, one by one, crept through the wood to pray before their Bhagat. They saw the *barasingh* standing over him, who fled when they came near, and they heard the *langurs* wailing in the branches, and Sona moaning up the hill; but their Bhagat was dead, sitting cross-legged, his back against a tree, his crutch under his armpit, and his face turned to the north-east.

The priest said: 'Behold a miracle after a miracle, for in this very attitude must all Sunnyasis be buried! Therefore where he now is we will build the temple to our holy man.'

They built the temple before a year was ended—a little stone-and-earth shrine—and they called the hill the Bhagat's hill, and they worship there with lights and flowers and offerings to this day. But they do not know that the saint of their worship is the late Sir Purun Dass, K.C.I.E., D.C.L., PH.D., etc., once Prime Minister of the progressive and enlightened State of Mohiniwala, and honorary or corresponding member of more learned and scientific societies than will ever do any good in this world or the next.

1894

# The King's Ankus

These are the Four that are never content, that have
never been filled since the Dews began—
Jacala's mouth, and the glut of the Kite, and the
hands of the Ape, and the eyes of Man.

*Jungle Saying.*

KAA, the big Rock Python, had changed his skin for perhaps the
two hundredth time since his birth; and Mowgli, who never
forgot that he owed his life to Kaa for a night's work at Cold
Lairs, which you may perhaps remember, went to congratulate
him. Skin-changing always makes a snake moody and depressed
till the new skin begins to shine and look beautiful. Kaa never
made fun of Mowgli any more, but accepted him, as the other
Jungle People did, for the Master of the Jungle, and brought him
all the news that a python of his size would naturally hear. What
Kaa did not know about the Middle Jungle, as they call it—the
life that runs close to the earth or under it, the boulder, burrow,
and the tree-bole life—might have been written upon the smallest
of his scales.

That afternoon Mowgli was sitting in the circle of Kaa's great
coils, fingering the flaked and broken old skin that lay looped and
twisted among the rocks just as Kaa had left it. Kaa had very
courteously packed himself under Mowgli's broad bare shoulders,
so that the boy was really resting in a living armchair.

'Even to the scales of the eyes it is perfect,' said Mowgli, under
his breath, playing with the old skin. 'Strange to see the covering
of one's own head at one's own feet!'

'Ay, but I lack feet,' said Kaa; 'and since this is the custom of
all my people, I do not find it strange. Does thy skin never feel
old and harsh?'

'Then go I and wash, Flathead; but, it is true, in the great heats
I have wished I could slough my skin without pain, and run
skinless.'

'I wash, and *also* I take off my skin. How looks the new coat?'

Mowgli ran his hand down the diagonal checkerings of the
immense back. 'The Turtle is harder-backed, but not so gay,' he
said judgmatically. 'The Frog, my name-bearer, is more gay, but
not so hard. It is very beautiful to see—like the mottling in the
mouth of a lily.'

'It needs water. A new skin never comes to full colour before
the first bathe. Let us go bathe.'

'I will carry thee,' said Mowgli; and he stooped down, laugh-

ing, to lift the middle section of Kaa's great body, just where the
barrel was thickest. A man might just as well have tried to heave
up a two-foot water-main; and Kaa lay still, puffing with quiet
amusement. Then the regular evening game began—the Boy in
the flush of his great strength, and the Python in his sumptuous
new skin, standing up one against the other for a wrestling match
—a trial of eye and strength. Of course, Kaa could have crushed
a dozen Mowglis if he had let himself go; but he played carefully,
and never loosed one-tenth of his power. Ever since Mowgli was
strong enough to endure a little rough handling, Kaa had taught
him this game, and it suppled his limbs as nothing else could.
Sometimes Mowgli would stand lapped almost to his throat in
Kaa's shifting coils, striving to get one arm free and catch him by
the throat. Then Kaa would give way limply, and Mowgli, with
both quick-moving feet, would try to cramp the purchase of that
huge tail as it flung backward feeling for a rock or a stump. They
would rock to and fro, head to head, each waiting for his chance,
till the beautiful, statue-like group melted in a whirl of black-and-
yellow coils and struggling legs and arms, to rise up again and
again. 'Now! now! now!' said Kaa, making feints with his head
that even Mowgli's quick hand could not turn aside. 'Look!
I touch thee here, Little Brother! Here, and here! Are thy hands
numb? Here again!'

The game always ended in one way—with a straight, driving
blow of the head that knocked the boy over and over. Mowgli
could never learn the guard for that lightning lunge, and, as Kaa
said, there was not the least use in trying.

'Good hunting!' Kaa grunted at last; and Mowgli, as usual, was
shot away half a dozen yards, gasping and laughing. He rose with
his fingers full of grass, and followed Kaa to the wise snake's pet
bathing-place—a deep, pitchy-black pool surrounded with rocks,
and made interesting by sunken tree-stumps. The boy slipped
in, Jungle-fashion, without a sound, and dived across; rose,
too, without a sound, and turned on his back, his arms behind
his head, watching the moon rising above the rocks, and breaking
up her reflection in the water with his toes. Kaa's diamond-
shaped head cut the pool like a razor, and came to rest on
Mowgli's shoulder. They lay still, soaking luxuriously in the cool
water.

'It is *very* good,' said Mowgli at last, sleepily. 'Now, in the
Man-Pack, at this hour, as I remember, they laid them down
upon hard pieces of wood in the inside of a mud-trap, and having
carefully shut out all the clean winds, drew foul cloth over their
heavy heads and made evil songs through their noses. It is better
in the Jungle.'

A hurrying cobra slipped down over a rock and drank, gave them 'Good hunting!' and went away.

'Sssh!' said Kaa, as though he had suddenly remembered something. 'So the Jungle gives thee all that thou hast ever desired, Little Brother?'

'Not all,' said Mowgli, laughing; 'else there would be a new and strong Shere Khan to kill once a moon. Now, I could kill with my own hands, asking no help of buffaloes. And also I have wished the sun to shine in the middle of the Rains, and the Rains to cover the sun in the deep of summer; and also I have never gone empty but I wished that I had killed a goat; and also I have never killed a goat but I wished it had been buck: nor buck but I wished it had been nilghai. But thus do we feel, all of us.'

'Thou hast no other desire?' the big snake demanded.

'What more can I wish? I have the Jungle, and the favour of the Jungle! Is there more anywhere between sunrise and sunset?'

'Now, the Cobra said——' Kaa began.

'What cobra? He that went away just now said nothing. He was hunting.'

'It was another.'

'Hast thou many dealings with the Poison People? I give them their own path. They carry death in the fore-tooth, and that is not good—for they are so small. But what hood is this thou hast spoken with?'

Kaa rolled slowly in the water like a steamer in a beam sea. 'Three or four moons since,' said he, 'I hunted in Cold Lairs, which place thou hast not forgotten. And the thing I hunted fled shrieking past the tanks and to that house whose side I once broke for thy sake, and ran into the ground.'

'But the people of Cold Lairs do not live in burrows.' Mowgli knew that Kaa was telling of the Monkey People.

'This thing was not living, but seeking to live,' Kaa replied, with a quiver of his tongue. 'He ran into a burrow that led very far. I followed, and having killed, I slept. When I waked I went forward.'

'Under the earth?'

'Even so, coming at last upon a White Hood [a white cobra], who spoke of things beyond my knowledge, and showed me many things I had never before seen.'

'New game? Was it good hunting?' Mowgli turned quickly on his side.

'It was no game, and would have broken all my teeth; but the White Hood said that a man—he spoke as one that knew the breed—that a man would give the breath under his ribs for only the sight of those things.'

'We will look,' said Mowgli. 'I now remember that I was once a man.'

'Slowly—slowly. It was haste killed the Yellow Snake that ate the sun. We two spoke together under the earth, and I spoke of thee, naming thee as a man. Said the White Hood (and he is indeed as old as the Jungle): "It is long since I have seen a man. Let him come, and he shall see all these things, for the least of which very many men would die."'

'That *must* be new game. And yet the Poison People do not tell us when game is afoot. They are an unfriendly folk.'

'It is *not* game. It is—it is—I cannot say what it is.'

'We will go there. I have never seen a White Hood, and I wish to see the other things. Did he kill them?'

'They are all dead things. He says he is the keeper of them all.'

'Ah! As a wolf stands above meat he has taken to his own lair. Let us go.'

Mowgli swam to bank, rolled on the grass to dry himself, and the two set off for Cold Lairs, the deserted city of which you may have heard. Mowgli was not the least afraid of the Monkey People in those days, but the Monkey People had the liveliest horror of Mowgli. Their tribes, however, were raiding in the Jungle, and so Cold Lairs stood empty and silent in the moonlight. Kaa led up to the ruins of the queens' pavilion that stood on the terrace, slipped over the rubbish, and dived down the half-choked staircase that went underground from the centre of the pavilion. Mowgli gave the snake-call—'We be of one blood, ye and I,'—and followed on his hands and knees. They crawled a long distance down a sloping passage that turned and twisted several times, and at last came to where the root of some great tree, growing thirty feet overhead, had forced out a solid stone in the wall. They crept through the gap, and found themselves in a large vault, whose domed roof had been also broken away by tree-roots so that a few streaks of light dropped down into the darkness.

'A safe lair,' said Mowgli, rising to his firm feet, 'but over-far to visit daily. And now what do we see?'

'Am I nothing?' said a voice in the middle of the vault; and Mowgli saw something white move till, little by little, there stood up the hugest cobra he had ever set eyes on—a creature nearly eight feet long, and bleached by being in darkness to an old ivory-white. Even the spectacle-marks of his spread hood had faded to faint yellow. His eyes were a red as rubies, and altogether he was most wonderful.

'Good hunting!' said Mowgli, who carried his manners with his knife, and that never left him.

'What of the city?' said the White Cobra, without answering the greeting. 'What of the great, the walled city—the city of a hundred elephants and twenty thousand horses, and cattle past counting—the city of the King of Twenty Kings? I grow deaf here and it is long since I heard their war-gongs.'

'The Jungle is above our heads,' said Mowgli. 'I know only Hathi and his sons among elephants. Bagheera has slain all the horses in one village, and—what is a King?'

'I told thee,' said Kaa softly to the Cobra—'I told thee, four moons ago, that thy city was not.'

'The city—the great city of the forest whose gates are guarded by the King's towers—can never pass. They builded it before my father's father came from the egg, and it shall endure when my son's sons are as white as I! Salomdhi, son of Chandrabija, son of Viyeja, son of Yegasuri, made it in the days of Bappa Rawal. Whose cattle are *ye*?'

'It is a lost trail,' said Mowgli, turning to Kaa. 'I know not his talk.'

'Nor I. He is very old. Father of Cobras, there is only the Jungle here, as it has been since the beginning.'

'Then who is *he*,' said the White Cobra, 'sitting down before me, unafraid, knowing not the name of the King, talking our talk through a man's lips? Who is he with the knife and the snake's tongue?'

'Mowgli they call me,' was the answer. 'I am of the Jungle. The wolves are my people, and Kaa here is my brother. Father of Cobras, who art thou?'

'I am the Warden of the King's Treasure. Kurrun Raja built the stone above me, in the days when my skin was dark, that I might teach death to those who came to steal. Then they let down the treasure through the stone, and I heard the song of the Brahmins my masters.'

'Umm!' said Mowgli to himself. 'I have dealt with one Brahmin already, in the Man-Pack, and—I know what I know. Evil comes here in a little.'

'Five times since I came here has the stone been lifted, but always to let down more, and never to take away. There are no riches like these riches—the treasures of a hundred kings. But it is long and long since the stone was last moved, and I think that my city has forgotten.'

'There is no city. Look up. Yonder are roots of the great trees tearing the stones apart. Trees and men do not grow together,' Kaa insisted.

'Twice and thrice have men found their way here,' the White Cobra answered savagely; 'but they never spoke till I came upon them groping in the dark, and then they cried only a little time. But *ye* come with lies, Man and Snake both, and would have me believe the city is not, and that my wardship ends. Little do men change in the years. But *I* change never! Till the stone is lifted, and the Brahmins come down singing the songs that I know, and feed me with warm milk, and take me to the light again, I—I—*I*, and no other, am the Warden of the King's Treasure! The city is dead, ye say, and here are the roots of the trees? Stoop down, then, and take what ye will. Earth has no treasure like to these. Man with the snake's tongue, if thou canst go alive by the way that thou hast entered at, the lesser Kings will be thy servants!'

'Again the trail is lost,' said Mowgli coolly. 'Can any jackal have burrowed so deep and bitten this great White Hood? He is surely mad. Father of Cobras, I see nothing here to take away.'

'By the God of the Sun and Moon, it is the madness of death upon the boy!' hissed the Cobra. 'Before thine eyes close I will allow thee this favour. Look thou, and see what man has never seen before!'

'They do not well in the Jungle who speak to Mowgli of favours,' said the boy, between his teeth; 'but the dark changes all, as I know. I will look, if that please thee.'

He stared with puckered-up eyes round the vault, and then lifted up from the floor a handful of something that glittered.

'Oho!' said he, 'this is like the stuff they play with in the Man-Pack: only this is yellow and the other was brown.'

He let the gold piece fall, and moved forward. The floor of the vault was buried some five or six feet deep in coined gold and silver that had burst from the sacks it had been originally stored in, and, in the long years, the metal had packed and settled as sand packs at low tide. On it and in it, and rising through it, as wrecks lift through the sand, were jewelled elephant-howdahs of embossed silver, studded with plates of hammered gold, and adorned with carbuncles and turquoises. There were palanquins and litters for carrying queens, framed and braced with silver and enamel, with jade-handled poles and amber curtain-rings; there were golden candlesticks hung with pierced emeralds that quivered on the branches; there were studded images, five feet high, of forgotten gods, silver with jewelled eyes; there were coats of mail, gold inlaid on steel, and fringed with rotted and blackened seed-pearls; there were helmets, crested and beaded with pigeon's-blood rubies; there were shields of lacquer, of tortoise-shell and rhinoceros-hide, strapped and bossed with red gold and set with emeralds at the edge; there were sheaves of diamond-hilted swords, daggers, and hunting-knives; there were

golden sacrificial bowls and ladles, and portable altars of a shape
that never sees the light of day; there were jade cups and brace-
lets; there were incense-burners, combs, and pots for perfume,
henna, and eye-powder, all in embossed gold; there were nose-
rings, armlets, head-bands, finger-rings, and girdles past any
counting; there were belts, seven fingers broad, of square-cut
diamonds and rubies, and wooden boxes, trebly clamped with
iron, from which the wood had fallen away in powder, showing
the pile of uncut star-sapphires, opals, cat's-eyes, sapphires,
rubies, diamonds, emeralds, and garnets within.

The White Cobra was right. No mere money would begin to
pay the value of this treasure, the sifted pickings of centuries of
war, plunder, trade, and taxation. The coins alone were priceless,
leaving out of count all the precious stones; and the dead weight
of the gold and silver alone might be two or three hundred tons.
Every native ruler in India today, however poor, has a hoard to
which he is always adding; and though, once in a long while,
some enlightened prince may send off forty or fifty bullock-cart
loads of silver to be exchanged for Government securities, the
bulk of them keep their treasure and the knowledge of it very
closely to themselves.

But Mowgli naturally did not understand what these things
meant. The knives interested him a little, but they did not
balance so well as his own, and so he dropped them. At last he
found something really fascinating laid on the front of a howdah
half buried in the coins. It was a three-foot ankus, or elephant-
goad—something like a small boat hook. The top was one round,
shining ruby, and eight inches of the handle below it were
studded with rough turquoises close together, giving a most
satisfactory grip. Below them was a rim of jade with a flower-
pattern running round it—only the leaves were emeralds, and the
blossoms were rubies sunk in the cool, green stone. The rest of
the handle was a shaft of pure ivory, while the point—the spike
and hook—was gold-inlaid steel with pictures of elephant-
catching; and the pictures attracted Mowgli, who saw that they
had something to do with his friend Hathi the Silent.

The White Cobra had been following him closely.

'Is this not worth dying to behold?' he said. 'Have I not done
thee a great favour?'

'I do not understand,' said Mowgli. 'The things are hard and
cold, and by no means good to eat. But this'—he lifted the ankus
—'I desire to take away, that I may see it in the sun. Thou sayest
they are all thine? Wilt thou give it to me, and I will bring thee
frogs to eat?'

The White Cobra fairly shook with evil delight. 'Assuredly

I will give it,' he said. 'All that is here I will give thee—till thou goest away.'

'But I go now. This place is dark and cold, and I wish to take the thorn-pointed thing to the Jungle.'

'Look by thy foot! What is that there?'

Mowgli picked up something white and smooth. 'It is the bone of a man's head,' he said quietly. 'And here are two more.'

'They came to take the treasure away many years ago. I spoke to them in the dark, and they lay still.'

'But what do I need of this that is called treasure? If thou wilt give me the ankus to take away, it is good hunting. If not, it is good hunting none the less. I do not fight with the Poison People, and I was also taught the Master-word of thy tribe.'

'There is but one Master-word here. It is mine!'

Kaa flung himself forward with blazing eyes. 'Who bade me bring the Man?' he hissed.

'I surely,' the old Cobra lisped. 'It is long since I have seen Man, and this Man speaks our tongue.'

'But there was no talk of killing. How can I go to the Jungle and say that I have led him to his death?' said Kaa.

'I talk not of killing till the time. And as to thy going or not going, there is the hole in the wall. Peace, now, thou fat monkey-killer! I have but to touch thy neck, and the Jungle will know thee no longer. Never Man came here that went away with the breath under his ribs. I am the Warden of the Treasure of the King's City!'

'But, thou white worm of the dark, I tell thee there is neither king nor city! The Jungle is all about us!' cried Kaa.

'There is still the Treasure. But this can be done. Wait awhile, Kaa of the Rocks, and see the boy run. There is room for great sport here. Life is good. Run to and fro awhile, and make sport, boy!'

Mowgli put his hand on Kaa's head quietly.

'The white thing has dealt with men of the Man-Pack until now. He does not know me,' he whispered. 'He has asked for this hunting. Let him have it.' Mowgli had been standing with the ankus held point down. He flung it from him quickly and it dropped crossways just behind the great snake's hood, pinning him to the floor. In a flash, Kaa's weight was upon the writhing body, paralysing it from hood to tail. The red eyes burned. and the six spare inches of the head struck furiously right and left.

'Kill!' said Kaa, as Mowgli's hand went to his knife.

'No,' he said, as he drew the blade; 'I will never kill again save for food. But look you, Kaa!' He caught the snake behind the hood, forced the mouth open with the blade of the knife, and showed the terrible poison-fangs of the upper jaw lying black and withered in the gum. The White Cobra had outlived his poison, as a snake will.

'*Thuu*' ('It is dried up'),[1] said Mowgli; and motioning Kaa away, he picked up the ankus, setting the White Cobra free.

'The King's Treasure needs a new Warden,' he said gravely. 'Thuu, thou hast not done well. Run to and fro and make sport, Thuu!'

'I am ashamed. Kill me!' hissed the White Cobra.

'There has been too much talk of killing. We will go now. I take the thorn-pointed thing, Thuu, because I have fought and worsted thee.'

'See, then, that the thing does not kill thee at last. It is Death! Remember, it is Death! There is enough in that thing to kill the men of all my city. Not long wilt thou hold it, Jungle Man, nor he who takes it from thee. They will kill, and kill, and kill for its sake! My strength is dried up, but the ankus will do my work. It is Death! It is Death! It is Death!'

Mowgli crawled out through the hole into the passage again, and the last that he saw was the White Cobra striking furiously with his harmless fangs at the stolid golden faces of the gods that lay on the floor, and hissing, 'It is Death!'

They were glad to get to the light of day once more; and when they were back in their own Jungle and Mowgli made the ankus glitter in the morning light, he was almost as pleased as though he had found a bunch of new flowers to stick in his hair.

'This is brighter than Bagheera's eyes,' he said delightedly, as he twirled the ruby. 'I will show it to him; but what did the Thuu mean when he talked of death?'

'I cannot say. I am sorrowful to my tail's tail that he felt not thy knife. There is always evil at Cold Lairs—above ground or below. But now I am hungry. Dost thou hunt with me this dawn?' said Kaa.

'No; Bagheera must see this thing. Good hunting!' Mowgli danced off, flourishing the great ankus, and stopping from time to time to admire it, till he came to that part of the Jungle Bagheera chiefly used, and found him drinking after a heavy kill. Mowgli told him all his adventures from beginning to end, and Bagheera sniffed at the ankus between whiles. When Mowgli came to the White Cobra's last words, the Panther purred approvingly.

'Then the White Hood spoke the thing which is?' Mowgli asked quickly.

[1] Literally, a rotted-out tree-stump.

'I was born in the King's cages at Oodeypore, and it is in my stomach that I know some little of Man. Very many men would kill thrice in a night for the sake of that one big red stone alone.'

'But the stone makes it heavy to the hand. My little bright knife is better; and—see! the red stone is not good to eat. Then *why* would they kill?'

'Mowgli, go thou and sleep. Thou hast lived among men, and——'

'I remember. Men kill because they are not hunting;—for idleness and pleasure. Wake again, Bagheera. For what use was this thorn-pointed thing made?'

Bagheera half opened his eyes—he was very sleepy—with a malicious twinkle.

'It was made by men to thrust into the head of the sons of Hathi, so that the blood should pour out. I have seen the like in the street of Oodeypore, before our cages. That thing has tasted the blood of many such as Hathi.'

'But why do they thrust into the heads of elephants?'

'To teach them Man's Law. Having neither claws nor teeth, men make these things—and worse.'

'Always more blood when I come near, even to the things the Man-Pack have made,' said Mowgli disgustedly. He was getting a little tired of the weight of the ankus. 'If I had known this, I would not have taken it. First it was Messua's blood on the thongs, and now it is Hathi's. I will use it no more. Look!'

The ankus flew sparkling, and buried itself point down thirty yards away, between the trees. 'So my hands are clean of death,' said Mowgli, rubbing his palms on the fresh, moist earth. 'The Thuu said Death would follow me. He is old and white and mad.'

'White or black, or death or life, *I* am going to sleep, Little Brother. I cannot hunt all night and howl all day, as do some folk.'

Bagheera went off to a hunting-lair that he knew, about two miles off. Mowgli made an easy way for himself up a convenient tree, knotted three or four creepers together, and in less time than it takes to tell was swinging in a hammock fifty feet above ground. Though he had no positive objection to strong daylight, Mowgli followed the custom of his friends, and used it as little as he could. When he waked among the very loud-voiced peoples that live in the trees, it was twilight once more, and he had been dreaming of the beautiful pebbles he had thrown away.

'At least I will look at the thing again,' he said, and slid down a creeper to the earth; but Bagheera was before him. Mowgli could hear him snuffing in the half light.

'Where is the thorn-pointed thing?' cried Mowgli.

'A man has taken it. Here is the trail.'

'Now we shall see whether the Thuu spoke truth. If the pointed thing is Death, that man will die. Let us follow.'

'Kill first,' said Bagheera. 'An empty stomach makes a careless eye. Men go very slowly, and the Jungle is wet enough to hold the lightest mark.'

They killed as soon as they could, but it was nearly three hours before they finished their meat and drink and buckled down to the trail. The Jungle People know that nothing makes up for being hurried over your meals.

'Think you the pointed thing will turn in the man's hand and kill him?' Mowgli asked. 'The Thuu said it was Death.'

'We shall see when we find,' said Bagheera, trotting with his head low. 'It is single-foot' (he meant that there was only one man), 'and the weight of the thing has pressed his heel far into the ground.'

'Hai! This is as clear as summer lightning,' Mowgli answered; and they fell into the quick, choppy trail-trot in and out through the checkers of the moonlight, following the marks of those two bare feet.

'Now he runs swiftly,' said Mowgli. 'The toes are spread apart.' They went on over some wet ground. 'Now why does he turn aside here?'

'Wait!' said Bagheera, and flung himself forward with one superb bound as far as ever he could. The first thing to do when a trail ceases to explain itself is to cast forward without leaving your own confusing foot-marks on the ground. Bagheera turned as he landed, and faced Mowgli, crying, 'Here comes another trail to meet him. It is a smaller foot, this second trail, and the toes turn inward.'

Then Mowgli ran up and looked. 'It is the foot of a Gond hunter,' he said. 'Look! Here he dragged his bow on the grass. That is why the first trail turned aside so quickly. Big Foot hid from Little Foot.'

'That is true,' said Bagheera. 'Now, lest by crossing each other's tracks we foul the signs, let each take one trail. I am Big Foot, Little Brother, and thou are Little Foot, the Gond.'

Bagheera leaped back to the original trail, leaving Mowgli stooping above the curious track of the wild little man of the woods.

'Now,' said Bagheera, moving step by step along the chain of footprints. 'I, Big Foot, turn aside here. Now I hide me behind a rock and stand still, not daring to shift my feet. Cry thy trail, Little Brother.'

'Now, I, Little Foot, come to the rock,' said Mowgli, running up his trail. 'Now, I sit down under the rock, leaning upon my right hand, and resting my bow between my toes. I wait long, for the mark of my feet is deep here.'

'I also,' said Bagheera, hidden behind the rock. 'I wait, resting the end of the thorn-pointed thing upon a stone. It slips, for here is a scratch upon the stone. Cry thy trail, Little Brother.'

'One, two twigs and a big branch are broken here,' said Mowgli, in an undertone. 'Now, how shall I cry *that*? Ah! it is plain now. I, Little Foot, go away making noises and tramplings so that Big Foot may hear me.' He moved away from the rock pace by pace among the trees, his voice rising in the distance as he approached a little cascade. 'I—go—far—away—to—where—the — noise — of — falling — water — covers — my — noise; and—here—I—wait. Cry thy trail, Bagheera, Big Foot!'

The panther had been casting in every direction to see how Big Foot's trail led away from behind the rock. Then he gave tongue:

'I come from behind the rock upon my knees, dragging the thorn-pointed thing. Seeing no one, I run. I, Big Foot, run swiftly. The trail is clear. Let each follow his own. I run!'

Bagheera swept on along the clearly-marked trail, and Mowgli followed the steps of the Gond. For some time there was silence in the Jungle.

'Where art thou, Little Foot?' cried Bagheera. Mowgli's voice answered him not fifty yards to the right.

'Um!' said the Panther, with a deep cough. 'The two run side by side, drawing nearer!'

They raced on another half-mile, always keeping about the same distance, till Mowgli, whose head was not so close to the ground as Bagheera's, cried: 'They have met. Good hunting—look! Here stood Little Foot, with his knee on a rock—and yonder is Big Foot indeed!'

Not ten yards in front of them, stretched across a pile of broken rocks, lay the body of a villager of the district, a long, small-feathered Gond arrow through his back and breast.

'Was the Thuu so old and so mad, Little Brother?' said Bagheera gently. 'Here is one death, at least.'

'Follow on. But where is the drinker of elephant's blood—the red-eyed thorn?'

'Little Foot has it—perhaps. It is single-foot again now.'

The single trail of a light man who had been running quickly and bearing a burden on his left shoulder held on round a long, low spur of dried grass, where each footfall seemed, to the sharp eyes of the trackers, marked in hot iron.

Neither spoke till the trail ran up to the ashes of a camp-fire hidden in a ravine.

'Again!' said Bagheera, checking as though he had been turned into stone.

The body of a little wizened Gond lay with its feet in the ashes, and Bagheera looked inquiringly at Mowgli.

'That was done with a bamboo,' said the boy, after one glance. 'I have used such a thing among the buffaloes when I served in the Man-Pack. The Father of Cobras—I am sorrowful that I made a jest of him—knew the breed well, as I might have known. Said I not that men kill for idleness?'

'Indeed, they killed for the sake of the red and blue stones,' Bagheera answered. 'Remember, I was in the King's cages at Oodeypore.'

'One, two, three, four tracks,' said Mowgli, stooping over the ashes. 'Four tracks of men with shod feet. They do not go so quickly as Gonds. Now, what evil had the little woodman done to them? See, they talked together, all five, standing up, before they killed him. Bagheera, let us go back. My stomach is heavy in me, and yet it heaves up and down like an oriole's nest at the end of a branch.'

'It is not good hunting to leave game afoot. Follow!' said the panther. 'Those eight shod feet have not gone far.'

No more was said for fully an hour, as they worked up the broad trail of the four men with shod feet.

It was clear, hot daylight now, and Bagheera said, 'I smell smoke.'

'Men are always more ready to eat than to run,' Mowgli answered, trotting in and out between the low scrub bushes of the new Jungle they were exploring. Bagheera, a little to his left, made an indescribable noise in his throat.

'Here is one that has done with feeding,' said he. A tumbled bundle of gay-coloured clothes lay under a bush, and round it was some spilt flour.

'That was done by the bamboo again,' said Mowgli. 'See! that white dust is what men eat. They have taken the kill from this one—he carried their food—and given him for a kill to Chil, the Kite.'

'It is the third,' said Bagheera.

'I will go with new, big frogs to the Father of Cobras, and feed him fat,' said Mowgli to himself. 'The drinker of elephant's blood is Death himself—but still I do not understand!'

'Follow!' said Bagheera.

They had not gone half a mile farther when they heard Ko, the Crow, singing the death-song in the top of a tamarisk under whose shade three men were lying. A half-dead fire smoked in the centre of the circle, under an iron plate which held a blackened and burned cake of unleavened bread. Close to the fire, and blazing in the sunshine, lay the ruby-and-turquoise ankus.

'The thing works quickly; all ends here,' said Bagheera. 'How did *these* die, Mowgli? There is no mark on any.'

A Jungle-dweller gets to learn by experience as much as many doctors know of poisonous plants and berries. Mowgli sniffed the smoke that came up from the fire, broke off a morsel of the blackened bread, tasted it, and spat it out again.

'Apple of Death,' he coughed. 'The first must have made it ready in the food for *these*, who killed him, having first killed the Gond.'

'Good hunting, indeed! The kills follow close,' said Bahgeera.

'Apple of Death' is what the Jungle call thorn-apple or dhatura, the readiest poison in all India.

'What now?' said the panther. 'Must thou and I kill each other for yonder red-eyed slayer?'

'Can it speak?' said Mowgli in a whisper. 'Did I do it a wrong when I threw it away? Between us two it can do no wrong, for we do not desire what men desire. If it be left here, it will assuredly continue to kill men one after another as fast as nuts fall in a high wind. I have no love to men, but even I would not have them die six in a night.'

'What matter? They are only men. They killed one another, and were well pleased,' said Bagheera. 'That first little woodman hunted well.'

'They are cubs none the less; and a cub will drown himself to bite the moon's light on the water. The fault was mine,' said Mowgli, who spoke as though he knew all about everything. 'I will never again bring into the Jungle strange things—not though they be as beautiful as flowers. This'—he handled the ankus gingerly—'goes back to the Father of Cobras. But first we must sleep, and we cannot sleep near these sleepers. Also we must bury *him*, lest he run away and kill another six. Dig me a hole under that tree.'

'But, Little Brother,' said Bagheera, moving off to the spot, 'I tell thee it is no fault of the blood-drinker. The trouble is with the men.'

'All one,' said Mowgli. 'Dig the hole deep. When we wake I wil take him up and carry him back.'

Two nights later, as the White Cobra sat mourning in the darkness of the vault, ashamed, and robbed, and alone, the turquoise ankus whirled through the hole in the wall, and clashed on the floor of golden coins.

'Father of Cobras,' said Mowgli (he was careful to keep the

other side of the wall), 'get thee a young and ripe one of thine
own people to help thee guard the King's Treasure, so that no
man may come away alive any more.'

'Ah-ha! It returns, then. I said the thing was Death. How
comes it that thou art still alive?' the old Cobra mumbled,
twining lovingly round the ankus-haft.

'By the Bull that bought me, I do not know! That thing has
killed six times in a night. Let him go out no more.'

1895

# Slaves Of The Lamp

## [PART I]

THE music-room on the top floor of Number Five was filled with the 'Aladdin' company at rehearsal. Dickson Quartus, commonly known as Dick Four, was Aladdin, stage-manager, ballet-master, half the orchestra, and largely librettist, for the 'book' had been rewritten and filled with local allusions. The pantomime was to be given next week, in the downstairs study occupied by Aladdin, Abanazar, and the Emperor of China. The Slave of the Lamp, with the Princess Badroulbadour and the Widow Twankey, owned Number Five study across the same landing, so that the company could be easily assembled. The floor shook to the stamp-and-go of the ballet, while Aladdin, in pink cotton tights, a blue and tinsel jacket, and a plumed hat, banged alternately on the piano and his banjo. He was the moving spirit of the game, as befitted a senior who had passed his Army Preliminary and hoped to enter Sandhurst next spring.

Aladdin came to his own at last, Abanazar lay poisoned on the floor, the Widow Twankey danced her dance, and the company decided it would 'come all right on the night'.

'What about the last song, though?' said the Emperor, a tallish, fair-headed boy with a ghost of a moustache, at which he pulled manfully. 'We need a rousing old tune.'

'"John Peel"? "Drink, Puppy Drink"?' suggested Abanazar, smoothing his baggy lilac pyjamas. 'Pussy' Abanazar never looked more than one-half awake, but he owned a soft, slow smile which well suited the part of the Wicked Uncle.

'Stale,' said Aladdin. 'Might as well have "Grandfather's Clock". What's that thing you were humming at prep. last night, Stalky?'

Stalky, the Slave of the Lamp, in black tights and doublet, a black silk half-mask on his forehead, whistled lazily where he lay on the top of the piano. It was a catchy music-hall tune.

Dick Four cocked his head critically, and squinted down a large red nose.

'Once more, and I can pick it up,' he said, strumming. 'Sing the words.'

'Arrah, Patsy, mind the baby! Arrah Patsy, mind, the child!
Wrap him up in an overcoat, he's surely goin' wild!

53

        Arrah, Patsy, mind the baby; just ye mind the child
           awhile!
        He'll kick an' bite an' cry all night! Arrah, Patsy,
           mind the child!'

'Rippin'! Oh, rippin'!' said Dick Four. 'Only we shan't have
any piano on the night. We must work it with the banjos—play
an' dance at the same time. You try, Tertius.'

The Emperor pushed aside his pea-green sleeves of state, and
followed Dick Four on a heavy nickel-plated banjo.

'Yes, but I'm dead all this time. Bung in the middle of the
stage, too,' said Abanazar.

'Oh, that's Beetle's biznai,' said Dick Four. 'Vamp it up,
Beetle. Don't keep us waiting all night. You've got to get Pussy
out of the light somehow, and bring us all in dancin' at the end.'

'All right. You two play it again,' said Beetle, who, in a grey
skirt and a wig of chestnut sausage-curls, set slantwise above a
pair of spectacles mended with an old bootlace, represented the
Widow Twankey. He waved one leg in time to the hammered
refrain, and the banjos grew louder.

'Um! Ah! Er—"Aladdin now has won his wife",' he sang,
and Dick Four repeated it.

'"Your Emperor is appeased".' Tertius flung out his chest as
he delivered his line.

'Now jump up, Pussy! Say, "I think I'd better come to life!"
Then we all take hands and come forward: "We hope you've all
been pleased". *Twiggez-vous?*'

'*Nous twiggons*. Good enough. What's the chorus for the final
ballet? It's four kicks and a turn,' said Dick Four.

'Oh! Er!

        John Short will ring the curtain down,
          And ring the prompter's bell;
        We hope you know before you go,
          That we all wish you well.'

'Rippin'! Rippin'! Now for the Widow's scene with the
Princess. Hurry up, Turkey.'

M'Turk, in a violet silk skirt and a coquettish blue turban,
slouched forward as one thoroughly ashamed of himself. The
Slave of the Lamp climbed down from the piano, and dis-
passionately kicked him. 'Play up, Turkey,' he said; 'this is
serious.' But there fell on the door the knock of authority. It
happened to be King, in gown and mortar-board, enjoying a
Saturday evening prowl before dinner.

'Locked doors! Locked doors!' he snapped with a scowl.

'What's the meaning of this; and what, may I ask, is the intention of this—this epicene attire?'

'Pantomime, sir. The Head gave us leave,' said Abanazar, as the only member of the Sixth concerned. Dick Four stood firm in the confidence born of well-fitting tights, but Beetle strove to efface himself behind the piano. A grey princess-skirt borrowed from a day-boy's mother and a spotted cotton-bodice unsystematically padded with imposition-paper make one ridiculous. And in other regards Beetle had a bad conscience.

'As usual!' sneered King. 'Futile foolery just when your careers, such as they may be, are hanging in the balance. I see! Ah, I see! The old gang of criminals—allied forces of disorder— Corkran'—the Slave of the Lamp smiled politely—'M'Turk'— the Irishman smiled—'and, of course, the unspeakable Beetle, our friend Gigadibs.' Abanazar, the Emperor, and Aladdin had more or less of characters, and King passed them over. 'Come forth, my inky buffoon, from behind yonder instrument of music! You supply, I presume, the doggerel for this entertainment. Esteem yourself to be, as it were, a poet?'

'He's found one of 'em,' thought Beetle, noting the flush on King's cheek-bone.

'I have just had the pleasure of reading an effusion of yours to my address, I believe—an effusion intended to rhyme. So—so you despise me, Master Gigadibs, do you? I am quite aware— you need not explain—that it was ostensibly *not* intended for my edification. I read it with laughter—yes, with laughter. These paper pellets of inky boys—still a boy we are, Master Gigadibs— do not disturb my equanimity.'

''Wonder which it was,' thought Beetle. He had launched many lampoons on an appreciative public ever since he discovered that it was possible to convey reproof in rhyme.

In sign of his unruffled calm, King proceeded to tear Beetle, whom he called Gigadibs, slowly asunder. From his untied shoe-strings to his mended spectacles (the life of a poet at a big school is hard) he held him up to the derision of his associates—with the usual result. His wild flowers of speech—King had an unpleasant tongue—restored him to good humour at the last. He drew a lurid picture of Beetle's latter end as a scurrilous pamphleteer dying in an attic, scattered a few compliments over M'Turk and Corkran, and, reminding Beetle that he must come up for judgment when called upon, went to Common-room, where he triumphed anew over his victims.

'And the worst of it,' he explained in a loud voice over his soup, 'is that I waste such gems of sarcasm on their thick heads. It's miles above them, I'm certain.'

'We-ell,' said the school chaplain slowly. 'I don't know what Corkran's appreciation of your style may be, but young M'Turk reads Ruskin for his amusement.'

'Nonsense! He does it to show off. I mistrust the dark Celt.'

'He does nothing of the kind. I went into their study the other night, unofficially, and M'Turk was gluing up the back of four odd numbers of *Fors Clavigera*.'

'I don't know anything about their private lives,' said a mathematical master hotly, 'but I've learned by bitter experience that Number Five study are best left alone. They are utterly soulless young devils.' He blushed as the others laughed.

But in the music-room there was wrath and bad language. Only Stalky, Slave of the Lamp, lay on the piano unmoved.

'That little swine Manders minor must have shown him your stuff. He's always suckin' up to King. Go and kill him,' he drawled. 'Which one was it, Beetle?'

'Dunno,' said Beetle, struggling out of the skirt. 'There was one about his hunting for popularity with the small boys, and the other one was one about him in hell, tellin' the Devil he was a Balliol man. I swear both of 'em rhymed all right. By gum! P'raps Manders minor showed him both! *I*'ll correct his cæsuras for him.'

He disappeared down two flights of stairs, flushed a small pink and white boy in a form-room next door to King's study, which, again, was immediately below his own, and chased him up the corridor into a form-room sacred to the revels of the Lower Third. Thence he came back, greatly disordered, to find M'Turk, Stalky, and the others of the company in his study enjoying an unlimited 'brew'—coffee, cocoa, buns, new bread hot and steaming, sardine, sausage, ham-and-tongue paste, pilchards, three jams, and at least as many pounds of Devonshire cream.

'My Hat!' said he, throwing himself upon the banquet. 'Who stumped up for this, Stalky?' It was within a month of term end, and blank starvation had reigned in the studies for weeks.

'You,' said Stalky serenely.

'Confound you! You haven't been popping my Sunday bags, then?'

'Keep your hair on. It's only your watch.'

'Watch! I lost it—weeks ago. Out on the Burrows, when we tried to shoot the old ram—the day our pistol burst.'

'It dropped out of your pocket (you're so beastly careless, Beetle), and M'Turk and I kept it for you. I've been wearing it for a week, and you never noticed. 'Took it into Bideford after dinner today. 'Got thirteen and sevenpence. Here's the ticket.'

'Well, that's pretty average cool,' said Abanazar behind a slab of cream and jam, as Beetle, reassured upon the safety of his

Sunday trousers, showed not even surprise, much less resentment. Indeed, it was M'Turk who grew angry, saying:

'You gave him the ticket, Stalky? You pawned it? You unmitigated beast! Why, last month you and Beetle sold mine! 'Never got a sniff of any ticket.'

'Ah, that was because you locked your trunk and we wasted half the afternoon hammering it open. We might have pawned it if you'd behaved like a Christian, Turkey.'

'My Aunt!' said Abanazar, 'you chaps are communists. Vote of thanks to Beetle, though.'

'That's beastly unfair,' said Stalky, 'when I took all the trouble to pawn it. Beetle never knew he had a watch. Oh, I say, Rabbits-Eggs gave me a lift into Bideford this afternoon.'

Rabbits-Eggs was the local carrier—an outcrop of the early Devonian formation. It was Stalky who had invented his unlovely name. 'He was pretty average drunk, or he wouldn't have done it. Rabbits-Eggs is a little shy of me, somehow. But I swore it was *pax* between us, and gave him a bob. He stopped at two pubs on the way in, so he'll be howling drunk tonight. Oh, don't begin reading, Beetle; there's a council of war on. What the deuce is the matter with your collar?'

''Chivied Manders minor into the Lower Third box-room. 'Had all his beastly little friends on top of me,' said Beetle, from behind a jar of pilchards and a book.

'You ass! Any fool could have told you where Manders would bunk to,' said M'Turk.

'I didn't think,' said Beetle meekly, scooping out pilchards with a spoon.

''Course you didn't. You never do.' M'Turk adjusted Beetle's collar with a savage tug. 'Don't drop oil all over my "Fors", or I'll scrag you!'

'Shut up, you—you Irish Biddy! 'Tisn't your beastly "Fors". It's one of mine.'

The book was a fat, brown-backed volume of the later Sixties, which King had once thrown at Beetle's head that Beetle might see whence the name Gigadibs came. Beetle had quietly annexed the book, and had seen—several things. The quarter-comprehended verses lived and ate with him, as the be-dropped pages showed. He removed himself from all that world, drifting at large with wondrous Men and Women, till M'Turk hammered the pilchard spoon on his head and he snarled.

'Beetle! You're oppressed and insulted and bullied by King. Don't you feel it?'

'Let me alone! I can write some more poetry about him if I am, I suppose.'

'Mad! Quite mad!' said Stalky to the visitors, as one exhibiting strange beasts. 'Beetle reads an ass called Brownin', and M'Turk reads an ass called Ruskin; and——'

'Ruskin isn't an ass,' said M'Turk. 'He's almost as good as the Opium-Eater. He says "we're children of noble races trained by surrounding art". That means me, and the way I decorate the study when you two badgers would have stuck up brackets and Christmas cards. Child of a noble race, trained by surrounding art, stop reading, or I'll shove a pilchard down your neck!'

'It's two to one,' said Stalky warningly, and Beetle closed the book, in obedience to the law under which he and his companions had lived for six checkered years.

The visitors looked on delighted. Number Five study had a reputation for more variegated insanity than the rest of the school put together; and, so far as its code allowed friendship with outsiders, it was polite and open-hearted to its neighbours on the same landing.

'What rot do you want now?' said Beetle.

'King! War!' said M'Turk, jerking his head toward the wall, where hung a small wooden West-African war-drum, a gift to M'Turk from a naval uncle.

'Then we shall be turned out of the study again,' said Beetle, who loved his flesh-pots. 'Mason turned us out for—just warbling on it.' Mason was that mathematical master who had testified in Common-room.

'Warbling?—Oh, Lord!' said Abanazar. 'We couldn't hear ourselves speak in our study when you played the infernal thing. What's the good of getting turned out of your study, anyhow?'

'We lived in the form-rooms for a week, too,' said Beetle tragically. 'And it was beastly cold.'

'Ye-es; but Mason's rooms were filled with rats every day we were out. It took him a week to draw the inference,' said M'Turk. 'He loathes rats. 'Minute he let us go back the rats stopped. Mason's a little shy of us now, but there was no evidence.'

'Jolly well there wasn't,' said Stalky, 'when I got out on the roof and dropped the beastly things down his chimney. But, look here—question is, are our characters good enough just now to stand a study row?'

'Never mind mine,' said Beetle. 'King swears I haven't any.'

'I'm not thinking of you,' Stalky returned scornfully. 'You aren't going up for the Army, you old bat. I don't want to be expelled—and the Head's getting rather shy of us, too.'

'Rot!' said M'Turk. 'The Head never expels except for beastliness or stealing. But I forgot; you and Stalky *are* thieves—regular burglars.'

The visitors gasped, but Stalky interpreted the parable with large grins.

'Well, you know, that little beast Manders minor saw Beetle and me hammerin' M'Turk's trunk open in the dormitory when we took his watch last month. Of course Manders sneaked to Mason, and Mason solemnly took it up as a case of theft, to get even with us about the rats.'

'That just put Mason into our giddy hands,' said M'Turk blandly. 'We were nice to him, 'cause he was a new master and wanted to win the confidence of the boys. 'Pity he draws inferences, though. Stalky went to his study and pretended to blub, and told Mason he'd lead a new life if Mason would let him off this time, but Mason wouldn't. 'Said it was his duty to report him to the Head.'

'Vindictive swine!' said Beetle. 'It was all those rats! Then *I* blubbed, too, and Stalky confessed that he'd been a thief in regular practice for six years, ever since he came to the school; and that I'd taught him—*à la* Fagin. Mason turned white with joy. He thought he had us on toast.'

'Gorgeous! Oh, fids!' said Dick Four. 'We never heard of this.'

''Course not. Mason kept it jolly quiet. He wrote down all our statements on impot-paper. There wasn't anything he wouldn't believe,' said Stalky.

'And handed it all up to the Head, *with* an extempore prayer. It took about forty pages,' said Beetle. 'I helped him a lot.'

'And then, you crazy idiots?' said Abanazar.

'Oh, we were sent for; and Stalky asked to have the "depositions" read out, and the Head knocked him spinning into a wastepaper basket. Then he gave us eight cuts apiece—welters—for—for—takin' unheard-of liberties with a new master. I saw his shoulders shaking when we went out. Do you know,' said Beetle pensively, 'that Mason can't look at us now in second lesson without blushing? We three stare at him sometimes till he regularly trickles. He's an awfully sensitive beast.'

'He read *Eric; or, Little by Little*,' said M'Turk; 'so we gave him *St Winifred's; or, The World of School*. They spent all their spare time stealing at St Winifred's, when they weren't praying or getting drunk at pubs. Well, that was only a week ago, and the Head's a little bit shy of us. He called it constructive deviltry. Stalky invented it all.'

''Not the least good having a row with a master unless you can make use of him,' said Stalky, extended at ease on the hearth-rug. 'If Mason didn't know Number Five—well, he's learnt, that's all. Now, my dearly beloved 'earers'—Stalky curled his legs under him and addressed the company—'we've got that strong, perse-

verin' man King on our hands. He went miles out of his way to
provoke a conflict.' (Here Stalky snapped down the black silk
domino and assumed the air of a judge.) 'He has oppressed
Beetle, M'Turk, and me, *privatim et seriatim*, one by one, as he
could catch us. But now he has insulted Number Five up in the
music-room, and in the presence of these—these ossifers of the
Ninety-third, wot look like hairdressers. Binjimin, we must
make him cry "*Capivi!*"'

Stalky's reading did not include Browning or Ruskin.

'And, besides,' said M'Turk, 'he's a Philistine, a basket-
hanger. He wears a tartan tie. Ruskin says that any man who
wears a tartan tie will, without doubt, be damned everlastingly.'

'Bravo, M'Turk,' cried Tertius; 'I thought he was only a beast.'

'He's that, too, of course, but he's worse. He has a china
basket with blue ribbons and a pink kitten on it, hung up in his
window to grow musk in. You know when I got all that old oak
carvin' out of Bideford Church, when they were restoring it
(Ruskin says that any man who'll restore a church is an unmiti-
gated sweep), and stuck it up here with glue? Well, King came in
and wanted to know whether we'd done it with a fret-saw! Yah!
He is the king of basket-hangers!'

Down went M'Turk's inky thumb over an imaginary arena full
of bleeding Kings. '*Placetne*, child of a generous race?' he cried
to Beetle.

'Well,' began Beetle doubtfully, 'he comes from Balliol, but
I'm going to give the beast a chance. You see I can always make
him hop with some more poetry. He can't report me to the Head,
because it makes him ridiculous. (Stalky's quite right.) But he
shall have his chance.'

Beetle opened the book on the table, ran his finger down a
page, and began at random:

> 'Or who in Moscow toward the Czar
>     With the demurest of footfalls,
>     Over the Kremlin's pavement white
>     With serpentine and syenite,
> Steps with five other generals——'

'That's no good. Try another,' said Stalky.

'Hold on a shake; I know what's coming.' M'Turk was
reading over Beetle's shoulder—

> 'That simultaneously take snuff,
>     For each to have pretext enough,
>     To kerchiefwise unfold his sash,
>     Which—softness' self—is yet the stuff

(Gummy! What a sentence!)

> To hold fast where a steel chain snaps
> And leave the grand white neck no gash.

(Full stop.)'

''Don't understand a word of it,' said Stalky.

'More fool you! Construe,' said M'Turk. 'Those six bargees scragged the Czar and left no evidence. *Actum est* with King.'

'He gave me that book, too,' said Beetle, licking his lips:

> 'There's a great text in Galatians
> Once you trip on it entails
> Twenty-nine distinct damnations,
> One sure if another fails.'

Then irrelevantly:

> 'Setebos! Setebos! and Setebos!
> Thinketh he liveth in the cold of the moon.'

'He's just come in from dinner,' said Dick Four, looking through the window. 'Manders minor is with him.'

''Safest place for Manders minor just now,' said Beetle.

'Then you chaps had better clear out,' said Stalky politely to the visitors. ''Tisn't fair to mix you up in a study row. Besides, we can't afford to have evidence.'

'Are you going to begin at once?' said Aladdin.

'Immediately, if not sooner,' said Stalky, and turned out the gas. 'Strong, perseverin' man—King. Make him cry "*Capivi*". G'way, Binjimin.'

The company retreated to their neat and spacious study with expectant souls.

'When Stalky blows out his nostrils like a horse,' said Aladdin to the Emperor of China, 'he's on the war-path. 'Wonder what King will get.'

'Beans,' said the Emperor. 'Number Five generally pays in full.'

''Wonder if I ought to take any notice of it officially,' said Abanazar, who had just remembered that he was a prefect.

'It's none of your business, Pussy. Besides, if you did, we'd have them hostile to us; and we shouldn't be able to do any work,' said Aladdin. 'They've begun already.'

Now that West-African war-drum had been made to signal across estuaries and deltas. Number Five was forbidden to wake the engine within earshot of the school. But a deep devastating drone filled the passages as M'Turk and Beetle scientifically rubbed its top. Anon it changed to the blare of trumpets—of savage pursuing trumpets. Then, as M'Turk slapped one side, smooth with the blood of ancient sacrifice, the roar broke into short coughing howls such as the wounded gorilla throws in his native forest. These were followed by the wrath of King—three steps at a time, up the staircase, with a dry whirr of the gown. Aladdin and company, listening, squeaked with excitement as the door crashed open. King stumbled into the darkness, and cursed those performers by the gods of Balliol and quiet repose.

'Turned out for a week,' said Aladdin, holding the study door on the crack. 'Key to be brought down to his study in five minutes. "Brutes! Barbarians! Savages! Children!" He's rather agitated. "Arrah, Patsy, mind the baby",' he sang in a whisper as he clung to the door-knob, dancing a noiseless war-dance.

King went downstairs again, and Beetle and M'Turk lit the gas to confer with Stalky. But Stalky had vanished.

''Looks like no end of a mess,' said Beetle, collecting his books and mathematical instrument case. 'A week in the form-room isn't any advantage to us.'

'Yes, but don't you see that Stalky isn't here, you owl?' said M'Turk. 'Take down the key, and look sorrowful. King'll only jaw for half an hour. I'm goin' to read in the lower form-room.'

'But it's always me,' mourned Beetle.

'Wait till we see,' said M'Turk hopefully. 'I don't know any more than you do what Stalky means, but it's something. Go down and draw King's fire. You're used to it.'

No sooner had the key turned in the door than the lid of the coal-box, which was also the window-seat, lifted cautiously. It had been a tight fit, even for the lithe Stalky, his head between his knees, and his stomach under his right ear. From a drawer in the table he took a well-worn catapult, a handful of buckshot, and a duplicate key of the study; noiselessly he raised the window and kneeled by it, his face turned to the road, the wind-sloped trees, the dark levels of the Burrows, and the white line of breakers falling nine-deep along the Pebbleridge. Far down the steep-banked Devonshire lane he heard the husky hoot of the carrier's horn. There was a ghost of melody in it, as it might have been the wind in a gin-bottle essaying to sing 'It's a way we have in the Army.'

Stalky smiled a tight-lipped smile, and at extreme range opened fire: the old horse half wheeled in the shafts.

'Where be gwaine tu?' hiccoughed Rabbits-Eggs. Another buckshot tore through the rotten canvas tilt with a vicious zipp.

'*Habet!*' murmured Stalky, as Rabbits-Eggs swore into the patient night, protesting that he saw the 'dommed colleger' who was assaulting him.

'And so,' King was saying in a high head voice to Beetle, whom he had kept to play with before Manders minor, well knowing that it hurts a Fifth-form boy to be held up to a fag's derision—'and so, Master Beetle, in spite of all our verses, of which we are so proud, when we presume to come into direct conflict with even so humble a representative of authority as myself, for instance, we are turned out of our studies, are we not?'

'Yes, sir,' said Beetle, with a sheepish grin on his lips and murder in his heart. Hope had nearly left him, but he clung to a well-established faith that never was Stalky so dangerous as when he was invisible.

'You are not required to criticize, thank you. Turned out of our studies are we, just as if we were no better than little Manders minor. Only inky schoolboys we are, and must be treated as such.'

Beetle pricked up his ears, for Rabbits-Eggs was swearing savagely on the road, and some of the language entered at the upper sash. King believed in ventilation. He strode to the window, gowned and majestic, very visible in the gas-light.

'I zee 'un! I zee 'un!' roared Rabbits-Eggs, now that he had found a visible foe—another shot from the darkness above. 'Yiss, yeou, yeou long-nosed, fower-eyed, gingy-whiskered beggar! Yeu'm tu old for such goin's on. Aie! Poultice yeour nose, I tall 'ee! Poultice yeour long nose!'

Beetle's heart leapt up within him. Somewhere, somehow, he knew, Stalky moved behind these manifestations. There was hope and the prospect of revenge. He would embody the suggestion about the nose in deathless verse. King threw up the window, and sternly rebuked Rabbits-Eggs. But the carrier was beyond fear or fawning. He had descended from the cart, and was stooping by the roadside.

It all fell swiftly as a dream. Manders minor raised his hand to his head with a cry, as a jagged flint cannoned on to some rich tree-calf bindings in the bookshelf. Another quoited along the writing-table. Beetle made a zealous feint to stop it, and in that endeavour overturned a student's lamp, which dripped, *viâ* King's papers and some choice books, greasily on to a Persian rug. There was much broken glass on the window-seat; the china basket—M'Turk's aversion—cracked to flinders, had dropped her musk plant and its earth over the red rep cushions; Manders minor was bleeding profusely from a cut on the cheek-bone; and King, using strange words, every one of which Beetle treasured, ran forth to find the school-sergeant, that Rabbits-Eggs might be instantly cast into jail.

'Poor chap!' said Beetle, with a false, feigned sympathy. 'Let it bleed a little. That'll prevent apoplexy,' and he held the blind head skilfully over the table, and the papers on the table, as he guided the howling Manders to the door.

Then did Beetle, alone with the wreckage, return good for evil. How, in that office, a complete set of 'Gibbon' was scarred all along the back as by a flint; how so much black and copying ink chanced to mingle with Manders's gore on the table-cloth; why the big gum-bottle, unstoppered, had rolled semicircularly across the floor; and in what manner the white china door-knob grew to be painted with yet more of Manders's young blood, were matters which Beetle did not explain when the rabid King returned to find him standing politely over the reeking hearth-rug.

'You never told me to go, sir,' he said, with the air of Casabianca, and King consigned him to the outer darkness.

But it was to a boot-cupboard under the staircase on the ground floor that he hastened, to loose the mirth that was destroying him. He had not drawn breath for a first whoop of triumph when two hands choked him dumb.

'Go to the dormitory and get me my things. Bring 'em to Number Five lavatory. I'm still in tights,' hissed Stalky, sitting on his head. 'Don't run. Walk.'

But Beetle staggered into the form-room next door, and delegated his duty to the yet unenlightened M'Turk, with an hysterical *précis* of the campaign thus far. So it was M'Turk, of the wooden visage, who brought the clothes from the dormitory while Beetle panted on a form. Then the three buried themselves in Number Five lavatory, turned on all the taps, filled the place with steam, and dropped weeping into the baths, where they pieced out the war.

'*Moi! Je! Ich! Ego!*' gasped Stalky. 'I waited till I couldn't hear myself think, while you played the drum! Hid in the coal-locker—and tweaked Rabbits-Eggs—and Rabbits-Eggs rocked King. Wasn't it beautiful? Did you hear the glass?'

'Why, he—he—he,' shrieked M'Turk, one trembling finger pointed at Beetle.

'Why, I—I—I was through it all,' Beetle howled; 'in his study, being jawed.'

'Oh, my soul!' said Stalky, with a yell, disappearing under water.

'The—the glass was nothing. Manders minor's head's cut open. La-la-lamp upset all over the rug. Blood on the books and papers.

The gum! The gum! The gum! The ink! The ink! The ink! Oh, Lord!'

Then Stalky leaped out, all pink as he was, and shook Beetle into some sort of coherence; but his tale prostrated them afresh.

'I bunked for the boot-cupboard the second I heard King go downstairs. Beetle tumbled in on top of me. The spare key's hid behind the loose board. There isn't a shadow of evidence,' said Stalky. They were all chanting together.

'And he turned us out himself—himself—him*self*!' This from M'Turk. 'He can't begin to suspect us. Oh, Stalky, it's the loveliest thing we've ever done.'

'Gum! Gum! Dollops of gum!' shouted Beetle, his spectacles gleaming through a sea of lather. 'Ink and blood all mixed. I held the little beast's head all over the Latin proses for Monday. Golly, how the oil stunk! And Rabbits-Eggs told King to poultice his nose! Did you hit Rabbits-Eggs, Stalky?'

'Did I jolly well not? Tweaked him all over. Did you hear him curse? Oh, I shall be sick in a minute if I don't stop.'

But dressing was a slow process, because M'Turk was obliged to dance when he heard that the musk basket was broken, and, moreover, Beetle retailed all King's language with emendations and purple insets.

'Shockin'!' said Stalky, collapsing in a helpless welter of half-hitched trousers. 'So dam' bad, too, for innocent boys like us! Wonder what they'd say at "St Winifred's, *or* The World of School." By gum! That reminds me we owe the Lower Third one for assaultin' Beetle when he chivied Manders minor. Come on! It's an alibi, Samivel; and besides, if we let 'em off they'll be worse next time.'

The Lower Third had set a guard upon their form-room for the space of a full hour, which to a boy is a lifetime. Now they were busy with their Saturday evening businesses—cooking sparrows over the gas with rusty nibs; brewing unholy drinks in gallipots; skinning moles with pocket-knives: attending to paper trays full of silkworms, or discussing the iniquities of their elders with a freedom, fluency, and point that would have amazed their parents. The blow fell without warning. Stalky upset a crowded form of small boys among their own cooking utensils; M'Turk raided the untidy lockers as a terrier digs at a rabbit-hole; while Beetle poured ink upon such heads as he could not appeal to with a Smith's Classical Dictionary. Three brisk minutes accounted for many silk-worms, pet larvæ, French exercises, school caps, half-prepared bones and skulls, and a dozen pots of home-made sloe jam. It was a great wreckage, and the form-room looked as though three conflicting tempests had smitten it.

'Phew!' said Stalky, drawing breath outside the door (amid groans of 'Oh, you beastly ca-ads! You think yourselves awful funny,' and so forth). '*That*'s all right. Never let the sun go down upon your wrath. Rummy little devils, fags. 'Got no notion o' combinin'.'

'Six of 'em sat on my head when I went in after Manders minor,' said Beetle. 'I warned 'em what they'd get, though.'

'Everybody paid in full—beautiful feelin',' said M'Turk absently, as they strolled along the corridor. ''Don't think we'd better say much about King, though, do you, Stalky?'

'Not much. Our line is injured innocence, of course—same as when old Foxibus reported us on suspicion of smoking in the Bunkers. If I hadn't thought of buyin' the pepper and spillin' it all over our clothes, he'd have smelt us. King was gha-astly facetious about that. 'Called us bird-stuffers in form for a week.'

'Ah, King hates the Natural History Society because little Hartopp is president. 'Mustn't do anything in the Coll. without glorifyin' King,' said M'Turk. 'But he must be a putrid ass, you know, to suppose at our time o' life we'd go out and stuff birds like fags.'

'Poor old King!' said Beetle. 'He's awf'ly unpopular in Common-room, and they'll chaff his head off about Rabbits-Eggs. Golly! How lovely! How beautiful! How holy! But you should have seen his face when the first rock came in! *And* the earth from the basket!'

So they were all stricken helpless for five minutes.

They repaired at last to Abanazar's study, and were received reverently.

'What's the matter?' said Stalky, quick to realize new atmospheres.

'You know jolly well,' said Abanazar. 'You'll be expelled if you get caught. King is a gibbering maniac.'

'Who? Which? What? Expelled for how? We only played the war-drum. We've got turned out for that already.'

'Do you chaps mean to say you didn't make Rabbits-Eggs drunk and bribe him to rock King's rooms?'

'Bribe him? No, that I'll swear we didn't,' said Stalky, with a relieved heart, for he loved not to tell lies. 'What a low mind you've got, Pussy! We've been down having a bath. Did Rabbits-Eggs rock King? Strong, perseverin' man King? Shockin'!'

'Awf'ly. King's frothing at the mouth. There's bell for prayers. come on.'

'Wait a sec,' said Stalky, continuing the conversation in a loud and cheerful voice, as they descended the stairs. 'What did Rabbits-Eggs rock King for?'

'I know,' said Beetle, as they passed King's open door. 'I was in his study.'

'Hush, you ass!' hissed the Emperor of China.

'Oh, he's gone down to prayers,' said Beetle, watching the shadow of the house-master on the wall. 'Rabbits-Eggs was only a bit drunk, swearin' at his horse, and King jawed him through the window, and then, of course, he rocked King.'

'Do you mean to say,' said Stalky, 'that King began it?'

King was behind them, and every well-weighed word went up the staircase like an arrow. 'I can only swear,' said Beetle, 'that King cursed like a bargee. Simply disgustin'. I'm goin' to write to my father about it.'

'Better report it to Mason,' suggested Stalky. 'He knows our tender consciences. Hold on a shake. I've got to tie my bootlace.'

The other study hurried forward. They did not wish to be dragged into stage asides of this nature. So it was left to M'Turk to sum up the situation beneath the guns of the enemy.

'You see,' said the Irishman, hanging on the banister, 'he begins by bullying the little chaps; then he bullies the big chaps; then he bullies someone who isn't connected with the College, and then he catches it. Serves him jolly well right. . . . I beg your pardon, sir. I didn't see you were coming down the staircase.'

The black gown tore past like a thunderstorm, and in its wake, three abreast, arms linked, the Aladdin Company rolled up the big corridor to prayers, singing with most innocent intention:

> 'Arrah, Patsy, mind the baby! Arrah, Patsy, mind
> the child!
> Wrap him up in an overcoat, he's surely goin' wild!
> Arrah, Patsy, mind the baby; just ye mind the child
> awhile!
> He'll kick an' bite an' cry all night! Arrah, Patsy,
> mind the child!'

1897

# The Cat That Walked By Himself

HEAR and attend and listen; for this befell and be-happened and became and was, O my Best Beloved, when the Tame animals were wild. The Dog was wild, and the Horse was wild, and the Cow was wild, and the Sheep was wild, and the Pig was wild—as wild as wild could be—and they walked in the Wet Wild Woods by their wild lones. But the wildest of all the wild animals was the Cat. He walked by himself, and all places were alike to him.

Of course the Man was wild too. He was dreadfully wild. He didn't even begin to be tame till he met the Woman, and she told him that she did not like living in his wild ways. She picked out a nice dry Cave, instead of a heap of wet leaves, to lie down in; and she strewed clean sand on the floor; and she lit a nice fire of wood at the back of the Cave; and she hung a dried wild-horse skin, tail-down, across the opening of the Cave; and she said, 'Wipe your feet, dear, when you come in, and now we'll keep house.'

That night, Best Beloved, they ate wild sheep roasted on the hot stones, and flavoured with wild garlic and wild pepper; and wild duck stuffed with wild rice and wild fenugreek and wild coriander; and marrow-bones of wild oxen; and wild cherries, and wild grenadillas. Then the Man went to sleep in front of the fire ever so happy; but the Woman sat up, combing her hair. She took the bone of the shoulder of mutton—the big flat blade-bone —and she looked at the winderful marks on it, and she threw more wood on the fire, and she made a Magic. She made the First Singing Magic in the world.

Out in the Wet Wild Woods all the wild animals gathered together where they could see the light of the fire a long way off, and they wondered what it meant.

Then Wild Horse stamped with his wild foot and said, 'O my Friends and O my Enemies, why have the Man and the Woman made that great light in that great Cave, and what harm will it do us?'

Wild Dog lifted up his wild nose and smelled the smell of the roast mutton, and said, 'I will go up and see and look, and say; for I think it is good. Cat, come with me.'

'Nenni!' said the Cat. 'I am the Cat who walks by himself, and all places are alike to me. I will not come.'

'Then we can never be friends again,' said Wild Dog, and he trotted off to the Cave. But when he had gone a little way the Cat said to himself, 'All places are alike to me. Why should I not go too and see and look and come away at my own liking?' So he slipped after Wild Dog softly, very softly, and hid himself where he could hear everything.

When Wild Dog reached the mouth of the Cave he lifted up the dried horse-skin with his nose and sniffed the beautiful smell of the roast mutton, and the Woman, looking at the blade-bone, heard him, and laughed, and said, 'Here comes the first. Wild Thing out of the Wild Woods, what do you want?'

Wild Dog said, 'O my Enemy and Wife of my Enemy, what is this that smells so good in the Wild Woods?'

Then the Woman picked up a roasted mutton-bone and threw it to Wild Dog, and said, 'Wild Thing out of the Wild Woods, taste and try.' Wild Dog gnawed the bone, and it was more delicious than anything he had ever tasted, and he said, 'O my Enemy and Wife of my Enemy, give me another.'

The Woman said, 'Wild Thing out of the Wild Woods, help my Man to hunt through the day and guard this Cave at night, and I will give you as many roast bones as you need.'

'Ah!' said the Cat, listening. 'This is a very wise Woman, but she is not so wise as I am.'

Wild Dog crawled into the Cave and laid his head on the Woman's lap, and said, 'O my Friend and Wife of my Friend, I will help your Man to hunt through the day, and at night I will guard your Cave.'

'Ah!' said the Cat, listening. 'That is a very foolish Dog.' And he went back through the Wet Wild Woods waving his wild tail, and walked by his wild lone. But he never told anybody.

When the Man waked up he said, 'What is Wild Dog doing here?' And the Woman said, 'His name is not Wild Dog any more, but the First Friend, because he will be our friend for always and always and always. Take him with you when you go hunting.'

Next night the Woman cut great green armfuls of fresh grass from the water-meadows, and dried it before the fire, so that it smelt like new-mown hay, and she sat at the mouth of the Cave and plaited a halter out of horse-hide, and she looked at the shoulder-of-mutton bone—at the big broad blade-bone—and she made a Magic. She made the Second Singing Magic in the world.

Out in the Wild Woods all the wild animals wondered what had happened to Wild Dog, and at last Wild Horse stamped with his foot and said, 'I will go and see and say why Wild Dog has not returned. Cat, come with me.'

'Nenni!' said the Cat. 'I am the Cat who walks by himself, and all places are alike to me. I will not come.' But all the same he followed Wild Horse softly, very softly, and hid himself where he could hear everything.

When the Woman heard Wild Horse tripping and stumbling on his long mane, she laughed and said, 'Here comes the second. Wild Thing out of the Wild Woods, what do you want?'

Wild Horse said, 'O my Enemy and Wife of my Enemy, where is Wild Dog?'

The Woman laughed, and picked up the blade-bone and looked at it, and said, 'Wild Thing out of the Wild Woods, you did not come here for Wild Dog, but for the sake of this good grass.'

And Wild Horse, tripping and stumbling on his long mane, said, 'That's true; give it me to eat.'

The Woman said, 'Wild Thing out of the Wild Woods, bend your wild head and wear what I give you, and you shall eat the wonderful grass three times a day.'

'Ah!' said the Cat, listening. 'This is a clever Woman, but she is not so clever as I am.'

Wild Horse bent his wild head, and the Woman slipped the plaited-hide halter over it, and Wild Horse breathed on the Woman's feet and said, 'O my Mistress, and Wife of my Master, I will be your servant for the sake of the wonderful grass.'

'Ah!' said the Cat, listening. 'That is a very foolish Horse.' And he went back through the Wet Wild Woods, waving his wild tail and walking by his wild lone. But he never told anybody.

When the Man and the Dog came back from hunting, the Man said, 'What is Wild Horse doing here?' And the Woman said, 'His name is not Wild Horse any more, but the First Servant, because he will carry us from place to place for always and always and always. Ride on his back when you go hunting.'

Next day, holding her wild head high that her wild horns should not catch in the wild trees, Wild Cow came up to the Cave, and the Cat followed, and hid himself just the same as before; and everything happened just the same as before; and the Cat said the same things as before; and when Wild Cow had promised to give her milk to the Woman every day in exchange for the wonderful grass, the Cat went back through the Wet Wild Woods waving his wild tail and walking by his wild lone, just the same as before. But he never told anybody. And when the Man and the Horse and the Dog came home from hunting and asked the same questions same as before, the Woman said, 'Her name is not Wild Cow any more, but the Giver of Good Food. She will give us the warm white milk for always and always and always, and I will take care of her while you and the First Friend and the First Servant go hunting.'

Next day the Cat waited to see if any other Wild Thing would go up to the Cave, but no one moved in the Wet Wild Woods, so the Cat walked there by himself; and he saw the Woman milking the Cow, and he saw the light of the fire in the cave, and he smelt the smell of the warm white milk.

Cat said, 'O my Enemy and Wife of my Enemy, where did Wild Cow go?'

The Woman laughed and said, 'Wild Thing out of the Wild Woods, go back to the Woods again, for I have braided up my hair, and I have put away the magic blade-bone, and we have no more need of either friends or servants in our Cave.'

Cat said, 'I am not a friend, and I am not a servant. I am the Cat who walks by himself, and I wish to come into your Cave.'

Woman said, 'Then why did you not come with First Friend on the first night?'

Cat grew very angry and said, 'Has Wild Dog told tales of me?'

Then the Woman laughed and said, 'You are the Cat who walks by himself, and all places are alike to you. You are neither a friend nor a servant. You have said it yourself. Go away and walk by yourself in all places alike.'

Then Cat pretended to be sorry and said, 'Must I never come into the Cave? Must I never sit by the warm fire? Must I never drink the warm white milk? You are very wise and very beautiful. You should not be cruel even to a Cat.'

Woman said, 'I knew I was wise, but I did not know I was beautiful. So I will make a bargain with you. If ever I say one word in your praise, you may come into the Cave.'

'And if you say two words in my praise?' said the Cat.

'I never shall,' said the Woman, 'but if I say two words in your praise, you may sit by the fire in the Cave.'

'And if you say three words?' said the Cat.

'I never shall,' said the Woman, 'but if I say three words in your praise, you may drink the warm white milk three times a day for always and always and always.'

Then the Cat arched his back and said, 'Now let the Curtain at the mouth of the Cave, and the Fire at the back of the Cave, and the Milk-pots that stand beside the Fire, remember what my Enemy and the Wife of my Enemy has said.' And he went away through the Wet Wild Woods waving his wild tail and walking by his wild lone.

That night when the Man and the Horse and the Dog came home from hunting, the Woman did not tell them of the bargain that she had made with the Cat, because she was afraid that they might not like it.

Cat went far and far away and hid himself in the Wet Wild Woods by his wild lone for a long time till the Woman forgot all about him. Only the Bat—the little upside-down Bat—that hung inside the Cave knew where Cat hid; and every evening Bat would fly to Cat with news of what was happening.

One evening Bat said, 'There is a Baby in the Cave. He is new and pink and fat and small, and the Woman is very fond of him.'

'Ah,' said the Cat, listening. 'But what is the Baby fond of?'

'He is fond of things that are soft and tickle,' said the Bat. 'He is fond of warm things to hold in his arms when he goes to sleep. He is fond of being played with. He is fond of all those things.'

'Ah,' said the Cat, listening. 'Then my time has come.'

Next night Cat walked through the Wet Wild Woods and hid very near the Cave till morning-time, and Man and Dog and Horse went hunting. The Woman was busy cooking that morning, and the Baby cried and interrupted. So she carried him outside the Cave and gave him a handful of pebbles to play with. But still the Baby cried.

Then the Cat put out his paddy paw and patted the Baby on the cheek, and it cooed; and the Cat rubbed against its fat knees and tickled it under its fat chin with his tail. And the Baby laughed; and the Woman heard him and smiled.

Then the Bat—the little upside-down Bat—that hung in the mouth of the Cave said, 'O my Hostess and Wife of my Host and Mother of my Host's Son, a Wild Thing from the Wild Woods is most beautifully playing with your Baby.'

'A blessing on that Wild Thing whoever he may be,' said the Woman, straightening her back, 'for I was a busy woman this morning and he has done me a service.'

That very minute and second, Best Beloved, the dried horse-skin Curtain that was stretched tail-down at the mouth of the Cave fell down—*woosh!*—because it remembered the bargain she had made with the Cat; and when the Woman went to pick it up —lo and behold!—the Cat was sitting quite comfy inside the Cave.

'O my Enemy and Wife of my Enemy and Mother of my Enemy,' said the Cat, 'it is I: for you have spoken a word in my praise, and now I can sit within the Cave for always and always and always. But still I am the Cat who walks by himself, and all places are alike to me.'

The Woman was very angry, and shut her lips tight and took up her spinning-wheel and began to spin.

But the Baby cried because the Cat had gone away, and the Woman could not hush it, for it struggled and kicked and grew black in the face.

'O my Enemy and Wife of my Enemy and Mother of my Enemy,' said the Cat, 'take a strand of the thread that you are spinning and tie it to your spindle-whorl and drag it along the floor, and I will show you a Magic that shall make your Baby laugh as loudly as he is now crying.'

'I will do so,' said the Woman, 'because I am at my wits' end; but I will not thank you for it.'

She tied the thread to the little clay spindle-whorl and drew it across the floor, and the Cat ran after it and patted it with his paws and rolled head over heels, and tossed it backward over his shoulder and chased it between his hind legs and pretended to lose it, and pounced down upon it again, till the Baby laughed as loudly as it had been crying, and scrambled after the Cat and frolicked all over the Cave till it grew tired and settled down to sleep with the Cat in its arms.

'Now,' said Cat, 'I will sing the Baby a song that shall keep him asleep for an hour.' And he began to purr, loud and low, low and loud, till the Baby fell fast asleep. The Woman smiled as she looked down upon the two of them and said, 'That was wonderfully done. No question but you are very clever, O Cat.'

That very minute and second, Best Beloved, the smoke of the Fire at the back of the Cave came down in clouds from the roof—*puff!*—because it remembered the bargain she had made with the Cat; and when it had cleared away—lo and behold!—the Cat was sitting quite comfy close to the fire.

'O my Enemy and Wife of my Enemy and Mother of my Enemy,' said the Cat, 'it is I: for you have spoken a second word in my praise, and now I can sit by the warm fire at the back of the Cave for always and always and always. But still I am the Cat who walks by himself, and all places are alike to me.'

Then the Woman was very angry, and led down her hair and put more wood on the fire and brought out the broad blade-bone of the shoulder of mutton and began to make a Magic that should prevent her from saying a third word in praise of the Cat. It was not a Singing Magic, Best Beloved, it was a Still Magic; and by and by the Cave grew so still that a little wee-wee mouse crept out of a corner and ran across the floor.

'O my Enemy and Wife of my Enemy and Mother of my Enemy,' said the Cat, 'is that little mouse part of your Magic?'

'Ouh! Chee! No indeed!' said the Woman, and she dropped the blade-bone and jumped upon the footstool in front of the fire and braided up her hair very quick for fear that the mouse should run up it.

'Ah,' said the Cat, watching. 'Then the mouse will do me no harm if I eat it?'

'No,' said the Woman, braiding up her hair, 'eat it quickly and I will ever be grateful to you.'

Cat made one jump and caught the little mouse, and the

Woman said, 'A hundred thanks. Even the First Friend is not quick enough to catch little mice as you have done. You must be very wise.'

That very minute and second, O Best Beloved, the Milk-pot that stood by the fire cracked in two pieces—*ffft!*—because it remembered the bargain she had made with the Cat; and when the Woman jumped down from the footstool—lo and behold—the Cat was lapping up the warm white milk that lay in one of the broken pieces.

'O my Enemy and Wife of my Enemy and Mother of my Enemy,' said the Cat, 'it is I: for you have spoken three words in my praise, and now I can drink the warm white milk three times a day for always and always and always. But *still* I am the Cat who walks by himself, and all places are alike to me.'

Then the Woman laughed and set the Cat a bowl of the warm white milk and said, 'O Cat, you are as clever as a man, but remember that your bargain was not made with the Man or the Dog, and I do not know what they will do when they come home.'

'What is that to me?' said the Cat. 'If I have my place in the Cave by the fire and my warm white milk three times a day I do not care what the Man or the Dog can do.'

That evening when the Man and the Dog came into the Cave, the Woman told them all the story of the bargain, while the Cat sat by the fire and smiled. Then the Man said, 'Yes, but he has not made a bargain with *me* or with all proper Men after me.' Then he took off his two leather boots and he took up his little stone axe (that makes three) and he fetched a piece of wood and a hatchet (that is five altogether), and he set them out in a row and he said, 'Now we will make *our* bargain. If you do not catch mice when you are in the Cave for always and always and always, I will throw these five things at you whenever I see you, and so shall all proper Men do after me.'

'Ah!' said the Woman, listening. 'This is a very clever Cat, but he is not so clever as my Man.'

The Cat counted the five things (and they looked very knobby) and he said, 'I will catch mice when I am in the Cave for always and always and always; but *still* I am the Cat who walks by himself, and all places are alike to me.'

'Not when I am near,' said the Man. 'If you had not said that last I would have put all these things away for always and always and always; but now I am going to throw my two boots and my little stone axe (that makes three) at you whenever I meet you. And so shall all proper Men do after me!'

Then the Dog said, 'Wait a minute. He has not made a bargain with *me* or with all proper Dogs after me.' And he showed his teeth and said, 'If you are not kind to the Baby while I am in the Cave for always and always and always, I will hunt you till I catch you, and when I catch you I will bite you. And so shall all proper Dogs do after me.'

'Ah!' said the Woman, listening. 'This is a very clever Cat, but he is not so clever as the Dog.'

Cat counted the Dog's teeth (and they looked very pointed) and he said, 'I will be kind to the Baby while I am in the Cave, as long as he does not pull my tail too hard, for always and always and always. But *still* I am the Cat who walks by himself, and all places are alike to me.'

'Not when I am near,' said the Dog. 'If you had not said that last I would have shut my mouth for always and always and always; but *now* I am going to hunt you up a tree whenever I meet you. And so shall all proper Dogs do after me.'

Then the Man threw his two boots and his little stone axe (that makes three) at the Cat, and the Cat ran out of the Cave and the Dog chased him up a tree; and from that day to this, Best Beloved, three proper Men out of five will always throw things at a Cat whenever they meet him, and all proper Dogs will chase him up a tree. But the Cat keeps his side of the bargain too. He will kill mice, and he will be kind to Babies when he is in the house, as long as they do not pull his tail too hard. But when he has done that, and between times, and when the moon gets up and night comes, he is the Cat that walks by himself, and all places are alike to him. Then he goes out to the Wet Wild Woods or up the Wet Wild Trees or on the Wet Wild Roofs, waving his wild tail and walking by his wild lone.

1902

# 'They'

ONE view called me to another; one hill top to its fellow, half across the county, and since I could answer at no more trouble than the snapping forward of a lever, I let the county flow under my wheels. The orchid-studded flats of the East gave way to the thyme, ilex, and grey grass of the Downs; these again to the rich cornland and fig-trees of the lower coast, where you carry the beat of the tide on your left hand for fifteen level miles; and when at last I turned inland through a huddle of rounded hills and woods I had run myself clean out of my known marks. Beyond that precise hamlet which stands godmother to the capital of the United States, I found hidden villages where bees, the only things awake, boomed in eighty-foot lindens that overhung grey Norman churches; miraculous brooks diving under stone bridges built for heavier traffic than would ever vex them again; tithe-barns larger than their churches, and an old smithy that cried out aloud how it had once been a hall of the Knights of the Temple. Gipsies I found on a common where the gorse, bracken, and heath fought it out together up a mile of Roman road; and a little farther on I disturbed a red fox rolling dog-fashion in the naked sunlight.

As the wooded hills closed about me I stood up in the car to take the bearings of that great Down whose ringed head is a landmark for fifty miles across the low countries. I judged that the lie of the country would bring me across some westward-running road that went to his feet, but I did not allow for the confusing veils of the woods. A quick turn plunged me first into a green cutting brim-full of liquid sunshine, next into a gloomy tunnel where last year's dead leaves whispered and scuffled about my tyres. The strong hazel stuff meeting overhead had not been cut for a couple of generations at least, nor had any axe helped the moss-cankered oak and beech to spring above them. Here the road changed frankly into a carpeted ride on whose brown velvet spent primrose-clumps showed like jade, and a few sickly, white-stalked blue-bells nodded together. As the slope favoured I shut off the power and slid over the whirled leaves, expecting every moment to meet a keeper; but I only heard a jay, far off, arguing against the silence under the twilight of the trees.

Still the track descended. I was on the point of reversing and working my way back on the second speed ere I ended in some swamp, when I saw sunshine through the tangle ahead and lifted the brake.

It was down again at once. As the light beat across my face my

fore-wheels took the turf of a great still lawn from which sprang
horsemen ten feet high with levelled lances, monstrous peacocks,
and sleek round-headed maids of honour—blue, black, and
glistening—all of clipped yew. Across the lawn—the marshalled
woods besieged it on three sides—stood an ancient house of
lichened and weather-worn stone, with mullioned windows and
roofs of rose-red tile. It was flanked by semi-circular walls, also
rose-red, that closed the lawn on the fourth side, and at their feet
a box hedge grew man-high. There were doves on the roof about
the slim brick chimneys, and I caught a glimpse of an octagonal
dove-house behind the screening wall.

Here, then, I stayed; a horseman's green spear laid at my
breast; held by the exceeding beauty of that jewel in that setting.

'If I am not packed off for a trespasser, or if this knight does
not ride a wallop at me,' thought I, 'Shakespeare and Queen
Elizabeth at least must come out of that half-open garden door
and ask me to tea.'

A child appeared at an upper window, and I thought the little
thing waved a friendly hand. But it was to call a companion, for
presently another bright head showed. Then I heard a laugh
among the yew-peacocks, and turning to make sure (till then I
had been watching the house only) I saw the silver of a fountain
behind a hedge thrown up against the sun. The doves on the roof
cooed to the cooing water; but between the two notes I caught the
utterly happy chuckle of a child absorbed in some light mischief.

The garden door—heavy oak sunk deep in the thickness of the
wall—opened further: a woman in a big garden hat set her foot
slowly on the time-hollowed stone step and as slowly walked
across the turf. I was forming some apology when she lifted up
her head and I saw that she was blind.

'I heard you,' she said. 'Isn't that a motor car?'

'I'm afraid I've made a mistake in my road. I should have
turned off up above—I never dreamed——' I began.

'But I'm very glad. Fancy a motor car coming into the garden!
It will be such a treat——' She turned and made as though look-
ing about her. 'You—you haven't seen anyone, have you—
perhaps?'

'No one to speak to, but the children seemed interested at a
distance.'

'Which?'

'I saw a couple up at the window just now, and I think I heard
a little chap in the grounds.'

'Oh, lucky you!' she cried, and her face brightened. 'I hear
them, of course, but that's all. You've seen them and heard
them?'

'Yes,' I answered. 'And if I know anything of children, one of them's having a beautiful time by the fountain yonder. Escaped, I should imagine.'

'You're fond of children?'

I gave her one or two reasons why I did not altogether hate them.

'Of course, of course,' she said. 'Then you understand. Then you won't think it foolish if I ask you to take your car through the gardens, once or twice—quite slowly. I'm sure they'd like to see it. They see so little, poor things. One tries to make their life pleasant, but——' she threw out her hands towards the woods. 'We're so out of the world here.'

'That will be splendid,' I said. 'But I can't cut up your grass.'

She faced to the right. 'Wait a minute,' she said. 'We're at the South gate, aren't we? Behind those peacocks there's a flagged path. We call it the Peacocks' Walk. You can't see it from here, they tell me, but if you squeeze along by the edge of the wood you can turn at the first peacock and get on to the flags.'

It was sacrilege to wake that dreaming house-front with the clatter of machinery, but I swung the car to clear the turf, brushed along the edge of the wood and turned in on the broad stone path where the fountain-basin lay like one star-sapphire.

'May I come too?' she cried. 'No, please don't help me. They'll like it better if they see me.'

She felt her way lightly to the front of the car, and with one foot on the step she called: 'Children, oh, children! Look and see what's going to happen!'

The voice would have drawn lost souls from the Pit, for the yearning that underlay its sweetness, and I was not surprised to hear an answering shout behind the yews. It must have been the child by the fountain, but he fled at our approach, leaving a little toy boat in the water. I saw the glint of his blue blouse among the still horsemen.

Very disposedly we paraded the length of the walk and at her request backed again. This time the child had got the better of his panic, but stood far off and doubting.

'The little fellow's watching us,' I said. 'I wonder if he'd like a ride.'

'They're very shy still. Very shy. But, oh, lucky you to be able to see them! Let's listen.'

I stopped the machine at once, and the humid stillness, heavy with the scent of box, cloaked us deep. Shears I could hear where some gardener was clipping; a mumble of bees and broken voices that might have been the doves.

'Oh, unkind!' she said wearily.

'Perhaps they're only shy of the motor. The little maid at the window looks tremendously interested.'

'Yes?' She raised her head. 'It was wrong of me to say that. They are really fond of me. It's the only thing that makes life worth living—when they're fond of you, isn't it? I daren't think what the place would be without them. By the way, is it beautiful?'

'I think it is the most beautiful place I have ever seen.'

'So they tell me. I can feel it, of course, but that isn't quite the same thing.'

'Then have you never——?' I began, but stopped abashed.

'Not since I can remember. It happened when I was only a few months old, they tell me. And yet I must remember something, else how could I dream about colours. I see light in my dreams, and colours, but I never see *them*. I only hear them just as I do when I'm awake.'

'It's difficult to see faces in dreams. Some people can, but most of us haven't the gift,' I went on, looking up at the window where the child stood all but hidden.

'I've heard that too,' she said. 'And they tell me that one never sees a dead person's face in a dream. Is that true?'

'I believe it is—now I come to think of it.'

'But how is it with yourself—yourself?' The blind eyes turned towards me.

'I have never seen the faces of my dead in any dream,' I answered.

'Then it must be as bad as being blind.'

The sun had dipped behind the woods and the long shades were possessing the insolent horsemen one by one. I saw the light die from off the top of a glossy-leaved lance and all the brave hard green turn to soft black. The house, accepting another day at end, as it had accepted an hundred thousand gone, seemed to settle deeper into its rest among the shadows.

'Have you ever wanted to?' she said after the silence.

'Very much sometimes,' I replied. The child had left the window as the shadows closed upon it.

'Ah! So've I, but I don't suppose it's allowed. . . . Where d'you live?'

'Quite the other side of the county—sixty miles and more, and I must be going back. I've come without my big lamp.'

'But it's not dark yet. I can feel it.'

'I'm afraid it will be by the time I get home. Could you lend me someone to set me on my road at first? I've utterly lost myself.'

'I'll send Madden with you to the crossroads. We are so out of the world, I don't wonder you were lost! I'll guide you round to the front of the house; but you will go slowly, won't you, till you're out of the grounds? It isn't foolish, do you think?'

'I promise you I'll go like this,' I said, and let the car start herself down the flagged path.

We skirted the left wing of the house, whose elaborately cast lead guttering alone was worth a day's journey; passed under a great rose-grown gate in the red wall, and so round to the high front of the house which in beauty and stateliness as much excelled the back as that all others I had seen.

'Is it so very beautiful?' she said wistfully when she heard my raptures. 'And you like the lead-figures too? There's the old azalea garden behind. They say that this place must have been made for children. Will you help me out, please? I should like to come with you as far as the crossroads, but I mustn't leave them. Is that you, Madden? I want you to show this gentleman the way to the crossroads. He has lost his way but—he has seen them.'

A butler appeared noiselessly at the miracle of old oak that must be called the front door, and slipped aside to put on his hat. She stood looking at me with open blue eyes in which no sight lay, and I saw for the first time that she was beautiful.

'Remember,' she said quietly, 'if you are fond of them you will come again,' and disappeared within the house.

The butler in the car said nothing till we were nearly at the lodge gates, where catching a glimpse of a blue blouse in a shrubbery I swerved amply lest the devil that leads little boys to play should drag me into child-murder.

'Excuse me,' he asked of a sudden, 'but why did you do that, Sir?'

'The child yonder.'

'Our young gentleman in blue?'

'Of course.'

'He runs about a good deal. Did you see him by the fountain, Sir?'

'Oh, yes, several times. Do we turn here?'

'Yes, Sir. And did you 'appen to see them upstairs too?'

'At the upper window? Yes.'

'Was that before the mistress come out to speak to you, Sir?'

'A little before that. Why d'you want to know?'

He paused a little. 'Only to make sure that—that they had seen the car, Sir, because with children running about, though I'm sure you're driving particularly careful, there might be an accident. That was all, Sir. Here are the crossroads. You can't miss your way from now on. Thank you, Sir, but that isn't *our* custom, not with——'

'I beg your pardon,' I said, and thrust away the British silver.

'Oh, it's quite right with the rest of 'em as a rule. Goodbye, Sir.'

He retired into the armour-plated conning tower of his caste and walked away. Evidently a butler solicitous for the honour of his house, and interested, probably through a maid, in the nursery.

Once beyond the signposts at the crossroads I looked back, but the crumpled hills interlaced so jealously that I could not see where the house had lain. When I asked its name at a cottage along the road, the fat woman who sold sweetmeats there gave me to understand that people with motor cars had small right to live—much less to 'go about talking like carriage folk'. They were not a pleasant-mannered community.

When I retraced my route on the map that evening I was little wiser. Hawkin's Old Farm appeared to be the Survey title of the place, and the old County Gazetteer, generally so ample, did not allude to it. The big house of those parts was Hodnington Hall, Georgian with early Victorian embellishments, as an atrocious steel engraving attested. I carried my difficulty to a neighbour—a deep-rooted tree of that soil—and he gave me a name of a family which conveyed no meaning.

A month or so later—I went again, or it may have been that my car took the road of her own volition. She over-ran the fruit-less Downs, threaded every turn of the maze of lanes below the hills, drew through the high-walled woods, impenetrable in their full leaf, came out at the crossroads where the butler had left me, and a little farther on developed an internal trouble which forced me to turn her in on a grass way-waste that cut into a summer-silent hazel wood. So far as I could make sure by the sun and a six-inch Ordnance map, this should be the road flank of that wood which I had first explored from the heights above. I made a mighty serious business of my repairs and a glittering shop of my repair kit, spanners, pump, and the like, which I spread out orderly upon a rug. It was a trap to catch all childhood, for on such a day, I argued, the children would not be far off. When I paused in my work I listened, but the wood was so full of the noises of summer (though the birds had mated) that I could not at first distinguish these from the tread of small cautious feet stealing across the dead leaves. I rang my bell in an alluring manner, but the feet fled, and I repented, for to a child a sudden noise is very real terror. I must have been at work half an hour when I heard in the wood the voice of the blind woman crying: 'Children, oh, children! Where are you?' and the stillness made slow to close on the perfection of that cry. She came towards me, half feeling her way between the tree boles, and though a child it seemed clung to her skirt, it swerved into the leafage like a rabbit as she drew nearer.

'Is that you?' she said, 'from the other side of the county?'

'Yes, it's me from the other side of the county.'

'Then why didn't you come through the upper woods? They were there just now.'

'They were here a few minutes ago. I expect they knew my car had broken down, and came to see the fun.'

'Nothing serious, I hope? How do cars break down?'

'In fifty different ways. Only mine has chosen the fifty-first.'

She laughed merrily at the tiny joke, cooed with delicious laughter, and pushed her hat back.

'Let me hear,' she said.

'Wait a moment,' I cried, 'and I'll get you a cushion.'

She set her foot on the rug all covered with spare parts, and stooped above it eagerly 'What delightful things!' The hands through which she saw them glanced in the chequered sunlight. 'A box here—another box! Why you've arranged them like playing shop!'

'I confess now that I put it out to attract them. I don't need half those things really.'

'How nice of you! I heard your bell in the upper wood. You say they were here before that?'

'I'm sure of it. Why are they so shy? That little fellow in blue who was with you just now ought to have got over his fright. He's been watching me like a Red Indian.'

'It must have been your bell,' she said. 'I heard one of them go past me in trouble when I was coming down. They're shy—so shy even with me.' She turned her face over her shoulder and cried again: 'Children, oh, children! Look and see!'

'They must have gone off together on their own affairs,' I suggested, for there was a murmur behind us of lowered voices broken by the sudden squeaking giggles of childhood. I returned to my tinkerings and she leaned forward, her chin on her hand, listening interestedly.

'How many are they?' I said at last. The work was finished, but I saw no reason to go.

Her forehead puckered a little in thought. 'I don't quite know,' she said simply. 'Sometimes more—sometimes less. They come and stay with me because I love them, you see.'

'That must be very jolly,' I said, replacing a drawer, and as I spoke I heard the inanity of my answer.

'You—you aren't laughing at me,' she cried. 'I—I haven't any of my own. I never married. People laugh at me sometimes about them because—because——'

'Because they're savages,' I returned. 'It's nothing to fret for. That sort laugh at everything that isn't in their own fat lives.'

'I don't know. How should I? I only don't like being laughed at about *them*. It hurts; and when one can't see. . . . I don't want to seem silly,' her chin quivered like a child's as she spoke, 'but we blindies have only one skin, I think. Everything outside hits straight at our souls. It's different with you. You've such good defences in your eyes—looking out—before anyone can really pain you in your soul. People forget that with us.'

I was silent reviewing that inexhaustible matter—the more than inherited (since it is also carefully taught) brutality of the Christian peoples, beside which the mere heathendom of the West Coast nigger is clean and restrained. It led me a long distance into myself.

'Don't do that!' she said of a sudden, putting her hands before her eyes.

'What?'

She made a gesture with her hand.

'That! It's—it's all purple and black. Don't! That colour hurts.'

'But, how in the world do you know about colours?' I exclaimed, for here was a revelation indeed.

'Colours as colours?' she asked.

'No. *Those* Colours which you saw just now.'

'You know as well as I do,' she laughed, 'else you wouldn't have asked that question. They aren't in the world at all. They're in *you*—when you went so angry.'

'D'you mean a dull purplish patch, like port wine mixed with ink?' I said.

'I've never seen ink or port wine, but the colours aren't mixed. They are separate—all separate.'

'Do you mean black streaks and jags across the purple?'

She nodded. 'Yes—if they are like this,' and zig-zagged her finger again, 'but it's more red than purple—that bad colour.'

'And what are the colours at the top of the—whatever you see?'

Slowly she leaned forward and traced on the rug the figure of the Egg itself.

'I see them so,' she said, pointing with a grass stem, 'white, green, yellow, red, purple, and when people are angry or bad, black across the red—as you were just now.'

'Who told you anything about it—in the beginning?' I demanded.

'About the colours? No one. I used to ask what colours were when I was little—in table-covers and curtains and carpets, you

see—because some colours hurt me and some made me happy.
People told me; and when I got older that was how I saw people.'
Again she traced the outline of the Egg which it is given to very
few of us to see.

'All by yourself?' I repeated.

'All by myself. There wasn't anyone else. I only found out
afterwards that other people did not see the Colours.'

She leaned against the tree-bole plaiting and unplaiting chance-
plucked grass stems. The children in the wood had drawn nearer.
I could see them with the tail of my eye frolicking like squirrels.

'Now I am sure you will never laugh at me,' she went on after
a long silence. 'Nor at *them*.'

'Goodness! No!' I cried, jolted out of my train of thought. 'A
man who laughs at a child—unless the child is laughing too—is
a heathen!'

'I didn't mean that, of course. You'd never laugh *at* children,
but I thought—I used to think—that perhaps you might laugh
about *them*. So now I beg your pardon. . . . What are you going
to laugh at?'

I had made no sound, but she knew.

'At the notion of your begging my pardon. If you had done
your duty as a pillar of the State and a landed proprietress you
ought to have summoned me for trespass when I barged through
your woods the other day. It was disgraceful of me—inexcusable.'

She looked at me, her head against the tree trunk—long and
steadfastly—this woman who could see the naked soul.

'How curious,' she half whispered. 'How very curious.'

'Why, what have I done?'

'You don't understand . . . and yet you understood about the
Colours. Don't you understand?'

She spoke with a passion that nothing had justified, and I faced .
her bewilderedly as she rose. The children had gathered them-
selves in a roundel behind a bramble bush. One sleek head bent
over something smaller, and the set of the little shoulders told me
that fingers were on lips. They, too, had some child's tremendous
secret. I alone was hopelessly astray there in the broad sunlight.

'No,' I said, and shook my head as though the dead eyes could
note. 'Whatever it is, I don't understand yet. Perhaps I shall later
—if you'll let me come again.'

'You will come again,' she answered. 'You will surely come
again and walk in the wood.'

'Perhaps the children will know me well enough by that time to
let me play with them—as a favour. You know what children are
like.'

'It isn't a matter of favour but of right,' she replied, and while

I wondered what she meant, a dishevelled woman plunged round the bend of the road, loose-haired, purple, almost lowing with agony as she ran. It was my rude, fat friend of the sweetmeat shop. The blind woman heard and stepped forward. 'What is it, Mrs Madehurst?' she asked.

The woman flung her apron over her head and literally grovelled in the dust, crying that her grandchild was sick to death, that the local doctor was away fishing, that Jenny the mother was at her wits' end, and so forth, with repetitions and bellowings.

'Where's the next nearest doctor?' I asked between paroxysms.

'Madden will tell you. Go round to the house and take him with you. I'll attend to this. Be quick!' She half supported the fat woman into the shade. In two minutes I was blowing all the horns of Jericho under the front of the House Beautiful, and Madden, in the pantry, rose to the crisis like a butler and a man.

A quarter of an hour at illegal speeds caught us a doctor five miles away. Within the half-hour we had decanted him, much interested in motors, at the door of the sweetmeat shop, and drew up the road to await the verdict.

'Useful things cars,' said Madden, all man and no butler. 'If I'd had one when mine took sick she wouldn't have died.'

'How was it?' I asked.

'Croup. Mrs Madden was away. No one knew what to do. I drove eight miles in a tax cart for the doctor. She was choked when we came back. This car 'd ha' saved her. She'd have been close on ten now.'

'I'm sorry,' I said. 'I thought you were rather fond of children from what you told me going to the crossroads the other day.'

'Have you seen 'em again, Sir—this mornin'?'

'Yes, but they're well broke to cars. I couldn't get any of them within twenty yards of it.'

He looked at me carefully as a scout considers a stranger—not as a menial should lift his eyes to his divinely appointed superior.

'I wonder why,' he said just above the breath that he drew.

We waited on. A light wind from the sea wandered up and down the long lines of the woods, and the wayside grasses, whitened already with summer dust, rose and bowed in sallow waves.

A woman, wiping the suds off her arms, came out of the cottage next the sweetmeat shop.

'I've be'n listenin' in de back-yard,' she said cheerily. 'He says Arthur's unaccountable bad. Did ye hear him shruck just now? Unaccountable bad. I reckon t'will come Jenny's turn to walk in de wood nex' week along, Mr Madden.'

'Excuse me, Sir, but your lap-robe is slipping,' said Madden deferentially. The woman started, dropped a curtsey, and hurried away.

'What does she mean by "walking in the wood"?' I asked.

'It must be some saying they use hereabouts. I'm from Norfolk myself,' said Madden. 'They're an independent lot in this county. She took you for a chauffeur, Sir.'

I saw the Doctor come out of the cottage followed by a draggle-tailed wench who clung to his arm as though he could make treaty for her with Death. 'Dat sort,' she wailed—'dey're just as much to us dat has 'em as if dey was lawful born. Just as much—just as much! An' God he'd be just as pleased if you saved 'un, Doctor. Don't take it from me. Miss Florence will tell ye de very same. Don't leave 'im, Doctor!'

'I know, I know,' said the man; 'but he'll be quiet for a while now. We'll get the nurse and the medicine as fast as we can.' He signalled me to come forward with the car, and I strove not to be privy to what followed; but I saw the girl's face, blotched and frozen with grief, and I felt the hand without a ring clutching at my knees when we moved away.

The Doctor was a man of some humour, for I remember he claimed my car under the Oath of Æsculapius, and used it and me without mercy. First we convoyed Mrs Madehurst and the blind woman to wait by the sick bed till the nurse should come. Next we invaded a neat county town for prescriptions (the Doctor said the trouble was cerebro-spinal meningitis), and when the County Institute, banked and flanked with scared market cattle, reported itself out of nurses for the moment we literally flung ourselves loose upon the county. We conferred with the owners of great houses—magnates at the ends of overarching avenues whose big-boned womenfolk strode away from their tea-tables to listen to the imperious Doctor. At last a white-haired lady sitting under a cedar of Lebanon and surrounded by a court of magnificent Borzois—all hostile to motors—gave the Doctor, who received them as from a princess, written orders which we bore many miles at top speed, through a park, to a French nunnery, where we took over in exchange a pallid-faced and trembling Sister. She knelt at the bottom of the tonneau telling her beads without pause till, by short cuts of the Doctor's invention, we had her to the sweetmeat shop once more. It was a long afternoon crowded with mad episodes that rose and dissolved like the dust of our wheels; cross-sections of remote and incomprehensible lives through which we raced at right angles; and I went home in the dusk, wearied out, to dream of the clashing horns of cattle; round-eyed nuns walking in a garden of graves; pleasant tea-parties beneath shaded trees; the carbolic-scented, grey-painted corridors of the County Institute; the steps of shy children in the wood, and the hands that clung to my knees as the motor began to move.

I had intended to return in a day or two, but it pleased Fate to hold me from that side of the county, on many pretexts, till the elder and the wild rose had fruited. There came at last a brilliant day, swept clear from the south-west, that brought the hills within hand's reach—a day of unstable airs and high filmy clouds. Through no merit of my own I was free, and set the car for the third time on that known road. As I reached the crest of the Downs I felt the soft air change, saw it glaze under the sun; and, looking down at the sea, in that instant beheld the blue of the Channel turn through polished silver and dulled steel to dingy pewter. A laden collier hugging the coast steered outward for deeper water, and, across copper-coloured haze, I saw sails rise one by one on the anchored fishing-fleet. In a deep dene behind me an eddy of sudden wind drummed through sheltered oaks, and spun aloft the first dry sample of autumn leaves. When I reached the beach road the sea-fog fumed over the brickfields, and the tide was telling all the groins of the gale beyond Ushant. In less than an hour summer England vanished in chill grey. We were again the shut island of the North, all the ships of the world bellowing at our perilous gates; and between their outcries ran the piping of bewildered gulls. My cap dropped moisture, the folds of the rug held it in pools or sluiced it away in runnels, and the salt-rime stuck to my lips.

Inland the smell of autumn loaded the thickened fog among the trees, and the drip became a continuous shower. Yet the late flowers—mallow of the wayside, scabious of the field, and dahlia of the garden—showed gay in the mist, and beyond the sea's breath there was little sign of decay in the leaf. Yet in the villages the house doors were all open, and bare-legged, bare-headed children sat at ease on the damp doorsteps to shout 'pip-pip' at the stranger.

I made bold to call at the sweetmeat shop, where Mrs Madehurst met me with a fat woman's hospitable tears. Jenny's child, she said, had died two days after the nun had come. It was, she felt, best out of the way, even though insurance offices, for reasons which she did not pretend to follow, would not willingly insure such stray lives. 'Not but what Jenny didn't tend to Arthur as though he'd come all proper at de end of de first years—like Jenny herself.' Thanks to Miss Florence, the child had been buried with a pomp which, in Mrs Madehurst's opinion, more than covered the small irregularity of its birth. She described the

coffin, within and without, the glass hearse, and the evergreen
lining of the grave.

'But how's the mother?' I asked.

'Jenny? Oh, she'll get over it. I've felt dat way with one or two
o' my own. She'll get over. She's walkin' in de wood now.'

'In this weather?'

Mrs Madehurst looked at me with narrowed eyes across the
counter.

'I dunno but it opens de 'eart like. Yes, it opens de 'eart. Dat's
where losin' and bearin' comes so alike in de long run, we do say.'

Now the wisdom of the old wives is greater that that of all the
Fathers, and this last oracle sent me thinking so extendedly as I
went up the road, that I nearly ran over a woman and a child at
the wooded corner by the lodge gates of the House Beautiful.

'Awful weather!' I cried, as I slowed dead for the turn.

'Not so bad,' she answered placidly out of the fog. 'Mine's
used to 'un. You'll find yours indoors, I reckon.'

Indoors, Madden received me with professional courtesy, and
kind inquiries for the health of the motor, which he would put
under cover.

I waited in a still, nut-brown hall, pleasant with late flowers and
warmed with a delicious wood fire—a place of good influence and
great peace. (Men and women may sometimes, after great effort,
achieve a creditable lie; but the house, which is their temple,
cannot say anything save the truth of those who have lived in it.)
A child's cart and a doll lay on the black-and-white floor, where a
rug had been kicked back. I felt that the children had only just
hurried away—to hide themselves, most like—in the many turns
of the great adzed staircase that climbed statelily out of the hall,
or to crouch at gaze behind the lions and roses of the carven
gallery above. Then I heard her voice above me, singing as the
blind sing—from the soul:

> In the pleasant orchard-closes.

And all my early summer came back at the call.

> In the pleasant orchard-closes,
>   God bless all our gains say we—
> But may God bless all our losses,
>   Better suits with our degree.

She dropped the marring fifth line, and repeated—

> Better suits with our degree!

I saw her lean over the gallery, her linked hands white as pearl
against the oak.

'Is that you—from the other side of the county?' she called.

'Yes, me—from the other side of the county,' I answered, laughing.

'What a long time before you had to come here again.' She ran down the stairs, one hand lightly touching the broad rail. 'It's two months and four days. Summer's gone!'

'I meant to come before, but Fate prevented.'

'I knew it. Please do something to that fire. They won't let me play with it, but I can feel it's behaving badly. Hit it!'

I looked on either side of the deep fireplace, and found but a half-charred hedge-stake with which I punched a black log into flame.

'It never goes out, day or night,' she said, as though explaining. 'In case anyone comes in with cold toes, you see.'

'It's even lovelier inside than it was out,' I murmured. The red light poured itself along the age-polished dusky panels till the Tudor roses and lions of the gallery took colour and motion. An old eagle-topped convex mirror gathered the picture into its mysterious heart, distorting afresh the distorted shadows, and curving the gallery lines into the curves of a ship. The day was shutting down in half a gale as the fog turned to stringy scud. Through the uncurtained mullions of the broad window I could see valiant horsemen of the lawn rear and recover against the wind that taunted them with legions of dead leaves.

'Yes, it must be beautiful,' she said. 'Would you like to go over it? There's still light enough upstairs.'

I followed her up the unflinching, wagon-wide staircase to the gallery whence opened the thin fluted Elizabethan doors.

'Feel how they put the latch low down for the sake of the children.' She swung a light door inward.

'By the way, where are they?' I asked. 'I haven't even heard them today.'

She did not answer at once. Then, 'I can only hear them,' she replied softly. 'This is one of their rooms—everything ready, you see.'

She pointed into a heavily-timbered room. There were little low gate tables and children's chairs. A doll's house, its hooked front half open, faced a great dappled rocking-horse, from whose padded saddle it was but a child's scramble to the broad window-seat overlooking the lawn. A toy gun lay in a corner beside a gilt wooden cannon.

'Surely they've only just gone,' I whispered. In the failing light a door creaked cautiously. I heard the rustle of a frock and the patter of feet—quick feet through a room beyond.

'I heard that,' she cried triumphantly. 'Did you? Children, oh, children! Where are you?'

The voice filled the walls that held it lovingly to the last perfect note, but there came no answering shout such as I had heard in the garden. We hurried on from room to oak-floored room; up a step here, down three steps there; among a maze of passages; always mocked by our quarry. One might as well have tried to work an unstopped warren with a single ferret. There were bolt-holes innumerable—recesses in walls, embrasures of deep slitten windows now darkened, whence they could start up behind us; and abandoned fireplaces, six feet deep in the masonry, as well as the tangle of communicating doors. Above all, they had the twilight for their helper in our game. I had caught one or two joyous chuckles of evasion, and once or twice had seen the silhouette of a child's frock against some darkening window at the end of a passage; but we returned empty-handed to the gallery, just as a middle-aged woman was setting a lamp in its niche.

'No, I haven't seen her either this evening, Miss Florence,' I heard her say, 'but that Turpin he says he wants to see you about his shed.'

'Oh, Mr Turpin must want to see me very badly. Tell him to come to the hall, Mrs Madden.'

I looked down into the hall whose only light was the dulled fire, and deep in the shadow I saw them at last. They must have slipped down while we were in the passages, and now thought themselves perfectly hidden behind an old gilt leather screen. By child's law, my fruitless chase was as as good as an introduction, but since I had taken so much trouble I resolved to force them to come forward later by the simple trick, which children detest, of pretending not to notice them. They lay close, in a little huddle, no more than shadows except when a quick flame betrayed an outline.

'And now we'll have some tea,' she said. 'I believe I ought to have offered it you at first, but one doesn't arrive at manners somehow when one lives alone and is considered—h'm—peculiar.' Then with very pretty scorn, 'Would you like a lamp to see to eat by?'

'The firelight's much pleasanter, I think.' We descended into that delicious gloom and Madden brought tea.

I took my chair in the direction of the screen ready to surprise or be surprised as the game should go, and at her permission, since a hearth is always sacred, bent forward to play with the fire.

'Where do you get these beautiful short faggots from?' I asked idly. 'Why, they are tallies!'

'Of course,' she said. 'As I can't read or write I'm driven back on the early English tally for my accounts. Give me one and I'll tell you what it meant.'

I passed her an unburned hazel-tally, about a foot long, and she ran her thumb down the nicks.

'This is the milk-record for the home farm for the month of April last year, in gallons,' said she, 'I don't know what I should have done without tallies. An old forester of mine taught me the system. It's out of date now for everyone else; but my tenants respect it. One of them's coming now to see me. Oh, it doesn't matter. He has no business here out of office hours. He's a greedy, ignorant man—very greedy or—he wouldn't come here after dark.'

'Have you much land then?'

'Only a couple of hundred acres in hand, thank goodness. The other six hundred are nearly all let to folk who knew my folk before me, but this Turpin is quite a new man—and a highway robber.'

'But are you sure I shan't be——?'

'Certainly not. You have the right. He hasn't any children.'

'Ah, the children!' I said, and slid my low chair back till it nearly touched the screen that hid them. 'I wonder whether they'll come out for me.'

There was a murmur of voices—Madden's and a deeper note—at the low, dark side door, and a ginger-headed, canvas-gaitered giant of the unmistakable tenant-farmer type stumbled or was pushed in.

'Come to the fire, Mr Turpin,' she said.

'If—if you please, Miss, I'll—I'll be quite as well by the door.' He clung to the latch as he spoke like a frightened child. Of a sudden I realized that he was in the grip of some almost overpowering fear.

'Well?'

'About that new shed for the young stock—that was all. These first autumn storms settin' in . . . but I'll come again, Miss.' His teeth did not chatter much more than the door latch.

'I think not,' she answered levelly. 'The new shed—m'm. What did my agent write you on the 15th?'

'I—fancied p'raps that if I came to see you—ma—man to man like, Miss. But——'

His eyes rolled into every corner of the room wide with horror. He half opened the door through which he had entered, but I noticed it shut again—from without and firmly.

'He wrote what I told him,' she went on. 'You are overstocked already. Dunnett's Farm never carried more than fifty bullocks—even in Mr Wright's time. And *he* used cake. You've sixty-seven and you don't cake. You've broken the lease in that respect. You're dragging the heart out of the farm.'

'I'm—I'm getting some minerals—superphosphates—next week. I've as good as ordered a truck-load already. I'll go down to the station tomorrow about 'em. Then I can come and see you man to man like, Miss, in the daylight. . . . That gentleman's not going away, is he?' He almost shrieked.

I had only slid the chair a little farther back, reaching behind me to tap on the leather of the screen, but he jumped like a rat.

'No. Please attend to me, Mr Turpin.' She turned in her chair and faced him with his back to the door. It was an old and sordid little piece of scheming that she forced from him—his plea for the new cow-shed at his landlady's expense, that he might with the covered manure pay his next year's rent out of the valuation after, as she made clear, he had bled the enriched pastures to the bone. I could not but admire the intensity of his greed, when I saw him out-facing for its sake whatever terror it was that ran wet on his forehead.

I ceased to tap the leather—was, indeed, calculating the cost of the shed—when I felt my relaxed hand taken and turned softly between the soft hands of a child. So at last I had triumphed. In a moment I would turn and acquaint myself with those quick-footed wanderers. . . .

The little brushing kiss fell in the centre of my palm—as a gift on which the fingers were, once, expected to close: as the all-faithful half-reproachful signal of a waiting child not used to neglect even when grown-ups were busiest—a fragment of the mute code devised very long ago.

Then I knew. And it was as though I had known from the first day when I looked across the lawn at the high window.

I heard the door shut. The woman turned to me in silence, and I felt that she knew.

What time passed after this I cannot say. I was roused by the fall of a log, and mechanically rose to put it back. Then I returned to my place in the chair very close to the screen.

'Now you understand,' she whispered, across the packed shadows.

'Yes, I understand—now. Thank you.'

'I—I only hear them.' She bowed her head in her hands. 'I have no right, you know—no other right. I have neither borne nor lost—neither borne nor lost!'

'Be very glad then,' said I, for my soul was torn open within me.

'Forgive me!'

She was still, and I went back to my sorrow and my joy.

'It was because I loved them so,' she said at last, brokenly. '*That* was why it was, even from the first—even before I knew that they—they were all I should ever have. And I loved them so!'

She stretched out her arms to the shadows and the shadows within the shadow.

'They came because I loved them—because I needed them. I—I must have made them come. Was that wrong, think you?'

'No—no.'

'I—I grant you that the toys and—and all that sort of thing were nonsense, but—but I used to so hate empty rooms myself when I was little.' She pointed to the gallery. 'And the passages all empty. . . . And how could I ever bear the garden door shut? Suppose——'

'Don't! For pity's sake, don't!' I cried. The twilight had brought a cold rain with gusty squalls that plucked at the leaded windows.

'And the same thing with keeping the fire in all night. *I* don't think it so foolish—do you?'

I looked at the broad brick hearth, saw, through tears I believe, that there was no unpassable iron on or near it, and bowed my head.

'I did all that and lots of other things—just to make believe. Then they came. I heard them, but I didn't know that they were not mine by right till Mrs Madden told me——'

'The butler's wife? What?'

'One of them—I heard—she saw. And knew. Hers! *Not* for me. I didn't know at first. Perhaps I was jealous. Afterwards, I began to understand that it was only because I loved them, not because—— . . . Oh, you *must* bear or lose,' she said piteously. 'There is no other way—and yet they love me. They must! Don't they?'

There was no sound in the room except the lapping voices of the fire, but we two listened intently, and she at least took comfort from what she heard. She recovered herself and half rose. I sat still in my chair by the screen.

'Don't think me a wretch to whine about myself like this, but—but I'm all in the dark, you know, and *you* can see.'

In truth I could see, and my vision confirmed me in my resolve, though that was like the very parting of spirit and flesh. Yet a little longer I would stay since it was the last time.

'You think it is wrong, then?' she cried sharply, though I had said nothing.

'Not for you. A thousand times no. For you it is right. . . . I am grateful to you beyond words. For me it would be wrong. For me only. . . .'

'Why?' she said, but passed her hand before her face as she had done at our second meeting in the wood. 'Oh, I see,' she went on simply as a child. 'For you it would be wrong.' Then with a little indrawn laugh, 'and, d'you remember, I called you lucky—once—at first. You who must never come here again!'

She left me to sit a little longer by the screen, and I heard the sound of her feet die out along the gallery above.

1904

# An Habitation Enforced

My friend, if cause doth wrest thee,
Ere folly hath much oppressed thee,
Far from acquaintance kest thee
Where country may digest thee . . .
Thank God that so hath blessed thee,
And sit down, Robin, and rest thee.

THOMAS TUSSER.

IT CAME without warning, at the very hour his hand was out-
stretched to crumple the Holz and Gunsberg Combine. The New
York doctors called it overwork, and he lay in a darkened room,
one ankle crossed above the other, tongue pressed into palate,
wondering whether the next brain surge of prickly fires would
drive his soul from all anchorages. At last they gave judgment.
With care he might in two years return to the arena, but for the
present he must go across the water and do no work whatever.
He accepted the terms. It was capitulation; but the Combine that
had shivered beneath his knife gave him all the honours of war.
Gunsberg himself, full of condolences, came to the steamer and
filled the Chapins' suite of cabins with overwhelming flower-
works.

'Smilax,' said George Chapin when he saw them. 'Fitz is right.
I'm dead; only I don't see why he left out the "In Memoriam" on
the ribbons!'

'Nonsense!' his wife answered, and poured him his tincture.
'You'll be back before you can think.'

He looked at himself in the mirror, surprised that his face had
not been branded by the hells of the past three months. The noise
of the decks worried him, and he lay down, his tongue only a little
pressed against his palate.

An hour later he said: 'Sophie, I feel sorry about taking you
away from everything like this. I—I suppose we're the two
loneliest people on God's earth tonight.'

Said Sophie his wife, and kissed him: 'Isn't it something to you
that we're going together?'

They drifted about Europe for months—sometimes alone,
sometimes with chance-met gipsies of their own land. From the
North Cape to the Blue Grotto at Capri they wandered, because
the next steamer headed that way, or because someone had set
them on the road. The doctors had warned Sophie that Chapin
was not to take interest even in other men's interests; but a

95

familiar sensation at the back of the neck after one hour's keen talk with a Nauheimed railway magnate saved her any trouble. He nearly wept.

'And I'm over thirty,' he cried; 'with all I meant to do!'

'Let's call it a honeymoon,' said Sophie. 'D'you know, in all the six years we've been married, you've never told me what you meant to do with your life?'

'With my life? What's the use? It's finished now.' Sophie looked up quickly from the Bay of Naples. 'As far as my business goes, I shall have to live on my rents like that architect at San Moritz.'

'You'll get better if you don't worry; and even if it takes time, there are worse things than—— How much have you?'

'Between four and five million. But it isn't the money. You know it isn't. It's the principle. How could you respect me? You never did, the first year after we married, till I went to work like the others. Our tradition and upbringing are against it. We can't accept *those* ideals.'

'Well, I suppose I married you for some sort of ideal,' she answered, and they returned to their forty-third hotel.

In England they missed the alien tongues of Continental streets that reminded them of their own polyglot cities. In England all men spoke one tongue, speciously like American to the ear, but on cross-examination unintelligible.

'Ah, but you have not seen England,' said a lady with iron-grey hair. They had met her in Vienna, Bayreuth, and Florence, and were grateful to find her again at Claridge's, for she commanded situations, and knew where prescriptions are most carefully made up. 'You ought to take an interest in the home of our ancestors—as I do.'

'I've tried for a week, Mrs Shonts,' said Sophie, 'but I never get further than tipping German waiters.'

'These are not the true type,' Mrs Shonts went on. 'I know where you should go.'

Chapin pricked up his ears, anxious to run anywhere from the streets on which quick men something of his kidney did the business denied to him.

'We hear and we obey, Mrs Shonts,' said Sophie, feeling his unrest as he drank the loathed British tea.

Mrs Shonts smiled, and took them in hand. She wrote widely and telegraphed far on their behalf, till, armed with her letter of introduction, she drove them into that wilderness which is reached from an ash-barrel of a station called Charing Cross. They were to go to Rocketts—the farm of one Cloke, in the southern counties—where, she assured them, they would meet the genuine England of folklore and song.

Rocketts they found after some hours, four miles from a station, and, so far as they could judge in the bumpy darkness, twice as many from a road. Trees, kine, and the outlines of barns showed shadowy about them when they alighted, and Mr and Mrs Cloke, at the open door of a deep stone-floored kitchen, made them slowly welcome. They lay in an attic beneath a wavy whitewashed ceiling, and because it rained, a wood fire was made in an iron basket on a brick hearth, and they fell asleep to the chirping of mice and the whimper of flames.

When they woke it was a fair day, full of the noises of birds, the smell of box, lavender, and fried bacon, mixed with an elemental smell they had never met before.

'This,' said Sophie, nearly pushing out the thin casement in an attempt to see round the corner, 'is—what did the hack—cabman say to the railway porter about my trunk—"quite on the top"?'

'No; "a little bit of all right". I feel farther away from anywhere than I've ever felt in my life. We must find out where the telegraph office is.'

'Who cares?' said Sophie, wandering about, hairbrush in hand, to admire the illustrated weekly pictures pasted on door and cupboard.

But there was no rest for the alien soul till he had made sure of the telegraph office. He asked the Clokes's daughter, laying breakfast, while Sophie plunged her face in the lavender bush outside the low window.

'Go to the stile a-top o' the Barn field,' said Mary, 'and look across Pardons to the next spire. It's directly under. You can't miss it—not if you keep to the footpath. My sister's the telegraphist there. But you're in the three-mile radius, sir. The boy delivers telegrams directly to this door from Pardons village.'

'One has to take a good deal on trust in this country,' he murmured.

Sophie looked at the close turf, scarred only with last night's wheels, at two ruts which wound round a rickyard, and at the circle of still orchard about the half-timbered house.

'What's the matter with it?' she said. 'Telegrams delivered to the Vale of Avalon, of course,' and she beckoned in an earnest-eyed hound of engaging manners and no engagements, who answered, at times, to the name of Rambler. He led them, after breakfast, to the rise behind the house where the stile stood against the skyline, and, 'I wonder what we shall find now,' said Sophie, frankly prancing with joy on the grass.

It was a slope of gap-hedged fields possessed to their centres by clumps of brambles. Gates were not, and the rabbit-mined, cattle-rubbed posts leaned out and in. A narrow path doubled among the bushes, scores of white tails twinkled before the racing hound, and a hawk rose, whistling shrilly.

'No roads, no nothing!' said Sophie, her short skirt hooked by briers. 'I thought all England was a garden. There's your spire, George, across the valley. How curious!'

They walked toward it through an all-abandoned land. Here they found the ghost of a patch of lucerne that had refused to die; there a harsh fallow surrendered to yard-high thistles; and here a breadth of rampant kelk feigning to be lawful crop. In the un-grazed pastures swaths of dead stuff caught their feet, and the ground beneath glistened with sweat. At the bottom of the valley a little brook had undermined its footbridge, and frothed in the wreckage. But there stood great woods on the slopes beyond— old, tall, and brilliant, like unfaded tapestries against the walls of a ruined house.

'All this within a hundred miles of London,' he said. ''Looks as if it had had nervous prostration, too.' The footpath turned the shoulder of a slope, through a thicket of rank rhododendrons, and crossed what had once been a carriage drive, which ended in the shadow of two gigantic holm-oaks.

'A house!' said Sophie, in a whisper. 'A colonial house!'

Behind the blue-green of the twin trees rose a dark-bluish brick Georgian pile, with a shell-shaped fan-light over its pillared door. The hound had gone off on his own foolish quests. Except for some stir in the branches and the flight of four startled magpies, there was neither life nor sound about the square house, but it looked out of its long windows most friendlily.

'Cha-armed to meet you, I'm sure,' said Sophie, and curtsied to the ground. 'George, this is history I can understand. *We* began here.' She curtsied again.

The June sunshine twinkled on all the lights. It was as though an old lady, wise in three generations' experience, but for the present sitting out, bent to listen to her flushed and eager grand-child.

'I *must* look!' Sophie tiptoed to a window, and shaded her eyes with her hand. 'Oh, this room's half-full of cotton-bales—wool, I suppose! But I can see a bit of the mantelpiece. George, do come! Isn't that someone?'

She fell back behind her husband. The front door opened slowly, to show the hound, his nose white with milk, in charge of an ancient of days clad in a blue linen ephod curiously gathered on breast and shoulders.

'Certainly,' said George, half aloud. 'Father Time himself. This is where he lives, Sophie.'

'We came,' said Sophie weakly. 'Can we see the house? I'm afraid that's our dog.'

'No, 'tis Rambler,' said the old man. 'He's been at my swill-pail again. Staying at Rocketts, be ye? Come in. Ah! you runagate!'

The hound broke from him, and he tottered after him down the drive. They entered the hall—just such a high light hall as such a house should own. A slim-balustered staircase, wide and shallow and once creamy-white, climbed out of it under a long oval window. On either side delicately-moulded doors gave on to wool-lumbered rooms, whose sea-green mantelpieces were adorned with nymphs, scrolls, and Cupids in low relief.

'What's the firm that makes these things?' cried Sophie, enraptured. 'Oh, I forgot! These must be the originals. Adams, is it? I never dreamed of anything like that steel-cut fender. Does he mean us to go everywhere?'

'He's catching the dog,' said George, looking out. 'We don't count.'

They explored the first or ground floor, delighted as children playing burglars.

'This is like all England,' she said at last. 'Wonderful, but no explanation. You're expected to know it beforehand! Now, let's try upstairs.'

The stairs never creaked beneath their feet. From the broad landing they entered a long, green-panelled room lighted by three full-length windows, which overlooked the forlorn wreck of a terraced garden, and wooded slopes beyond.

'The drawing-room, of course,' Sophie swam up and down it. 'That mantelpiece—Orpheus and Euridice—is the best of them all. Isn't it marvellous? Why, the room seems furnished with nothing in it! How's that, George?'

'It's the proportions. I've noticed it.'

'I saw a Hepplewhite couch once'—Sophie laid her finger to her flushed cheek and considered. 'With two of them—one on each side—you wouldn't need anything else. Except—there must be one perfect mirror over that mantelpiece.'

'Look at that view. It's a framed Constable,' her husband cried.

'No; it's a Morland—a parody of a Morland. But about that couch, George. Don't you think Empire might be better than Hepplewhite? Dull gold against that pale green? It's a pity they don't make spinets nowadays.'

'I believe you can get them. Look at that oak wood behind the pines.'

'"While you sat and played toccatas stately at the clavi-chord,"' Sophie hummed, and, head on one side, nodded to where the perfect mirror should hang.

Then they found bedrooms with dressing-rooms and powder-ing-closets, and steps leading up and down—boxes of rooms, round, square, and octagonal, with enriched ceilings and chased door-locks.

'Now about servants. Oh!' She had darted up the last stairs to the chequered darkness of the top floor, where loose tiles lay among broken laths, and the walls were scrawled with names, sentiments, and hop records. 'They've been keeping pigeons here,' she cried.

'And you could drive a buggy through the roof anywhere,' said George.

'That's what *I* say,' the old man cried below them on the stairs. 'Not a dry place for my pigeons at all.'

'But why was it allowed to get like this?' said Sophie.

''Tis with housen as teeth,' he replied. 'Let 'em go too far, and there's nothing *to* be done. Time was they was minded to sell her, but none would buy. She was too far away along from any place. Time was they'd ha' lived here theyselves, but they took and died.'

'Here?' Sophie moved beneath the light of a hole in the roof.

'Nah—none dies here excep' falling off ricks and such. In London they died.' He plucked a lock of wool from his blue smock. 'They was no staple—neither the Elphicks nor the Moones. Shart and brittle all of 'em. Dead they be seventeen year, for I've been here caretakin' twenty-five.'

'Who does all the wool belong to downstairs?' George asked.

'To the estate. I'll show you the back parts if ye like. You're from America, ain't ye? I've had a son there once myself.' They followed him down the main stairway. He paused at the turn and swept one hand towards the wall. 'Plenty room here for your coffin to come down. Seven foot and three men at each end wouldn't brish the paint. If I die in my bed they'll 'ave to up-end me like a milk-can. 'Tis all luck, d'ye see?'

He led them on and on, through a maze of back-kitchens, dairies, larders, and sculleries, that melted along covered ways into a farm-house, visibly older than the main building, which again rambled out among barns, byres, pig-pens, stalls and stables to the dead fields behind.

'Somehow,' said Sophie, sitting exhausted on an ancient well-curb—'somehow one wouldn't insult these lovely old things by filling them with hay.'

George looked at long stone walls upholding reaches of silvery oak weather-boarding; buttresses of mixed flint and bricks; outside stairs, stone upon arched stone; curves of thatch where grass sprouted; roundels of house-leeked tiles, and a huge paved yard populated by two cows and the repentant Rambler. He had not thought of himself or of the telegraph office for two and a half hours.

'But why,' said Sophie, as they went back through the crater of stricken fields—'why is one expected to know everything in England? Why do they never tell?'

'You mean about the Elphicks and the Moones?' he answered.

'Yes—and the lawyers and the estate. Who are they? I wonder whether those painted floors in the green room were real oak. Don't you like us exploring things together—better than Pompeii?'

George turned once more to look at the view. 'Eight hundred acres go with the house—the old man told me. Five farms altogether. Rocketts is one of 'em.'

'I like Mrs Cloke. But what is the old house called?'

George laughed. 'That's one of the things you're expected to know. He never told me.'

The Clokes were more communicative. That evening and thereafter for a week they gave the Chapins the official history, as one gives it to lodgers, of Friars Pardon the house and its five farms. But Sophie asked so many questions, and George was so humanly interested, that, as confidence in the strangers grew, they launched, with observed and acquired detail, into the lives and deaths and doings of the Elphicks and the Moones and their collaterals, the Haylings and the Torrells. It was a tale told serially by Cloke in the barn, or his wife in the dairy, the last chapters reserved for the kitchen o' nights by the big fire, when the two had been half the day exploring about the house, where old Iggulden, of the blue smock, cackled and chuckled to see them. The motives that swayed the characters were beyond their comprehension; the fates that shifted them were gods they had never met; the side-lights Mrs Cloke threw on act and incident were more amazing than anything in the record. Therefore the Chapins listened delightedly, and blessed Mrs Shonts.

'But why—why—why—did So-and-so do so-and-so?' Sophie would demand from her seat by the pothook; and Mrs Cloke would answer, smoothing her knees, 'For the sake of the place.'

'I give it up,' said George one night in their own room. 'People don't seem to matter in this country compared to the places they live in. The way she tells it, Friars Pardon was a sort of Moloch.'

'Poor old thing!' They had been walking round the farms as usual before tea. 'No wonder they loved it. Think of the sacrifices

they made for it. Jane Elphick married the younger Torrell to
to keep it in the family. The octagonal room with the moulded
ceiling next to the big bedroom was hers. Now what did *he* tell
you while he was feeding the pigs?' said Sophie.

'About the Torrell cousins and the uncle who died in Java.
They lived at Burnt House—behind High Pardons, where that
brook is all blocked up.'

'No; Burnt House is under High Pardons Wood, *before* you
come to Gale Anstey,' Sophie corrected.

'Well, old man Cloke said——'

Sophie threw open the door and called down into the kitchen,
where the Clokes were covering the fire: 'Mrs Cloke, isn't Burnt
House under High Pardons?'

'Yes, my dear, of course,' the soft voice answered absently. A
cough. 'I beg your pardon, Madam. What was it you said?'

'Never mind. I prefer it the other way,' Sophie laughed, and
George re-told the missing chapter as she sat on the bed.

'Here today an' gone tomorrow,' said Cloke warningly.
'They've paid their first month, but we've only that Mrs Shonts's
letter for guarantee.'

'None she sent never cheated us yet. It slipped out before I
thought. She's a most humane young lady. They'll be going away
in a little. An' *you've* talked a lot too, Alfred.'

'Yes, but the Elphicks are all dead. No one can bring my loose
talking home to me. But why do they stay on and stay on so?'

In due time George and Sophie asked each other that question,
and put it aside. They argued that the climate—a pearly blend
unlike the hot and cold ferocities of their native land—suited
them, as the thick stillness of the nights certainly suited George.
He was saved even the sight of a metalled road, which, as pre-
sumably leading to business, wakes desire in a man; and the
telegraph office at the village of Friars Pardon, where they sold
picture postcards and peg-tops, was two walking miles across the
fields and woods. For all that touched his past among his fellows,
or their remembrance of him, he might have been in another
planet; and Sophie, whose life had been very largely spent among
husbandless wives of lofty ideals, had no wish to leave this
present of God. The unhurried meals, the foreknowledge of
deliciously empty hours to follow, the breadths of soft sky under
which they walked together and reckoned time only by their
hunger or thirst; the good grass beneath their feet that cheated
the miles; their discoveries, always together, amid the farms—
Griffons, Rocketts, Burnt House, Gale Anstey, and the Home
Farm, where Iggulden of the blue smock-frock would waylay
them, and they would ransack the old house once more; the long

wet afternoons when they tucked up their feet on the bedroom's deep window-sill over against the apple-trees, and talked together as never till then had they found time to talk—these things contented her soul, and her body throve.

'Have you realized,' she asked one morning, 'that we've been here absolutely alone for the last thirty-four days?'

'Have you counted them?' he asked.

'Did you like them?' she replied.

'I must have. I didn't think about them. Yes, I have. Six months ago I should have fretted myself sick. Remember at Cairo? I've only had two or three bad times. Am I getting better, or is it senile decay?'

'Climate, all climate.' Sophie swung her new-bought English boots, as she sat on the stile overlooking Friars Pardon, behind the Clokes's barn.

'One must take hold of things though,' he said, 'if it's only to keep one's hand in.' His eyes did not flicker now as they swept the empty fields. 'Mustn't one?'

'Lay out a Morristown links over Gale Anstey. I dare say you could hire it.'

'No, I'm not as English as that—nor as Morristown. Cloke says all the farms here could be made to pay.'

'Well, I'm Anastasia in the *Treasure of Franchard*. I'm content to be alive and purr. There's no hurry.'

'No.' He smiled. 'All the same, I'm going to see after my mail.'

'You promised you wouldn't have any.'

'There's some business coming through that's amusing me. Honest. It doesn't get on my nerves at all.'

''Want a secretary?'

'No, thanks, old thing! Isn't that quite English?'

'Too English! Go away.' But none the less in broad daylight she returned the kiss. 'I'm off to Pardons. I haven't been to the house for nearly a week.'

'How've you decided to furnish Jane Elphick's bedroom?' he laughed, for it had come to be a permanent Castle in Spain between them.

'Black Chinese furniture and yellow silk brocade,' she answered, and ran downhill. She scattered a few cows at a gap with a flourish of a ground-ash that Iggulden had cut for her a week ago, and singing as she passed under the holm-oaks, sought the farmhouse at the back of Friars Pardon. The old man was not to be found, and she knocked at his half-opened door, for she needed him to fill her idle forenoon. A blue-eyed sheep-dog, a new friend, and Rambler's old enemy, crawled out and besought her to enter.

Iggulden sat in his chair by the fire, a thistle-spud between his knees, his head drooped. Though she had never seen death before, her heart, that missed a beat, told her that he was dead. She did not speak or cry, but stood outside the door, and the dog licked her hand. When he threw up his nose, she heard herself saying: 'Don't howl! Please don't begin to howl, Scottie, or I shall run away!'

She held her ground while the shadows in the rickyard moved toward noon; sat after a while on the steps by the door, her arms round the dog's neck, waiting till someone should come. She watched the smokeless chimneys of Friars Pardon slash its roofs with shadow, and the smoke of Iggulden's last lighted fire gradually thin and cease. Against her will she fell to wondering how many Moones, Elphicks, and Torrells had been swung round the turn of the broad hall stairs. Then she remembered the old man's talk of being 'up-ended like a milk-can', and buried her face on Scottie's neck. At last a horse's feet clinked upon flags, rustled in the old grey straw of the rickyard, and she found herself facing the vicar—a figure she had seen at church declaiming impossibilities (Sophie was a Unitarian) in an unnatural voice.

'He's dead,' she said, without preface.

'Old Iggulden? I was coming for a talk with him.' The vicar passed in uncovered. 'Ah!' she heard him say. 'Heart-failure! How long have you been here?'

'Since a quarter to eleven.' She looked at her watch earnestly and saw that her hand did not shake.

'I'll sit with him now till the doctor comes. D'you think you could tell him, and—yes, Mrs Betts in the cottage with the wistaria next the blacksmith's? I'm afraid this has been rather a shock to you.'

Sophie nodded, and fled toward the village. Her body failed her for a moment; she dropped beneath a hedge, and looked back at the great house. In some fashion its silence and stolidity steadied her for her errand.

Mrs Betts, small, black-eyed and dark, was almost as unconcerned as Frairs Pardon.

'Yiss, yiss, of course. Dear me! Well, Iggulden he had had his day in my father's time. Muriel, get me my little blue bag, please. Yiss, ma'am. They come down like ellum-branches in still weather. No warnin' at all. Muriel, my bicycle's be'ind the fowl-house. I'll tell Dr Dallas, ma'am.'

She trundled off on her wheel like a brown bee, while Sophie—heaven above and earth beneath changed—walked stiffly home, to fall over George at his letters, in a muddle of laughter and tears.

'It's all quite natural for *them*,' she gasped. '"They come down like ellum-branches in still weather. Yiss, ma'am".' No, there wasn't anything in the least horrible, only—only—oh George, that poor shiny stick of his between his poor thin knees. I couldn't have borne it if Scottie had howled. I didn't know the vicar was —so sensitive. He said he was afraid it was ra-rather a shock. Mrs Betts told me to go home, and I wanted to collapse on her floor. But I didn't disgrace myself. I—I couldn't have left him— could I?'

'You're sure you've took no 'arm?' cried Mrs Cloke, who had heard the news by farm-telegraphy, which is older but swifter than Marconi's.

'No. I'm perfectly well,' Sophie protested.

'You lay down till tea-time.' Mrs Cloke patted her shoulder. '*They*'ll be very pleased, though she 'as 'ad no proper understandin' for twenty years.'

'They' came before twilight—a black-bearded man in moleskins, and a little palsied old woman, who chirruped like a wren.

'I'm his son,' said the man to Sophie, among the lavender bushes. 'We 'ad a difference—twenty year back, and didn't speak since. But I'm his son all the same, and we thank you for the watching.'

'I'm only glad I happened to be there,' she answered, and from the bottom of her heart she meant it.

'We heard he spoke a lot o' you—one time an' another since you came. We thank you kindly,' the man added.

'Are you the son that was in America?' she asked.

'Yes, ma'am. On my uncle's farm, in Connecticut. He was what they call road-master there.'

'Whereabouts in Connecticut?' asked George over her shoulder.

'Veering Holler was the name. I was there six year with my uncle.'

'How small the world is!' Sophie cried. 'Why, all my mother's people come from Veering Hollow. There must be some there still—the Lashmars. Did you ever hear of them?'

'I remember hearing that name, seems to me,' he answered, but his face was blank as the back of a spade.

A little before dusk a woman in grey, striding like a footsoldier, and bearing on her arm a long pole, crashed through the orchard calling for food. George, upon whom the unannounced English worked mysteriously, fled to the parlour; but Mrs Cloke came forward beaming. Sophie could not escape.

'We've only just heard of it,' said the stranger, turning on her. 'I've been out with the otter-hounds all day. It was a splendidly sportin' thing——'

'Did you—er—kill?' said Sophie. She knew from books she could not go far wrong here.

'Yes, a dry bitch—seventeen pounds,' was the answer. 'A splendidly sportin' thing of you to do. Poor old Iggulden——'

'Oh—that!' said Sophie, enlightened.

'If there had been any people at Pardons it would never have happened. He'd have been looked after. But what can you expect from a parcel of London solicitors?'

Mrs Cloke murmured something.

'No. I'm soaked from the knees down. If I hang about I shall get chilled. A cup of tea, Mrs Cloke, and I can eat one of your sandwiches as I go.' She wiped her weather-worn face with a green and yellow silk handkerchief.

'Yes, my lady!' Mrs Cloke ran and returned swiftly.

'Our land marches with Pardons for a mile on the south,' she explained, waving the full cup, 'but one has quite enough to do with one's own people without poachin'. Still, if I'd known, I'd have sent Dora, of course. Have you seen her this afternoon, Mrs Cloke? No? I wonder whether that girl did sprain her ankle. Thank you.' It was a formidable hunk of bread and bacon that Mrs Cloke presented. 'As I was sayin', Pardons is a scandal! Lettin' people die like dogs. There ought to be people there who do their duty. You've done yours, though there wasn't the faintest call upon you. Good night. Tell Dora, if she comes, I've gone on.'

She strode away, munching her crust, and Sophie reeled breathless into the parlour, to shake the shaking George.

'Why did you keep catching my eye behind the blind? Why didn't you come out and do your duty?'

'Because I should have burst. Did you see the mud on its cheek?' he said.

'Once. I daren't look again. Who is she?'

'God—a local deity then. Anyway, she's another of the things you're expected to know by instinct.'

Mrs Cloke, shocked at their levity, told them that it was Lady Conant, wife of Sir Walter Conant, Baronet, a large landholder in the neighbourhood, and if not God, at least His visible Providence.

George made her talk of that family for an hour.

'Laughter,' said Sophie afterward in their own room, 'is the mark of the savage. Why couldn't you control your emotions? It's all real to *her*.'

'It's all real to me. That's my trouble,' he answered in an altered tone. 'Anyway, it's real enough to mark time with. Don't you think so?'

'What d'you mean?' she asked quickly, though she knew his voice.

'That I'm better. I'm well enough to kick.'

'What at?'

'This!' he waved his hand round the one room. 'I must have something to play with till I'm fit for work again.'

'Ah!' She sat on the bed and leaned forward, her hands clasped. 'I wonder if it's good for you.'

'We've been better here than anywhere,' he went on slowly. 'One could always sell it again.'

She nodded gravely, but her eyes sparkled.

'The only thing that worries me is what happened this morning. I want to know how you feel about it. If it's on your nerves in the least we can have the old farm at the back of the house pulled down, or perhaps it has spoiled the notion for you?'

'Pull it down?' she cried. 'You've no business faculty. Why, that's where we could live while we're putting the big house in order. It's almost under the same roof. No! What happened this morning seemed to be more of a —of a leading than anything else. There *ought* to be people at Pardons. Lady Conant's quite right.'

'I was thinking more of the woods and the roads. I could double the value of the place in six months.'

'What do they want for it?' She shook her head, and her loosened hair fell glowingly about her cheeks.

'Seventy-five thousand dollars. They'll take sixty-eight.'

'Less than half what we paid for our old yacht when we married. And we didn't have a good time in her. You were——'

'Well, I discovered I was too much of an American to be content to be a rich man's son. You aren't blaming me for that?'

'Oh no. Only it was a very businesslike honeymoon. How far are you going along with the deal, George?'

'I can mail the deposit on the purchase money tomorrow morning, and we can have the thing completed in a fortnight or three weeks—if you say so.'

'Friars Pardon—Friars Pardon!' Sophie chanted rapturously, her dark grey eyes big with delight. 'All the farms? Gale Anstey, Burnt House, Rocketts, the Home Farm, and Griffons? Sure you've got 'em all?'

'Sure.' He smiled.

'And the woods? High Pardons Wood, Lower Pardons, Suttons, Dutton's Shaw, Reuben's Ghyll, Maxey's Ghyll, and both the Oak Hangers? Sure you've got 'em all?'

'Every last stick. Why, you know them as well as I do.' He laughed. 'They say there's five thousand—a thousand pounds' worth of lumber—timber they call it—in the Hangers alone.'

'Mrs Cloke's oven must be mended first thing, *and* the kitchen roof. I think I'll have all this whitewashed,' Sophie broke in, pointing to the ceiling. 'The whole place is a scandal. Lady Conant is quite right. George, when did you begin to fall in love with the house? In the green room—that first day? I did.'

'I'm not in love with it. One must do something to mark time till one's fit for work.'

'Or when we stood under the oaks, and the door opened? Oh! Ought I to go to poor Iggulden's funeral?' She sighed with utter happiness.

'Wouldn't they call it a liberty—*now*?' said he.

'But I liked him.'

'But you didn't own him at the date of his death.'

'That wouldn't keep me away. Only, they made such a fuss about the watching'—she caught her breath—'it might be ostentatious from that point of view, too. Oh, George,'—she reached for his hand—'we're two little orphans moving in worlds not realized, and we shall make some bad breaks. But we're going to have the time of our lives.'

'We'll run up to London tomorrow and see if we can hurry those English law—solicitors. I want to get to work.'

They went. They suffered many things ere they returned across the fields in a fly one Saturday night, nursing a two by two-and-a-half box of deeds and maps—lawful owners of Friars Pardon and the five decayed farms therewith.

'I do most sincerely 'ope and trust you'll be 'appy, Madam,' Mrs Cloke gasped, when she was told the news by the kitchen fire.

'Goodness! It isn't a marriage!' Sophie exclaimed, a little awed; for to them the joke, which to an American means work, was only just beginning.

'If it's took in a proper spirit'—Mrs Cloke's eye turned toward her oven.

'Send and have that mended tomorrow,' Sophie whispered.

'We couldn't 'elp noticing,' said Cloke slowly, 'from the times you walked there, that you an' your lady was drawn to it, but—but I don't know as we ever precisely thought——' His wife's glance checked him.

'That we were that sort of people,' said George. 'We aren't sure of it ourselves yet.'

'Perhaps,' said Cloke, rubbing his knees, just for the sake of saying something, 'perhaps you'll park it?'

'What's that?' said George.

'Turn it all into a fine park like Violet Hill'—he jerked a thumb to westward—'that Mr Sangres bought. It was four farms, and Mr Sangres made a fine park of them, with a herd of faller deer.'

'Then it wouldn't be Friars Pardon,' said Sophie. 'Would it?'

'I don't know as I've heard Pardons was ever anything but wheat an' wool. Only some gentlemen say that parks are less trouble than tenants.' He laughed nervously. 'But the gentry, o' course, they keep on pretty much as they was used to.'

'I see,' said Sophie. 'How did Mr Sangres make his money?'

'I never rightly heard. It was pepper an' spices, or it may ha' been gloves. No. Gloves was Sir Reginald Liss at Marley End. Spices was Mr Sangres. He's a Brazilian gentleman—very sunburnt like.'

'Be sure o' one thing. You won't 'ave any trouble,' said Mrs Cloke, just before they went to bed.

Now the news of the purchase was told to Mr and Mrs Cloke alone at 8 p.m. of a Saturday. None left the farm till they set out for church next morning. Yet when they reached the church and were about to slip aside into their usual seats, a little beyond the font, where they could see the red-furred tails of the bell-ropes waggle and twist at ringing time, they were swept forward irresistibly, a Cloke on either flank (and yet they had not walked with the Clokes), upon the ever-retiring bosom of a black-gowned verger, who ushered them into a room of a pew at the head of the left aisle, under the pulpit.

'This,' he sighed reproachfully, 'is the Pardons' Pew,' and shut them in.

They could see little more than the choir boys in the chancel, but to the roots of the hair of their necks they felt the congregation behind mercilessly devouring them by look.

'*When the wicked man turneth away.*' The strong alien voice of the priest vibrated under the hammer-beam roof, and a loneliness unfelt before swamped their hearts, as they searched for places in the unfamiliar Church of England service. The Lord's Prayer—'Our Father, *which* art'—set the seal on that desolation. Sophie found herself thinking how in other lands their purchase would long ere this have been discussed from every point of view in a dozen prints, forgetting that George for months had not been allowed to glance at those black and bellowing headlines. Here was nothing but silence—not even hostility! The game was up to them; the other players hid their cards and waited. Suspense, she felt, was in the air, and when her sight cleared, saw indeed, a mural tablet of a footless bird brooding upon the carven motto, 'Wayte awhyle—wayte awhyle.'

At the Litany George had trouble with an unstable hassock, and drew the slip of carpet under the pew-seat. Sophie pushed her end back also, and shut her eyes against a burning that felt like tears. When she opened them she was looking at her mother's maiden name, fairly carved on a blue flagstone on the pew floor:

Ellen Lashmar . ob. 1796. ætat. 27.

She nudged George and pointed. Sheltered, as they knelt, they looked for more knowledge, but the rest of the slab was blank.

'Ever hear of her?' he whispered.

'Never knew any of us came from here.'

'Coincidence?'

'Perhaps. But it makes me feel better,' and she smiled and winked away a tear on her lashes, and took his hand while they prayed for 'all women labouring of child'—not 'in the perils of childbirth'; and the sparrows who had found their way through the guards behind the glass windows chirped above the faded gilt and alabaster family tree of the Conants.

The baronet's pew was on the right of the aisle. After service its inhabitants moved forth without haste, but so as to effectively block a dusky person with a large family who champed in their rear.

'Spices, I think,' said Sophie, deeply delighted as the Sangres closed up after the Conants. 'Let 'em get away, George.'

But when they came out many folk whose eyes were one still lingered by the lych-gate.

'I want to see if any more Lashmars are buried here,' said Sophie.

'Not now. This seems to be show day. Come home quickly,' he replied.

A group of families, the Clokes a little apart, opened to let them through. The men saluted with jerky nods, the women with remnants of a curtsey. Only Iggulden's son, his mother on his arm, lifted his hat as Sophie passed.

'Your people,' said the clear voice of Lady Conant in her car.

'I suppose so,' said Sophie, blushing, for they were within two yards of her; but it was not a question.

'Then that child looks as if it were coming down with mumps. You ought to tell the mother she shouldn't have brought it to church.'

'I can't leave 'er be'ind, my lady,' the woman said. 'She'd set the 'ouse afire in a minute, she's that forward with the matches. Ain't you, Maudie dear?'

'Has Dr Dallas seen her?'

'Not yet, my lady.'

'He must. You can't get away, of course. M—m! My idiotic maid is coming in for her teeth tomorrow at twelve. She shall pick her up—at Gale Anstey, isn't it?—at eleven.'

'Yes. Thank you very much, my lady.'

'I oughtn't to have done it,' said Lady Conant apologetically, 'but there has been no one at Pardons for so long that you'll forgive my poaching. Now, can't you lunch with us? The vicar usually comes too. I don't use the horses on a Sunday,'—she glanced at the Brazilian's silver-plated chariot. 'It's only a mile across the fields.'

'You—you're very kind,' said Sophie, hating herself because her lip trembled.

'My dear,' the compelling tone dropped to a soothing gurgle, 'd'you suppose I don't know how it feels to come to a strange county—country I should say—away from one's own people? When I first left the Shires—I'm Shropshire, you know—I cried for a day and a night. But fretting doesn't make loneliness any better. Oh, here's Dora. She *did* sprain her leg that day.'

'I'm as lame as a tree still,' said the tall maiden frankly. 'You ought to go out with the otter-hounds, Mrs Chapin; I believe they're drawing your water next week.'

Sir Walter had already led off George, and the vicar came up on the other side of Sophie. There was no escaping the swift procession or the leisurely lunch, where talk came and went in low-voiced eddies that had the village for their centre. Sophie heard the vicar and Sir Walter address her husband lightly as Chapin! (She also remembered many women known in a previous life who habitually addressed their husbands as Mr Such-an-one.) After lunch Lady Conant talked to her explicitly of maternity as that is achieved in cottages and farmhouses remote from aid, and of the duty thereto of the mistress of Pardons.

A gap in a beech hedge, reached across triple lawns, let them out before teatime into the unkempt south side of their land.

'I want your hand, please,' said Sophie as soon as they were safe among the beech boles and the lawless hollies. 'D'you remember the old maid in *Providence and the Guitar* who heard the Commissary swear, and hardly reckoned herself a maiden lady afterward? Because I'm a relative of hers. Lady Conant is——'

'Did you find out anything about the Lashmars?' he interrupted.

'I didn't ask. I'm going to write to Aunt Sydney about it first, Oh, Lady Conant said something at lunch about their having bought some land from some Lashmars a few years ago. I found it was at the beginning of last century.'

'What did you say?'

'I said, "Really, how interesting!" Like that. I'm not going to push myself forward. I've been hearing about Mr Sangres's efforts in that direction. And you? I couldn't see you behind the flowers. Was it very deep water, dear?'

George mopped a brow already browned by outdoor exposure.

'Oh no—dead easy,' he answered. 'I've bought Friars Pardon to prevent Sir Walter's birds straying.'

A cock pheasant scuttered through the dry leaves and exploded almost under their feet. Sophie jumped.

'That's one of 'em,' said George calmly.

'Well, your nerves are better, at any rate,' said she. 'Did you tell 'em you'd bought the thing to play with?'

'No. That was where my nerve broke down. I only made one bad break—I think. I said I couldn't see why hiring land to men to farm wasn't as much a business proposition as anything else.'

'And what did they say?'

'They smiled. I shall know what that smile means some day. They don't waste their smiles. D'you see that track by Gale Anstey?'

They looked down from the edge of the hanger over a cup-like hollow. People by twos and threes in their Sunday best filed slowly along the paths that connected farm to farm.

'I've seen ever so many on our land before,' said Sophie. 'Why is it?'

'To show us we mustn't shut up their rights of way.'

'Those cow-tracks we've been using cross lots?' said Sophie forcibly.

'Yes. Any one of 'em would cost us two thousand pounds each in legal expenses to close.'

'But we don't want to,' she said.

'The whole community would fight if we did.'

'But it's our land. We can do what we like.'

'It's *not* our land. We've only paid for it. We belong to it, and it belongs to the people—our people they call 'em. I've been to lunch with the English too.'

They passed slowly from one bracken-dotted field to the next— flushed with pride of ownership, plotting alterations and restorations at each turn; halting in their tracks to argue, spreading apart to embrace two views at once, or closing in to consider one. Couples moved out of their way, but smiling covertly.

'We shall make some bad breaks,' he said at last.

'Together, though. You won't let anyone else in, will you?'

'Except the contractors. This syndicate handles this proposition by its little lone.'

'But you might feel the want of someone,' she insisted.

'I shall—but it will be you. It's business, Sophie, but it's going to be good fun.'

'Please God,' she answered flushing, and cried to herself as they went back to tea. 'It's worth it. Oh, it's worth it.'

The repairing and moving into Friars Pardon was business of the most varied and searching, but all done English fashion, without friction. Time and money alone were asked. The rest lay in the hand of beneficent advisers from London, or spirits, male and female, called up by Mr and Mrs Cloke from the wastes of the farms. In the centre stood George and Sophie, a little aghast, their interests reaching out on every side.

'I ain't sayin' anything against Londoners,' said Cloke, self-appointed Clerk of the outer works, consulting engineer, head of the immigration bureau, and superintendent of woods and forests; 'but your own people won't go about to make more than a fair profit out of you.'

'How is one to know?' said George.

'Five years from now, or so on, maybe, you'll be lookin' over your first year's accounts, and, knowin' what you'll know then, you'll say: "Well, Billy Beartup"—or Old Cloke as it might be—"did me proper when I was new." No man likes to have that sort of thing laid up against him.'

'I think I see,' said George. 'But five years is a long time to look ahead.'

'I doubt if that oak Billy Beartup throwed in Reuben's Ghyll will be fit for her drawin'-room floor in less than seven,' Cloke drawled.

'Yes, that's my work,' said Sophie. (Billy Beartup of Griffons, a woodman by training and birth, a tenant farmer by misfortune of marriage, had laid his broad axe at her feet a month before.) 'Sorry if I've committed you to another eternity.'

'And we shan't even know where we've gone wrong with *your* new carriage-drive before that time either,' said Cloke, ever anxious to keep the balance true—with an ounce or two in Sophie's favour. The past four months had taught George better than to reply. The carriage road winding up the hill was his present keen interest. They set off to look at it, and the imported American scraper which had blighted the none too sunny soul of 'Skim' Winsh, the carter. But young Iggulden was in charge now, and under his guidance Buller and Roberts, the great horses, moved mountains.

'You lif' her like that, an' you tip her like that,' he explained to the gang. 'My uncle he was road-master in Connecticut.'

'Are they roads yonder?' said Skim, sitting under the laurels.

'No better than accommodation-roads. Dirt, they call 'em. They'd suit you, Skim.'

'Why?' said the incautious Skim.

''Cause you'd take no hurt when you fall out of your cart drunk of a Saturday,' was the answer.

'I didn't last time neither,' Skim roared.

After the loud laugh old Whybarne of Gale Anstey piped feebly, 'Well, dirt or no dirt, there's no denyin' Chapin knows a good job when he sees it. 'E don't build one day and dee-stroy the next, like that nigger Sangres.'

'*She's* the one that knows her own mind,' said Pinky, brother to Skim Winsh, and a Napoleon among carters who had helped to bring the grand piano across the fields in the autumn rains.

'She had ought to,' said Iggulden. 'Whoa, Buller! She's a Lashmar. They never was double-thinking.'

'Oh, you found that? Has the answer come from your uncle?' said Skim, doubtful whether so remote a land as America had posts.

The others looked at him scornfully. Skim was always a day behind the fair.

Iggulden rested from his labours. 'She's a Lashmar right enough. I started up to write to my uncle at once—the month after she said her folks came from Veering Holler.'

'Where there ain't any roads?' Skim interrupted, but none laughed.

'My uncle he married an American woman for his second, and she took it up like a—like the coroner. She's a Lashmar out of the old Lashmar place, 'fore they sold to Conants. She ain't no Toot Hill Lashmar, nor any o' the Crayford lot. Her folk come out of the ground here, neither chalk nor forest, but wildishers. They sailed over to America—I've got it all writ down by my uncle's woman—in eighteen hundred an' nothing. My uncle says they're all slow begetters like.'

'Would they be gentry yonder now?' Skim asked.

'Nah—there's no gentry in America, no matter how long you're there. It's against their law. There's only rich and poor allowed. They've been lawyers and such like over yonder for a hundred years—but she's a Lashmar for all that.'

'Lord! What's a hundred years?' said Whybarne, who had seen seventy-eight of them.

'An' they write too, from yonder—my uncle's woman writes—that you can still tell 'em by headmark. Their hair's foxy-red still —an' they throw out when they walk. *He's* in-toed—treads like a gipsy; but you watch, an' you'll see 'er throw out—like a colt.'

'Your trace wants taking up.' Pinky's large ears had caught

the sound of voices, and as the two broke through the laurels the men were hard at work, their eyes on Sophie's feet.

She had been less fortunate in her inquiries than Iggulden, for her Aunt Sydney of Meriden (a badged and certificated Daughter of the Revolution to boot) answered her inquiries with a two-paged discourse on patriotism, the leaflets of a Village Improvement Society, of which she was president, and a demand for an overdue subscription to a Factory Girls' Reading Circle. Sophie burned it all in the Orpheus and Eurydice grate, and kept her own counsel.

'What I want to know,' said George, when spring was coming, and the gardens needed thought, 'is who will ever pay me for my labour? I've put in at least half a million dollars' worth already.'

'Sure you're not taking too much out of yourself?' his wife asked.

'Oh no; I haven't been conscious of myself all winter.' He looked at his brown English gaiters and smiled. 'It's all behind me now. I believe I could sit down and think of all that—those months before we sailed.'

'Don't—ah, don't!' she cried.

'But I must go back one day. You don't want to keep me out of business always—or do you?' He ended with a nervous laugh.

Sophie sighed as she drew her own ground-ash (of old Iggulden's cutting) from the hall rack.

'Aren't you overdoing it too? You look a little tired,' he said.

'You make me tired. I'm going to Rocketts to see Mrs Cloke about Mary.' (This was the sister of the telegraphist, promoted to be sewing-maid at Pardons.) 'Coming?'

'I'm due at Burnt House to see about the new well. By the way, there's a sore throat at Gale Anstey——'

'That's my province. Don't interfere. The Whybarne children always have sore throats. They do it for jujubes.'

'Keep away from Gale Anstey till I make sure, honey. Cloke ought to have told me.'

'These people don't tell. Haven't you learnt that yet? But I'll obey, me lord. See you later!'

She set off afoot, for within the three main roads that bounded the blunt triangle of the estate (even by night one could scarcely hear the carts on them), wheels were not used except for farm work. The footpaths served all other purposes. And though at first they had planned improvements, they had soon fallen in with the customs of their hidden kingdom, and moved about the soft-footed ways by woodland, hedgerow, and shaw as freely as the rabbits. Indeed, for the most part Sophie walked bareheaded beneath her helmet of chestnut hair; but she had been plagued of late by vague toothaches, which she explained to Mrs Cloke, who asked some questions. How it came about Sophie never knew, but after a while behold Mrs Cloke's arm was about her waist, and her head was on that deep bosom behind the shut kitchen door.

'My dear! my dear!' the elder woman almost sobbed. 'An' d'you mean to tell me you never suspicioned? Why—why—where *was* you ever taught anything at all? Of *course* it is. It's what we've been only waitin' for, all of us. Time and again I've said to Lady——' she checked herself. 'An' now we shall be as we should be.'

'But—but—but——' Sophie whimpered.

'An' to see you buildin' your nest so busy—pianos and books —an' never thinkin' of a nursery!'

'No more I did.' Sophie sat bolt upright, and began to laugh.

'Time enough yet.' The fingers tapped thoughtfully on the broad knee. 'But—they must be strange-minded folk over yonder with you! Have you thought to send for your mother? She dead? My dear, my dear! Never mind! She'll be happy where she knows. 'Tis God's work. An' we was only waitin' for it, for you've never failed in your duty yet. It ain't your way. *What* did you say about my Mary's doings?' Mrs Cloke's face hardened as she pressed her chin on Sophie's forehead. 'If any of your girls thinks to be'ave arbitrary now, I'll—— But they won't, my dear. I'll see they do their duty too. Be sure you'll 'ave no trouble.'

When Sophie walked back across the fields, heaven and earth changed about her as on the day of old Iggulden's death. For an instant she thought of the wide turn of the staircase, and the new ivory-white paint that no coffin corner could scar, but presently the shadow passed in a pure wonder and bewilderment that made her reel. She leaned against one of their new gates and looked over their lands for some other stay.

'Well,' she said resignedly, half aloud, 'we must try to make him feel that he isn't a third in our party,' and turned the corner that looked over Friars Pardon, giddy, sick, and faint.

Of a sudden the house they had bought for a whim stood up as she had never seen it before, low-fronted, broad-winged, ample, prepared by course of generations for all such things. As it had steadied her when it lay desolate, so now that it had meaning from their few months of life within, it soothed and promised good. She went alone and quickly into the hall, and kissed either door-post, whispering: 'Be good to me. *You* know! You've never failed in your duty yet.'

When the matter was explained to George, he would have sailed at once to their own land, but this Sophie forbade.

'I don't want science,' she said. 'I just want to be loved, and there isn't time for that at home. Besides,' she added, looking out of the window, 'it would be desertion.'

George was forced to soothe himself with linking Friars Pardon to the telegraph system of Great Britain by telephone—three-quarters of a mile of poles, put in by Whybarne and a few friends. One of these was a foreigner from the next parish. Said he when the line was being run: 'There's an old ellum right in our road. Shall us throw her?'

'Toot Hill parish folk, neither grace nor good luck, God help 'em.' Old Whybarne shouted the local proverb from three poles down the line. '*We* ain't goin' to lay any axe-iron to coffin-wood here—not till we know where we are yet awhile. Swing round 'er, swing round!'

To this day, then, that sudden kink in the straight line across the upper pasture remains a mystery to Sophie and George. Nor can they tell why Skim Winsh, who came to his cottage under Dutton Shaw most musically drunk at 10.45 p.m. of every Saturday night, as his father had done before him, sang no more at the bottom of the garden steps, where Sophie always feared he would break his neck. The path was undoubtedly an ancient right of way, and at 10.45 p.m. on Saturdays Skim remembered it was his duty to posterity to keep it open—till Mrs Cloke spoke to him —once. She spoke likewise to her daughter Mary, sewing-maid at Pardons, and to Mary's best new friend, the five-foot-seven imported London housemaid, who taught Mary to trim hats, and found the country dullish.

But there was no noise—at no time was there any noise—and when Sophie walked abroad she met no one in her path unless she had signified a wish that way. Then they appeared to protest that all was well with them and their children, their chickens, their roofs, their water-supply, and their sons in the police or the railway service.

'But don't you find it dull, dear?' said George, loyally doing his best not to worry as the months went by.

'I've been so busy putting my house in order I haven't had time to think,' said she. 'Do you?'

'No—no. If I could only be sure of you.'

She turned on the green drawing-room's couch (it was Empire, not Hepplewhite after all), and laid aside a list of linen and blankets.

'It has changed everything, hasn't it?' she whispered.

'Oh Lord, yes. But I still think if we went back to Baltimore——'

'And missed our first real summer together. No thank you, me lord.'

'But we're absolutely alone.'

'Isn't that what I'm doing my best to remedy? Don't you worry. I like it—like it to the marrow of my little bones. You don't realize what her house means to a woman. We thought we were living in it last year, but we hadn't begun to. Don't you rejoice in your study, George?'

'I prefer being here with you.' He sat down on the floor by the couch and took her hand.

'Seven,' she said as the French clock struck. 'Year before last you'd just be coming back from business.'

He winced at the recollection, then laughed. 'Business! I've been at work ten solid hours today.'

'Where did you lunch? With the Conants?'

'No; at Dutton Shaw, sitting on a log, with my feet in a swamp. But we've found out where the old spring is, and we're going to pipe it down to Gale Anstey next year.'

'I'll come and see tomorrow. Oh, please open the door, dear. I want to look down the passage. Isn't that corner by the stair-head lovely where the sun strikes in?' She looked through half-closed eyes at the vista of ivory-white and pale green all steeped in liquid gold.

'There's a step out of Jane Elphick's bedroom,' she went on—'and *his* first step in the world ought to be up. I shouldn't wonder if those people hadn't put it there on purpose. George, will it make any odds to you if he's a girl?'

He answered, as he had many times before, that his interest was his wife, not the child.

'Then you're the only person who thinks so.' She laughed. 'Don't be silly, dear. It's expected. *I* know. It's my duty. I shan't be able to look our people in the face if I fail.'

'What concern is it of theirs, confound 'em!'

'You'll see. Luckily the tradition of the house is boys, Mrs Cloke says, so I'm provided for. Shall you ever begin to understand these people? I shan't.'

'And we bought it for fun—for fun?' he groaned. 'And here we are held up for goodness knows how long!'

'Why? Were you thinking of selling it?' He did not answer. 'Do you remember the second Mrs Chapin?' she demanded.

This was a bold, brazen little black-browed woman—a widow for choice—who on Sophie's death was guilefully to marry George for his wealth, and ruin him in a year. George being busy, Sophie had invented her some two years after her marriage, and conceived she was alone among wives in so doing.

'You aren't going to bring *her* up again?' he asked anxiously.

'I only want to say that I should hate anyone who bought

Pardons ten times worse than I used to hate the second Mrs Chapin. Think what we've put into it of our two selves.'

'At least a couple of million dollars. I know I could have made——' He broke off.

'The beasts!' she went on. 'They'd be sure to build a red-brick lodge at the gates, and cut the lawn up for bedding out. You must leave instructions in your will that *he's* never to do that, George, won't you?'

He laughed and took her hand again but said nothing till it was time to dress. Then he muttered: 'What the devil use is a man's country to him when he can't do business in it?'

Friars Pardon stood faithful to its tradition. At the appointed time was born, not that third in their party to whom Sophie meant to be so kind, but a godling; in beauty, it was manifest, excelling Eros, as in wisdom Confucius; an enhancer of delights, a renewer of companionships and an interpreter of Destiny. This last George did not realize till he met Lady Conant striding through Dutton Shaw a few days after the event.

'My dear fellow,' she cried, and slapped him heartily on the back, 'I can't tell you how glad we all are.—Oh, *she*'ll be all right. (There's never been any trouble over the birth of an heir at Pardons.) Now where the dooce is it?' She felt largely in her leather-bound skirt and drew out a small silver mug. 'I sent a note to your wife about it, but my silly ass of a groom forgot to take this. You can save me a tramp. Give her my love.' She marched off amid her guard of grave Airedales.

The mug was worn and dented: above the twined initials, G. L., was the crest of a footless bird and the motto: 'Wayte awhyle—wayte awhyle'.

'That's the other end of the riddle,' Sophie whispered, when he saw her that evening. 'Read her note. The English write beautiful notes.'

The warmest of welcomes to your little man. I hope he will appreciate his native land now he has come to it. Though you have said nothing we cannot, of course, look on him as a little stranger, and so I am sending him the old Lashmar christening mug. It has been with us since Gregory Lashmar, your great-grandmother's brother—

George stared at his wife.
'Go on,' she twinkled from the pillows.

—mother's brother, sold his place to Walter's family. We seem to have acquired some of your household gods at that time, but nothing survives except the mug and the old cradle, which I found in the potting-shed and am having put in order for you. I hope little George—Lashmar, he will be too, won't he?—will live to see his grandchildren cut their teeth on his mug.

Affectionately yours,
ALICE CONANT.

P.S.—How quiet you've kept about it all!

'Well, I'm——'

'Don't swear,' said Sophie. 'Bad for the infant mind.'

'But how in the world did she get at it? Have you ever said a word about the Lashmars?'

'You know the only time—to young Iggulden at Rocketts—when Iggulden died.'

'Your great-grandmother's brother! She's traced the whole connection—more than your Aunt Sydney could do. What does she mean about our keeping quiet?'

Sophie's eyes sparkled. 'I've thought that out too. We've got back at the English at last. Can't you see that *she* thought that we thought my mother's being a Lashmar was one of those things we'd expect the English to find out for themselves, and that's impressed her?' She turned the mug in her white hands, and sighed happily. '"Wyate awhyle—wayte awhyle." That's not a bad motto, George. It's been worth it.'

'But still I don't quite see——'

'I shouldn't wonder if they don't think our coming here was part of a deep-laid scheme to be near our ancestors. *They*'d understand that. And look how they've accepted us, all of them.'

'Are we so undesirable in ourselves?' George grunted.

'Be just, me lord. That wretched Sangres man has twice our money. Can you see Marm Conant slapping him between the shoulders? Not by a jugful! The poor beast doesn't exist!'

'Do you think it's that then?' He looked toward the cot by the fire where the godling snorted.

'The minute I get well I shall find out from Mrs Cloke what every Lashmar gives in doles (that's nicer than tips) every time a Lashmite is born. I've done my duty thus far, but there's much expected of me.'

Entered here Mrs Cloke, and hung worshipping over the cot. They showed her the mug and her face shone. 'Oh, now Lady Conant's sent it, it'll be all proper, ma'am, won't it? "George" of course he'd have to be, but seein' what he is we was hopin'—all your people was hopin'—it 'ud be "Lashmar" too, and that 'ud just round it out. A very 'andsome mug—quite unique, I

should imagine. "Wayte awhyle—wayte awhyle." That's true
with the Lashmars, I've heard. Very slow to fill their houses, they
are. Most like Master George won't open 'is nursery till he's thirty.'

'Poor lamb!' cried Sophie. 'But how did you know my folk
were Lashmars?'

Mrs Cloke thought deeply. 'I'm sure I can't quite say, ma'am,
but I've a belief likely that it was something you may have let
drop to young Iggulden when you was at Rocketts. That *may*
have been what give us an inkling. An' so it came out, one thing
in the way o' talk leading to another, and those American people
at Veering Holler was very obligin' with news, I'm told, ma'am.'

'Great Scott!' said George, under his breath. 'And this is the
simple peasant!'

'Yiss,' Mrs Cloke went on. 'An' Cloke was only wonderin' this
afternoon—your pillow's slipped, my dear, you mustn't lie that
a-way—just for the sake o' sayin' something, whether you
wouldn't think well now of getting the Lashmar farms back, sir.
They don't rightly round off Sir Walter's estate. They come
caterin' across us more. Cloke, 'e 'ud be glad to show you over
any day.'

'But Sir Walter doesn't want to sell, does he?'

'We can find out from his bailiff, sir, but'—with cold contempt
—'I think that trained nurse is just comin' up from her dinner, so
I'm afraid we'll 'ave to ask you, sir . . . Now, Master George—
Ai-ie! Wake a litty minute, lammie!'

A few months later the three of them were down at the brook
in the Gale Anstey woods to consider the rebuilding of a foot-
bridge carried away by spring floods. George Lashmar wanted
all the bluebells on God's earth that day to eat, and Sophie
adored him in a voice like to the cooing of a dove; so business
was delayed.

'Here's the place,' said his father at last among the water
forget-me-nots. 'But where the deuce are the larch-poles, Cloke?
I told you to have them down here ready.'

'We'll get 'em down *if* you say so,' Cloke answered, with a
thrust of the underlip they both knew.

'But I did say so. What on earth have you brought that timber-
tug here for? We aren't building a railway bridge. Why, in
America, half a dozen two-by-four bits would be ample.'

'I don't know nothin' about that,' said Cloke. 'An' I've nothin'
to say against larch—*if* you want to make a temp'ry job of it. I
ain't 'ere to tell you what isn't so, sir; an' you can't say I ever
come creepin' up on you, or tryin' to lead you farther in than you
set out——'

A year ago George would have danced with impatience. Now he scraped a little mud off his old gaiters with his spud, and waited.

'All I say is that you can put up larch and make a temp'ry job of it; and by the time the young master's married it'll have to be done again. Now, I've brought down a couple of as sweet six-by-eight oak timbers as we've ever drawed. You put 'em in an' it's off your mind for good an' all. Y'other way—I don't say it ain't right, I'm only just sayin' what I think—but t'other way, he'll no sooner be married than we'll 'ave it *all* to do again. You've no call to regard my words, but you can't get out of *that*.'

'No,' said George after a pause; 'I've been realizing that for some time. Make it oak then; we can't get out of it.'

1905

# Marklake Witches

WHEN Dan took up boat-building, Una coaxed Mrs Vincey, the farmer's wife at Little Lindens, to teach her to milk. Mrs Vincey milks in the pasture in summer, which is different from milking in the shed, because the cows are not tied up, and until they know you they will not stand still. After three weeks Una could milk Red Cow or Kitty Shorthorn quite dry, without her wrists aching, and then she allowed Dan to look. But milking did not amuse him, and it was pleasanter for Una to be alone in the quiet pastures with quiet-spoken Mrs Vincey. So, evening after evening, she slipped across to Little Lindens, took her stool from the fern-clump beside the fallen oak, and went to work, her pail between her knees, and her head pressed hard into the cow's flank. As often as not, Mrs Vincey would be milking cross Pansy at the other end of the pasture, and would not come near till it was time to strain and pour off.

Once, in the middle of milking, Kitty Shorthorn boxed Una's ear with her tail.

'You old pig!' said Una, nearly crying, for a cow's tail can hurt.

'Why didn't you tie it down, child?' said a voice behind her.

'I meant to, but the flies are so bad I let her off—and this is what she's done!' Una looked round, expecting Puck, and saw a curly-haired girl, not much taller than herself, but older, dressed in a curious high-waisted, lavender-coloured riding-habit, with a high hunched collar and a deep cape and a belt fastened with a steel clasp. She wore a yellow velvet cap and tan gauntlets, and carried a real hunting-crop. Her cheeks were pale except for two pretty pink patches in the middle, and she talked with little gasps at the end of her sentences, as though she had been running.

'You don't milk so badly, child,' she said, and when she smiled her teeth showed small and even and pearly.

'Can you milk?' Una asked, and then flushed, for she heard Puck's chuckle.

He stepped out of the fern and sat down, holding Kitty Shorthorn's tail. 'There isn't much,' he said, 'that Miss Philadelphia doesn't know about milk—or, for that matter, butter and eggs. She's a great housewife.'

'Oh,' said Una. 'I'm sorry I can't shake hands. Mine are all milky; but Mrs Vincey is going to teach me butter-making this summer.'

'Ah! I'm going to London this summer,' the girl said, 'to my aunt in Bloomsbury.' She coughed as she began to hum, '"Oh, what a town! What a wonderful metropolis!"'

'You've got a cold,' said Una.

'No. Only my stupid cough. But it's vastly better than it was last winter. It will disappear in London air. Everyone says so. D'you like doctors, child?'

'I don't know any,' Una replied. 'But I'm sure I shouldn't.'

'Think yourself lucky, child. I beg your pardon,' the girl laughed, for Una frowned.

'I'm not a child, and my name's Una,' she said.

'Mine's Philadelphia. But everybody except René calls me Phil. I'm Squire Bucksteed's daughter—over at Marklake yonder.' She jerked her little round chin towards the south behind Dallington. 'Sure-ly you know Marklake?'

'We went a picnic to Marklake Green once,' said Una. 'It's awfully pretty. I like all those funny little roads that don't lead anywhere.'

'They lead over our land,' said Philadelphia stiffly, 'and the coach road is only four miles away. One can go anywhere from the Green. I went to the Assize Ball at Lewes last year.' She spun round and took a few dancing steps, but stopped with her hand to her side.

'It gives me a stitch,' she explained. 'No odds. 'Twill go away in London air. That's the latest French step, child. René taught it me. D'you hate the French, chi—Una?'

'Well, I hate French, of course, but I don't mind Ma'm'selle. She's rather decent. Is René your French governess?'

Philadelphia laughed till she caught her breath again.

'Oh no! René's a French prisoner—on parole. That means he's promised not to escape till he has been properly exchanged for an Englishman. He's only a doctor, so I hope they won't think him worth exchanging. My uncle captured him last year in the *Ferdinand* privateer, off Belle Isle, and he cured my uncle of a r-r-raging toothache. Of course, after *that* we couldn't let him lie among the common French prisoners at Rye, and so he stays with us. He's of very old family—a Breton, which is nearly next door to being a true Briton, my father says—and he wears his hair clubbed—not powdered. *Much* more becoming, don't you think?'

'I don't know what you're——' Una began, but Puck, the other side of the pail, winked, and she went on with her milking.

'He's going to be a great French physician when the war is over. He makes me bobbins for my lace-pillow now—he's very clever with his hands; but he'd doctor our people on the Green if they would let him. Only our Doctor—Doctor Break—says he's an emp—— or imp something—worse than impostor. But my nurse says——'

'Nurse! You're ever so old. What have you got a nurse for?'

Una finished milking, and turned round on her stool as Kitty Shorthorn grazed off.

'Because I can't get rid of her. Old Cissie nursed my mother, and she says she'll nurse me till she dies. The idea! She never lets me alone. She thinks I'm delicate. She has grown infirm in her understanding, you know. Mad—quite mad, poor Cissie!'

'Really mad?' said Una. 'Or just silly?'

'Crazy, I should say—from the things she does. Her devotion to me is terribly embarrassing. You know I have all the keys of the Hall except the brewery and the tenants' kitchen. I give out all stores and the linen and plate.'

'How jolly! I love store-rooms and giving out things.'

'Ah, it's a great responsibility, you'll find, when you come to my age. Last year Dad said I was fatiguing myself with my duties, and he actually wanted me to give up the keys to old Amoore, our housekeeper. I wouldn't. I hate her. I said, "No, sir. I am Mistress of Marklake Hall just as long as I live, because I'm never going to be married, and I shall give out stores and linen till I die!"'

'And what did your father say?'

'Oh, I threatened to pin a dishclout to his coat-tail. He ran away. Everyone's afraid of Dad, except me.' Philadelphia stamped her foot. 'The idea! If I can't make my own father happy in his house, I'd like to meet the woman that can, and—and—I'd have the living hide off her!'

She cut with her long-thonged whip. It cracked like a pistol-shot across the still pasture. Kitty Shorthorn threw up her head and trotted away.

'I beg your pardon,' Philadelphia said; 'but it makes me furious. Don't you hate those ridiculous old quizzes with their feathers and fronts, who come to dinner and call you "child" in your own chair at your own table?'

'I don't always come to dinner,' said Una, 'but I hate being called "child". Please tell me about store-rooms and giving out things.'

'Ah, it's a great responsibility—particularly with that old cat Amoore looking at the lists over your shoulder. And such a shocking thing happened last summer! Poor crazy Cissie, my nurse that I was telling you of, she took three solid silver tablespoons.'

'Took! But isn't that stealing?' Una cried.

'Hsh!' said Philadelphia, looking round at Puck. 'All I say is she took them without my leave. I made it right afterwards. So, as Dad says—and he's a magistrate—it wasn't a legal offence; it was only compounding a felony.'

'It sounds awful,' said Una.

'It was. My dear, I was furious! I had had the keys for ten months, and I'd never lost anything before. I said nothing at first, because a big house offers so many chances of things being mislaid, and coming to hand later. "Fetching up in the lee-scuppers," my uncle calls it. But next week I spoke to old Cissie about it when she was doing my hair at night, and she said I wasn't to worry my heart for trifles!'

'Isn't it like 'em?' Una burst out. 'They see you're worried over something that really matters, and they say, "Don't worry"; as if *that* did any good!'

'I quite agree with you, my dear; quite agree with you! I told Ciss the spoons were solid silver, and worth forty shillings, so if the thief were found, he'd be tried for his life.'

'Hanged, do you mean?' Una said.

'They ought to be; but Dad says no jury will hang a man nowadays for a forty-shilling theft. They transport 'em into penal servitude at the uttermost ends of the earth beyond the seas, for the term of their natural life. I told Cissie that, and I saw her tremble in my mirror. Then she cried, and caught hold of my knees, and I couldn't for my life understand what it was all about —she cried so. *Can* you guess, my dear, what that poor crazy thing had done? It was midnight before I pieced it together. She had given the spoons to Jerry Gamm, the Witchmaster on the Green, so that he might put a charm on me! Me!'

'Put a charm on you? Why?'

'That's what *I* asked; and then I saw how mad poor Cissie was! You know this stupid little cough of mine? It will disappear as soon as I go to London. She was troubled about *that*, and about my being so thin, and she told me Jerry had promised her, if she would bring him three silver spoons, that he'd charm my cough away and make me plump—"flesh up", she said. I couldn't help laughing; but it was a terrible night! I had to put Cissie into my own bed, and stroke her hand till she cried herself to sleep. What else could I have done? When she woke, and I coughed—I suppose I *can* cough in my own room if I please—she said that she'd killed me, and asked me to have her hanged at Lewes sooner than send her to the uttermost ends of the earth away from me.'

'How awful! What did you do, Phil?'

'Do? I rode off at five in the morning to talk to Master Jerry, with a new lash on my whip. Oh, I was *furious*! Witchmaster or no Witchmaster, I meant to——'

'Ah! what's a Witchmaster?'

'A master of witches, of course. *I* don't believe there are witches; but people say every village has a few, and Jerry was the master of all ours at Marklake. He has been a smuggler, and a man-of-war's man, and now he pretends to be a carpenter and joiner—he can make almost anything—but he really is a white wizard. He cures people by herbs and charms. He can cure them after Doctor Break has given them up, and that's why Doctor Break hates him so. He used to make me toy carts, and charm off my warts when I was a child.' Philadelphia spread out her hands with the delicate shiny little nails. 'It isn't counted lucky to cross him. He has his ways of getting even with you, they say. But *I* wasn't afraid of Jerry! I saw him working in his garden, and I leaned out of my saddle and double-thonged him between the shoulders, over the hedge. Well, my dear, for the first time since Dad gave him to me, my Troubadour (I wish you could see the sweet creature!) shied across the road, and I spilled out into the hedge-top. *Most* undignified! Jerry pulled me through to his side and brushed the leaves off me. I was horribly pricked, but I didn't care. "Now, Jerry," I said, "I'm going to take the hide off you first, and send you to Lewes afterwards. You well know why." "Oh!" he said, and he sat down among his bee-hives. "Then I reckon you've come about old Cissie's business, my dear." "I reckon I justabout have," I said. "Stand away from these hives. I can't get at you there." "That's why I be where I be," he said. "If you'll excuse me, Miss Phil, I don't hold with bein' flogged before breakfast, at my time o' life." He's a huge big man, but he looked so comical squatting among the hives that—I know I oughtn't to—I laughed, and he laughed. I always laugh at the wrong time. But I soon recovered my dignity, and I said, "Then give me back what you made poor Cissie steal!"

'"Your pore Cissie," he said. "She's a hatful o' trouble. But you shall have 'em, Miss Phil. They're all ready put by for you." And, would you believe it, the old sinner pulled my three silver spoons out of his dirty pocket, and polished them on his cuff! "Here they be," he says, and he gave them to me, just as cool as though I'd come to have my warts charmed. That's the worst of people having known you when you were young. But I preserved my composure. "Jerry," I said, "what in the world are we to do? If you'd been caught with these things on you, you'd have been hanged."

'"I know it," he said. "but they're yours now."

'"But you made my Cissie steal them," I said.

'"That I didn't," he said. "Your Cissie, she was pickin' at me an' tarrifyin' me all the long day an' every day for weeks, to put a charm on you, Miss Phil, an' take away your little spitty cough."

'"Yes. I knew that, Jerry, and to make me flesh-up!" I said.

"I'm much obliged to you, but I'm not one of your pigs!"

"'Ah! I reckon she've been talking to you, then," he said. "Yes, she give me no peace, and bein' tarrified—for I don't hold with old women—I laid a task on her which I thought 'ud silence her. *I* never reckoned the old scrattle 'ud risk her neckbone at Lewes Assizes for your sake, Miss Phil. But she did. She up an' stole, I tell ye, as cheerful as a tinker. You might ha' knocked me down with any one of them liddle spoons when she brung 'em in her apron."

"'Do you mean to say, then, that you did it to try my poor Cissie?" I screamed at him.

"'What else for, dearie?" he said. "*I* don't stand in need of hedge-stealings. I'm a freeholder, with money in the bank; and now I won't trust women no more! Silly old besom! I do beleft she'd ha' stole the Squire's big fob-watch, if I'd required her."

"'Then you're a wicked, wicked old man," I said, and I was so angry that I couldn't help crying, and of course that made me cough.

'Jerry was in a fearful taking. He picked me up and carried me into his cottage—it's full of foreign curiosities—and he got me something to eat and drink, and he said he'd be hanged by the neck any day if it pleased me. He said he'd even tell old Cissie he was sorry. That's a great come-down for a Witchmaster, you know.

'I was ashamed of myself for being so silly, and I dabbed my eyes and said, "The least you can do now is to give poor Ciss some sort of a charm for me."

"'Yes, that's only fair dealings," he said. "You know the names of the Twelve Apostles, dearie? You say them names, one by one, before your open window, rain or storm, wet or shine, five times a day fasting. But mind you, 'twixt every name you draw in your breath through your nose, right down to your pretty liddle toes, as long and as deep as you can, and let it out slow through your pretty liddle mouth. There's virtue for your cough in those names spoke that way. And I'll give you something you can see, moreover. Here's a stick of maple, which is the warmest tree in the wood."'

'That's true,' Una interrupted. 'You can feel it almost as warm as yourself when you touch it.'

"'It's cut one inch long for your every year," Jerry said. "That's sixteen inches. You set it in your window so that it holds up the sash, and thus you keep it, rain or shine, or wet or fine, day and night. I've said words over it which will have virtue on your complaints."

"'I haven't any complaints, Jerry," I said. "It's only to please Cissie."

'"I know that as well as you do, dearie," he said. And—and that was all that came of my going to give him a flogging. I wonder whether he made poor Troubadour shy when I lashed at him? Jerry has his ways of getting even with people.'

'I wonder,' said Una. 'Well, did you try the charm? Did it work?'

'What nonsense! I told René about it, of course, because he's a doctor. He's going to be a most famous doctor. That's why our doctor hates him. René said, "Oho! Your Master Gamm, he is worth knowing," and he put up his eyebrows—like this. He made joke of it all. He can see my window from the carpenter's shed, where he works, and if ever the maple stick fell down, he pretended to be in a fearful taking till I propped the window up again. He used to ask me whether I had said my Apostles properly, and how I took my deep breaths. Oh yes, and the next day, though he had been there ever so many times before, he put on his new hat and paid Jerry Gamm a visit of state—as a fellow-physician. Jerry never guessed René was making fun of him, and so he told René about the sick people in the village, and how he cured them with herbs after Doctor Break had given them up. Jerry could talk smugglers' French, of course, and I had taught René plenty of English, if only he wasn't so shy. They called each other Monsieur Gamm and Mosheur Lanark, just like gentlemen. I suppose it amused poor René. He hasn't much to do, except to fiddle about in the carpenter's shop. He's like all the French prisoners—always making knick-knacks; and Jerry had a little lathe at his cottage, and so—and so—René took to being with Jerry much more than I approved of. The Hall is so big and empty when Dad's away, and I will *not* sit with old Amoore—she talks so horridly about everyone—specially about René.

'I was rude to René, I'm afraid; but I was properly served out for it. One always is. You see, Dad went down to Hastings to pay his respects to the General who commanded the brigade there, and to bring him to the Hall afterwards. Dad told me he was a very brave soldier from India—he was Colonel of Dad's Regiment, the Thirty-third Foot, after Dad left the Army, and then he changed his name from Wesley to Wellesley, or else the other way about; and Dad said I was to get out all the silver for him, and I knew that meant a big dinner. So I sent down to the sea for early mackerel, and had *such* a morning in the kitchen and the store-rooms. Old Amoore nearly cried.

'However, my dear, I made all my preparations in ample time, but the fish didn't arrive—it never does—and I wanted René to ride to Pevensey and bring it himself. He had gone over to Jerry, of course, as he always used, unless I requested his presence beforehand. *I* can't send for René every time I want him. He should be there. Now, don't you ever do what I did, child, because it's in the highest degree unladylike; but—but one of our woods runs up to Jerry's garden, and if you climb—it's ungenteel, but I can climb like a kitten—there's an old hollow oak just above the pigsty where you can hear and see everything below. Truthfully, I only went to tell René about the mackerel, but I saw him and Jerry sitting on the seat playing with wooden toy trumpets. So I slipped into the hollow, and choked down my cough, and listened. René had never shown *me* any of these trumpets.'

'Trumpets? Aren't you too old for trumpets?' said Una.

'They weren't real trumpets, because Jerry opened his shirt-collar, and René put one end of his trumpet against Jerry's chest, and put his ear to the other. Then Jerry put his trumpet against René's chest, and listened while René breathed and coughed. I was afraid *I* would cough too.

'"This hollywood one is the best," said Jerry. "'Tis won'erful like hearin' a man's soul whisperin' in his innards; but unless I've a buzzin' in my ears, Mosheur Lanark, you make much about the same kind o' noises as old Gaffer Macklin—but not quite so loud as young Copper. It sounds like breakers on a reef—a long way off. Comprenny?"

'"Perfectly," said René. "I drive on the breakers. But before I strike, I shall save hundreds, thousands, millions perhaps, by my little trumpets. Now tell me what sounds the old Gaffer Macklin have made in his chest, and what the young Copper also."

'Jerry talked for nearly a quarter of an hour about sick people in the village, while René asked questions. Then he sighed, and said, "You explain very well, Monsieur Gamm, but if only I had your opportunities to listen for myself! Do you think these poor people would let me listen to them through my trumpet—for a little money? No?"—René's as poor as a church mouse.

'"They'd kill you, Mosheur. It's all I can do to coax 'em to abide it, and I'm Jerry Gamm," said Jerry. He's very proud of his attainments.

'"Then these poor people are alarmed—No?" said René.

'"They've had it in at me for some time back because o' my tryin' your trumpets on their sick; and I reckon by the talk at the alehouse they won't stand much more. Tom Dunch an' some of his kidney was drinkin' themselves riot-ripe when I passed along after noon. Charms an' mutterin's an' bits o' red wool an' black hens is in the way o' nature to these fools, Mosheur; but anything likely to do 'em real service is devil's work by their estimation. If I was you, I'd go home before they come." Jerry spoke quite quietly, and René shrugged his shoulders.

'"I am prisoner on parole, Monsieur Gamm," he said. "I have no home."

'Now that was unkind of René. He's often told me that he looked on England as his home. I suppose it's French politeness.

'"Then we'll talk o' something that matters," said Jerry. "Not to name no names, Mosheur Lanark, what might be your own opinion o' some one who ain't old Gaffer Macklin nor young Copper? Is that person better or worse?"

'"Better—for time that is," said René. He meant for the time being, but I never could teach him some phrases.

'"I thought so too," said Jerry. "But how about time to come?"

'René shook his head, and then he blew his nose. You don't know how odd a man looks blowing his nose when you are sitting directly above him.

'"I've thought that too," said Jerry. He rumbled so deep I could scarcely catch. "It don't make much odds to me, because I'm old. But you're young, Mosheur—you're young," and he put his hand on René's knee, and René covered it with his hand. I didn't know they were such friends.

'"Thank you, *mon ami*," said René. "I am much oblige. Let us return to our trumpet-making. But I forget"—he stood up—"it appears that you receive this afternoon!"

'You can't see into Gamm's Lane from the oak, but the gate opened, and fat little Doctor Break stumped in, mopping his head, and half-a-dozen of our people followed him, very drunk.

'You ought to have seen René bow; he does it beautifully.

'"A word with you, Laennec," said Doctor Break. "Jerry has been practising some devilry or other on these poor wretches, and they've asked me to be arbiter."

'"Whatever that means, I reckon it's safer than asking you to be doctor," said Jerry, and Tom Dunch, one of our carters, laughed.

'"That ain't right feeling of you, Tom," Jerry said, "seeing how clever Doctor Break put away your thorn in the flesh last winter." Tom's wife had died at Christmas, though Doctor Break bled her twice a week. Doctor Break danced with rage.

'"This is all beside the mark," he said. "These good people are willing to testify that you've been impudently prying into God's secrets by means of some papistical contrivance which this person"—he pointed to poor René—"has furnished you with. Why, here are the things themselves!" René was holding a trumpet in his hand.

'Then all the men talked at once. They said old Gaffer Macklin was dying from stitches in his side where Jerry had put the trumpet—they called it the devil's ear-piece; and they said it left round red witch-marks on people's skins, and dried up their lights, and made 'em spit blood, and threw 'em into sweats. Terrible things they said. You never heard such a noise. I took advantage of it to cough.

'René and Jerry were standing with their backs to the pigsty. Jerry fumbled in his big flap pockets and fished up a pair of pistols. You ought to have seen the men give back when he cocked his. He passed one to René.

'"Wait! Wait!" said René. "I will explain to the doctor if he permits." He waved a trumpet at him, and the men at the gate shouted," Don't touch it, Doctor! Don't lay a hand to the thing.'

'"Come, come!" said René. "You are not so big fool as you pretend. No?"

'Doctor Break backed toward the gate, watching Jerry's pistol, and René followed him with his trumpet, like a nurse trying to amuse a child, and put the ridiculous thing to his ear to show how it was used, and talked of *la Gloire*, and *l'Humanité*, and *la Science*, while Doctor Break watched Jerry's pistol and swore. I nearly laughed aloud.

'"Now listen! Now listen!" said René. "This will be moneys in your pockets, my dear *confrère*. You will become rich."

'Then Doctor Break said something about adventurers who could not earn an honest living in their own country creeping into decent houses and taking advantage of gentlemen's confidence to enrich themselves by base intrigues.

'René dropped his absurd trumpet and made one of his best bows. I knew he was angry from the way he rolled his "r's".

'"Ver-r-ry good," said he. "For that I shall have much pleasure to kill you now and here. Monsieur Gamm,"—another bow to Jerry—"you will please lend him your pistol, or he shall have mine. I give you my word I know not which is best; and if he will choose a second from his friends over there"—another bow to our drunken yokels at the gate—"we will commence."

'"That's fair enough," said Jerry. "Tom Dunch, you owe it to the Doctor to be his second. Place your man."

'"No," said Tom. "No mixin' in gentry's quarrels for me." And he shook his head and went out, and the others followed him.

'"Hold on," said Jerry. "You've forgot what you set out to do up at the alehouse just now. You was goin' to search me for witch-marks; you was goin' to duck me in the pond; you was goin' to drag all my bits o' sticks out o' my little cottage here. What's the matter with you? Wouldn't you like to be with your old woman tonight, Tom?"

'But they didn't even look back, much less come. They ran to the village alehouse like hares.

'"No matter for these *canaille*," said René, buttoning up his coat so as not to show any linen. All gentlemen do that before a duel, Dad says—and he's been out five times. "You shall be his second, Monsieur Gamm. Give him the pistol."

'Doctor Break took it as if it was red-hot, but he said that if René resigned his pretensions in certain quarters he would pass over the matter. René bowed deeper than ever.

'"As for that," he said, "if you were not the ignorant which you are, you would have known long ago that the subject of your remarks is not for any living man."

'I don't know what the subject of his remarks might have been, but he spoke in a simply dreadful voice, my dear, and Doctor Break turned quite white, and said René was a liar; and then René caught him by the throat, and choked him black.

'Well, my dear, as if this wasn't deliciously exciting enough, just exactly at that minute I heard a strange voice on the other side of the hedge say, "What's this? What's this, Bucksteed?" and there was my father and Sir Arthur Wesley on horseback in the lane; and there was René kneeling on Doctor Break, and there was I up in the oak, listening with all my ears.

'I must have leaned forward too much, and the voice gave me such a start that I slipped. I had only time to make one jump on to the pigsty roof—another, before the tiles broke, on to the pigsty wall—and then I bounced down into the garden, just behind Jerry, with my hair full of bark. Imagine the situation!'

'Oh, I can!' Una laughed till she nearly fell off the stool.

'Dad said, "Phil—a—del—phia!" and Sir Arthur Wesley said, "Good Ged!" and Jerry put his foot on the pistol René had dropped. But René was splendid. He never even looked at me. He began to untwist Doctor Break's neckcloth as fast as he'd twisted it, and asked him if he felt better.

'"What's happened? What's happened?" said Dad.

'"A fit!" said René. "I fear my *confrère* has had a fit. Do not be alarmed. He recovers himself. Shall I bleed you a little, my dear Doctor?" Doctor Break was very good too. He said, "I am vastly obliged, Monsieur Laennec, but I am restored now." And as he went out of the gate he told Dad it was a syncope—I think. Then Sir Arthur said, "Quite right, Bucksteed. Not another word! They are both gentlemen." And he took off his cocked hat to Doctor Break and René.

'But poor Dad wouldn't let well alone. He kept saying, "Philadelphia, what does all this mean?"

'"Well, sir," I said, "I've only just come down. As far as I

could see, it looked as though Doctor Break had had a sudden
seizure." That was quite true—if you'd seen René seize him. Sir
Arthur laughed. "Not much change there, Bucksteed," he said.
"She's a lady—a thorough lady."

'"Heaven knows she doesn't look like one," said poor Dad.
"Go home, Philadelphia."

'So I went home, my dear—don't laugh so!—right under Sir
Arthur's nose—a most enormous nose—feeling as though I were
twelve years old, going to be whipped. Oh, I *beg* your pardon,
child!'

'It's all right,' said Una. 'I'm getting on for thirteen. I've never
been whipped, but I know how you felt. All the same, it must have
been funny!'

'Funny! If you'd heard Sir Arthur jerking out, "Good Ged,
Bucksteed!" every minute as they rode behind me; and poor
Dad saying, "'Pon my honour, Arthur, I can't account for it!"
Oh, how my cheeks tingled when I reached my room! But Cissie
had laid out my very best evening dress, the white satin one, van-
dyked at the bottom with spots of morone foil, and the pearl
knots, you know, catching up the drapery from the left shoulder.
I had poor mother's lace tucker and her coronet comb.'

'Oh, you lucky!' Una murmured. '*And* gloves?'

'French kid, my dear'—Philadelphia patted her shoulder—
'and morone satin shoes and a morone and gold crape fan. That
restored my calm. Nice things always do. I wore my hair banded
on my forehead with a little curl over the left ear. And when I
descended the stairs, *en grande tenue*, old Amoore curtsied to me
without my having to stop and look at her, which, alas! is too
often the case. Sir Arthur highly approved of the dinner, my dear:
the mackerel *did* come in time. We had all the Marklake silver
out, and he toasted my health, and he asked me where my little
bird's-nesting sister was. I *know* he did it to quiz me, so I looked
him straight in the face, my dear, and I said, "I always send her
to the nursery, Sir Arthur, when I receive guests at Marklake
Hall".'

'Oh, how chee—clever of you. What did he say?' Una cried.

'He said, "Not much change there, Bucksteed. Ged, I deserved
it," and he toasted me again. They talked about the French and
what a shame it was that Sir Arthur only commanded a brigade
at Hastings, and he told Dad of a battle in India at a place called
Assaye. Dad said it was a terrible fight, but Sir Arthur described
it as though it had been a whist-party—I suppose because a lady
was present.'

'Of course you were the lady. I wish I'd seen you,' said Una.

'I wish you had, child. I had *such* a triumph after dinner. René and Doctor Break came in. They had quite made up their quarrel, and they told me they had the highest esteem for each other, and I laughed and said, "I heard every word of it up in the tree." You never saw two men so frightened in your life, and when I said, "What *was* 'the subject of your remarks', René?" neither of them knew where to look. Oh, I quizzed them unmercifully. They'd seen me jump off the pigsty roof, remember.'

'But what *was* the subject of their remarks?' said Una.

'Oh, Dr Break said it was a professional matter, so the laugh was turned on me. I was horribly afraid it might have been something unladylike and indelicate. But *that* wasn't my triumph. Dad asked me to play on the harp. Between just you and me, child, I had been practising a new song from London—I don't always live in trees—for weeks; and I gave it them for a surprise.'

'What was it?' said Una. 'Sing it.'

'"I have given my heart to a flower." Not very difficult fingering, but r-r-ravishing sentiment.'

Philadelphia coughed and cleared her throat.

'I've a deep voice for my age and size,' she explained. 'Contralto, you know, but it ought to be stronger,' and she began, her face all dark against the last of the soft pink sunset:

> 'I have given my heart to a flower,
> Though I know it is fading away,
> Though I know it will live but an hour
> And leave me to mourn its decay!

'Isn't that touchingly sweet? Then the last verse—I wish I had my harp, dear—goes as low as my register will reach.' She drew in her chin, and took a deep breath:

> 'Ye desolate whirlwinds that rave,
> I charge you be good to my dear!
> She is all—she is all that I have,
> And the time of our parting is near!'

'Beautiful!' said Una. 'And did they like it?'

'Like it? They were overwhelmed—*accablés*, as René says. My dear, if I hadn't seen it, I shouldn't have believed that I could have drawn tears, genuine tears, to the eyes of four grown men. But I did! René simply couldn't endure it! He's all French sensibility. He hid his face and said, "*Assez, Mademoiselle! C'est plus fort que moi! Assez!*" And Sir Arthur blew his nose and said, "Good Ged! This is worse than Assaye!" While Dad sat with the tears simply running down his cheeks.'

'And what did Doctor Break do?'

'He got up and pretended to look out of the window, but I saw his little fat shoulders jerk as if he had the hiccoughs. That *was* a triumph. I never suspected him of sensibility.'

'Oh, I wish I'd seen! I wish I'd been you,' said Una, clasping her hands. Puck rustled and rose from the fern, just as a big blundering cockchafer flew smack against Una's cheek.

When she had finished rubbing the place, Mrs Vincey called to her that Pansy had been fractious, or she would have come long before to help her strain and pour off.

'It didn't matter,' said Una; 'I just waited. Is that old Pansy barging about the lower pasture now?'

'No,' said Mrs Vincey, listening. 'It sounds more like a horse being galloped middlin' quick through the woods; but there's no road there. I reckon it's one of Gleason's colts loose. Shall I see you up to the house, Miss Una?'

'Gracious, no! thank you. What's going to hurt me?' said Una, and she put her stool away behind the oak, and strolled home through the gaps that old Hobden kept open for her.

1910

# The Gardener

One grave to me was given,
  One watch till Judgment Day;
And God looked down from Heaven
  And rolled the stone away.

*One day in all the years,*
  *One hour in that one day,*
*His Angels saw my tears,*
  *And rolled the stone away!*

EVERYONE in the village knew that Helen Turrell did her duty by all her world, and by none more honourably than by her only brother's unfortunate child. The village knew, too, that George Turrell had tried his family severely since early youth, and were not surprised to be told that, after many fresh starts given and thrown away, he, an Inspector of Indian Police, had entangled himself with the daughter of a retired non-commissioned officer, and had died of a fall from a horse a few weeks before his child was born. Mercifully, George's father and mother were both dead, and though Helen, thirty-five and independent, might well have washed her hands of the whole disgraceful affair, she most nobly took charge, though she was, at the time, under threat of lung trouble which had driven her to the South of France. She arranged for the passage of the child and a nurse from Bombay, met them at Marseilles, nursed the baby through an attack of infantile dysentery due to the carelessness of the nurse, whom she had had to dismiss, and at last, thin and worn but triumphant, brought the boy late in the autumn, wholly restored, to her Hampshire home.

All these details were public property, for Helen was as open as the day, and held that scandals are only increased by hushing them up. She admitted that George had always been rather a black sheep, but things might have been much worse if the mother had insisted on her right to keep the boy. Luckily, it seemed that people of that class would do almost anything for money, and, as George had always turned to her in his scrapes, she felt herself justified—her friends agreed with her—in cutting the whole non-commissioned officer connection, and giving the child every advantage. A christening, by the Rector, under the name of Michael, was the first step. So far as she knew herself, she was not, she said, a child-lover, but, for all his faults, she had been very fond of George, and she pointed out that little Michael had his father's mouth to a line; which made something to build upon.

As a matter of fact, it was the Turrell forehead, broad, low, and well-shaped, with the widely spaced eyes beneath it, that Michael had most faithfully reproduced. His mouth was somewhat better cut than the family type. But Helen, who would concede nothing good to his mother's side, vowed he was a Turrell all over, and, there being no one to contradict, the likeness was established.

In a few years Michael took his place, as accepted as Helen had always been—fearless, philosophical, and fairly good-looking. At six, he wished to know why he could not call her 'Mummy', as other boys called their mothers. She explained that she was only his auntie, and that aunties were not quite the same as mummies, but that, if it gave him pleasure, he might call her 'Mummy' at bedtime, for a pet-name between themselves.

Michael kept his secret most loyalty, but Helen, as usual, explained the fact to her friends; which when Michael heard, he raged.

'Why did you tell? *Why* did you tell?' came at the end of the storm.

'Because it's always best to tell the truth,' Helen answered, her arm round him as he shook in his cot.

'All right, but when the troof's ugly I don't think it's nice.'

'Don't you, dear?'

'No, I don't, and'—she felt the small body stiffen—'now you've told, I won't call you "Mummy" any more—not even at bedtimes.'

'But isn't that rather unkind?' said Helen softly.

'I don't care! I don't care! You've hurted me in my insides and I'll hurt you back. I'll hurt you as long as I live!'

'Don't, oh, don't talk like that, dear! You don't know what——'

'I will! And when I'm dead I'll hurt you worse!'

'Thank goodness, I shall be dead long before you, darling.'

'Huh! Emma says, "'Never know your luck".' (Michael had been talking to Helen's elderly, flat-faced maid.) 'Lots of little boys die quite soon. So'll I. *Then* you'll see!'

Helen caught her breath and moved towards the door, but the wail of 'Mummy! Mummy!' drew her back again, and the two wept together.

At ten years old, after two terms at a prep. school, something or somebody gave him the idea that his civil status was not quite regular. He attacked Helen on the subject, breaking down her stammered defences with the family directness.

''Don't believe a word of it,' he said, cheerily, at the end. 'People wouldn't have talked like they did if my people had been married. But don't you bother, Auntie. I've found out all about my sort in English His'try and the Shakespeare bits. There was William the Conqueror to begin with, and—oh, heaps more, and they all got on first-rate. 'Twon't make any difference to you, my being *that*—will it?'

'As if anything could——' she began.

'All right. We won't talk about it any more if it makes you cry.' He never mentioned the thing again of his own will, but when, two years later, he skilfully managed to have measles in the holidays, as his temperature went up to the appointed one hundred and four he muttered of nothing else, till Helen's voice, piercing at last his delirium, reached him with assurance that nothing on earth or beyond could make any difference between them.

The terms at his public school and the wonderful Christmas, Easter, and summer holidays followed each other, variegated and glorious as jewels on a string; and as jewels Helen treasured them. In due time Michael developed his own interests, which ran their courses and gave way to others; but his interest in Helen was constant and increasing throughout. She repaid it with all that she had of affection or could command of counsel and money; and since Michael was no fool, the War took him just before what was like to have been a most promising career.

He was to have gone up to Oxford, with a scholarship, in October. At the end of August he was on the edge of joining the first holocaust of public-school boys who threw themselves into the Line; but the captain of his O.T.C., where he had been sergeant for nearly a year, headed him off and steered him directly to a commission in a battalion so new that half of it still wore the old Army red, and the other half was breeding meningitis through living overcrowdedly in damp tents. Helen had been shocked at the idea of direct enlistment.

'But it's in the family,' Michael laughed.

'You don't mean to tell me that you believed that old story all this time?' said Helen. (Emma, her maid, had been dead now several years.) 'I gave you my word of honour—and I give it again—that—that it's all right. It is indeed.'

'Oh, *that* doesn't worry me. It never did,' he replied valiantly. 'What I meant was, I should have got into the show earlier if I'd enlisted—like my grandfather.'

'Don't talk like that! Are you afraid of its ending so soon, then?'

'No such luck. You know what K. says.'

'Yes. But my banker told me last Monday it couldn't *possibly* last beyond Christmas—for financial reasons.'

''Hope he's right, but our Colonel—and he's a Regular—says it's going to be a long job.'

Michael's battalion was fortunate in that, by some chance which meant several 'leaves', it was used for coast-defence among shallow trenches on the Norfolk coast; thence sent north to watch the mouth of a Scotch estuary, and, lastly, held for weeks on a baseless rumour of distant service. But, the very day that Michael was to have met Helen for four whole hours at a railway-junction up the line, it was hurled out, to help make good the wastage of Loos, and he had only just time to send her a wire of farewell.

In France luck again helped the battalion. It was put down near the Salient, where it led a meritorious and unexacting life, while the Somme was being manufactured; and enjoyed the peace of the Armentières and Laventie sectors when that battle began. Finding that it had sound views on protecting its own flanks and could dig, a prudent Commander stole it out of its own Division, under pretence of helping to lay telegraphs, and used it round Ypres at large.

A month later, and just after Michael had written Helen that there was nothing special doing and therefore no need to worry, a shell-splinter dropping out of a wet dawn killed him at once. The next shell uprooted and laid down over the body what had been the foundation of a barn wall, so neatly that none but an expert would have guessed that anything unpleasant had happened.

By this time the village was old in experience of war, and, English fashion, had evolved a ritual to meet it. When the post-mistress handed her seven-year-old daughter the official telegram to take to Miss Turrell, she observed to the Rector's gardener: 'It's Miss Helen's turn now.' He replied, thinking of his own son: 'Well, he's lasted longer than some.' The child herself came to the front-door weeping aloud, because Master Michael had often given her sweets. Helen, presently, found herself pulling down the house-blinds one after one with great care, and saying earnestly to each: 'Missing *always* means dead.' Then she took her place in the dreary procession that was impelled to go through an inevitable series of unprofitable emotions. The Rector, of course, preached hope and prophesied word, very soon, from a prison camp. Several friends, too, told her perfectly truthful tales, but always about other women, to whom, after months and months of silence, their missing had been miraculously restored. Other people urged her to communicate with infallible Secretaries of organizations who could communicate with benevolent neutrals, who could extract accurate information from the most secretive of Hun prison commandants. Helen did and wrote and signed everything that was suggested or put before her.

Once, on one of Michael's leaves, he had taken her over a munition factory, where she saw the progress of a shell from blank-iron to the all but finished article. It struck her at the time that the wretched thing was never left alone for a single second; and 'I'm being manufactured into a bereaved next of kin', she told herself, as she prepared her documents.

In due course, when all the organizations had deeply or sincerely regretted their inability to trace, etc., something gave way within her and all sensation—save of thankfulness for the release—came to an end in blessed passivity. Michael had died and her world had stood still and she had been one with the full shock of that arrest. Now she was standing still and the world was going forward, but it did not concern her—in no way or relation did it touch her. She knew this by the ease with which she could slip Michael's name into talk and incline her head to the proper angle, at the proper murmur of sympathy.

In the blessed realization of that relief, the Armistice with all its bells broke over her and passed unheeded. At the end of another year she had overcome her physical loathing of the living and returned young, so that she could take them by the hand and almost sincerely wish them well. She had no interest in any aftermath, national or personal, of the war, but, moving at an immense distance, she sat on various relief committees and held strong views—she heard herself delivering them—about the site of the proposed village War Memorial.

Then there came to her, as next of kin, an official intimation, backed by a page of a letter to her in indelible pencil, a silver identity-disc, and a watch, to the effect that the body of Lieutenant Michael Turrell had been found, identified, and reinterred in Hagenzeele Third Military Cemetery—the letter of the row and the grave's number in that row duly given.

So Helen found herself moved on to another process of the manufacture—to a world full of exultant or broken relatives, now strong in the certainty that there was an altar upon earth where they might lay their love. These soon told her, and by means of time-tables made clear, how easy it was and how little it interfered with life's affairs to go and see one's grave.

'*So* different,' as the Rector's wife said, 'if he'd been killed in Mesopotamia, or even Gallipoli.'

The agony of being waked up to some sort of second life drove Helen across the Channel, where, in a new world of abbreviated titles, she learnt that Hagenzeele Third could be comfortably reached by an afternoon train which fitted in with the morning boat, and that there was a comfortable little hotel not three kilometres from Hagenzeele itself, where one could spend quite a comfortable night and see one's grave next morning. All this she had from a Central Authority who lived in a board and tar-paper shed on the skirts of a razed city full of whirling lime-dust and blown papers.

'By the way,' said he, 'you know your grave, of course?'

'Yes, thank you,' said Helen, and showed its row and number typed on Michael's own little typewriter. The officer would have checked it, out of one of his many books; but a large Lancashire woman thrust between them and bade him tell her where she might find her son, who had been corporal in the A.S.C. His proper name, she sobbed, was Anderson, but, coming of respectable folk he had of course enlisted under the name of Smith; and had been killed at Dickiebush, in early 'Fifteen. She had not his number nor did she know which of his two Christian names he might have used with his alias; but her Cook's tourist ticket expired at the end of Easter week, and if by then she could not find her child she should go mad. Whereupon she fell forward on Helen's breast; but the officer's wife came out quickly from a little bedroom behind the office, and the three of them lifted the woman on to the cot.

'They are often like this,' said the officer's wife, loosening the tight bonnet-strings. 'Yesterday she said he'd been killed at Hooge. Are you sure you know your grave? It makes such a difference.'

'Yes, thank you,' said Helen, and hurried out before the woman on the bed should begin to lament again.

Tea in a crowded mauve and blue striped wooden structure, with a false front, carried her still further into the nightmare. She paid her bill beside a stolid, plain-featured Englishwoman, who, hearing her inquire about the train to Hagenzeele, volunteered to come with her.

'I'm going to Hagenzeele myself,' she explained. 'Not to Hagenzeele Third; mine is Sugar Factory, but they call it La Rosière now. It's just south of Hagenzeele Three. Have you got your room at the hotel there?'

'Oh yes, thank you. I've wired.'

'That's better. Sometimes the place is quite full, and at others there's hardly a soul. But they've put bathrooms into the old Lion d'Or—that's the hotel on the west side of Sugar Factory—and it draws off a lot of people, luckily.'

'It's all new to me. This is the first time I've been over.'

'Indeed! This is my ninth time since the Armistice. Not on my own account. *I* haven't lost anyone, thank God—but, like everyone else, I've a lot of friends at home who have. Coming over as often as I do, I find it helps them to have someone just look at the —the place and tell them about it afterwards. And one can take photos for them, too. I get quite a list of commissions to execute.' She laughed nervously and tapped her slung Kodak. 'There are two or three to see at Sugar Factory this time, and plenty of others in the cemeteries all about. My system is to save them up, and arrange them, you know. And when I've got enough commissions for one area to make it worth while, I pop over and execute them. It *does* comfort people.'

'I suppose so,' Helen answered, shivering as they entered the little train.

'Of course it does. (Isn't it lucky we've got window-seats?) It must do or they wouldn't ask one to do it, would they? I've a list of quite twelve or fifteen commissions here'—she tapped the Kodak again—'I must sort them out tonight. Oh, I forgot to ask you. What's yours?'

'My nephew,' said Helen. 'But I was very fond of him.'

'Ah, yes! I sometimes wonder whether *they* know after death? What do you think?'

'Oh, I don't—I haven't dared to think much about that sort of thing,' said Helen, almost lifting her hands to keep her off.

'Perhaps that's better,' the woman answered. 'The sense of loss must be enough, I expect. Well, I won't worry you any more.'

Helen was grateful, but when they reached the hotel Mrs Scarsworth (they had exchanged names) insisted on dining at the same table with her, and after the meal, in the little, hideous salon full of low-voiced relatives, took Helen through her 'commissions' with biographies of the dead, where she happened to know them, and sketches of their next of kin. Helen endured till nearly half-past nine, ere she fled to her room.

Almost at once there was a knock at her door and Mrs Scarsworth entered; her hands, holding the dreadful list, clasped before her.

'Yes—yes—*I* know,' she began. 'You're sick of me, but I want to tell you something. You—you aren't married, are you? Then perhaps you won't . . . But it doesn't matter. I've *got* to tell someone. I can't go on any longer like this.'

'But please——' Mrs Scarsworth had backed against the shut door, and her mouth worked dryly.

'In a minute,' she said. 'You—you know about these graves of mine I was telling you about downstairs, just now? They really *are* commissions. At least several of them are.' Her eye wandered round the room. 'What extraordinary wall-papers they have in

Belgium, don't you think? ... Yes. I swear they are commissions.
But there's *one*, d'you see, and—and he was more to me than any-
thing else in the world. Do you understand?'

Helen nodded.

'More than anyone else. And, of course, he oughtn't to have
been. He ought to have been nothing to me. But he *was*. He *is*.
That's why I do the commissions, you see. That's all.'

'But why do you tell me?' Helen asked desperately.

'Because I'm *so* tired of lying. Tired of lying—always lying—
year in and year out. When I don't tell lies I've got to act 'em and
I've got to think 'em, always. *You* don't know what that means.
He was everything to me that he oughtn't to have been—the one
real thing—the only thing that ever happened to me in all my life;
and I've had to pretend he wasn't. I've had to watch every word
I said, and think out what lie I'd tell next, for years and years!'

'How many years?' Helen asked.

'Six years and four months before, and two and three-quarters
after. I've gone to him eight times, since. Tomorrow'll make the
ninth, and—and I can't—I *can't* go to him again with nobody in
the world knowing. I want to be honest with someone before I go.
Do you understand? It doesn't matter about *me*. I was never
truthful, even as a girl. But it isn't worthy of *him*. So—so I—I had
to tell you. I can't keep it up any longer. Oh, I can't!'

She lifted her joined hands almost to the level of her mouth,
and brought them down sharply, still joined, to full arms' length
below her waist. Helen reached forward, caught them, bowed her
head over them, and murmured: 'Oh, my dear! My dear!' Mrs
Scarsworth stepped back, her face all mottled.

'My God!' said she. 'Is *that* how you take it?'

Helen could not speak, and the woman went out; but it was a
long while before Helen was able to sleep.

Next morning Mrs Scarsworth left early on her round of com-
missions, and Helen walked alone to Hagenzeele Third. The
place was still in the making, and stood some five or six feet above
the metalled road, which it flanked for hundreds of yards. Cul-
verts across a deep ditch served for entrances through the
unfinished boundary wall. She climbed a few wooden-faced
earthen steps and then met the entire crowded level of the thing
in one held breath. She did not know that Hagenzeele Third
counted twenty-one thousand dead already. All she saw was a
merciless sea of black crosses, bearing little strips of stamped tin
at all angles across their faces. She could distinguish no order or
arrangement in their mass; nothing but a waist-high wilderness as
of weeds stricken dead, rushing at her. She went forward, moved

to the left and the right hopelessly, wondering by what guidance she should ever come to her own. A great distance away there was a line of whiteness. It proved to be a block of some two or three hundred graves whose headstones had already been set, whose flowers were planted out, and whose new-sown grass showed green. Here she could see clear-cut letters at the ends of the rows, and, referring to her slip, realized that it was not here she must look.

A man knelt behind a line of headstones—evidently a gardener, for he was firming a young plant in the soft earth. She went towards him, her paper in her hand. He rose at her approach and without prelude or salutation asked: 'Who are you looking for?'

'Lieutenant Michael Turrell—my nephew,' said Helen slowly, and word for word, as she had many thousands of times in her life.

The man lifted his eyes and looked at her with infinite compassion before he turned from the fresh-sown grass toward the naked black crosses.

'Come with me,' he said, 'and I will show you where your son lies.'

When Helen left the Cemetery she turned for a last look. In the distance she saw the man bending over his young plants; and she went away, supposing him to be the gardener.

1926

# The Eye Of Allah

THE Cantor of St Illod's being far too enthusiastic a musician to concern himself with its Library, the Sub-Cantor, who idolized every detail of the work, was tidying up, after two hours' writing and dictation in the Scriptorium. The copying-monks handed him in their sheets—it was a plain Four Gospels ordered by an Abbot at Evesham—and filed out to vespers. John Otho, better known as John of Burgos, took no heed. He was burnishing a tiny boss of gold in his miniature of the Annunciation for his Gospel of St Luke, which it was hoped that Cardinal Falcodi, the Papal Legate, might later be pleased to accept.

'Break off, John,' said the Sub-Cantor in an undertone.

'Eh? Gone, have they? I never heard. Hold a minute, Clement.'

The Sub-Cantor waited patiently. He had known John more than a dozen years, coming and going at St Illod's, to which monastery John, when abroad, always said he belonged. The claim was gladly allowed, for, more even than other Fitz Othos, he seemed to carry all the Arts under his hand, and most of their practical receipts under his hood.

The Sub-Cantor looked over his shoulder at the pinned-down sheet where the first words of the Magnificat were built up in gold washed with red-lac for a background to the Virgin's hardly yet fired halo. She was shown, hands joined in wonder, at a lattice of infinitely intricate arabesque, round the edges of which sprays of orange-bloom seemed to load the blue hot air that carried back over the minute parched landscape in the middle distance.

'You've made her all Jewess,' said the Sub-Cantor, studying the olive-flushed cheek and the eyes charged with foreknowledge.

'What else was Our Lady?' John slipped out the pins. 'Listen, Clement. If I do not come back, this goes into my Great Luke, whoever finishes it.' He slid the drawing between its guard-papers.

'Then you're for Burgos again—as I heard?'

'In two days. The new Cathedral yonder—but they're slower than the Wrath of God, those masons—is good for the soul.'

'*Thy* soul?' The Sub-Cantor seemed doubtful.

'Even mine, by your permission. And down south—on the edge of the Conquered Countries—Granada way—there's some Moorish diaper-work that's wholesome. It allays vain thought and draws it toward the picture—as you felt, just now, in my Annunciation.'

'She—it was very beautiful. No wonder you go. But you'll not forget your absolution, John?'

'Surely.' This was a precaution John no more omitted on the

eve of his travels than he did the recutting of the tonsure which he had provided himself with in his youth, somewhere near Ghent. The mark gave him privilege of clergy at a pinch, and a certain consideration on the road always.

'You'll not forget, either, what we need in the Scriptorium. There's no more true ultramarine in this world now. They mix it with that German blue. And as for vermilion——'

'I'll do my best always.'

'And Brother Thomas' (this was the Infirmarian in charge of the monastery hospital) 'he needs——'

'He'll do his own asking. I'll go over his side now, and get me re-tonsured.'

John went down the stairs to the lane that divides the hospital and cookhouse from the back-cloisters. While he was being barbered, Brother Thomas (St Illod's meek but deadly persistent infirmarian) gave him a list of drugs that he was to bring back from Spain by hook, crook, or lawful purchase. Here they were surprised by the lame, dark Abbot Stephen, in his fur-lined night-boots. Not that Stephen de Sautré was any spy; but as a young man he had shared an unlucky Crusade, which had ended, after a battle at Mansura, in two years' captivity among the Saracens at Cairo where men learn to walk softly. A fair huntsman and hawker, a reasonable disciplinarian, but a man of science above all, and a Doctor of Medicine under one Ranulphus, Canon of St Paul's, his heart was more in the monastery's hospital work than its religious. He checked their list interestedly, adding items of his own. After the Infirmarian had withdrawn, he gave John generous absolution, to cover lapses by the way; for he did not hold with chance-bought Indulgences.

'And what seek you *this* journey?' he demanded, sitting on the bench beside the mortar and scales in the little warm cell for stored drugs.

'Devils, mostly,' said John, grinning.

'In Spain? Are not Abana and Pharpar——?'

John, to whom men were but matter for drawings, and well-born to boot (since he was a de Sanford on his mother's side), looked the Abbot full in the face and—'Did *you* find it so?' said he.

'No. They were in Cairo too. But what's your special need of 'em?'

'For my Great Luke. He's the master-hand of all Four when it comes to devils.'

'No wonder. He was a physician. You're not.'

'Heaven forbid! But I'm weary of our Church-pattern devils. They're only apes and goats and poultry conjoined. 'Good

enough for plain red-and-black Hells and Judgment Days—but
not for me.'

'What makes you so choice in them?'

'Because it stands to reason and Art that there are all musters
of devils in Hell's dealing. Those Seven, for example, that were
haled out of the Magdalene. They'd be she-devils—no kin at all
to the beaked and horned and bearded devils-general.'

The Abbot laughed.

'And see again! The devil that came out of the dumb man.
What use is snout or bill to *him*? He'd be faceless as a leper.
Above all—God send I live to do it!—the devils that entered the
Gadarene swine. They'd be—they'd be—I know not yet what
they'd be, but they'd be surpassing devils. I'd have 'em diverse as
the Saints themselves. But now, they're all one pattern, for wall,
window, or picture-work.'

'Go on, John. You're deeper in this mystery than I.'

'Heaven forbid! But I say there's respect due to devils, damned
tho' they be.'

'Dangerous doctrine.'

'My meaning is that if the shape of anything be worth man's
thought to picture to man, it's worth his best thought.'

'That's safer. But I'm glad I've given you Absolution.'

'There's less risk for a craftsman who deals with the outside
shapes of things—for Mother Church's glory.'

'Maybe so, but, John'—the Abbot's hand almost touched
John's sleeve—'tell me, now, is—is she Moorish or—or Hebrew?'

'She's mine,' John returned.

'Is that enough?'

'I have found it so.'

'Well—ah well! It's out of my jurisdiction, but—how do they
look at it down yonder?'

'Oh, they drive nothing to a head in Spain—neither Church nor
King, bless them! There's too many Moors and Jews to kill them
all, and if they chased 'em away there'd be no trade nor farming.
Trust me, in the Conquered Countries, from Seville to Granada,
we live lovingly enough together—Spaniard, Moor, and Jew.
Ye see, *we* ask no questions.'

'Yes—yes,' Stephen sighed. 'And always there's the hope she
may be converted.'

'Oh yes, there's always hope.'

The Abbot went on into the hospital. It was an easy age before
Rome tightened the screw as to clerical connections. If the lady
were not too forward, or the son too much his father's beneficiary
in ecclesiastical preferments and levies, a good deal was over-
looked. But, as the Abbot had reason to recall, unions between

Christian and Infidel led to sorrow. None the less, when John with mule, mails, and man, clattered off down the lane for Southampton and the sea, Stephen envied him.

He was back, twenty months later, in good hard case, and loaded down with fairings. A lump of richest lazuli, a bar of orange-hearted vermilion, and a small packet of dried beetles which make most glorious scarlet, for the Sub-Cantor. Besides that, a few cubes of milky marble, with yet a pink flush in them, which could be slaked and ground down to incomparable background-stuff. There were quite half the drugs that the Abbot and Thomas had demanded, and there was a long deep-red cornelian necklace for the Abbot's Lady—Anne of Norton. She received it graciously, and asked where John had come by it.

'Near Granada,' he said.

'You left all well there?' Anne asked. (Maybe the Abbot had told her something of John's confession.)

'I left all in the hands of God.'

'Ah me! How long since?'

'Four months less eleven days.'

'Were you—with her?'

'In my arms. Childbed.'

'And?'

'The boy too. There is nothing now.'

Anne of Norton caught her breath.

'I think you'll be glad of that,' she said after a while.

'Give me time, and maybe I'll compass it. But not now.'

'You have your handiwork and your art, and—John—remember there's no jealousy in the grave.'

'Ye-es! I have my Art, and Heaven knows I'm jealous of none.'

'Thank God for that at least,' said Anne of Norton, the always ailing woman who followed the Abbot with her sunk eyes. 'And be sure I shall treasure this'—she touched the beads—'as long as I shall live.'

'I brought—trusted—it to you for that,' he replied, and took leave. When she told the Abbot how she had come by it, he said nothing, but as he and Thomas were storing the drugs that John handed over in the cell which backs on to the hospital kitchen-chimney, he observed, of a cake of dried poppy-juice: 'This has power to cut off all pain from a man's body.'

'I have seen it,' said John.

'But for pain of the soul there is, outside God's Grace, but one drug; and that is a man's craft, learning, or other helpful motion of his own mind.'

'That is coming to me, too,' was the answer.

John spent the next fair May day out in the woods with the monastery swineherd and all the porkers; and returned loaded with flowers and sprays of spring, to his own carefully kept place in the north bay of the Scriptorium. There, with his travelling sketch-books under his left elbow, he sunk himself past all recollections in his Great Luke.

Brother Martin, Senior Copyist (who spoke about once a fortnight), ventured to ask, later, how the work was going.

'All here!' John tapped his forehead with his pencil. 'It has been only waiting these months to—ah God!—be born. Are ye free of your plain-copying, Martin?'

Brother Martin nodded. It was his pride that John of Burgos turned to him, in spite of his seventy years, for really good pagework.

'Then see!' John laid out a new vellum—thin but flawless. 'There's no better than this sheet from here to Paris. Yes! Smell it if you choose. Wherefore—give me the compasses and I'll set it out for you—if ye make one letter lighter or darker than its next, I'll stick ye like a pig.'

'Never, John!' The old man beamed happily.

'But I will! Now, follow! Here and here, as I prick, and in script of just this height to the hair's-breadth, ye'll scribe the thirty-first and thirty-second verses of Eighth Luke.'

'Yes, the Gadarene Swine! "*And they besought him that he would not command them to go out into the abyss. And there was a herd of many swine*"'—— Brother Martin naturally knew all the Gospels by heart.

'Just so! Down to "*and he suffered them*". Take your time to it. My Magdalene has to come off my heart first.'

Brother Martin achieved the work so perfectly that John stole some soft sweetmeats from the Abbot's kitchen for his reward. The old man ate them; then repented; then confessed and insisted on penance. At which, the Abbot, knowing there was but one way to reach the real sinner, set him a book called *De Virtutibus Herbarum* to fair-copy. St Illod's had borrowed it from the gloomy Cistercians, who do not hold with pretty things, and the crabbed text kept Martin busy just when John wanted him for some rather specially spaced letterings.

'See now,' said the Sub-Cantor improvingly. 'You should not do such things, John. Here's Brother Martin on penance for your sake——'

'No—for my Great Luke. But I've paid the Abbot's cook. I've drawn him till his own scullions cannot keep straight-faced. *He*'ll not tell again.'

'Unkindly done! And you're out of favour with the Abbot too.

He's made no sign to you since you came back—never asked you to high table.'

'I've been busy. Having eyes in his head, Stephen knew it. Clement, there's no Librarian from Durham to Torre fit to clean up after you.'

The Sub-Cantor stood on guard; he knew where John's compliments generally ended.

'But outside the Scriptorium——'

'Where I never go,' The Sub-Cantor had been excused even digging in the garden, lest it should mar his wonderful book-binding hands.

'In all things outside the Scriptorium you are the master-fool of Christendie. Take it from me, Clement. I've met many.'

'I take everything from you,' Clement smiled benignly. 'You use me worse than a singing-boy.'

They could hear one of that suffering breed in the cloister below, squalling as the Cantor pulled his hair.

'God love you! So I do! But have you ever thought how I lie and steal daily on my travels—yes, and for aught you know, murder—to fetch you colours and earths?'

'True,' said just and conscience-stricken Clement. 'I have often thought that were I in the world—which God forbid!—I might be a strong thief in some matters.'

Even Brother Martin, bent above his loathed *De Virtutibus*, laughed.

But about mid-summer, Thomas the Infirmarian conveyed to John the Abbot's invitation to supper in his house that night, with the request that he would bring with him anything that he had done for his Great Luke.

'What's toward?' said John, who had been wholly shut up in his work.

'Only one of his "wisdom" dinners. You've sat at a few since you were a man.'

'True: and mostly good. How would Stephen have us——?'

'Gown and hood over all. There will be a doctor from Salerno —one Roger, an Italian. Wise and famous with the knife on the body. He's been in the Infirmary some ten days, helping me— even me!'

''Never heard the name. But our Stephen's *physicus* before *sacerdos*, always.'

'And his Lady has a sickness of some time. Roger came hither in chief because of her.'

'Did he? Now I think of it, I have not seen the Lady Anne for a while.'

'Ye've seen nothing for a long while. She has been housed near a month—they have to carry her abroad now.'

'So bad as that, then?'

'Roger of Salerno will not yet say what he thinks. But——'

'God pity Stephen! . . . Who else at table, besides thee?'

'An Oxford friar. Roger is his name also. A learned and famous philosopher. And he holds his liquor too, valiantly.'

'Three doctors—counting Stephen. I've always found that means two atheists.'

Thomas looked uneasily down his nose. 'That's a wicked proverb,' he stammered. 'You should not use it.'

'Hoh! Never come you the monk over me, Thomas! You've been Infirmarian at St Illod's eleven years—and a lay-brother still. Why have you never taken orders, all this while?'

'I—I am not worthy.'

'Ten times worthier than that new fat swine—Henry Who's-his-name—that takes the Infirmary Masses. He bullocks in with the Viaticum, under your nose, when a sick man's only faint from being bled. So the man dies—of pure fear. Ye know it! I've watched your face at such times. Take Orders, Didymus. You'll have a little more medicine and a little less Mass with your sick then; and they'll live longer.'

'I am unworthy—unworthy,' Thomas repeated pitifully.

'Not you—but—to your own master you stand or fall. And now that my work releases me for awhile, I'll drink with any philosopher out of any school. And, Thomas,' he coaxed, 'a hot bath for me in the infirmary before vespers.'

When the Abbot's perfectly cooked and served meal had ended, and the deep-fringed naperies were removed, and the Prior had sent in the keys with word that all was fast in the Monastery, and the keys had been duly returned with the word, 'Make it so till Prime', the Abbot and his guests went out to cool themselves in an upper cloister that took them, by way of the leads, to the South Choir side of the Triforium. The summer sun was still strong, for it was barely six o'clock, but the Abbey Church, of course, lay in her wonted darkness. Lights were being lit for choir-practice thirty feet below.

'Our Cantor gives them no rest,' the Abbot whispered. 'Stand by this pillar and we'll hear what he's driving them at now.'

'Remember, all!' the Cantor's hard voice came up. 'This is the soul of Bernard himself, attacking our evil world. Take it quicker than yesterday, and throw all your words clean-bitten from you. In the loft there! Begin!'

The organ broke out for an instant, alone and raging. Then the voices crashed together into that first fierce line of the '*De Contemptu Mundi.*'[1]

'*Hora novissima—tempora pessima*'—a dead pause till the assenting *sunt* broke, like a sob, out of the darkness, and one boy's voice, clearer than silver trumpets, returned the long-drawn *vigilemus.*

'*Ecce minaciter, imminet Arbiter*' (organ and voices were leashed together in terror and warning, breaking away liquidly to the '*ille supremus*'). Then the tone-colours shifted for the prelude to—'*Imminet, imminet, ut mala terminet——*'

'Stop! Again!' cried the Cantor; and gave his reasons a little more roundly than was natural at choir-practice.

'Ah! Pity o' man's vanity! He's guessed we are here. Come away!' said the Abbot. Anne of Norton, in her carried chair, had been listening too, further along the dark Triforium, with Roger of Salerno. John heard her sob. On the way back, he asked Thomas how her health stood. Before Thomas could reply the sharp-featured Italian doctor pushed between them. 'Following on our talk together, I judged it best to tell her,' said he to Thomas.

'What?' John asked simply enough.

'What she knew already.' Roger of Salerno launched into a Greek quotation to the effect that every woman knows all about everything.

'I have no Greek,' said John stiffly. Roger of Salerno had been giving them a good deal of it, at dinner.

'Then I'll come to you in Latin. Ovid hath it neatly. "*Utque malum late solet immedicabile cancer——*" but doubtless you know the rest, worthy Sir.'

'Alas! My school-Latin's but what I've gathered by the way from fools professing to heal sick women. "*Hocus-pocus——*" but doubtless you know the rest, worthy Sir.'

Roger of Salerno was quite quiet till they regained the dining-room, where the fire had been comforted and the dates, raisins, ginger, figs, and cinnamon-scented sweetmeats set out, with the choicer wines, on the after-table. The Abbot seated himself, drew off his ring, dropped it, that all might hear the tinkle, into an empty silver cup, stretched his feet towards the hearth, and looked at the great gilt and carved rose in the barrel-roof. The silence that keeps from Compline to Matins had closed on their world. The bull-necked Friar watched a ray of sunlight split itself into colours on the rim of a crystal salt-cellar; Roger of Salerno had re-opened some discussion with Brother Thomas on a type of spotted fever that was baffling them both in England and abroad;

[1] Hymn No. 226, A. and M., 'The world is very evil.'

John took note of the keen profile, and—it might serve as a note for the Great Luke—his hand moved to his bosom. The Abbot saw, and nodded permission. John whipped out silver-point and sketchbook.

'Nay—modesty is good enough—but deliver your own opinion,' the Italian was urging the Infirmarian. Out of courtesy to the foreigner nearly all the talk was in table-Latin; more formal and more copious than monk's patter. Thomas began with his meek stammer.

'I confess myself at a loss for the cause of the fever unless—as Varro saith in his *De Re Rustica*—certain small animals which the eye cannot follow enter the body by the nose and mouth, and set up grave diseases. On the other hand, this is not in Scripture.'

Roger of Salerno hunched head and shoulders like an angry cat. 'Always *that*!' he said, and John snatched down the twist of the thin lips.

'Never at rest, John.' The Abbot smiled at the artist. 'You should break off every two hours for prayers, as we do. St Benedict was no fool. Two hours is all that a man can carry the edge of his eye or hand.'

'For copyists—yes. Brother Martin is not sure after one hour. But when a man's work takes him, he must go on till it lets him go.'

'Yes, that is the Demon of Socrates,' the Friar from Oxford rumbled above his cup.

'The doctrine leans toward presumption,' said the Abbot. 'Remember, "Shall mortal man be more just than his Maker?"'

'There is no danger of justice'; the Friar spoke bitterly. 'But at least Man might be suffered to go forward in his Art or his thought. Yet if Mother Church sees or hears him move anyward, what says she? "No!" Always "No".'

'But if the little animals of Varro be invisible'—this was Roger of Salerno to Thomas—'how are we any nearer to a cure?'

'By experiment'—the Friar wheeled round on them suddenly. 'By reason and experiment. The one is useless without the other. But Mother Church——'

'Ay!' Roger de Salerno dashed at the fresh bait like a pike. 'Listen, Sirs. Her bishops—our Princes—strew our roads in Italy with carcasses that they make for their pleasure or wrath. Beautiful corpses! Yet if I—if we doctors—so much as raise the skin of one of them to look at God's fabric beneath, what says Mother Church? "Sacrilege! Stick to your pigs and dogs, or you burn!".'

'And not Mother Church only!' the Friar chimed in. '*Every* way we are barred—barred by the words of some man, dead a thousand years, which are held final. Who is any son of Adam that his one say-so should close a door towards truth? I would not except even Peter Peregrinus, my own great teacher.'

'Nor I Paul of Aegina,' Roger of Salerno cried. 'Listen, Sirs! Here is a case to the very point. Apuleius affirmeth, if a man eat fasting of the juice of the cut-leaved buttercup—*sceleratus* we call it, which means "rascally"'—this with a condescending nod towards John—'his soul will leave his body laughing. Now this is the lie more dangerous than truth, since truth of a sort is in it.'

'He's away!' whispered the Abbot despairingly.

'For the juice of that herb, I know by experiment, burns, blisters, and wries the mouth. I know also the *rictus*, or pseudo-laughter, on the face of such as have perished by the strong poisons of herbs allied to this ranunculus. Certainly that spasm resembled laughter. It seems then, in my judgment, that Apuleius, having seen the body of one thus poisoned, went off at score and wrote that the man died laughing.'

'Neither staying to observe, nor to confirm observation by experiment,' added the Friar, frowning.

Stephen the Abbot cocked an eyebrow toward John.

'How think *you*?' said he.

'I'm no doctor,' John returned, 'but I'd say Apuleius in all these years might have been betrayed by his copyists. They take short-cuts to save 'emselves trouble. Put case that Apuleius wrote the soul *seems to* leave the body laughing, after this poison. There's not three copyists in five (*my* judgment) would not leave out the "seems to". For who'd question Apuleius? If it seemed so to him, so it must be. Otherwise any child knows cut-leaved buttercup.'

'Have you knowledge of herbs?' Roger of Salerno asked curtly.

'Only that, when I was a boy in convent, I've made tetters round my mouth and on my neck with buttercup-juice, to save going to prayer o' cold nights.'

'Ah! said Roger. 'I profess no knowledge of tricks.' He turned aside, stiffly.

'No matter! Now for your own tricks, John,' the tactful Abbot broke in. 'You shall show the doctors your Magdalene and your Gadarene Swine and the devils.'

'Devils? Devils? *I* have produced devils by means of drugs; and have abolished them by the same means. Whether devils be external to mankind or immanent, I have not yet pronounced.' Roger of Salerno was still angry.

'Ye dare not,' snapped the Friar from Oxford. 'Mother Church makes Her own devils.'

'Not wholly! Our John has come back from Spain with brand-new ones.' Abbot Stephen took the vellum handed to him, and laid it tenderly on the table. They gathered to look. The Magdalene was drawn in palest, almost transparent, grisaille, against a raging, swaying background of woman-faced devils, each broke to and by her special sin, and each, one could see, frenziedly straining against the Power that compelled her.

'I've never seen the like of this grey shadow-work,' said the Abbot. 'How came you by it?'

'*Non nobis!* It came to me,' said John, not knowing he was a generation or so ahead of his time in the use of that medium.

'Why is she so pale?' the Friar demanded.

'Evil has all come out of her—she'd take any colour now.'

'Ay, like light through glass. *I* see.'

Roger of Salerno was looking in silence—his nose nearer and nearer the page. 'It is so,' he pronounced finally. 'Thus it is in epilepsy—mouth, eyes, and forehead—even to the droop of her wrist there. Every sign of it! She will need restoratives, that woman, and, afterwards, sleep natural. No poppy-juice, or she will vomit on her waking. And thereafter—but I am not in my Schools.' He drew himself up. 'Sir,' said he, 'you should be of Our calling. For, by the Snakes of Aesculapius, you *see*!'

The two struck hands as equals.

'And how think you of the Seven Devils?' the Abbot went on.

These melted into convoluted flower- or flame-like bodies, ranging in colour from phosphorescent green to the black purple of outworn iniquity, whose hearts could be traced beating through their substance. But, for sign of hope and the sane workings of life, to be regained, the deep border was of conventionalized spring flowers and birds, all crowned by a kingfisher in haste, atilt through a clump of yellow iris.

Roger of Salerno identified the herbs and spoke largely of their virtues.

'And now, the Gadarene Swine,' said Stephen. John laid the picture on the table.

Here were devils dishoused, in dread of being abolished to the Void, huddling and hurtling together to force lodgment by every opening into the brute bodies offered. Some of the swine fought the invasion, foaming and jerking; some were surrendering to it, sleepily, as to a luxurious back-scratching; others, wholly possessed, whirled off in bucking droves for the lake beneath. In one corner the freed man stretched out his limbs all restored to his control, and Our Lord, seated, looked at him as questioning what he would make of his deliverance.

'Devils indeed!' was the Friar's comment. 'But wholly a new sort.'

Some devils were mere lumps, with lobes and protuberances—
a hint of a fiend's face peering through jelly-like walls. And there
was a family of impatient, globular devillings who had burst open
the belly of their smirking parent, and were revolving desperately
toward their prey. Others patterned themselves into rods, chains
and ladders, single or conjoined, round the throat and jaws of a
shrieking sow, from whose ear emerged the lashing, glassy tail of
a devil that had made good his refuge. And there were granulated
and conglomerate devils, mixed up with the foam and slaver
where the attack was fiercest. Thence the eye carried on to the
insanely active backs of the downward-racing swine, the swine-
herd's aghast face, and his dog's terror.

Said Roger of Salerno, 'I pronounce that these were begotten
of drugs. They stand outside the rational mind.'

'Not these,' said Thomas the Infirmarian, who as a servant of
the Monastery should have asked his Abbot's leave to speak.
'Not *these*—look!—in the bordure.'

The border to the picture was a diaper of irregular but balanced
compartments or cellules, where sat, swam, or weltered, devils in
blank, so to say—things as yet uninspired by Evil—indifferent,
but lawlessly outside imagination. Their shapes resembled, again,
ladders, chains, scourges, diamonds, aborted buds, or gravid
phosphorescent globes—some well-nigh star-like.

Roger of Salerno compared them to the obsessions of a
Churchman's mind.

'Malignant?' the Friar from Oxford questioned.

'"Count everything unknown for horrible,"' Roger quoted
with scorn.

'Not I. But they are marvellous—marvellous. I think——'

The Friar drew back. Thomas edged in to see better, and half
opened his mouth.

'Speak,' said Stephen, who had been watching him. 'We are
all in a sort doctors here.'

'I would say then'—Thomas rushed at it as one putting out his
life's belief at the stake—'that these lower shapes in the bordure
may not be so much hellish and malignant as models and patterns
upon which John has tricked out and embellished his proper
devils among the swine above there!'

'And that would signify?' said Roger of Salerno sharply.

'In my poor judgment, that he may have seen such shapes—
without help of drugs.'

'Now who—*who*,' said John of Burgos, after a round and
unregarded oath, 'has made thee so wise of a sudden, my
Doubter?'

'I wise? God forbid! Only John, remember—one winter six

years ago—the snow-flakes melting on your sleeve at the cook-house-door. You showed me them through a little crystal, that made small things larger.'

'Yes. The Moors call such a glass the Eye of Allah,' John confirmed.

'You showed me them melting—six-sided. You called them, then, your patterns.'

'True. Snow-flakes melt six-sided. I have used them for diaper-work often.'

'Melting snowflakes as seen through a glass? By art optical?' the Friar asked.

'Art optical? *I* have never heard!' Roger of Salerno cried.

'John,' said the Abbot of St Illod's commandingly, 'was it—is it so?'

'In some sort,' John replied, 'Thomas has the right of it. Those shapes in the bordure were my workshop-patterns for the devils above. In *my* craft, Salerno, we dare not drug. It kills hand and eye. My shapes are to be seen honestly, in nature.'

The Abbot drew a bowl of rose-water towards him. 'When I was prisoner with—with the Saracens after Mansura,' he began, turning up the fold of his long sleeve, 'there were certain magi-cians—physicians—who could show—' he dipped his third finger delicately in the water—'all the firmament of Hell, as it were, in —' he shook off one drop from his polished nail on to the polished table—'even such a supernaculum as this.'

'But it must be foul water—not clean,' said John.

'Show us then—all—all,' said Stephen. 'I would make sure—once more.' The Abbot's voice was official.

John drew from his bosom a stamped leather box, some six or eight inches long, wherein, bedded on faded velvet, lay what looked like silver-bound compasses of old box-wood, with a screw at the head which opened or closed the legs to minute fractions. The legs terminated, not in points, but spoon-shapedly, one spatula pierced with a metal-lined hole less than a quarter of an inch across, the other with a half-inch hole. Into this latter John, after carefully wiping with a silk rag, slipped a metal cylinder that carried glass or crystal, it seemed, at each end.

'Ah! Art optic!' said the Friar. 'But what is that beneath it?'

It was a small swivelling sheet of polished silver no bigger than a florin, which caught the light and concentrated it on the lesser hole. John adjusted it without the Friar's proffered help.

'And now to find a drop of water,' said he, picking up a small brush.

'Come to my upper cloister. The sun is on the leads still,' said the Abbot, rising.

They followed him there. Half-way along, a drip from a gutter had made a greenish puddle in a worn stone. Very carefully, John dropped a drop of it into the smaller hole of the compass-leg, and, steadying the apparatus on a coping, worked the screw in the compass-joint, screwed the cylinder, and swung the swivel of the mirror till he was satisfied.

'Good!' He peered through the thing. 'My Shapes are all here. Now look, Father! If they do not meet your eye at first, turn this nicked edge here, left- or right-handed.'

'I have not forgotten,' said the Abbot, taking his place. 'Yes! They are here—as they were in my time—my time past. There is no end to them, I was told. . . . There *is* no end!'

'The light will go. Oh, let me look! Suffer me to see, also!' the Friar pleaded, almost shouldering Stephen from the eye-piece. The Abbot gave way. His eyes were on time past. But the Friar, instead of looking, turned the apparatus in his capable hands.

'Nay, nay,' John interrupted, for the man was already fiddling at the screws. 'Let the Doctor see.'

Roger of Salerno looked, minute after minute. John saw his blue-veined cheek-bones turn white. He stepped back at last, as though stricken.

'It is a new world—a new world, and—Oh, God Unjust!—I am old!'

'And now Thomas,' Stephen ordered.

John manipulated the tube for the Infirmarian, whose hands shook, and he too looked long. 'It is Life,' he said presently in a breaking voice. 'No Hell! Life created and rejoicing—the work of the Creator. They live, even as I have dreamed. Then it was no sin for me to dream. No sin—O God—no sin!'

He flung himself on his knees and began hysterically the *Benedicite omnia Opera*.

'And now I will see how it is actuated,' said the Friar from Oxford, thrusting forward again.

'Bring it within. The place is all eyes and ears,' said Stephen.

They walked quietly back along the leads, three English counties laid out in evening sunshine around them; church upon church, monastery upon monastery, cell after cell, and the bulk of a vast cathedral moored on the edge of the banked shoals of sunset.

When they were at the after-table once more they sat down, all except the Friar, who went to the window and huddled bat-like over the thing. 'I see! I see!' he was repeating to himself.

'He'll not hurt it,' said John. But the Abbot, staring in front of him, like Roger of Salerno, did not hear. The Infirmarian's head was on the table between his shaking arms.

John reached for a cup of wine.

'It was shown to me,' the Abbot was speaking to himself, 'in Cairo, that man stands ever between two infinities—of greatness and littleness. Therefore, there is no end—either to life—or——'

'And *I* stand on the edge of the grave,' snarled Roger of Salerno. 'Who pities *me*?'

'Hush!' said Thomas the Infirmarian. 'The little creatures shall be sanctified—sanctified to the service of His sick.'

'What need?' John of Burgos wiped his lips. 'It shows no more than the shapes of things. It gives good pictures. I had it at Granada. It was brought from the East, they told me.'

Roger of Salerno laughed with an old man's malice. 'What of Mother Church? Most Holy Mother Church? If it comes to Her ears that we have spied into Her Hell without Her leave, where do we stand?'

'At the stake,' said the Abbot of St Illod's, and, raising his voice a trifle, 'You hear that? Roger Bacon, heard you that?'

The Friar turned from the window, clutching the compasses tighter.

'No, no!' he appealed. 'Not with Falcodi—not with our English-hearted Foulkes made Pope. He's wise—he's learned. He reads what I have put forth. Foulkes would never suffer it.'

'"Holy Pope is one thing, Holy Church another",' Roger quoted.

'But I—*I* can bear witness it is no Art Magic,' the Friar went on. 'Nothing is it, except Art optical—wisdom after trial and experiment, mark you. I can prove it, and—my name weighs with men who dare think.'

'Find them!' croaked Roger of Salerno. 'Five or six in all the world. That makes less than fifty pounds by weight of ashes at the stake. I have watched such men—reduced.'

'I will not give this up!' The Friar's voice cracked in passion and despair. 'It would be to sin against the Light.'

'No, no! Let us—let us sanctify the little animals of Varro,' said Thomas.

Stephen leaned forward, fished his ring out of the cup, and slipped it on his finger. 'My sons,' said he, 'we have seen what we have seen.'

'That is no magic but simple Art,' the Friar persisted.

''Avails nothing. In the eyes of Mother Church we have seen more than is permitted to man.'

'But it was Life—created and rejoicing,' said Thomas.

'To look into Hell as we shall be judged—as we shall be proved —to have looked, is for priests only.'

'Or green-sick virgins on the road to saint-hood who, for cause any midwife could give you——'

The Abbot's half-lifted hand checked Roger of Salerno's out-pouring.

'Nor may even priests see more in Hell than Church knows to be there. John, there is respect due to Church as well as to Devils.'

'My trade's the outside of things,' said John quietly. 'I have my patterns.'

'But you may need to look again for more,' the Friar said.

'In my craft, a thing done is done with. We go on to new shapes after that.'

'And if we trespass beyond bounds, even in thought, we lie open to the judgment of the Church,' the Abbot continued.

'But thou knowest—*knowest*!' Roger of Salerno had returned to the attack. 'Here's all the world in darkness concerning the causes of things—from the fever across the lane to thy Lady's—thine own Lady's—eating malady. Think!'

'I have thought upon it, Salerno! I have thought indeed.'

Thomas the Infirmarian lifted his head again; and this time he did not stammer at all. 'As in the water, so in the blood must they rage and war with each other! I have dreamed these ten years—I thought it was a sin—but my dreams and Varro's are true! Think on it again! Here's the Light under our very hand!'

'Quench it! You'd no more stand to roasting than—any other. I'll give you the case as Church—as I myself—would frame it. Our John here returns from the Moors, and shows us a hell of devils contending in the compass of one drop of water. Magic past clearance! You can hear the faggots crackle.'

'But thou knowest! Thou hast seen it all before! For man's poor sake! For old friendship's sake—Stephen!' The Friar was trying to stuff the compasses into his bosom as he appealed.

'What Stephen de Sautré knows, you his friends know also. I would have you, now, obey the Abbot of St Illod's. Give to me!' He held out his ringed hand.

'May I—may John here—not even make a drawing of one—one screw?' said the broken Friar, in spite of himself.

'Nowise!' Stephen took it over. 'Your dagger, John. Sheathed will serve.'

He unscrewed the metal cylinder, laid it on the table, and with the dagger's hilt smashed some crystal to sparkling dust which he swept into a scooped hand and cast behind the hearth.

'It would seem,' said he, 'the choice lies between two sins. To deny the world a Light which is under our hand, or to enlighten the world before her time. What you have seen, I saw long since among the physicians at Cairo. And I know what doctrine they drew from it. Hast *thou* dreamed, Thomas? I also—with fuller knowledge. But this birth, my sons, is untimely. It will be but the mother of more death, more torture, more division, and greater darkness in this dark age. Therefore I, who know both my world and the Church, take this Choice on my conscience. Go! It is finished.'

He thrust the wooden part of the compasses deep among the beech logs till all was burned.

1926

# The Church That Was At Antioch

'But when Peter was come to Antioch, I with-
stood him to the face, because he was to be
blamed.'—St Paul's Epistle to the Galatians, ii, 11.

HIS mother, a devout and well-born Roman widow, decided that
he was doing himself no good in an Eastern Legion so near to
free-thinking Constantinople, and got him seconded for civil duty
in Antioch, where his uncle, Lucius Sergius, was head of the
urban Police. Valens obeyed as a son and as a young man keen to
see life, and, presently, cast up at his uncle's door.

'That sister-in-law of mine,' said the elder, 'never remembers
me till she wants something. What have you been doing?'

'Nothing, Uncle.'

'Meaning everything?'

'That's what mother thinks. But I haven't.'

'We shall see. Your quarters are across the inner courtyard.
Your—er—baggage is there already. . . . Oh, I shan't interfere
with your private arrangements! I'm not the uncle with the rough
tongue. Get your bath. We'll talk at supper.'

But before that hour 'Father Serga', as the Prefect of Police
was called, learned from the Treasury that his nephew had
marched overland from Constantinople in charge of a treasure-
convoy which, after a brush with brigands in the pass outside
Tarsus, he had duly delivered.

'Why didn't you tell me about it?' his uncle asked at the meal.

'I had to report to the Treasury first,' was the answer.

Serga looked at him. 'Gods! You *are* like your father,' said he.
'Cilicia is scandalously policed.'

'So I noticed. They ambushed us not five miles from Tarsus
town. Are we given to that sort of thing here?'

'You make yourself at home early. No. *We* are not, but Syria is
a Non-regulation Province—under the Emperor—not the Senate.
We've the entire unaccountable East to one side; the scum of the
Mediterranean on the other; and all hellicat Judaea southward.
Anything can happen in Syria. D'you like the prospect?'

'I shall—under you.'

'It's in the blood. The same with men as horses. Now what
have you done that distresses your mother so?'

'She's a little behind the times, sir. She follows the old school,
of course—the home-worships, and the strict Latin Trinity. I
don't think she recognizes any Gods outside Jupiter, Juno, and
Minerva.'

'I don't either—officially.'

'Nor I, as an officer, sir. But one wants more than that, and—
and—what I learned in Byzant squared with what I saw with the
Fifteenth.'

'You needn't go on. All Eastern Legions are alike. You mean
you follow Mithras—eh?'

The young man bowed his head slightly.

'No harm, boy. It's a soldier's religion, even if it comes from
outside.'

'So I thought. But Mother heard of it. She didn't approve and
—I suppose that's why I'm here.'

'Off the trident and into the net! Just like a woman! All Syria is
stuffed with Mithraism. *My* objection to fancy religions is that
they mostly meet after dark, and that means more work for the
Police. We've a College here of stiff-necked Hebrews who call
themselves Christians.'

'I've heard of them,' said Valens. 'There isn't a ceremony or
symbol they haven't stolen from the Mithras ritual.'

''No news to *me*! Religions are part of my office-work; and
they'll be part of yours. Our Synagogue Jews are fighting like
Scythians over this new faith.'

'Does that matter much?'

'So long as they fight each other, we've only to keep the ring.
Divide and rule—especially with Hebrews. Even these Christians
are divided now. You see—one part of their worship is to eat
together.'

'Another theft! The Supper is the essential Symbol with us,'
Valens interrupted.

'With *us*, it's the essential symbol of trouble for your uncle, my
dear. Anyone can become a Christian. A Jew may; but he still
lives by his Law of Moses (I've had to master that cursed code,
too) and it regulates all his doings. Then he sits down at a
Christian love-feast beside a Greek or Westerner, who doesn't
kill mutton or pig—No! No! Jews don't touch pork—as the
Jewish Law lays down. Then the tables are broken up—but not
by laughter—No! No! Riot!'

'That's childish,' said Valens.

''Wish it were. But my lictors are called in to keep order, and I
have to take the depositions of Synagogue Jews, denouncing
Christians as traitors to Caesar. If I chose to act on half the stuff
their Rabbis swear to, I'd have respectable little Jew shop-
keepers up every week for conspiracy. *Never* decide on the
evidence, when you're dealing with Hebrews! Oh, you'll get your
bellyfull of it! You're for Market-duty tomorrow in the Little
Circus ward, all among 'em. And now, sleep you well! I've been

on this frontier as far back as anyone remembers—that's why they call me the Father of Syria—and oh—it's good to see a sample of the old stock again!'

Next morning, and for many weeks after, Valens found himself on Market-inspection duty with a fat Aedile, who flew into rages because the stalls were not flushed down at the proper hour. A couple of his uncle's men were told off to him, and, of course, introduced him to the thieves' and prostitutes' quarters, to the leading gladiators, and so forth.

One day, behind the Little Circus, near Singon Street, he ran into a mob, where a race-course gang were trying to collect, or evade, some bets on recent chariot-races. The Aedile said it was none of his affair and turned back. The lictors closed up behind Valens, but left the situation in his charge. Then a small hard man with eyebrows was punted on to his chest, amid howls from all around that he was the ringleader of a conspiracy. 'Yes,' said Valens, 'that was an old trick in Byzant; but I think we'll take *you*, my friend.' Turning the small man loose, he gathered in the loudest of his accusers to appear before his uncle.

'You were quite right,' said Serga next day. 'That gentleman was put up to the job—by someone else. I ordered him one Roman dozen. Did you get the name of the man they were trying to push off on you?'

'Yes. Gaius Julius Paulus. Why?'

'I guessed as much. He's an old acquaintance of mine, a Cilician from Tarsus. Well-born—a citizen by descent, and well-educated, but his people have disowned him. So he works for his living.'

'He spoke like a well-born. He's in splendid training, too. 'Felt him. All muscle.'

'Small wonder. He can outmarch a camel. He is really the Prefect of this new sect. He travels all over our Eastern Provinces starting their Colleges and keeping them up to the mark. That's why the Synagogue Jews are hunting him. If they could run him in on the political charge, it would finish him.'

'Is he seditious, then?'

'Not in the least. Even if he were, I wouldn't feed him to the Jews just because they wanted it. One of our Governors tried that game down-coast—for the sake of peace—some years ago. He didn't get it. Do you like your Market-work, my boy?'

'It's interesting. D'you know, uncle, I think the Synagogue Jews are better at their slaughterhouse arrangements than we.'

'They are. That's what makes 'em so tough. A dozen stripes are nothing to Apella, though he'll howl the yard down while he's getting 'em. You've the Christians' College in your quarter. How do they strike you?'

''Quiet enough. They're worrying a bit over what they ought to eat at their love-feasts.'

'I know it. Oh, I meant to tell you—we mustn't try 'em too high just now, Valens. My office reports that Paulus, your small friend, is going down-country for a few days to meet another priest of the College, and bring him back to help smooth over their difficulties about their victuals. That means their congregation will be at loose ends till they return. Mass without mind always comes a cropper. So, *now* is when the Synagogue Jews will try to compromise them. I don't want the poor devils stampeded into what can be made to look like political crime. Understand?'

Valens nodded. Between his uncle's discursive evening talks, studded with kitchen-Greek and out-of-date Roman society-verses; his morning tours with the puffing Aedile; and the confidences of his lictors at all hours; he fancied he understood Antioch.

So he kept an eye on the rooms in the colonnade behind the Little Circus, where the new faith gathered. One of the many Jew butchers told him that Paulus had left affairs in the hands of some man called Barnabas, but that he would come back with one, Petrus—evidently a well-known character—who would settle all the food-differences between Greek and Hebrew Christians. The butcher had no spite against Greek Christians as such, if they would only kill their meat like decent Jews.

Serga laughed at this talk, but lent Valens an extra man or two, and said that this lion would be his to tackle, before long.

The boy found himself rushed into the arena one hot dusk, when word had come that this was to be a night of trouble. He posted his lictors in an alley within signal, and entered the common-room of the College, where the love-feasts were held. Everyone seemed as friendly as a Christian—to use the slang of the quarter—and Barnabas, a smiling, stately man by the door, specially so.

'I am glad to meet you,' he said. 'You helped our Paulus in that scuffle the other day. We can't afford to lose *him*. I wish he were back!'

He looked nervously down the hall, as it filled with people, of middle and low degree, setting out their evening meal on the bare tables, and greeting each other with a special gesture.

'I assure you,' he went on, his eyes still astray, '*we've* no intention of offending any of the brethren. Our differences can be settled if only——'

As though on a signal, clamour rose from half a dozen tables at once, with cries of 'Pollution! Defilement! Heathen! The Law!

The Law! Let Caesar know!' As Valens backed against the wall, the crowd pelted each other with broken meats and crockery, till at last stones appeared from nowhere.

'It's a put-up affair,' said Valens to Barnabas.

'Yes. They come in with stones in their breasts. Be careful! they're throwing your way,' Barnabas replied. The crowd was well embroiled now. A section of it bore down to where they stood, yelling for the Justice of Rome. His two lictors slid in behind Valens, and a man leaped at him with a knife.

Valens struck up the hand, and the lictors had the man helpless as the weapon fell on the floor. The clash of it stilled the tumult a little. Valens caught the lull, speaking slowly: 'Oh, citizens,' he called, '*must* you begin your love-feasts with battle? Our tripe-sellers' burial-club has better manners.'

A little laughter relieved the tension.

'The Synagogue has arranged this,' Barnabas muttered. 'The responsibility will be laid on me.'

'Who is the Head of your College?' Valens called to the crowd. The cries rose against each other.

'Paulus! Saul! *He* knows the world—— No! No! Petrus! Our Rock! *He* won't betray us. Petrus, the Living Rock.'

'When do they come back?' Valens asked. Several dates were given, sworn to, and denied.

'Wait to fight till they return. I'm not a priest; but if you don't tidy up these rooms, our Aedile (Valens gave him his gross nick-name in the quarter) will fine the sandals off your feet. And you mustn't trample good food either. When you've finished, I'll lock up after you. Be quick. *I* know our Prefect if you don't.'

They toiled, like children rebuked. As they passed out with baskets of rubbish, Valens smiled. The matter would not be pressed further.

'Here is our key,' said Barnabas at the end. 'The Synagogue will swear I hired this man to kill you.'

'Will they? Let's look at him.'

The lictors pushed their prisoner forward.

'Ill-fortune!' said the man. 'I owed you for my brother's death in Tarsus Pass.'

'Your brother tried to kill me,' Valens retorted.

The fellow nodded.

'Then we'll call it even-throws,' Valens signed to the lictors, who loosed hold. 'Unless you *really* want to see my uncle?'

The man vanished like a trout in the dusk. Valens returned the key to Barnabas, and said:

'If I were you, I shouldn't let your people in again till your leaders come back. You don't know Antioch as I do.'

He went home, the grinning lictors behind him, and they told his uncle, who grinned also, but said that he had done the right thing—even to patronizing Barnabas.

'Of course, *I* don't know Antioch as you do; but, seriously, my dear, I think you've saved their Church for the Christians this time. I've had three depositions already that your Cilician friend was a Christian hired by Barnabas. 'Just as well for Barnabas that you let the brute go.'

'You told me you didn't want them stampeded into trouble. Besides, it was fair-throws. I may have killed his brother after all. We had to kill two of 'em.'

'Good! You keep a level head in a tight corner. You'll need it. There's no lying about in secluded parks for *us*! I've got to see Paulus and Petrus when they come back, and find out what they've decided about their infernal feasts. Why can't they all get decently drunk and be done with it?'

'They talk of them both down-town as though they were Gods. By the way, uncle, all the riot was worked up by Synagogue Jews sent from Jerusalem—not by our lot at all.'

'You *don't* say so? Now, perhaps, you understand why I put you on market-duty with old Sow-Belly! You'll make a Police-officer yet.'

Valens met the scared, mixed congregation round the fountains and stalls as he went about his quarter. They were rather relieved at being locked out of their rooms for the time; as well as by the news that Paulus and Petrus would report to the Prefect of Police before addressing them on the great food-question.

Valens was not present at the first part of that interview, which was official. The second, in the cool, awning-covered courtyard, with drinks and *hors-d'œuvre*, all set out beneath the vast lemon and lavender sunset, was much less formal.

'You have met, I think,' said Serga to the little lean Paulus as Valens entered.

'Indeed, yes. Under God, we are twice your debtors,' was the quick reply.

'Oh, that was part of my duty. I hope you found our roads good on your journey,' said Valens.

'Why, yes. I think they were.' Paulus spoke as if he had not noticed them.

'We should have done better to come by boat,' said his companion, Petrus, a large fleshy man, with eyes that seemed to see nothing, and a half-palsied right hand that lay idle in his lap.

'Valens came overland from Byzant,' said his uncle. 'He rather fancies his legs.'

'He ought to at his age. What was your best day's march on the

Via Sebaste?' Paulus asked interestedly, and, before he knew, Valens was reeling off his mileage on mountain-roads every step of which Paulus seemed to have trod.

'That's good,' was the comment. 'And I expect you march in heavier order than I.'

'What would you call your best day's work?' Valens asked in turn.

'I have covered . . .' Paulus checked himself. 'And yet not I but the God,' he muttered. 'It's hard to cure oneself of boasting.'

A spasm wrenched Petrus's face.

'Hard indeed,' said he. Then he addressed himself to Paulus as though none other were present. 'It is true I have eaten with Gentiles and as the Gentiles ate. Yet, at the time, I doubted if it were wise.'

'That is behind us now,' said Paulus gently. 'The decision has been taken for the Church—that little Church which you saved, my son.' He turned on Valens with a smile that half-captured the boy's heart. 'Now—as a Roman and a Police-officer—what think you of us Christians?'

'That I have to keep order in my own ward.'

'Good! Caesar must be served. But—as a servant of Mithras, shall we say—how think you about our food disputes?'

Valens hesitated. His uncle encouraged him with a nod. 'As a servant of Mithras I eat with any initiate, so long as the food is clean,' said Valens.

'But,' said Petrus, '*that* is the crux.'

'Mithras also tells us,' Valens went on, 'to share a bone covered with dirt, if better cannot be found.'

'You observe no difference, then, between peoples at your feasts?' Paulus demanded.

'How dare we? We are all His children. Men make laws. Not Gods,' Valens quoted from the old Ritual.

'Say that again, child!'

'Gods do not make laws. They change men's hearts. The rest is the Spirit.'

'You heard it, Petrus? You heard that? It is the utter Doctrine itself!' Paulus insisted to his dumb companion.

Valens, a little ashamed of having spoken of his faith, went on:

'They tell me the Jew butchers here want the monopoly of killing for your people. Trade feeling's at the bottom of most of it.'

'A little more than that perhaps,' said Paulus. 'Listen a minute.' He threw himself into a curious tale about the God of the Christians, Who, he said, had taken the shape of a Man, and Whom the Jerusalem Jews, years ago, had got the authorities to deal with as a conspirator. He said that he himself, at that time a right Jew, quite agreed with the sentence, and had denounced all who followed the new God. But one day the Light and the Voice of the God broke over him, and he experienced a rending change of heart—precisely as in the Mithras creed. Then he met, and had been initiated by, some men who had walked and talked and, more particularly, had eaten, with the new God before He was killed, and who had seen Him after, like Mithras, He had risen from His grave. Paulus and those others—Petrus was one of them—had next tried to preach Him to the Jews, but that was no success; and, one thing leading to another, Paulus had gone back to his home at Tarsus, where his people disowned him for a renegade. There he had broken down with overwork and despair. Till then, he said, it had never occurred to any of them to show the new religion to any except right Jews; for their God had been born in the shape of a Jew. Paulus himself only came to realize the possibilities of outside work, little by little. He said he had all the foreign preaching in his charge now, and was going to change the whole world by it.

Then he made Petrus finish the tale, who explained, speaking very slowly, that he had, some years ago, received orders from the God to preach to a Roman officer of Irregulars down-country; after which that officer and most of his people wanted to become Christians. So Petras had initiated them the same night, although none of them were Hebrews. 'And,' Petrus ended, 'I saw there is nothing under heaven that we dare call unclean.'

Paulus turned on him like a flash and cried:

'You admit it! Out of your own mouth it is evident,' Petrus shook like a leaf and his right hand almost lifted.

'Do *you* too twit me with my accent?' he began, but his face worked and he choked.

'Nay! God forbid! And God once more forgive *me*!' Paulus seemed as distressed as he, while Valens stared at the extraordinary outbreak.

'Talking of clean and unclean,' his uncle said tactfully, 'there's that ugly song come up again in the City. They were singing it on the city-front yesterday, Valens. Did you notice?'

He looked at his nephew, who took the hint.

'If it was "Pickled Fish", sir, they were. Will it make trouble?'

'As surely as these fish'—a jar of them stood on the table—' 'make one thirsty. How does it go? Oh yes.' Serga hummed:

'Oie-eaah!
From the Shark and the Sardine—the clean and the unclean—
To the Pickled Fish of Galilee, said Petrus, shall be mine.'

He twanged it off to the proper gutter-drawl.

> '(Ha-ow?)
> In the nets or on the line,
> Till the Gods Themselves decline.
> (Whe-en?)
> When the Pickled Fish of Galilee ascend the Esquiline!

That'll be something of a flood—worse than live fish in trees!
Hey?'

'It will happen one day,' said Paulus.

He turned from Petrus, whom he had been soothing tenderly,
and resumed in his natural, hardish voice:

'Yes. We owe a good deal to that Centurion being converted
when he was. It taught us that the whole world could receive the
God; and it showed *me* my next work. I came over from Tarsus
to teach here for a while. And I shan't forget how good the
Prefect of Police was to us then.'

'For one thing, Cornelius was an early colleague,' Serga
smiled largely above his strong cup. '"Prime companion"—
how does it go?—"we drank the long, long Eastern day out
together," and so on. For another, I know a good workman
when I see him. That camel-kit you made for my desert-tours,
Paul, is as sound as ever. And for a third—which to a man of my
habits is most important—that Greek doctor you recommended
me is the only one who understands my tumid liver.'

He passed a cup of all but unmixed wine, which Paulus handed
to Petrus, whose lips were flaky white at the corners.

'But your trouble,' the Prefect went on, 'will come from your
own people. Jerusalem never forgives. They'll get you run in on
the charge of *laesa majestatis* soon or late.'

'Who knows better than I?' said Petrus. 'And the decision we
*all* have taken about our love-feasts may unite Hebrew and Greek
against us. As I told you, Prefect, we are asking Christian Greeks
not to make the feasts difficult for Christian Hebrews by eating
meat that has not been lawfully killed. (Our way is much more
wholesome, anyhow.) Still, we may get round that. But there's *one*
vital point. Some of our Greek Christians bring food to the love-
feasts that they've bought from your priests, after your sacrifices
have been offered. That we can't allow.'

Paulus turned to Valens imperiously.

'You mean they buy Altar-scraps,' the boy said. 'But only the
very poor do it; and it's chiefly block-trimmings. The sale's a
perquisite of the Altar-butchers. They wouldn't like its being
stopped.'

'Permit separate tables for Hebrew and Greek, as I once said,' Petrus spoke suddenly.

'That would end in separate churches. There shall be but *one* Church,' Pauius spoke over his shoulder, and the words fell like rods. 'You think there may be trouble, Valens?'

'My uncle——' Valens began.

'No, no!' the Prefect laughed. 'Singon Street Markets are your Syria. Let's hear what our Legate thinks of his Province.'

Valens flushed and tried to pull his wits together.

'Primarily,' he said, 'it's pig, I suppose. Hebrews hate pork.'

'Quite right, too. Catch *me* eating pig east the Adriatic! *I* don't want to die of worms. Give me a young Sabine tush-ripe boar! I have spoken!'

Serga mixed himself another raw cup and took some pickled Lake fish to bring out the flavour.

'But, still,' Petrus leaned forward like a deaf man, 'if we admitted Hebrew and Greek Christians to separate tables we should escape——'

'Nothing, except salvation,' said Paulus. 'We have broken with the whole Law of Moses. We live in and through and by our God only. Else we are nothing. What is the sense of harking back to the Law at meal times? Whom do we deceive? Jerusalem? Rome? The God? You yourself have eaten with Gentiles! You yourself have said——'

'One says more than one means when one is carried away,' Petrus answered, and his face worked again.

'This time you will say precisely what is meant,' Paulus spoke between his teeth. 'We will keep the Churches *one*—in and through the Lord. You dare not deny this?'

'I dare nothing—the God knows! But I have denied Him. . . . I denied Him. . . . And He said—He said I was the Rock on which His Church should stand.'

'*I* will see that it stands, and yet not I——' Paulus's voice dropped again. 'Tomorrow you will speak to the one Church of the one Table the world over.'

'That's *your* business,' said the Prefect. 'But I warn you again, it's your own people who will make you trouble.'

Paulus rose to say farewell, but in the act he staggered, put his hand to his forehead and, as Valens steered him to a divan, collapsed in the grip of that deadly Syrian malaria which strikes like a snake. Valens, having suffered, called to his rooms for his heavy travelling-fur. His girl, whom he had bought in Constantinople a few months before, fetched it. Petrus tucked it awkwardly round the shivering little figure; the Prefect ordered lime-juice and hot water, and Paulus thanked them and apologized, while his teeth rattled on the cup.

'Better today than tomorrow,' said the Prefect. 'Drink—sweat—and sleep here the night. Shall I send for my doctor?'

But Paulus said that the fit would pass naturally, and as soon as he could stand he insisted on going away with Petrus, late though it was, to prepare their announcement to the Church.

'Who was that big, clumsy man?' his girl asked Valens as she took up the fur. 'He made more noise than the small one, who was really suffering.'

'He's a priest of the new College by the Little Circus, dear. He believes, uncle told me, that he once denied his God, Who, he says, died for him.'

She halted in the moonlight, the glossy jackal skins over her arm.

'Does he? *My* God bought me from the dealers like a horse. Too much, too, he paid. Didn't he? 'Fess, thou?'

'No, thee!' emphatically.

'But I wouldn't deny *my* God—living or dead! . . . Oh—but *not* dead! My God's going to live—for me. Live—live, Thou, my heart's blood, for ever!'

It would have been better had Paulus and Petrus not left the Prefect's house so late; for the rumour in the city, as the Prefect knew, and as the long conference seemed to confirm, was that Caesar's own secretary of State in Rome was, through Paulus, arranging for a general defilement of the Hebrew with the Greek Christians, and that after this had been effected, by promiscuous eating of unlawful foods, all Jews would be lumped together as Christians—members, that is, of a mere free-thinking sect instead of the very particular and troublesome 'Nation of Jews within the Empire'. Eventually, the story went, they would lose their rights as Roman citizens, and could then be sold on any slave-stand.

'Of course,' Serga explained to Valens next day, 'that has been put about by the Jerusalem Synagogue. Our Antioch Jews aren't clever enough. Do you see their game? Petrus is a defiler of the Hebrew nation. If he is cut down tonight by some properly primed young zealot so much the better.'

'He won't be,' said Valens. 'I'm looking after him.'

''Hope so. But, if he isn't knifed,' Serga went on, 'they'll try to work up city riots on the grounds that, when all the Jews have lost their civil rights, he'll set up as a sort of King of the Christians.'

'At Antioch? In the present year of Rome? That's crazy, Uncle.'

'*Every* crowd is crazy. What else do we draw pay for? But, listen. Post a Mounted Police patrol at the back of the Little Circus. Use 'em to keep the people moving when the congregation comes out. Post two of your men in the Porch of their College itself. Tell Paulus and Petrus to wait there with them, till the streets are clear. Then fetch 'em both over here. Don't hit till you have to. Hit hard *before* the stones fly. Don't get my little horses knocked about more than you can help, and—look out for "Pickled Fish"!'

Knowing his own quarter, it seemed to Valens as he went on duty that evening, that his uncle's precautions had been excessive. The Christian Church, of course, was full, and a large crowd waited outside for word of the decision about the feasts. Most of them seemed to be Christians of sorts, but there was an element of gesticulating Antiochene loafers, and like all crowds they amused themselves with popular songs while they waited. Things went smoothly, till a group of Christians raised a rather explosive hymn, which ran:

> 'Enthroned above Caesar and Judge of the Earth!
> We wait on Thy coming—oh tarry not long!
>   As the Kings of the Sunrise
>   Drew sword at Thy Birth,
> So we arm in this midnight of insult and wrong!'

'Yes—and if one of their fish-stalls is bumped over by a camel —it's *my* fault!' said Valens. 'Now they've started it!'

Sure enough, voices on the outskirts broke into 'Pickled Fish', but before Valens could speak, they were suppressed by someone crying: 'Quiet there, or you'll get your pickle before your fish.'

It was close on twilight when a cry rose from within the packed Church, and its congregation breasted out into the crowd. They all talked about the new orders for their love-feasts, most of them agreeing that they were sensible and easy. They agreed, too, that Petrus (Paulus did not seem to have taken much part in the debate) had spoken like one inspired, and they were all extremely proud of being Christians. Some of them began to link arms across the alley, and strike into the 'Enthroned above Caesar' chorus.

'And this, I *think*,' Valens called to the young Commandant of the Mounted Patrol, 'is where we'll begin to steer 'em home. Oh! and "Let night also have her well-earned hymn," as Uncle 'ud say.'

There filed out from behind the Little Circus four blaring

trumpets, a standard, and a dozen Mounted Police. Their wise little grey Arabs sidled, passaged, shouldered, and nosed softly into the mob, as though they wanted petting, while the trumpets deafened the narrow street. An open square, near by, eased the pressure before long. Here the Patrol broke into fours, and grid-ironed it, saluting the images of the Gods at each corner and in the centre. People stopped, as usual, to watch how cleverly the incense was cast down over the withers into the spouting cressets; children reached up to pat horses which they said they knew; family groups re-found each other in the smoky dusk; hawkers offered cooked suppers; and soon the crowd melted into the main traffic avenues. Valens went over to the Church porch, where Petrus and Paulus waited between his lictors.

'That was well done,' Paulus began.

'How's the fever?' Valens asked.

'I was spared for today. I think, too, that by The Blessing we have carried our point.'

'Good hearing! My uncle bids me say you are welcome at his house.'

'That is always a command,' said Paulus, with a quick down-country gesture. 'Now that this day's burden is lifted, it will be a delight.'

Petrus joined up like a weary ox. Valens greeted him, but he did not answer.

'Leave him alone,' Paulus whispered. 'The virtue has gone out of me—him—for the while.' His own face looked pale and drawn.

The street was empty, and Valens took a short cut through an alley, where light ladies leaned out of windows and laughed. The three strolled easily together, the lictors behind them, and far off they heard the trumpets of the Night Horse saluting some statue of a Caesar, which marked the end of their round. Paulus was telling Valens how the whole Roman Empire would be changed by what the Christians had agreed to about their love-feasts, when an impudent little Jew boy stole up behind them, playing 'Pickled Fish' on some sort of desert bagpipe.

'Can't you stop that young pest, one of you?' Valens asked laughing. 'You shan't be mocked on this great night of yours, Paulus.'

The lictors turned back a few paces, and shook a torch at the brat, but he retreated and drew them on. Then they heard Paulus shout, and when they hurried back, found Valens prostrate and coughing—his blood on the fringe of the kneeling Paul's robe. Petrus stooped, waving a helpless hand above them.

'Someone ran out from behind that well-head. He stabbed him as he ran, and ran on. Listen!' said Paulus.

But there was not even the echo of a footfall for clue, and the Jew boy had vanished like a bat. Said Valens from the ground:

'Home! Quick! I have it!'

They tore a shutter out of a shop-front, lifted and carried him, while Paulus walked beside. They set him down in the lighted inner courtyard of the Prefect's house, and a lictor hurried for the Prefect's physician.

Paulus watched the boy's face, and, as Valens shivered a little, called to the girl to fetch last night's fur rug. She brought it, laid the head on her breast, and cast herself beside Valens.

'It isn't bad. It doesn't bleed much. So it *can't* be bad—can it?' she repeated. Valens's smile reassured her, till the Prefect came and recognized the deadly upward thrust under the ribs. He turned on the Hebrews.

'Tomorrow you will look for where your Church stood,' said he.

Valens lifted the hand that the girl was not kissing.

'No—no!' he gasped. 'The Cilician did it! For his brother! He said it.'

'The Cilician you let go to save these Christians because I——?' Valens signed to his uncle that it was so, while the girl begged him to steal strength from her till the doctor should come.

'Fogive me,' said Serga to Paulus. 'None the less I wish your God in Hades once for all. . . . But what am I to write his mother? Can't either of you two talking creatures tell me what I'm to tell his mother?'

'What has *she* to do with him?' the slave-girl cried. 'He is mine—mine! I testify before all Gods that he bought me! I am his. He is mine.'

'We can deal with the Cilician and his friends later,' said one of the lictors. 'But what now?'

For some reason, the man, though used to butcher-work, looked at Petrus.

'Give him drink and wait,' said Petrus. 'I have—seen such a wound.' Valens drank and a shade of colour came to him. He motioned the Prefect to stoop.

'What is it? Dearest of lives, what troubles?'

'The Cilician and his friends. . . . Don't be hard on them. . . They get worked up. . . . They don't know what they are doing. . . . Promise!'

'This is not I, child. It is the Law.'

''No odds. You're Father's brother. . . . Men make laws—not Gods. . . . Promise! . . . It's finished with me.'

Valens's head eased back on its yearning pillow.

Petrus stood like one in a trance. The tremor left his face as he repeated:

'"Forgive them, for they know not what they do." Heard you *that*, Paulus? He, a heathen and an idolator, said it!'

'I heard. What hinders now that we should baptize him?' Paulus answered promptly.

Petrus stared at him as though he had come up out of the sea.

'Yes,' he said at last. 'It is the little maker of tents. . . . And what does he *now*—command?'

Paulus repeated the suggestion.

Painfully, that other raised the palsied hand that he had once held up in a hall to deny a charge.

'Quiet!' said he. 'Think you that one who has spoken Those Words needs such as *we* are to certify him to any God?'

Paulus cowered before the unknown colleague, vast and commanding, revealed after all these years.

'As you please—as you please,' he stammered, overlooking the blasphemy. 'Moreover there is the concubine.'

The girl did not heed, for the brow beneath her lips was chilling, even as she called on her God who had bought her at a price that he should not die but live.

1929

# Proofs Of Holy Writ

THEY seated themselves in the heavy chairs on the pebbled floor beneath the eaves of the summer-house by the orchard. A table between them carried the wine and glasses, and a packet of papers, with pen and ink. The larger man of the two, his doublet unbuttoned, his broad face blotched and scarred, puffed a little as he came to rest. The other picked an apple from the grass, bit it, and went on with the thread of the talk that they must have carried out of doors with them.

'But why waste time fighting atomies who do not come up to your belly-button, Ben?' he asked.

'It breathes me—it breathes me, between bouts! *You'd* be better for a tussle or two.'

'But not to spend mind and verse on 'em. What was Dekker to you? Ye knew he'd strike back—and hard.'

'He and Marston had been baiting me like dogs . . . about my trade as they called it, though it was only my cursed stepfather's. "Bricks and mortar", Dekker said, and "hodman". And he mocked my face. 'Twas clean as curds in my youth. This humour has come on me since.'

'Ah! "Every man *and* his humour"? But why did ye not have at Dekker in peace—over the sack, as you do at me?'

'Because I'd have drawn on him—and he's no more worth a hanging than Gabriel. Setting aside what he wrote of me, too, the hireling dog has merit of a sort. His *Shoemaker's Holiday.* Hey? Though my *Bartlemy Fair*, when 'tis presented, will furnish out three of it and——'

'Ride all the easier. I have suffered two readings of it already. It creaks like an overloaded haywain', the other cut in. 'You give too much.'

Ben smiled loftily and went on. 'But I'm glad I lashed him in my *Poetaster* for all I've worked with him since. How comes it that I've never fought with thee, Will?'

'First, Behemoth'' the other drawled, 'it needs two to engender any sort of iniquity. Second, the betterment of this present age— and the next, maybe—lies, in chief, on our four shoulders. If the Pillars of the Temple fall out, Nature, Art, and Learning come to a stand. Last, I am not yet ass enough to hawk up my private spites before groundlings. What do the Court, citizens or 'prentices give for thy fallings-out or fallings-in with Dekker—or the Grand Devil?'

'They should be taught, then—taught.'

'Always *that*? What's your commission to enlighten us?'

'My own learning which I have heaped up, lifelong, at my own pains. My assured knowledge, also, of my craft and art. I'll suffer no man's mock or malice on it.'

'The one sure road to mockery.'

'I deny nothing of my brain-store to my lines. I—I build up my own works throughout.'

'Yet when Dekker cries "hodman" y'are not content.'

Ben half-heaved in his chair. 'I'll owe you a beating for that when I'm thinner. Meantime, here's on account. I say, *I* build upon my own foundations; devising and perfecting my own plots; adorning 'em justly as fits time, place and action. In all of which you sin damnably. *I* set no landward principalities on sea-beaches.'

'They pay their penny for pleasure—not learning,' Will answered above the apple-core.

'Penny or tester, you owe 'em justice. In the facture of plays— nay, listen, Will—at all points they must be dressed historically— *teres atque rotundus*—in ornament and temper. As my *Sejanus*, of which the mob was unworthy.'

Here Will made a doleful face, and echoed. 'Unworthy! I was —what did I play, Ben, in that long weariness. Some most grievous ass.'

'The part of Caius Silius,' said Ben, stiffly.

Will laughed aloud. 'True. "Indeed that place *was* not my sphere".'

It must have been a quotation, for Ben winced a little, ere he recovered himself and went on: 'Also my *Alchemist* which the world in part apprehends. The main of its learning is necessarily yet hid from 'em. To come to your works, Will——'

'I am a sinner on all sides. The drink's at your elbow.'

'Confession shall not save ye—bribery.' Ben filled his glass. 'Sooner than labour the right cold heat to devise your own plots, you filch, botch, and clap 'em together out o' ballads, broadsheets, old wives' tales, chapbooks——'

Will nodded with complete satisfaction. 'Say on,' quoth he.

''Tis so with nigh all yours. I've known honester jackdaws. And whom among the learned do ye deceive? Reckoning up those—forty is it?—your plays you've misbegot, there's not six which have not plots common as Moorditch.'

'Ye're out, Ben. There's not one. My *Love's Labour* (how I came to write it, I know not) is nearest to lawful issue. My *Tempest* (how I came to write *that*, I know) is, in some part, my own stuff. Of the rest, I stand guilty. Bastards all!'

'And no shame?'

'None! Our business must be fitted with parts hot and hot—

and the boys are more trouble than the men. Give me the bones of any stuff, I'll cover 'em as quickly as any. But to hatch new plots is to waste God's unreturning time like—' he chuckled, 'like a hen.'

'Yet see what ye miss! Invention next to Knowledge,—whence it proceeds, being the chief glory of Art——'

'Miss, say you? Dick Burbage—in my *Hamlet* that I botched for him when he had staled of our Kings? (Nobly he played it!) Was *he* a miss?'

Ere Ben could speak Will overbore him.

'And when poor Dick was at odds with the world in general and womenkind in special, I clapped him up my *Lear* for a vomit.'

'An hotch-potch of passion, outrunning reason,' was the verdict.

'Not altogether. Cast in a mould too large for any boards to bear (My fault!) Yet Dick evened it. And when he'd come out of his whoremongering aftermaths of repentance I served him my *Macbeth* to toughen him. Was that a miss?'

'I grant you, your *Macbeth* as nearest in spirit to my *Sejanus*; showing for example: "How fortune plies her sports when she begins To practise 'em." We'll see which of the two lives longest.'

'Amen! I'll bear no malice among the worms.'

A liveried serving-man, booted and spurred, led a saddlehorse through the gate into the orchard. At a sign from Will he tethered the beast to a tree, lurched aside and stretched on the grass. Ben, curious as a lizard, for all his bulk, wanted to know what it meant.

'There's a nosing Justice of the Peace lost in thee,' Will returned. 'Yon's a business I've neglected all this day for thy fat sake—and he by so much the drunker . . . Patience! It's all set out on the table. Have a care with the ink!'

Ben reached unsteadily for the packet of papers and read the superscription: '"To William Shakespeare, Gentleman, at his house of New Place in the town of Stratford, these—with diligence from M.S." Why does the fellow withold his name? Or is it one of your women? I'll look.'

Muzzy as he was, he opened and unfolded a mass of printed papers expertly enough.

'From the most learned divine, Miles Smith of Brazen Nose College,' Will explained. 'You know this business as well as I. The King has set all the scholars of England to make one Bible, which the Church shall be bound to, out of all the Bibles that men use.'

'*I* knew.' Ben could not lift his eyes from the printed page. 'I'm more about the Court than you think. The learning of Oxford and Cambridge—"most noble and most equal", as I have said—and Westminster, to sit upon a clutch of Bibles. Those 'ud be Geneva (my mother read to me out of it at her knee), Douai, Rheims, Coverdale, Matthews, the Bishops', the Great, and so forth.'

'They are all set down on the page there—text against text. And you call me a botcher of old clothes?'

'Justly. But what's your concern with this botchery? To keep peace among the Divines? There's fifty of 'em at it as I've heard.'

'I deal with but one. He came to know me when we played at Oxford—when the plague was too hot in London.'

'I remember this Miles Smith now. Son of a butcher? Hey?' Ben grunted.

'Is it so?' was the quiet answer. 'He was moved, he said, with some lines of mine in Dick's part. He said they were, to his godly apprehension, a parable, as it might be, of his reverend self, going down darkling to his tomb 'twixt cliffs of ice and iron.'

'What lines? I know none of thine of that power. But in my *Sejanus*——'

'These were in my *Macbeth*. They lost nothing at Dick's mouth:

> "Tomorrow and tomorrow and tomorrow
> Creeps in this petty pace from day to day
> To the last syllable of recorded time,
> And all our yesterdays have lighted fools
> The way to dusty death——"

or something in that sort. Condell writes 'em out fair for him, and tells him I am Justice of the Peace (wherein he lied) and *armiger*, which brings me within the pale of God's creatures and the Church. Little and little, then, this very reverend Miles Smith opens his mind to me. He and a half score others, his cloth, are cast to furbish up the Prophets—Isaiah to Malachi. In his opinion by what he'd heard, I had some skill in words, and he'd condescend——'

'How?' Ben barked. 'Condescend?'

'Why not? He'd condescend to inquire o' me privily, when direct illumination lacked, for a tricking out of his words or the turn of some figure. For example'—Will pointed to the papers— 'here be the first three verses of the Sixtieth of Isaiah, and the nineteenth and twentieth of that same. Miles has been at a stand over 'em a week or more.'

'They never called on *me*.' Ben caressed lovingly the hand-pressed proofs on their lavish linen paper. 'Here's the Latin atop

and'—his thick forefinger ran down the slip—'some three—four
—Englishings out of the other Bibles. They spare 'emselves
nothing. Let's do it together. Will you have the Latin first?'

'Could I choke ye from that, Holofernes?'

Ben rolled forth, richly: '"*Surge, illumare, Jerusalem, quia
venit lumen tuum, et gloria Domini super te orta est. Quia ecce
tenebrae operient terram et caligo populos. Super te autem orietur
Dominus, et gloria ejus in te videbitur. Et ambulabunt gentes in
lumine tuo, et reges in splendore ortus tui.*" Er-hum? Think you to
better that?'

'How have Smith's crew gone about it?'

'Thus.' Ben read from the paper. '"Get thee up, O Jerusalem,
and be bright, for thy light is at hand, and the glory of God has
risen up upon thee."'

'Up-pup-up!' Will stuttered, profanely.

Ben held on. '"See how darkness is upon the earth and the
peoples thereof."'

'That's no great stuff to put into Isaiah's mouth. And further,
Ben?'

'"But on thee God shew light and on——' . . . or "in" is it?'
(Ben held the proof closer to the deep furrow at the bridge of his
nose.) '"On thee shall His glory be manifest. So that all peoples
shall walk in the light and the Kings in the glory of thy
morning."'

'It may be mended. Read me the Coverdale of it now. 'Tis on
the same sheet—to the right, Ben.'

'Umm-umm. Coverdale saith, "And therefore get thee up
betimes for thy light cometh and the glory of the Lord shall rise
upon thee. For lo! while the darkness and cloud covereth the
earth and the people, the Lord shall show thee light and His glory
shall be seen in thee. The Gentiles shall come to thy light and the
Kings to the brightness that springs forth on thee." But "gentes"
is, for the most part, "peoples".'

'Eh?' said Will, indifferently. 'Art sure?'

This loosed an avalanche of instances from Ovid, Quintilian,
Terence, Columella, Seneca and others. Will took no heed till the
rush ceased, but stared into the orchard, through the September
haze. 'Now give me the Douai and Geneva for this "Get thee
up, O Jerusalem",' said he at last. 'They'll be all there.'

Ben referred to the proofs. ''Tis "arise" in both,' said he.
'"Arise and be bright" in Geneva. In the Douai 'tis "Arise and
be illuminated".'

'So? Give me the paper now.' Will took it from his companion,
rose, and paced towards a tree in the orchard, turning again,
when he had reached it, by a well-worn track through the grass,

Ben leaned forward in his chair. The other's free hand went up warningly.

'Quiet, man!' said he. 'I wait on my Demon!' He fell into the stage-stride of his art at that time, speaking to the air.

'How shall this open? "Arise" No! "Rise". Yes. And we'll have no weak coupling. 'Tis a call to a City! "Rise—shine" . . . Nor yet any schoolmaster's "because"—because Isaiah is not Holofernes. "*Rise—shine; for thy light is come, and——*!"' He refreshed himself from the apple and the proofs as he strode. '"And—and the glory of God!"—No! "God's" over-short. We need the long roll here. "*And the glory of the Lord is risen on thee.*" (Isaiah speaks the part. We'll have it from his own lips.) What's next in Smith's stuff? . . . "See now"? Oh, vile—vile! . . . And Geneva hath "Lo"? (Still, Ben! Still!) "Lo" is better by all odds: but to match the long roll of "the Lord" we'll have it "Behold". How goes it now? "*For, behold, darkness clokes the earth and—and—*" what's the colour and use of this cursed *caligo*, Ben?—"*Et caligo populos*".'

'"Mistiness" or, as in Pliny, "blindness". And further——'

'No-o . . . Maybe, though, *caligo* will piece out *tenebrae*. "*Quia ecce tenebrae operient terram et caligo populos.*" Nay! "Shadow" and "mist" are not men enough for this work . . . Blindness, did ye say, Ben? . . . The blackness of blindness atop of mere darkness? . . . By God, I've used it in my own stuff many times! "Gross" searches it to the hilts! "Darkness covers"—no, "clokes" (short always). "*Darkness clokes the earth and gross— gross darkness the people*"! (But Isaiah's prophesying, with the storm behind him. Can ye not *feel* it, Ben? It must be "shall")— "*Shall cloke the earth*" . . . The rest comes clearer. . . . "But on thee God shall arise" . . . (Nay, that's sacrificing the Creator to the Creature!) "*But the Lord shall arise on thee*", and—yes, we'll sound that "thee" again—"and on thee shall"—No! . . . "*And His glory shall be seen on thee*". Good!' He walked his beat a little in silence, mumbling the two verses before he mouthed them.

'I have it! Heark, Ben! "*Rise—shine; for thy light is come and the glory of the Lord is risen on thee. For, behold, darkness shall cloke the earth and gross darkness the people. But the Lord shall arise on thee and His glory shall be seen upon thee*".'

'There's something not all amiss there,' Ben conceded.

'My Demon never betrayed me yet, while I trusted him. Now for the verse that runs to the blast of ramshorns. "*Et ambulabunt gentes in lumine tuo, et reges in splendore ortus tui.*" How goes that in the Smithy? "The Gentiles shall come to thy light and Kings to the brightness that springs forth upon thee?' The same in Coverdale, and the Bishops'—eh? We'll keep "Gentiles", Ben,

for the sake of the indraught of the last syllable. But it might be
"And the Gentiles shall draw". No! The plainer the better! "The
Gentiles shall come to thy light and Kings to the splendour
of——" (Smith's out here! We'll need something that shall lift the
trumpet anew.) "Kings shall—shall—Kings to—" (Listen, Ben,
but on your life speak not!) "Gentiles shall come to thy light and
Kings to thy brightness"—No! "Kings to the brightness that
springeth—" Serves not! . . . One trumpet must answer another.
And the blast of a trumpet is always *ai-ai*. "The brightness of"—
"*Ortus*" signifies "rising", Ben—or what?'

'Ay, or "birth", or the East in general.'

'Ass! 'Tis the one word that answers to "light". "Kings to the
brightness of thy rising". Look! The thing shines now within and
without. God! That so much should lie on a word!' He repeated
the verse—'"*And the Gentiles shall come to thy light and Kings to
the brightness of thy rising*".'

He walked to the table and wrote rapidly on the proof margin
all three verses as he had spoken them. 'If they hold by this,' said
he, raising his head, 'they'll not go far astray. Now for the nine-
teenth and twentieth verses. On the other sheet, Ben. What?
What? Smith says he has held back his rendering till he hath seen
mine? Then we'll botch 'em as they stand. Read me first the Latin;
next the Coverdale, and last the Bishops'. There's a contagion of
sleep in the air.' He handed back the proofs, yawned, and took
up his walk.

Obedient, Ben began: '"*Non erit tibi amplius Sol ad lucendum
per diem, nec splendor Lunae illuminabit te*." Which Coverdale
rendereth, "The sun shall never go down and thy moon shall have
been taken away". The Bishops' read: "Thy sun shall never be
thy daylight and the light of the moon shall never shine on thee".'

'Coverdale is better,' said Will, and, wrinkling his nose a little,
'The Bishops put out their lights clumsily. Have at it, Ben.'

Ben pursed his lips and knit his brow. 'The two verses are in the
same mode, changing a hand's breadth in the second. By so much,
therefore, the more difficult.'

'Ye see *that*, then?' said the other, staring past him, and
muttering as he paced, concerning suns and moons. Presently he
took back the proof, chose him another apple and grunted.
'Umm-umm! "Thy Sun shall never go down." No! Flat as a split
viol. "*Non erit tibi amplius Sol—*" That *amplius* must give
tongue. Ah! . . . "Thy Sun shall not—shall not—shall no more be
thy light by day' . . . A fair entry. "Nor"?—No! Not on the heels
of "day". "Neither" it must be—"Neither the Moon"—but
here's *splendor* and the ramshorns again. (Therefore—*ai-ai*!)
"Neither for brightness shall the Moon." (Pest! It is the Lord

who is taking the Moon's place over Israel. It must be "thy Moon".) "Neither for brightness shall thy Moon light—give—make—give light unto thee." Ah! . . . Listen here! . . . "*The Sun shall no more be thy light by day: neither for brightness shall thy Moon give light unto thee.*" That serves, and more, for the first entry. What next, Ben?'

Ben nodded magisterially as Will neared him, reached out his hand for the proofs, and read: '"*Sed erit tibi Dominus in lucem sempiternam et Deus tuus in gloriam tuam*". Here is a jewel of Coverdale's that the Bishops have wisely stolen whole. Hear! "But the Lord Himself shall be thy everlasting light and thy God shall be thy Glory".' Ben paused. 'There's a handsbreadth of splendour for a simple man to gather!'

'Both hands rather. He's swept the strings as divinely as David before Saul,' Will assented. 'We'll convey it whole, too. . . . What's amiss now, Holofernes?'

For Ben was regarding him with a scholar's cold pity. 'Both hands! Will, hast thou *ever* troubled to master *any* shape or sort of prosody—the mere names of the measures and pulses of strung words?'

'I beget some such stuff and send it to you to christen. What's your wisdomhood in labour of?'

'Naught. Naught. But not to know the names of the tools of his trade!' Ben half muttered and pronounced some Greek word or other which conveyed nothing to the listener, who replied: 'Pardon then for whatever sin it was. I do but know words for my need of 'em, Ben. Hold still awhile!'

He went back to his pacings and mutterings. '"For the Lord Himself shall be thy—or thine?—everlasting light." Yes, We'll convey that.' He repeated it twice. 'Nay! Can be bettered. Hark ye, Ben. Here is the Sun going up to over-run and possess all Heaven for evermore. *There*fore (Still, man!) we'll harness the horses of the dawn. Hear their hooves? "The Lord Himself shall be unto thee thy everlasting light and——" Hold again! After that climbing thunder must be some smooth check—like great wings gliding. *There*fore we'll not have "shall be thy glory, but " *And thy God thy glory!*" Ay—even as an eagle alighteth! Good—good! Now again, the sun and moon of that twentieth verse, Ben.'

Ben read: '"*Non occidet ultra Sol tuus et Luna tua non minuetur: quia erit tibi Dominus in lucem sempiternam, et complebuntur dies luctus tui*".'

Will snatched the paper and read aloud from the Coverdale version. '"Thy Sun shall never go down and thy Moon shall never be taken away . . .' What a plague's Coverdale doing with his blocking *uts* and *urs*, Ben? What's *minuetur*? . . . I'll have it all anon.'

'Minish—make less—appease—abate, as in——'

'So?' . . . Will threw the proofs back. 'Then "wane" should serve. "Neither shall thy Moon wane" . . . "Wane" is good, but over-weak for place next to "moon"' . . . He swore softly. 'Isaiah hath abolished both earthly sun and moon. *Exeunt ambo.* Aha! I begin to see! . . . Sol, the man, goes down—downstairs or trap—as needs be. Therefore "Go down" shall stand. "Set" would have been better—as a sword sent home in the scabbard— but it jars—it jars. Now Luna must retire herself in some simple fashion . . . Which? Ass that I be! 'Tis common talk in all the plays . . . "Withdrawn" . . . "Favour withdrawn" . . . "Countenance withdrawn." "The Queen withdraws herself." . . . "Withdraw", it shall be! "Neither shall thy moon withdraw herself." (Hear her silver train rasp the boards, Ben?) "Thy Sun shall no more go down—neither shall thy Moon withdraw herself. For the Lord"—ay, "the Lord, simple of Himself","shall be thine"—yes, "thine" here—"everlasting light and" . . How goes the ending, Ben?"'

'"*Et complebuntur dies luctus tui*",' Ben read. '"And thy sorrowful days shall be rewarded thee", says Coverdale.'

'And the Bishops'?'

'"And thy sorrowful days shall be ended".'

'By no means. And Douai?'

'"Thy sorrow shall be ended".'

'And Geneva?'

'"And the days of thy mourning shall be ended".'

'The Switzers have it! Lay the tail of Geneva to the head of Coverdale and the last is without flaw.' He began to thump Ben on the shoulder. 'We have it! I have it all, Boanerges! Blessed be my Demon! Hear! "*The sun shall no more be thy light by day, neither for brightness the moon by night. But the Lord Himself shall be unto thee thy everlasting light and thy God thy glory.*"' He drew a deep breath and went on. '"*Thy sun shall no more go down, neither shall thy moon withdraw herself, for the Lord shall be thine everlasting light and the days of thy mourning shall be ended*".' The rain of triumphant blows began again. 'If those other seven devils in London let it stand on this sort, it serves. But God knows what they can *not* turn upsee-dejee!'

Ben wriggled. 'Let be!' he protested. 'Ye are more moved by this jugglery than if the Globe were burned.'

'Thatch—old thatch! And full of fleas! . . . But, Ben, ye should have heard my Ezekiel making mock of fallen Tyrus in his twenty-seventh chapter. Miles sent me the whole, for, he said, some small touches. I took it to the Bank—four o'clock of a summer morn; stretched out in one of our wherries—and watched London, Port and Town, up and down the river, waking all arrayed to heap more upon evident excess. Ay! "A merchant for the peoples of many isles" . . . "The ships of Tarshish did sing of thee in thy markets?" Yes! I saw all Tyre before me neighing her pride against lifted heaven . . . But what will they let stand of all mine at long last? Which? I'll never know.'

He had set himself neatly and quickly to refolding and cording the packet while he talked. 'That's secret enough,' he said at the finish.

'He'll lose it by the way.' Ben pointed to the sleeper beneath the tree. 'He's owl-drunk.'

'But not his horse,' said Will. He crossed the orchard, roused the man; slid the packet into an holster which he carefully re-buckled; saw him out of the gate, and returned to his chair.

'Who will know we had part in it?' Ben asked.

'God, may be—if He ever lay ear to earth. I've gained and lost enough—lost enough.' He lay back and sighed. There was long silence till he spoke half aloud. 'And Kit that was my master in the beginning, he died when all the world was young.'

'Knifed on a tavern reckoning—not even for a wench!' Ben nodded.

'Ay. But if he'd lived he'd have breathed me! 'Fore God, he'd have breathed me!'

'Was Marlowe, or any man, *ever* thy master, Will?'

'He alone. Very he. I envied Kit. Ye do not know that envy, Ben?'

'Not as touching my own works. When the mob is led to prefer a baser Muse, I have felt the hurt, and paid home. Ye know that —as ye know my doctrine of playwriting.'

'Nay—not wholly—tell it at large,' said Will, relaxing in his seat, for virtue had gone out of him. He put a few drowsy questions. In three minutes Ben had launched full-flood on the decayed state of the drama, which he was born to correct; on cabals and intrigues against him which he had fought without cease; and on the inveterate muddle-headedness of the mob unless duly scourged into approbation by his magisterial hand.

It was very still in the orchard now that the horse had gone. The heat of the day held though the sun sloped, and the wine had done its work. Presently, Ben's discourse was broken by a snort from the other chair.

'I was listening, Ben! Missed not a word—missed not a word.' Will sat up and rubbed his eyes. 'Ye held me throughout.' His head dropped again before he had done speaking.

Ben looked at him with a chuckle and quoted from one of his own plays:

> "'Mine earnest vehement botcher
> And deacon also, Will, I cannot dispute with you.'"

He drew out flint, steel and tinder, pipe and tobacco-bag from somewhere round his waist, lit and puffed against the midges till he, too, dozed.

1934

# POEMS

# The Story Of Uriah

*'Now there were two men in one city; the one rich, and the other poor.'*

JACK BARRETT went to Quetta
  Because they told him to.
He left his wife at Simla
  On three-fourths his monthly screw.
Jack Barrett died at Quetta
  Ere the next month's pay he drew.

Jack Barrett went to Quetta.
  He didn't understand
The reason of his transfer
  From the pleasant mountain-land.
The season was September,
  And it killed him out of hand.

Jack Barrett went to Quetta
  And there gave up the ghost,
Attempting two men's duty
  In that very healthy post;
And Mrs Barrett mourned for him
  Five lively months at most.

Jack Barrett's bones at Quetta
  Enjoy profound repose;
But I shouldn't be astonished
  If *now* his spirit knows
The reason of his transfer
  From the Himalayan snows.

And, when the Last Great Bugle Call
  Adown the Hurnai throbs,
And the last grim joke is entered
  In the big black Book of Jobs,
And Quetta graveyards give again
  Their victims to the air,
I shouldn't like to be the man
  Who sent Jack Barrett there.

1886

# Danny Deever

'WHAT are the bugles blowin' for?' said Files-on-Parade.
'To turn you out, to turn you out,' the Colour-Sergeant said.
'What makes you look so white, so white?' said Files-on-Parade.
'I'm dreadin' what I've got to watch,' the Colour-Sergeant said.
  For they're hangin' Danny Deever, you can hear the Dead
    March play,
  The Regiment's in 'ollow square—they're hangin' him today;
  They've taken of his buttons off an' cut his stripes away,
  An' they're hangin' Danny Deever in the mornin'.

'What makes the rear-rank breathe so 'ard?' said Files-on-
  Parade.
'It's bitter cold, it's bitter cold,' the Colour-Sergeant said.
'What makes that front-rank man fall down?' said Files-on-
  Parade.
'A touch o' sun, a touch o' sun,' the Colour-Sergeant said.
  They are hangin' Danny Deever, they are marchin' of 'im
    round,
  They 'ave 'alted Danny Deever by 'is coffin on the ground;
  An' 'e'll swing in 'arf a minute for a sneakin' shootin' hound—
  O they're hangin' Danny Deever in the mornin'!

''Is cot was right-'and cot to mine,' said Files-on-Parade.
''E's sleepin' out an' far tonight,' the Colour-Sergeant said.
'I've drunk 'is beer a score o' time,' said Files-on-Parade.
''E's drinkin' bitter beer alone,' the Colour-Sergeant said.
  They are hangin' Danny Deever, you must mark 'im to his
    place,
  For 'e shot a comrade sleepin'—you must look 'im in the face;
  Nine 'undred of 'is county an' the Regiment's disgrace,
  While they're hangin' Danny Deever in the mornin'.

'What's that so black agin the sun?' said Files-on-Parade.
'It's Danny fightin' 'ard for life,' the Colour-Sergeant said.
'What's that that whispers over'ead?' said Files-on-Parade.
'It's Danny's soul that's passin' now,' the Colour-Sergeant said.
  For they're done with Danny Deever, you can 'ear the quick-
    step play,
  The Regiment's in column, an' they're marchin' us away;
  Ho! the young recruits are shakin', an' they'll want their beer
    today,
  After hangin' Danny Deever in the mornin'!

1890

# Gunga Din

You may talk o' gin and beer
When you're quartered safe out 'ere,
An' you're sent to penny-fights an' Aldershot it;
But when it comes to slaughter
You will do your work on water,
An' you'll lick the bloomin' boots of 'im that's got it.
Now in Injia's sunny clime,
Where I used to spend my time
A-servin' of 'Er Majesty the Queen,
Of all them blackfaced crew
The finest man I knew
Was our regimental *bhisti*, Gunga Din.
          He was 'Din! Din! Din!
    'You limpin' lump o' brick-dust, Gunga Din!
          'Hi! Slippy *hitherao*!
          'Water, get it! *Panee lao*, [1]
    'You squidgy-nosed old idol, Gunga Din.'

The uniform 'e wore
Was nothin' much before,
An' rather less than 'arf o' that be'ind,
For a piece o' twisty rag
An' a goatskin water-bag
Was all the field-equipment 'e could find.
When the sweatin' troop-train lay
In a sidin' through the day,
Where the 'eat would make your bloomin' eyebrows crawl,
We shouted '*Harry By!*' [2]
Till our throats were bricky-dry,
Then we wopped 'im 'cause 'e couldn't serve us all.
          It was 'Din! Din! Din!
    'You 'eathen, where the mischief 'ave you been?
          'You put some *juldee* [3] in it
          'Or I'll *marrow* [4] you this minute
    'If you don't fill up my helmet, Gunga Din!'

'E would dot an' carry one
Till the longest day was done;
An' 'e didn't seem to know the use o' fear.
If we charged or broke or cut,
You could bet your bloomin' nut,
'E'd be waitin' fifty paces right flank rear.

[1] Bring water swiftly.          [2] O brother.
[3] Be quick.          [4] Hit.

193

With 'is *mussick* [1] on 'is back,
'E would skip with our attack,
An' watch us till the bugles made 'Retire',
An' for all 'is dirty 'ide
'E was white, clear white, inside
When 'e went to tend the wounded under fire!
      It was 'Din! Din! Din!'
  With the bullets kickin' dust-spots on the green.
     When the cartridges ran out,
      You could hear the front-ranks shout,
  'Hi! ammunition-mules an' Gunga Din!'

I shan't forget the night
When I dropped be'ind the fight
With a bullet where my belt-plate should 'a' been.
I was chokin' mad with thirst,
An' the man that spied me first
Was our good old grinnin', gruntin' Gunga Din.
'E lifted up my 'ead,
  An' he plugged me where I bled,
  An' 'e guv me 'arf-a-pint o' water green.
It was crawlin' and it stunk,
But of all the drinks I've drunk,
I'm gratefullest to one from Gunga Din.
      It was 'Din! Din! Din!
  ''Ere's a beggar with a bullet through 'is spleen;
    ''E's chawin' up the ground,
    'An' 'e's kickin' all around:
  'For Gawd's sake git the water, Gunga Din!'

'E carried me away
To where a *dooli* lay,
An' a bullet come an' drilled the beggar clean.
'E put me safe inside,
An' just before 'e died,
'I 'ope you liked your drink,' sez Gunga Din.
So I'll meet 'im later on
At the place where 'e is gone—
Where it's always double drill and no canteen.
'E'll be squattin' on the coals
Givin' drink to poor damned souls
An' I'll get a swig in hell from Gunga Din!
      Yes, Din! Din ! Din!
  You Lazarushian-leather Gunga Din!
     Though I've belted you and flayed you,
     By the livin' Gawd that made you,
  You're a better man than I am, Gunga Din!
               [1] Water-skin.

1890

# Mandalay

By the old Moulmein Pagoda, lookin' lazy at the sea,
There's a Burma girl a-settin', and I know she thinks o' me;
For the wind is in the palm-trees, and the temple-bells they say:
'Come you back, you British soldier; come you back to Manda-
lay!'
  Come you back to Mandalay,
  Where the old Flotilla lay:
  Can't you 'ear their paddles chunkin' from Rangoon to
    Mandalay?
  On the road to Mandalay,
  Where the flyin'-fishes play,
  An' the dawn comes up like thunder outer China 'crost the
    Bay!

'Er petticoat was yaller an' 'er little cap was green,
An' 'er name was Supi-yaw-lat—jes' the same as Theebaw's
Queen,
An' I seed her first a'smokin' of a whackin' white cheroot,
An' a-wastin' Christian kisses on an 'eathen idol's foot:
  Bloomin' idol made o' mud—
  Wot they called the Great Gawd Budd—
  Plucky lot she cared for idols when I kissed 'er where she
    stud!
  On the road to Mandalay . . .

When the mist was on the rice-fields an' the sun was droppin'
slow,
She'd git 'er little banjo an' she'd sing '*Kulla-lo-lo!*'
With 'er arm upon my shoulder an' 'er cheek agin my cheek
We useter watch the steamers an' the *hathis* pilin' teak.
  Eliphints a-pilin' teak
  In the sludgy, squdgy creek,
  Where the silence 'ung that 'eavy you was 'arf afraid to
    speak!
  On the road to Mandalay . . .

But that's all shove be'ind me—long ago an' fur away,
An' there ain't no 'buses runnin' from the Bank to Mandalay;
An' I'm learnin' 'ere in London what the ten-year soldier tells:
'If you've 'eard the East a-callin', you won't never 'eed naught
else.'
  No! you won't 'eed nothin' else
  But them spicy garlic smells,

An' the sunshine an' the palm-trees an' the tinkly temple-
  bells;
On the road to Mandalay . . .

I am sick o' wastin' leather on these gritty pavin'-stones,
An' the blasted English drizzle wakes the fever in my bones;
Tho' I walks with fifty 'ousemaids outer Chelsea to the Strand,
An' they talks a lot o' lovin', but wot do they understand?
    Beefy face an' grubby 'and—
    Law! wot do they understand?
    I've a neater, sweeter maiden in a cleaner, greener land!
    On the road to Mandalay . . .

Ship me somewheres east of Suez, where the best is like the worst,
Where there aren't no Ten Commandments an' a man can raise
  a thirst;
For the temple-bells are callin', an' it's there that I would be—
By the old Moulmein Pagoda, looking lazy at the sea;
    On the road to Mandalay,
    Where the old Flotilla lay,
    With our sick beneath the awnings when we went to
      Mandalay!
    O the road to Mandalay,
    Where the flyin'-fishes play,
    An' the dawn comes up like thunder outer China 'crost the
      Bay!

1890


# My New-cut Ashlar

### L'Envoi to *Life's Handicap*

My new-cut ashlar takes the light
Where crimson-blank the windows flare.
By my own work before the night,
Great Overseer, I make my prayer.

If there be good in that I wrought
Thy Hand compelled it, Master, Thine—
Where I have failed to meet Thy Thought
I know, through Thee, the blame was mine.

One instant's toil to Thee denied
Stands all Eternity's offence.
Of that I did with Thee to guide,
To Thee, through Thee, be excellence.

The depth and dream of my desire,
The bitter paths wherein I stray—
Thou knowest Who has made the Fire,
Thou knowest Who has made the Clay.

Who, lest all thought of Eden fade,
Bring'st Eden to the craftsman's brain—
Godlike to muse o'er his own Trade
And manlike stand with God again!

One stone the more swings into place
In that dread Temple of Thy worth.
It is enough that, through Thy Grace,
I saw naught common on Thy Earth.

Take not that vision from my ken—
Oh, whatsoe'er may spoil or speed.
Help me to need no aid from men
That I may help such men as need!

    1890

# The Long Trail

THERE'S a whisper down the field where the year has shot her
    yield,
  And the ricks stand grey to the sun,
Singing: 'Over then, come over, for the bee has quit the clover,
  'And your English summer's done.'

    You have heard the beat of the off-shore wind,
    And the thresh of the deep-sea rain;
    You have heard the song—how long? how long?
    Pull out on the trail again!

Ha' done with the Tents of Shem, dear lass,
    We've seen the seasons through,
And it's time to turn on the old trail, our own trail, the out
    trail,
Pull out, pull out, on the Long Trail—the trail that is always
    new!

It's North you may run to the rime-ringed sun
    Or South to the blind Horn's hate;
Or East all the way into Mississippi Bay,
    Or West to the Golden Gate—
        Where the blindest bluffs hold good, dear lass,
        And the wildest tales are true,
        And the men bulk big on the old trail, our own trail, the out
        trail,
        And life runs large on the Long Trail—the trail that is always
        new.

The days are sick and cold, and the skies are grey and old,
    And the twice-breathed airs blow damp;
And I'd sell my tired soul for the bucking beam-sea roll
    Of a black Bilbao tramp,
        With her load-line over her hatch, dear lass,
        And a drunken Dago crew,
        And her nose held down on the old trail, our own trail, the
        out trail
        From Cadiz south on the Long Trail—the trail that is always
        new.

There be triple ways to take, of the eagle or the snake,
    Or the way of a man with a maid;
But the sweetest way to me is a ship's upon the sea
    In the heel of the North-East Trade.
        Can you hear the crash on her bows, dear lass,
        And the drum of the racing screw,
        As she ships it green on the old trail, our own trail, the out
        trail,
        As she lifts and 'scends on the Long Trail—the trail that is
        always new?

See the shaking funnels roar, with the Peter at the fore,
    And the fenders grind and heave,
And the derricks clack and grate, as the tackle hooks the crate,
    And the fall-rope whines through the sheave;
        It's 'Gang-plank up and in', dear lass,
        It's 'Hawsers warp her through!'

And it's 'All clear aft' on the old trail, our own trail, the out trail,
  We're backing down on the Long Trail—the trail that is always new.

O the mutter overside, when the port-fog holds us tied,
  And the sirens hoot their dread,
When foot by foot we creep o'er the hueless, viewless deep
  To the sob of the questing lead!
    It's down by the Lower Hope, dear lass,
    With the Gunfleet Sands in view,
    Till the Mouse swings green on the old trail, our own trail, the out trail,
    And the Gull Light lifts on the Long Trail—the trail that is always new.

O the blazing tropic night, when the wake's a welt of light
  That holds the hot sky tame,
And the steady fore-foot snores through the planet-powdered floors
  Where the scared whale flukes in flame!
    Her plates are flaked by the sun, dear lass,
    And her ropes are taut with the dew,
    For we're booming down on the old trail, our own trail, the out trail,
    We're sagging south on the Long Trail—the trail that is always new.

Then home, get her home, where the drunken rollers comb,
  And the shouting seas drive by,
And the engines stamp and ring, and the wet bows reel and swing,
  And the Southern Cross rides high!
    Yes, the old lost stars wheel back, dear lass,
    That blaze in the velvet blue.
    They're all old friends on the old trail, our own trail, the out trail,
    They're God's own guides on the Long Trail—the trail that is always new.

Fly forward, O my heart, from the Foreland to the Start—
  We're steaming all too slow,
And it's twenty thousand mile to our little lazy isle
  Where the trumpet-orchids blow!
    You have heard the call of the off-shore wind
    And the voice of the deep-sea rain;
    You have heard the song—how long?—how long?
    Pull out on the trail again!

The Lord knows what we may find, dear lass,
And The Deuce knows what we may do—
But we're back once more on the old trail, our own trail, the out
 trail,
We're down, hull-down, on the Long Trail—the trail that is
 always new!

1891

# McAndrew's Hymn

LORD, Thou hast made this world below the shadow of a dream,
An', taught by time, I tak' it so—exceptin' always Steam.
From coupler-flange to spindle-guide I see Thy Hand, O God—
Predestination in the stride o' yon connectin'-rod.
John Calvin might ha' forged the same—enorrmous, certain,
 slow—
Ay, wrought it in the furnace-flame—*my* 'Institutio'.
I cannot get my sleep tonight; old bones are hard to please;
I'll stand the middle watch up here—alone wi' God an' these
My engines, after ninety days o' race an' rack an' strain
Through all the seas of all Thy world, slam-bangin' home again.
Slam-bang too much—they knock a wee—the crosshead-gibs are
 loose,
But thirty thousand mile o' sea has gied them fair excuse. . . .
Fine, clear an' dark—a full-draught breeze, wi' Ushant out o'
 sight,
An' Ferguson relievin' Hay. Old girl, ye'll walk tonight!
His wife's at Plymouth. . . . Seventy—One—Two—Three since he
 began—
Three turns for Mistress Ferguson . . . and who's to blame the man?
There's none at any port for me, by drivin' fast or slow,
Since Elsie Campbell went to Thee, Lord, thirty years ago.
(The year the *Sarah Sands* was burned. Oh, roads we used to
 tread,
Fra' Maryhill to Pollokshaws—fra' Govan to Parkhead!)
Not but they're ceevil on the Board. Ye'll hear Sir Kenneth say:
'Good morrn, McAndrew! Back again? An' how's your bilge
 today?'

Miscallin' technicalities but handin' me my chair
To drink Madeira wi' three Earls—the auld Fleet Engineer
That started as a boiler-whelp—when steam and he were low.
*I* mind the time we used to serve a broken pipe wi' tow!
Ten pound was all the pressure then—Eh! Eh!—a man wad drive;
An' here, our workin' gauges give one hunder sixty-five!
We're creepin' on wi' each new rig—less weight an' larger power;
There'll be the loco-boiler next an' thirty mile an hour!
Thirty an' more. What I ha' seen since ocean-steam began
Leaves me na doot for the machine; but what about the man?
The man that counts, wi' all his runs, one million mile o' sea:
Four time the span from earth to moon. . . . How far, O Lord, from Thee
That wast beside him night an' day? Ye mind my first typhoon?
It scoughed the skipper on his way to jock wi' the saloon.
Three feet were on the stokehold-floor—just slappin' to an' fro—
An' cast me on a furnace-door. I have the marks to show.
Marks! I ha' marks o' more than burns—deep in my soul an' black,
An' times like this, when things go smooth, my wickudness comes back.
The sins o' four an' forty years, all up an' down the seas,
Clack an' repeat like valves half-fed. . . . Forgie's our trespasses!
Nights when I'd come on deck to mark, wi' envy in my gaze,
The couples kittlin' in the dark between the funnel-stays;
Years when I raked the Ports wi' pride to fill my cup o' wrong—
Judge not, O Lord, my steps aside at Gay Street in Hong-Kong!
Blot out the wastrel hours of mine in sin when I abode—
Jane Harrigan's an' Number Nine, The Reddick an' Grant Road!
An' waur than all—my crownin' sin—rank blasphemy an' wild.
I was not four and twenty then—Ye wadna judge a child?
I'd seen the Tropics first that run—new fruit, new smells, new air—
How could I tell—blind-fou wi' sun—the Deil was lurkin' there?
By day like playhouse-scenes the shore slid past our sleepy eyes;
By night those soft, lasceevious stars leered from those velvet skies,
In port (we used no cargo-steam) I'd daunder down the streets—
An ijjit grinnin' in a dream—for shells an' parrakeets,
An' walkin'-sticks o' carved bamboo an' blowfish stuffed an' dried—
Fillin' my bunk wi' rubbishry the Chief put overside.
Till, off Sambawa Head, Ye mind, I heard a land-breeze ca',
Milk-warm wi' breath o' spice an' bloom; 'MacAndrew, come awa'!'

Firm, clear an' low—no haste, no hate—the ghostly whisper went,
Just statin' eevidential facts beyon' all argument:
'Your mither's God's a graspin' deil, the shadow o' yoursel',
'Got out o' books by meenisters clean daft on Heaven an' Hell.
'They mak' him in the Broomielaw, o' Glasgie cold an' dirt,
'A jealous, pridefu' fetich, lad, that's only strong to hurt.
'Ye'll not go back to Him again an' kiss His red-hot rod,
'But come wi' Us' (Now, who were *They*?) 'an' know the Leevin'
    God,
'That does not kipper souls for sport or break a life in jest,
'But swells the ripenin' cocoanuts an' ripes the woman's breast.'
An' there it stopped—cut off—no more—that quiet, certain
    voice—
For me, six months o' twenty-four, to leave or take at choice.
'Twas on me like a thunderclap—it racked me through an'
    through—
Temptation past the show o' speech, unnameable an' new—
The Sin against the Holy Ghost? . . . An' under all, our screw.

That storm blew by but left behind her anchor-shiftin' swell.
Thou knowest all my heart an' mind, Thou knowest, Lord, I
    fell—
Third on the *Mary Gloster* then, and first that night in Hell!
Yet was Thy Hand beneath my head, about my feet Thy Care—
Fra' Deli clear to Torres Strait, the trial o' despair,
But when we touched the Barrier Reef Thy answer to my
    prayer! . . .
We dared na run that sea by night but lay an' held our fire,
An' I was drowsin' on the hatch—sick—sick wi' doubt an' tire:
'*Better the sight of eyes that see than wanderin' o' desire!*'
Ye mind that word? Clear as our gongs—again, an' once again,
When rippin' down through coral-trash ran out our moorin'-
    chain:
An', by Thy Grace, I had the Light to see my duty plain.
Light on the engine-room—no more—bright as our carbons
    burn.
I've lost it since a thousand times, but never past return!

Obsairve! Per annum we'll have here two thousand souls
    aboard—
Think not I dare to justify myself before the Lord,
But—average fifteen hunder souls safe-borne fra' port to port—
I *am* o' service to my kind. Ye wadna blame the thought?
Maybe they steam from Grace to Wrath—to sin by folly led—
It isna mine to judge their path—their lives are on my head.

Mine at the last—when all is done it all comes back to me,
The fault that leaves six thousand ton a log upon the sea.
We'll tak' one stretch—three weeks an' odd by ony road ye steer—
Fra' Cape Town east to Wellington—ye need an engineer.
Fail there—ye've time to weld your shaft—ay, eat it, ere ye're spoke;
Or make Kerguelen under sail—three jiggers burned wi' smoke!
An' home again—the Rio run; it's no child's play to go
Steamin' to bell for fourteen days o' snow an' floe an' blow.
The bergs like kelpies overside that girn an' turn an' shift
Whair, grindin' like the Mills o' God, goes by the big South drift.
(Hail, Snow and Ice that praise the Lord. I've met them at their work,
An' wished we had anither route or they anither kirk.)
Yon's strain, hard strain, o' head an' hand, for though Thy Power brings
All skill to naught, Ye'll understand a man must think o' things.
Then, at the last, we'll get to port an' hoist their baggage clear—
The passengers, wi' gloves an' canes—an' this is what I'll hear:
'Well, thank ye for a pleasant voyage. The tender's comin' now.'
While I go testin' follower-bolts an' watch the skipper bow.
They've words for every one but me—shake hands wi' half the crew,
Except the dour Scots engineer, the man they never knew.
An' yet I like the wark for all we've dam'-few pickin's here—
No pension, an' the most we'll earn's four hunder pound a year.
Better myself abroad? Maybe. *I'd* sooner starve than sail
Wi' such as call a snifter-rod *ross*. . . . French for nightingale.
Commeesion on my stores? Some do; but I cannot afford
To lie like stewards wi' patty-pans. I'm older than the Board.
A bonus on the coal I save? Ou ay, the Scots are close,
But when I grudge the strength Ye gave I'll grudge their food to *those*.
(There's bricks that I might recommend—an' clink the fire-bars cruel.
No! Welsh—Wangarti at the worst—an' damn all patent fuel!)
Inventions? Ye must stay in port to mak' a patent pay.
My Deeferential Valve-Gear taught me how that business lay.
I blame no chaps wi' clearer heads for aught they make or sell.
*I* found that I could not invent an' look to these as well.
So, wrestled wi' Apollyon—Nah!—fretted like a bairn—
But burned the workin'-plans last run, wi' all I hoped to earn.
Ye know how hard an Idol dies, an' what that meant to me—
E'en tak' it for a sacrifice acceptable to Thee. . . .

*Below there! Oiler! What's your wark? Ye find it runnin' hard?*
*Ye needn't swill the cup wi' oil—this isn't the Cunard!*
*Ye thought? Ye are not paid to think. Go, sweat that off again!*
Tck! Tck! it's deeficult to sweer nor tak' The Name in vain!
Men, ay, an' women, call me stern. Wi' these to oversee,
Ye'll note I've little time to burn on social repartee.
The bairns see what their elders miss; they'll hunt me to an' fro,
'Till for the sake of—well, a kiss—I tak' 'em down below.
That minds me of our Viscount loon—Sir Kenneth's kin—the chap
Wi' Russia-leather tennis-shoon an' spar-decked yachtin-'cap.
I showed him round last week, o'er all—an' at the last says he:
'Mister McAndrew, don't you think steam spoils romance at sea?'
Damned ijjit! I'd been doon that morn to see what ailed the
　　throws,
Manholin', on my back—the cranks three inches off my nose.
Romance! Those first-class passengers they like it very well,
Printed an' bound in little books; but why don't poets tell?
I'm sick of all their quirks an' turns—the loves an' doves they dream—
Lord, send a man like Robbie Burns to sing the Song o' Steam!
To match wi' Scotia's noblest speech yon orchestra sublime
Whaurto—uplifted like the Just—the tail-rods mark the time.
The crank-throws give the double-bass, the feed-pump sobs an'
　　heaves,
An' now the main eccentrics start their quarrel on the sheaves:
Her time, her own appointed time, the rocking link-head bides,
Till—hear that note?—the rod's return whings glimmerin'
　　through the guides.
They're all awa'! True beat, full power, the clangin' chorus goes
Clear to the tunnel where they sit, my purrin' dynamos.
Interdependence absolute, foreseen, ordained, decreed,
To work, Ye'll note, at ony tilt an' every rate o' speed.
Fra' skylight-lift to furnace-bars, backed, bolted, braced an'
　　stayed,
An' singin' like the Mornin' Stars for joy that they are made;
While, out o' touch o' vanity, the sweatin' thrust-block says:
'Not unto us the praise, or man—not unto us the praise!'
Now, a' together, hear them lift their lesson—theirs an' mine:
'Law, Orrder, Duty an' Restraint, Obedience, Discipline!'
Mill, forge an' try-pit taught them that when roarin' they arose,
An' whiles I wonder if a soul was gied them wi' the blows.
Oh for a man to weld it then, in one trip-hammer strain,
Till even first-class passengers could tell the meanin' plain!
But no one cares except mysel' that serve an' understand
My seven-thousand horse-power here. Eh, Lord! They're grand—
　　they're grand!

Uplift am I? When first in store the new-made beasties stood,
Were Ye cast down that breathed the Word declarin' all things good?
Not so! O' that warld-liftin' joy no after-fall could vex,
Ye've left a glimmer still to cheer the Man—the Arrtifex!
*That* holds, in spite o' knock and scale, o' friction, waste an' slip,
An' by that light—now, mark my word—we'll build the Perfect
    Ship.
I'll never last to judge her lines or take her curve—not I.
But I ha' lived an' I ha' worked. Be thanks to Thee, Most High!
An' I ha done what I ha' done—judge Thou if ill or well—
Always Thy Grace preventin' me. . . .
                            Losh! Yon's the 'Stand-by' bell.
Pilot so soon? His flare it is. The mornin'-watch is set.
Well, God be thanked, as I was sayin', I'm no Pelagian yet.
Now I'll tak' on. . . .
    *'Morrn, Ferguson. Man, have ye ever thought*
*What your good leddy costs in coal? . . . I'll burn 'em down to port.*

1894


# The City Of Sleep

OVER the edge of the purple down,
    Where the single lamplight gleams,
Know ye the road to the Merciful Town
    That is hard by the Sea of Dreams—
Where the poor may lay their wrongs away,
    And the sick may forget to weep?
But we—pity us! Oh, pity us!
    We wakeful; ah, pity us!—
We must go back with Policeman Day—
    Back from the City of Sleep!

Weary they turn from the scroll and crown,
    Fetter and prayer and plough—
They that go up to the Merciful Town,
    For her gates are closing now.
It is their right in the Baths of Night
    Body and soul to steep,

But we—pity us! ah, pity us!
  We wakeful; oh, pity us!—
We must go back with Policeman Day—
  Back from the City of Sleep!


Over the edge of the purple down,
  Ere the tender dreams begin,
Look—we may look—at the Merciful Town,
  But we may not enter in!
Outcasts all, from her guarded wall
  Back to our watch we creep:
We—pity us! ah, pity us!
  We wakeful; ah, pity us!—
We that go back with Policeman Day—
  Back from the City of Sleep!

  1895




## The Flowers

*Buy my English posies!*
  *Kent and Surrey may—*
*Violets of the Undercliff*
  *Wet with Channel spray;*
*Cowslips from a Devon combe—*
  *Midland furze afire—*
*Buy my English posies*
  *And I'll sell your heart's desire!*


Buy my English posies!
  You that scorn the May,
Won't you greet a friend from home
  Half the world away?
Green against the draggled drift,
  Faint and frail but first—
Buy my Northern blood-root
  And I'll know where you were nursed!

Robin down the logging-road whistles, 'Come to me!'
Spring has found the maple-grove, the sap is running free.
All the winds of Canada call the ploughing-rain,
Take the flower and turn the hour, and kiss your love again!


Buy my English posies!
    Here's to match your need—
Buy a tuft of royal heath,
    Buy a bunch of weed
White as sand of Muizenberg
    Spun before the gale—
Buy my heath and lilies
    And I'll tell you whence you hail!
Under hot Constantia broad the vineyards lie—
Throned and thorned the aching berg props the speckless sky—
Slow below the Wynberg firs trails the tilted wain—
Take the flower and turn the hour, and kiss your love again!


Buy my English posies!
    You that will not turn—
Buy my hot-wood clematis,
    Buy a frond o' fern
Gathered where the Erskine leaps
    Down the road to Lorne—
Buy my Christmas creeper
    And I'll say where you were born!
West away from Melbourne dust holidays begin—
They that mock at Paradise woo at Cora Lynn—
Through the great South Otway gums sings the great South
    Main—
Take the flower and turn the hour, and kiss your love again!


Buy my English posies!
    Here's your choice unsold!
Buy a blood-red myrtle-bloom,
    Buy the kowhai's gold
Flung for gift on Taupo's face,
    Sign that spring is come—
Buy my clinging myrtle
    And I'll give you back your home!

Broom behind the windy town, pollen of the pine—
Bell-bird in the leafy deep where the *ratas* twine—
Fern above the saddle-bow, flax upon the plain—
Take the flower and turn the hour, and kiss your love again!

Buy my English posies!
    Ye that have your own
Buy them for a brother's sake
    Overseas, alone!
Weed ye trample underfoot
    Floods his heart abrim—
Bird ye never heeded,
    Oh, she calls his dead to him!
Far and far our homes are set round the Seven Seas;
Woe for us if we forget, we who hold by these!
Unto each his mother-beach, bloom and bird and land—
Masters of the Seven Seas, oh, love and understand!

1896

# Recessional

GOD of our fathers, known of old,
    Lord of our far-flung battle-line,
Beneath whose awful Hand we hold
    Dominion over palm and pine—
Lord God of Hosts, be with us yet,
Lest we forget—lest we forget!

The tumult and the shouting dies;
    The Captains and the Kings depart:
Still stands Thine ancient sacrifice,
    An humble and a contrite heart.
Lord God of Hosts, be with us yet,
Lest we forget—lest we forget!

Far-called, our navies melt away;
　　On dune and headland sinks the fire:
Lo, all our pomp of yesterday
　　Is one with Nineveh and Tyre!
Judge of the Nations, spare us yet,
Lest we forget—lest we forget!

If, drunk with sight of power, we loose
　　Wild tongues that have not Thee in awe,
Such boastings as the Gentiles use,
　　Or lesser breeds without the Law—
Lord God of Hosts, be with us yet,
Lest we forget—lest we forget!

For heathen heart that puts her trust
　　In reeking tube and iron shard,
All valiant dust that builds on dust,
　　And guarding, calls not Thee to guard,
For frantic boast and foolish word—
Thy mercy on Thy People, Lord!

1897

## Merrow Down

### I

THERE runs a road by Merrow Down—
　　A grassy track today it is—
An hour out of Guildford town,
　　Above the river Wey it is.

Here, where they heard the horse-bells ring,
　　The ancient Britons dressed and rode
To watch the dark Phœnicians bring
　　Their goods along the Western Road.

Yes, here, or hereabouts, they met
　　To hold their racial talks and such—
To barter beads for Whitby jet,
　　And tin for gay shell torques and such.

But long and long before that time
   (When bison used to roam on it)
Did Taffy and her Daddy climb
   That Down, and had their home on it.

Then beavers built in Broadstonebrook
   And made a swamp where Bramley stands;
And bears from Shere would come and look
   For Taffimai where Shamley stands.

The Wey, that Taffy called Wagai,
   Was more than six times bigger then;
And all the Tribe of Tegumai
   They cut a noble figure then!


II

Of all the Tribe of Tegumai
   Who cut that figure, none remain,—
On Merrow Down the cuckoos cry—
   The silence and the sun remain.

But as the faithful years return
   And hearts unwounded sing again,
Comes Taffy dancing through the fern
   To lead the Surrey spring again.

Her brows are bound with bracken-fronds,
   And golden elf-locks fly above;
Her eyes are bright as diamonds
   And bluer than the sky above.

In mocassins and deer-skin cloak,
   Unfearing, free and fair she flits,
And lights her little damp-wood smoke
   To show her Daddy where she flits.

For far—oh, very far behind,
   So far she cannot call to him,
Comes Tegumai alone to find
   The daughter that was all to him!

1902

# The Settler

South African War ended, May 1902

HERE, where my fresh-turned furrows run,
    And the deep soil glistens red,
I will repair the wrong that was done
    To the living and the dead.
Here, where the senseless bullet fell,
    And the barren shrapnel burst,
I will plant a tree, I will dig a well,
    Against the heat and the thirst.

Here, in a large and sunlit land,
    Where no wrong bites to the bone,
I will lay my hand in my neighbour's hand,
    And together we will atone
For the set folly and the red breach
    And the black waste of it all;
Giving and taking counsel each
    Over the cattle-kraal.

Here will we join against our foes—
    The hailstroke and the storm,
And the red and rustling cloud that blows
    The locust's mile-deep swarm.
Frost and murrain and flood let loose
    Shall launch us side by side
In the holy wars that have no truce
    'Twixt seed and harvest-tide.

Earth, where we rode to slay or be slain,
    Our love shall redeem unto life.
We will gather and lead to her lips again
    The waters of ancient strife,
From the far and the fiercely guarded streams
    And the pools where we lay in wait,
Till the corn cover our evil dreams
    And the young corn our hate.

And when we bring old fights to mind,
    We will not remember the sin—
If there be blood on his head of my kind,
    Or blood on my head of his kin—

For the ungrazed upland, the untilled lea
  Cry, and the fields forlorn:
'The dead must bury their dead, but ye—
  Ye serve an host unborn.'

Bless then, Our God, the new-yoked plough
  And the good beasts that draw,
And the bread we eat in the sweat of our brow
  According to Thy Law.
After us cometh a multitude—
  Prosper the work of our hands,
That we may feed with our land's food
  The folk of all our lands!

Here, in the waves and the troughs of the plains,
  Where the healing stillness lies,
And the vast, benignant sky restrains
  And the long days make wise—
Bless to our use the rain and the sun
  And the blind seed in its bed,
That we may repair the wrong that was done
  To the living and the dead!

  1903


# Sussex

GOD gave all men all earth to love,
  But, since our hearts are small,
Ordained for each one spot should prove
  Beloved over all;
That, as He watched Creation's birth,
  So we, in godlike mood,
May of our love create our earth
  And see that it is good.

So one shall Baltic pines content,
  As one some Surrey glade,
Or one the palm-grove's droned lament
  Before Levuka's Trade.

Each to his choice, and I rejoice
   The lot has fallen to me
In a fair ground—in a fair ground—
   Yea, Sussex by the sea!

No tender-hearted garden crowns,
   No bosomed woods adorn
Our blunt, bow-headed, whale-backed Downs,
   But gnarled and writhen thorn—
Bare slopes where chasing shadows skim,
   And, through the gaps revealed,
Belt upon belt, the wooded, dim,
   Blue goodness of the Weald.

Clean of officious fence or hedge,
   Half-wild and wholly tame,
The wise turf cloaks the white cliff-edge
   As when the Romans came.
What sign of those that fought and died
   At shift of sword and sword?
The barrow and the camp abide,
   The sunlight and the sward.

Here leaps ashore the full Sou'west
   All heavy-winged with brine,
Here lies above the folded crest
   The Channel's leaden line;
And here the sea-fogs lap and cling,
   And here, each warning each,
The sheep-bells and the ship-bells ring
   Along the hidden beach.

We have no waters to delight
   Our broad and brookless vales—
Only the dewpond on the height
   Unfed, that never fails—
Whereby no tattered herbage tells
   Which way the season flies—
Only our close-bit thyme that smells
   Like dawn in Paradise.

Here through the strong and shadeless days
   The tinkling silence thrills;
Or little, lost, Down churches praise
   The Lord who made the hills:
But here the Old Gods guard their round,
   And, in her secret heart,

The heathen kingdom Wilfrid found
    Dreams, as she dwells, apart.

Though all the rest were all my share,
    With equal soul I'd see
Her nine-and-thirty sisters fair,
    Yet none more fair than she.
Choose ye your need from Thames to Tweed,
    And I will choose instead
Such lands as lie 'twixt Rake and Rye,
    Black Down and Beachy Head.

I will go out against the sun
    Where the rolled scarp retires,
And the Long Man of Wilmington
    Looks naked toward the shires;
And east till doubling Rother crawls
    To find the fickle tide,
By dry and sea-forgotten walls,
    Our ports of stranded pride.

I will go north about the shaws
    And the deep ghylls that breed
Huge oaks and old, the which we hold
    No more than Sussex weed;
Or south where windy Piddinghoe's
    Begilded dolphin veers,
And red beside wide-bankèd Ouse
    Lie down our Sussex steers.

So to the land our hearts we give
    Till the sure magic strike,
And Memory, Use, and Love make live
    Us and our fields alike—
That deeper than our speech and thought,
    Beyond our reason's sway,
Clay of the pit whence we were wrought
    Yearns to its fellow-clay.

*God gives all men all earth to love,*
    *But, since man's heart is small,*
*Ordains for each one spot shall prove*
    *Belovèd over all,*
*Each to his choice, and I rejoice*
    *The lot has fallen to me*
*In a fair ground—in a fair ground—*
    *Yea, Sussex by the sea!*

1903

# 'Cities And Thrones And Powers'

CITIES and Thrones and Powers
    Stand in Time's eye,
Almost as long as flowers,
    Which daily die:
But, as new buds put forth
    To glad new men,
Out of the spent and unconsidered Earth
    The Cities rise again.

This season's Daffodil,
    She never hears
What change, what chance, what chill,
    Cut down last year's;
But with bold countenance,
    And knowledge small,
Esteems her seven days' continuance
    To be perpetual.

So Time that is o'er-kind
    To all that be,
Ordains us e'en as blind,
    As bold as she:
That in our very death,
    And burial sure,
Shadow to shadow, well persuaded, saith,
    'See how our works endure!'

1906

# The Harp Song Of The Dane Women

WHAT is a woman that you forsake her,
And the hearth-fire and the home-acre,
To go with the old grey Widow-maker?

She has no house to lay a guest in—
But one chill bed for all to rest in,
That the pale suns and the stray bergs nest in.

She has no strong white arms to fold you,
But the ten-times-fingering weed to hold you—
Out on the rocks where the tide has rolled you.

Yet, when the signs of summer thicken,
And the ice breaks, and the birch-buds quicken,
Yearly you turn from our side, and sicken—

Sicken again for the shouts and the slaughters.
You steal away to the lapping waters,
And look at your ship in her winter-quarters.

You forget our mirth, and talk at the tables,
The kine in the shed and the horse in the stables—
To pitch her sides and go over her cables.

Then you drive out where the storm-clouds swallow,
And the sound of your oar-blades, falling hollow,
Is all we have left through the months to follow.

Ah, what is Woman that you forsake her,
And the hearth-fire and the home-acre,
To go with the old grey Widow-maker?

   1906


# The Way Through The Woods

THEY shut the road through the woods
Seventy years ago.
Weather and rain have undone it again,
And now you would never know
There was once a road through the woods
Before they planted the trees.
It is underneath the coppice and heath
And the thin anemones.
Only the keeper sees
That, where the ring-dove broods,
And the badgers roll at ease,
There was once a road through the woods.

Yet, if you enter the woods
Of a summer evening late,
When the night-air cools on the trout-ringed pools
Where the otter whistles his mate,
(They fear not men in the woods,
Because they see so few.)
You will hear the beat of a horse's feet,
And the swish of a skirt in the dew,
Steadily cantering through
The misty solitudes,
As though they perfectly knew
The old lost road through the woods. . . .
But there is no road through the woods.

1910

# If—

If you can keep your head when all about you
    Are losing theirs and blaming it on you,
If you can trust yourself when all men doubt you,
    But make allowance for their doubting too;
If you can wait and not be tired of waiting,
    Or being lied about, don't deal in lies,
Or being hated, don't give way to hating,
    And yet don't look too good, nor talk too wise:

If you can dream—and not make dreams your master;
    If you can think—and not make thoughts your aim;
If you can meet with Triumph and Disaster
    And treat those two impostors just the same;
If you can bear to hear the truth you've spoken
    Twisted by knaves to make a trap for fools,
Or watch the things you gave your life to, broken,
    And stoop and build 'em up with worn-out tools:

If you can make one heap of all your winnings
    And risk it on one turn of pitch-and-toss,
And lose, and start again at your beginnings
    And never breathe a word about your loss;

If you can force your heart and nerve and sinew
    To serve your turn long after they are gone,
And so hold on when there is nothing in you
    Except the Will which says to them: 'Hold on!'

If you can talk with crowds and keep your virtue,
    Or walk with Kings—nor lose the common touch,
If neither foes nor loving friends can hurt you,
    If all men count with you, but none too much;
If you can fill the unforgiving minute
    With sixty seconds' worth of distance run,
Yours is the Earth and everything that's in it,
    And—which is more—you'll be a Man, my son!

    1910


# Eddi's Service

EDDI, priest of St Wilfrid
    In his chapel at Manhood End,
Ordered a midnight service
    For such as cared to attend.

But the Saxons were keeping Christmas,
    And the night was stormy as well.
Nobody came to service,
    Though Eddi rang the bell.

''Wicked weather for walking,'
    Said Eddi of Manhood End.
'But I must go on with the service
    For such as care to attend.'

The altar-lamps were lighted,—
    An old marsh-donkey came,
Bold as a guest invited,
    And stared at the guttering flame.

The storm beat on at the windows,
  The water splashed on the floor,
And a wet, yoke-weary bullock
  Pushed in through the open door.

'How do I know what is greatest,
  How do I know what is least?
That is My Father's business,'
  Said Eddi, Wilfrid's priest.

'But—three are gathered together—
  Listen to me and attend.
I bring good news, my brethren!'
  Said Eddi of Manhood End.

And he told the Ox of a Manger
  And a Stall in Bethlehem,
And he spoke to the Ass of a Rider
  That rode to Jerusalem.

They steamed and dripped in the chancel,
  They listened and never stirred,
While, just as though they were Bishops,
  Eddi preached them The Word,

Till the gale blew off on the marshes
  And the windows showed the day,
And the Ox and the Ass together
  Wheeled and clattered away.

And when the Saxons mocked him,
  Said Eddi of Manhood End,
'I dare not shut His chapel
  On such as care to attend.'

1910

# The Roman Centurion's Song

Roman occupation of Britain, A.D. 300

LEGATE, I had the news last night—my cohort ordered home
By ship to Portus Itius and thence by road to Rome.
I've marched the companies aboard, the arms are stowed below:
Now let another take my sword. Command me not to go!

I've served in Britain forty years, from Vectis to the Wall.
I have none other home than this, nor any life at all.
Last night I did not understand, but, now the hour draws near
That calls me to my native land, I feel that land is here.

Here where men say my name was made, here where my work was
done;
Here where my dearest dead are laid—my wife—my wife and
son;
Here where time, custom, grief and toil, age, memory, service,
love,
Have rooted me in British soil. Ah, how can I remove?

For me this land, that sea, these airs, those folks and field suffice.
What purple Southern pomp can match our changeful Northern
skies,
Black with December snows unshed or pearled with August
haze—
The clanging arch of steel-grey March, or June's long-lighted
days?

You'll follow widening Rhodanus till vine and olive lean
Aslant before the sunny breeze that sweeps Nemausus clean
To Arelate's triple gate; but let me linger on,
Here where our stiff-necked British oaks confront Euroclydon!

You'll take the old Aurelian Road through shore-descending
pines
Where, blue as any peacock's neck, the Tyrrhene Ocean shines.
You'll go where laurel crowns are won, but—will you e'er forget
The scent of hawthorn in the sun, or bracken in the wet?

Let me work here for Britain's sake—at any task you will—
A marsh to drain, a road to make or native troops to drill.
Some Western camp (I know the Pict) or granite Border keep,
Mid seas of heather derelict, where our old messmates sleep.

Legate, I come to you in tears—My cohort ordered home!
I've served in Britain forty years. What should I do in Rome?
Here is my heart, my soul, my mind—the only life I know.
I cannot leave it all behind. Command, me not to go!

1911

# The Glory Of The Garden

OUR England is a garden that is full of stately views,
Of borders, beds and shrubberies and lawns and avenues,
With statues on the terraces and peacocks strutting by;
But the Glory of the Garden lies in the more than meets the eye.

For where the old thick laurels grow, along the thin red wall,
You find the tool- and potting-sheds which are the heart of all;
The cold-frames and the hot-houses, the dungpits and the tanks,
The rollers, carts and drain-pipes, with the barrows and the planks.

And there you'll see the gardeners, the men and 'prentice boys
Told off to do as they are bid and do it without noise;
For, except when seeds are planted and we shout to scare the birds,
The Glory of the Garden it abideth not in words.

And some can pot begonias and some can bud a rose,
And some are hardly fit to trust with anything that grows;
But they can roll and trim the lawns and sift the sand and loam,
For the Glory of the Garden occupieth all who come.

Our England is a garden, and such gardens are not made
By singing:—'Oh, how beautiful!' and sitting in the shade,
While better men than we go out and start their working lives
At grubbing weeds from gravel-paths with broken dinner-knives.

There's not a pair of legs so thin, there's not a head to thick,
There's not a hand so weak and white, nor yet a heart so sick,
But it can find some needful job that's crying to be done,
For the Glory of the Garden glorifieth every one.

Then seek your job with thankfulness and work till further orders,
If it's only netting strawberries or killing slugs on borders;
And when your back stops aching and your hands begin to harden,
You will find yourself a partner in the Glory of the Garden.


Oh, Adam was a gardener, and God who made him sees
That half a proper gardener's work is done upon his knees,
So when your work is finished, you can wash your hands and
    pray
For the Glory of the Garden, that it may not pass away!
*And the Glory of the Garden it shall never pass away!*

    1911



# Lord Roberts

### Died in France 1914

He PASSED in the very battle-smoke
    Of the war that he had descried.
Three hundred mile of cannon spoke
    When the Master-Gunner died.


He passed to the very sound of the guns;
    But, before his eyes grew dim,
He had seen the faces of the sons
    Whose sires had served with him.


He had touched their sword-hilts and greeted each
    With the old sure word of praise;
And there was virtue in touch and speech
    As it had been in old days.


So he dismissed them and took his rest,
    And the steadfast spirit went forth
Between the adoring East and West
    And the tireless guns of the North.

Clean, simple, valiant, well-beloved,
Flawless in faith and fame,
Whom neither ease nor honours moved
An hair's-breadth from his aim.

Never again the war-wise face,
The weighed and urgent word
That pleaded in the market-place—
Pleaded and was not heard!

Yet from his life a new life springs
Through all the hosts to come,
And Glory is the least of things
That follow this man home.

1914


## My Boy Jack

The Great War: 1914-18

'HAVE you news of my boy Jack?'
*Not this tide.*
'When d'you think that he'll come back?'
*Not with this wind blowing, and this tide.*

'Has anyone else had word of him?'
*Not this tide.*
*For what is sunk will hardly swim,*
*Not with this wind blowing, and this tide.*

'Oh, dear, what comfort can I find?'
*None this tide,*
*Nor any tide,*
*Except he did not shame his kind—*
*Not even with that wind blowing, and that tide.*

*Then hold your head up all the more,*
*This tide,*
*And every tide;*
*Because he was the son you bore,*
*And gave to that wind blowing and that tide!*

1916

# The Land

WHEN Julius Fabricius, Sub-Prefect of the Weald,
In the days of Diocletian owned our Lower River-field,
He called to him Hobdenius—a Briton of the Clay,
Saying: 'What about that River-piece for layin' in to hay?'

And the aged Hobden answered: 'I remember as a lad
My father told your father that she wanted dreenin' bad.
An' the more that you neeglect her the less you'll get her clean.
Have it jest *as* you've a mind to, but, if I was you, I'd dreen.'

So they drained it long and crossways in the lavish Roman style—
Still we find among the river-drift their flakes of ancient tile,
And in drouthy middle August, when the bones of meadows
    show,
We can trace the lines they followed sixteen hundred years ago.

Then Julius Fabricius died as even Prefects do,
And after certain centuries, Imperial Rome died too.
Then did robbers enter Britain from across the Northern main
And our Lower River-field was won by Ogier the Dane.

Well could Ogier work his war-boat—well could Ogier wield his
    brand—
Much he knew of foaming water—not so much of farming land.
So he called to him a Hobden of the old unaltered blood,
Saying; 'What about that River-piece; she doesn't look no
    good?'

And that aged Hobden answered: ''Tain't for *me* to interfere,
But I've known that bit o' meadow now for five and fifty year.
Have it *jest* as you've a mind to, but I've proved it time on time,
If you want to change her nature you have *got* to give her lime!'

Ogier sent his wains to Lewes, twenty hours' solemn walk,
And drew back great abundance of the cool, grey, healing chalk.
And old Hobden spread it broadcast, never heeding what was
    in't.—
Which is why in cleaning ditches, now and then we find a flint.

Ogier died. His sons grew English—Anglo-Saxon was their
    name—
Till out of blossomed Normandy another pirate came;

For Duke William conquered England and divided with his men,
And our Lower River-field he gave to William of Warenne.

But the Brook (you know her habit) rose one rainy autumn night
And tore down sodden flitches of the bank to left and right.
So, said William to his Bailiff as they rode their dripping rounds:
'Hob, what about that River-bit—the Brook's got up no
   bounds?'

And that aged Hobden answered: ''Tain't my business to advise,
But ye might ha' known 'twould happen from the way the valley
   lies.
Where ye can't hold back the water you must try and save the
   sile.
Hev it jest as you've a *mind* to, but, if I was you, I'd spile!'

They spiled along the water-course with trunks of willow-trees,
And planks of elms behind 'em and immortal oaken knees.
And when the spates of Autumn whirl the gravel-beds away
You can see their faithful fragments, iron-hard in iron clay.

·       ·       ·       ·       ·       ·       ·

*Georgii Quinti Anno Sexto*, I, who own the River-field,
Am fortified with title-deed, attested, signed and sealed,
Guaranteeing me, my assigns, my executors and heirs
All sorts of powers and profits which—are neither mine nor
   theirs.

I have rights of chase and warren, as my dignity requires.
I can fish—but Hobden tickles. I can shoot—but Hobden wires.
I repair, but he reopens, certain gaps which, men allege,
Have been used by every Hobden since a Hobden swapped a
   hedge.

Shall I dog his morning progress o'er the track-betraying dew?
Demand his dinner-basket into which my pheasant flew?
Confiscate his evening faggot under which my conies ran,
And summons him to judgment? I would sooner summons Pan.

His dead are in the churchyard—thirty generations laid.
Their names were old in history when Domesday Book was
   made;
And the passion and the piety and prowess of his line
Have seeded, rooted, fruited in some land the Law calls mine.

Not for any beast that burrows, nor for any bird that flies,
Would I lose his large sound counsel, miss his keen amending
    eyes.
He is bailiff, woodman, wheelwright, field-surveyor, engineer,
And if flagrantly a poacher—'tain't for me to interfere.

'Hob, what about that River-bit?' I turn to him again,
With Fabricius and Ogier and William of Warenne.
'Hev it jest as you've a mind to, *but*'—and here he takes com-
    mand.
For whoever pays the taxes old Mus' Hobden owns the land.

   1917


## Hymn To Physical Pain

DREAD Mother of Forgetfulness
    Who, when Thy reign begins,
Wipest away the Soul's distress,
    And memory of her sins.

The trusty Worm that dieth not—
    The steadfast Fire also,
By Thy contrivance are forgot
    In a completer woe.

Thine are the lidless eyes of night
    That stare upon our tears,
Through certain hours which in our sight
    Exceed a thousand years:

Thine is the thickness of the Dark
    That presses in our pain,
As Thine the Dawn that bids us mark
    Life's grinning face again.

Thine is the weariness outworn
    No promise shall relieve,
That says at eve, 'Would God 'twere morn!'
    At morn, 'Would God 'twere eve!'

And when Thy tender mercies cease
And life unvexed is due,
Instant upon the false release
The Worm and Fire renew.

Wherefore we praise Thee in the deep,
And on our beds we pray
For Thy return that Thou may'st keep
The Pains of Hell at bay!

1932


# Four-Feet

I HAVE done mostly what most men do,
And pushed it out of my mind;
But I can't forget, if I wanted to,
Four-Feet trotting behind.

Day after day, the whole day through—
Wherever my road inclined—
Four-Feet said, 'I am coming with you!'
And trotted along behind.

Now I must go by some other round,—
Which I shall never find—
Somewhere that does not carry the sound
Of Four-Feet trotting behind.

1932

# 'Non Nobis Domine!'

Written for *The Pageant of Parliament*, 1934

*Non nobis Domine!*—
    Not unto us, O Lord!
The Praise or Glory be
    Of any deed or word;
For in Thy Judgment lies
    To crown or bring to nought
All knowledge or device
    That Man has reached or wrought.

And we confess our blame—
    How all too high we hold
That noise which men call Fame,
    That dross which men call Gold.
For these we undergo
    Our hot and godless days,
But in our hearts we know
    Not unto us the Praise.

O Power by Whom we live—
    Creator, Judge, and Friend,
Upholdingly forgive
    Nor fail us at the end:
But grant us well to see
    In all our piteous ways—
*Non nobis Domine!*—
    Not unto us the Praise!

1934

# Index Of First Lines

# Glossary

Arelate   220   Roman Arles

ashlar   196   squared stone used in building

Aurelian Road   220   an ancient road running north and west from Rome as far as Arles

*barasingh*   32   the Swamp Deer, *Rucervus duvaucellii*. Hindi

*bhisti*   193   water-carrier. Urdu

biznai   54   business. Slang

dandy   3   litter of cloth hammock slung from pole. Hindi

*dooli*   194   simple Indian litter, used as ambulance. Hindi

Euroclydon   220   a north-east wind blowing in the Mediterranean

*gram*   1   a kind of pulse

*Harry By!*   193   O brother. Hindi

*hathis*   195   elephants. Hindi

*juldee*   193   be quick. Urdu

Kali   30   Hindu goddess of destruction, wife of Siva

markhor   17   large wild goat of northern India, *Capra falconeri*. Persian

*marrow*   193   hit. Urdu

*mussick*   194   water-skin. Hindi

Nemausus   220   Roman Nîmes

nilghai   17   short-horned Indian antelope. Persian

*panee lao*   193   bring me water. Urdu

Pathan   15   warlike Afghan tribesman of the Indian frontier. Hindustani

Portus Itius   220   the Roman harbour on the north coast of Gaul from which Caesar set sail for Britain

Rhodanus   220   the Roman name for the river Rhône

rickshaw   3   abbreviation of *jinricksha*, light two-wheeled man-drawn vehicle. Japanese

sambhur   17   Indian Elk, *Rusa aristotelis*. Hindi

*shabash*   17   bravo. Urdu

sotnia   15   a squadron of Cossack cavalry. Russian

Theebaw's Queen   195   Supi-yaw-lat, wife of Theebaw, King of Upper Burma (1878–1885). She caused all his relatives, men, women and children, to be massacred

Tyrrhene Ocean   220   the Roman name for the Mediterranean Sea

Vectis   220   the Roman name for the Isle of Wight